"CAIN? YOU DECENT?"

Cain looked up to see Mariah framed in the doorway, her long black hair bathed in sunshine, and felt a jolt of desire. Decent? Not by a long shot.

She stumbled through the doorway and dumped the packages in her arms on the bed. "Zack bought ... up and try them on ...

"I don't know ... to unbutton his sh ... ine show will do a lo ... stays in this wagon."

"You've probably got a little stage fright."

Mariah rolled the sleeves of his flannel shirt down his arms and stripped it off. She tore open the smallest package and withdrew a white dress shirt. As she held the garment up to him, she couldn't help but notice the way the silk fabric whispered against his naked skin.

She had to turn away in order to catch her breath and her wits.

"Filled with tongue-in-cheek humor, clever dialogue, and strongly conceived characters who come alive for the reader. Great reading."
—*Rendezvous*

"A gourmet meal for the discriminating romantic palate. Five gold stars."
—*Heartland Critiques*

Also by Sharon Ihle

Wild Rose
Wildcat

Available from
HarperPaperbacks

The Law and
Miss Penny

 SHARON IHLE

HarperPaperbacks
A Division of HarperCollinsPublishers

HarperPaperbacks   *A Division of* HarperCollins*Publishers*
10 East 53rd Street, New York, N.Y. 10022

Copyright © 1994 by Sharon J. Ihle
All rights reserved. No part of this book may be used or
reproduced in any manner whatsoever without written
permission of the publisher, except in the case of brief
quotations embodied in critical articles and reviews. For
information address HarperCollins*Publishers*,
10 East 53rd Street, New York, N.Y. 10022.

Cover illustration by Jean Monti

First printing: May 1994

Printed in the United States of America

HarperPaperbacks, HarperMonogram, and colophon are
trademarks of HarperCollins*Publishers*

❖ 10 9 8 7 6 5 4 3 2 1

With all my love to my husband, Larry, and our children, the wildest wild west show I've ever seen, much less coproduced:
Lisa Ihle Kabouridis, Allen, Todd, & Sandy Ihle

and

In loving memory of my nephew and godson:
David Allen Schmuckle

1

New Mexico Territory

A profusion of springtime flowers painted the desert landscape, coloring the outskirts and the drab little settlement of Bucksnort in splotches of brilliant red, pink, and yellow. Casting a pall over the bright spring day, a man riding a big sorrel horse crested the knoll at the edge of town. His expression was dark, filled with singular purpose, and though his hat was white, the color of peace, the man beneath that hat was anything but peaceful.

Today marked his twenty-eighth birthday, but he felt much older than his years. The first quarter of 1888 had yet to pass, but since January he'd already killed three men. If he added to that number the outlaws felled by his guns over the past couple of years, the score would have tallied somewhere around two dozen. But United States Marshal Morgan Slater never dwelled on those figures, or on the men he'd cut down. As always, he focused all of his thoughts—and hatred—on the next assignment.

Now as he rode away from the town of Santa Fe and headed north, his thoughts were consumed with catching up to the Doolittle Gang and bringing them to justice. He would gain the latter through the courts if possible, but if forced to mete out the sentence himself, Morgan would do it without hesitation. Two members of the Doolittle Gang had already slipped through his fingers and the system by swaying a sympathetic jury. This time, one way or another, he'd see to it they weren't so lucky.

Morgan had not forgotten the ugly sneer on Billy Doolittle's pockmarked face when the judge pronounced him free to go—free after having taken part in one of the bloodiest train robberies of the century. Nor was he likely to forget the look in Billy's beady black eyes as he'd taunted Morgan, vowing to settle the score if their paths should ever cross again. Morgan swore on that day that if it was the last thing he ever did, their paths *would* cross again. And the sooner the better.

With his anger growing as he thought ahead to the hunt, Morgan urged his big red mount into an easy lope. He'd named the horse Amigo, and in many ways, the animal was his best and only friend, even though he'd castrated the beast early on in their partnership. Only a damn fool would ride a stallion on a manhunt, he had reasoned, and no one had ever had cause to call Morgan Slater a fool.

As he and his best friend rode into the town of Bucksnort, Morgan noticed a group of people crowded around the garishly painted wagon of a medicine show. Although he hadn't had much first-hand experience with such operations, what little he did know added more provocation to his already foul mood. Most of these "doctors" were quacks, and a swollen wallet was the only ailment their tonics could possibly cure. Since confidence games were second only to murder on Morgan's personal list of crimes against society, he nudged Amigo toward the gathering and watched as a middle-aged woman stepped out of the medicine wagon and began to beat on a tom-tom.

She wore a plain cabbage-green dress with leg-of-mutton sleeves, making her short, stout figure appear even more so. Her light brown hair was slicked back and tied into a large knot at the top of her head, and her features were plump and droopy. But the thing that caught Morgan's eye was her mouth—more correctly, the side of her mouth, which was stretched to accommodate the butt of a fat stogie.

This unladylike sight only added to his less-than-high opinion of the show. Morgan slid his rifle out of the scabbard, swung his body up and over the saddle, and dropped Amigo's reins to the ground to signal the horse to stay. Then he elbowed his way through the crowd for a better view of the action. By now the frantic drumbeats of the woman's tom-tom had been joined by the jangling of a tambourine. A tall, thin man wearing a swirling black cape and a top hat was slapping the instrument against his palm, encouraging the hoots and catcalls from the crowd. Morgan assumed this weathered old man to be "Doc Zachariah."

A younger woman stepped out of the back of the wagon then, gracefully made her way to the musicians, and bowed low from the waist. She was costumed in a white buckskin dress featuring rawhide strips at the elbows and knees, and blue beads fashioned into chevrons. At her neck she wore a breastplate made of cerulean beads woven into concentric circles, and at the crown of her head, a single eagle feather sprouted up from a blue-beaded headband. She was the very picture of what a real live Indian princess should be, Morgan supposed, and she lent the troupe a touch of legitimacy.

Morgan didn't buy it for a minute. He was sure that only one detail of this performance could be considered authentic. The girl appeared to be at least half Indian, tribe unknown. His gaze flickered to the signs nailed against the side of the bright red wagon. *Doc Zachariah's Kickapoo Medicine Show*, read one. The others made lofty claims: *Money-Back Guarantee, Certificate of Purity*, and *Cures All!* But the most outrageous proclamation of all was: *Purveyors of Kickapoo Wizard Oil, A Secret Formula Known Only by the Daughter of the Great Chief Sagawaka, Princess Tanacoa!*

Morgan studied the "princess" who now faced the audience in a trancelike state. Her skin was dusky, light cinnamon in color, and her blue-black hair was plaited into braids which reached the tops of her thighs. Although he was far from an expert on

Indians, Morgan doubted that she carried any actual Kickapoo blood in her lying, cheating veins. Nor had she lived amongst the tribe which sired her. Her features were too soft, and her expression too haughty, for her to have been raised by a band of savages.

She glanced at him then, catching his stare, and he saw that her eyes were a rich violet-blue color, fringed with thick lashes of the deepest ebony. She dared him with those eyes, alternating between a "come-get-me" look and a "try-it-and-I'll-carve-your-liver-into-a-whittle-stick" expression.

In spite of the fact that he never backed down from anyone, Morgan found that he was the one to break eye contact. He glanced at the dusty road, wondering briefly if she'd used some kind of hypnotic trick on him, and then heard the voice of the "doctor" resound as he gave his pitch.

"And don't we all know the signs of the first stage of liver disease? Ayuh! It's that painful ache which strikes so many of y'all right across the small of your back!"

Several men in the crowd, farmers who toiled over their crops daily, immediately swung their hands around to their backs and began to rub the aches and pains brought on by long hours of hard work.

"The kidneys . . . uric acid." The man shuddered dramatically. "The consequences of that horrifying malady are just too dreadful to even think about, but for today, thar is hope for one of y'all." He held up a small brown bottle. "I offer the last of Princess Tanacoa's Special Kickapoo Wizard Oil to the first man to offer me one paltry dollah!" At the gasps from the crowd, he added, "That's right! One measly dollah!"

Several voices erupted at once, and a few of the men began to argue over who had been the first to lay claim to the elixir. The man turned toward the back of the wagon where the younger woman stood, catching his wooden leg in the hem of his cape, and grasped the large back wheel to keep from falling. "I now call on Princess Tanacoa, true daughter of the great Kickapoo Medicine Man, Chief Sagawaka!"

As the "princess" stepped forward, eight men scrambled to the front of the small crowd, each one proclaiming terminal symptoms. The princess paused before each man long enough to brush her fingers across his forehead. Then she raised her hands and began to wail.

"Oh, great Sagawaka! Help me to chose correctly!" She squeezed her eyes shut, chanting all the while, and then suddenly opened them as if struck by lightning. Pointing to a flabbergasted farmer, she said, "Et tu, Brute!" and fell to her knees as if exhausted.

Morgan had seen enough. He remembered the warnings his father had issued during the one medicine show he'd attended as a young man as clearly as if he'd heard them yesterday. "Some poor farmer lucky enough to be deemed in the most ill of health will buy that bottle of medicine, son," Matt Slater had said, his tone stern and all-knowing. "Then that poor fool will guzzle it on a regular basis, and become addicted to the major ingredient therein— alcohol, cocaine, or even opium. This swill is nothing but the devil's brew, and you're watching the devil himself as he's brewing it!"

Egged on by memories of his father's harsh, unforgiving voice, Morgan broke through the crowd, shouting, "'Et tu, Brute,' *princess*? Don't you have your Romans mixed up with your Indians?"

Hearing the anger in the man's tone, Mariah Penny lifted one eyebrow and cautiously peered up at him. "Beg pardon?" she said, trying to sound as if she couldn't quite understand English.

"'Et tu, Brute,' my ass." Morgan dismissed the young woman with those words and turned to face the crowd. "Show's over, folks. These people don't have anything to sell you but grief. Go on back to your homes."

Mariah watched openmouthed as, incredibly enough, several members of the audience did just that. It was as if the stranger's deep, authoritative voice had snapped the crowd out of a collective fugue—and, just as easily, wrested command of the situation away from her father, Zachariah Penny.

Zack, who'd stepped between the stranger and his daughter, drew all six feet of his skinny frame up to meet the man's gaze, but fell some two inches short. "Begging your pardon, suh," he said. "But I'm afraid I'll have to ask y'all to kindly step back and—"

"The kindest thing I intend to do for you, old man, is keep you out of jail." Morgan shot him a glance filled with hot indignation as he tore his rawhide vest aside to reveal a shiny gold badge.

Zack went pale. "Oh, ayuh . . . in that case, I do believe I see your point."

"I thought you might."

Turning from the quack doctor, who by now had been joined by the older woman and the "princess," he addressed what was left of the crowd once again. "My name's Morgan Slater, U.S. Marshal, and I'm telling you for the last time to go back to your homes. This show is definitely over."

Whispering amongst themselves, the disappointed townsfolk slowly disbanded and went on their way.

Zack glanced at his wife and heaved a weary sigh. "Damned if it ain't time to move along, missus."

Oda struck a match against the side of the wagon and lit her stogie. "Damned if it ain't."

Only Mariah took exception to the marshal's orders. It certainly wasn't the first time the Penny family had been thrown out of a town, and it most likely wouldn't be the last, especially if they should venture too close to a Mormon settlement as they had done last spring. But she couldn't remember ever being asked to leave in such a rude and degrading manner.

The show wasn't quite legal in status in some areas, but they certainly had never done anything to invite prosecution. From town to town, and sheriff to sheriff, the terms of the ordinances varied, but even in the few places where the show was judged to be unacceptable, the law had always been polite about their dismissal, if not downright friendly. Exactly what had they done to anger this man so?

As Zack and Oda began to collect their props, Mariah approached the marshal, hands on hips.

"There's no call for you to talk to any of us that way, Marshal Slater. We're just good honest folks doing our best to make a living."

"Honest, you say?" Taking her by surprise, Morgan caught her chin in the web between his thumb and forefinger, and then turned her head from side to side, examining her. "What kind of *honest* Indian do we really have here beneath all the phony ceremonial baubles? Surely not a Kickapoo. How about a Comanche? Or should I have said . . . Apache?"

Her reaction was delayed by sheer astonishment, and the fact that the marshal seemed to know that something wasn't quite right about her. When Mariah finally took a swing at him, the lawman easily ducked the blow and stepped aside.

He laughed, and then issued an ultimatum. "You have exactly one second to get your crooked fanny aboard that wagon, *princess,* or I'll confiscate this entire operation just as it sits and drive it off a cliff." His gaze shot over to Zack and Oda. "And I'll give you folks five seconds more than that to pack up, or that's precisely what I'll do." Then he turned on his heel and whistled for Amigo.

Stunned by the hatred she'd seen in the marshal's green eyes, the sheer force of his malevolence, Mariah brought her hand to her chin. Worried the lawman may have left finger marks in the cinnamon-colored greasepaint she used to make her fair skin darker and redder, she smoothed the makeup and then walked backwards toward the wagon, muttering to herself under her breath. When she reached her parents, she turned to them wide-eyed, and whispered, "What a rotten . . . bastard. What a dirty, rotten *bastard*!"

Within the allotted time, Doc Zachariah's Kickapoo Medicine Show was packed and rolling down Main Street, dragging the supply wagon behind it. The pair of sturdy mules, used to the double load, moved along at a steady, if unspectacular clip, leaving Marshal Slater and his best friend to bring up the rear in uncharacteristically poky fashion.

They traveled for nearly three hours under increasingly overcast skies, and although it was early afternoon, the temperature began to drop to almost winterlike conditions. The folks riding on the front seat of the wagon didn't seem to notice the sudden chill, but Morgan tugged his hat lower on his forehead and buttoned the collar of his dark blue shirt. Cold and weary of the snail's pace set by the wagon, he decided that since he'd put some ten miles between Bucksnort and the medicine show and guided the troublemakers into an unpopulated area, it was time for a parting of the ways.

Morgan galloped up alongside the lead wagon and glanced over at the occupants. The man was driving the mules, with his wife silently puffing away on her stogie beside him, but there was no sign of the "Indian princess." In fact, now that he thought of it, he realized he had seen neither hide nor hair of her since she'd stormed into the wagon back in Bucksnort and slammed the door in his face. Nor did he care. All he really cared about was putting this particular medicine show and its quacks out of business. That and wiping the Doolittle Gang off the face of the earth.

He instructed the man to pull up the mules and then prepared to take his leave. That would have been the end of it, but as the medicine wagon skidded to a halt, the supply cart slid down off the edge of the muddy embankment, burying the wheels up to the axles.

Morgan sighed heavily, knowing his progress would be delayed even further. No matter how little he thought of the troupe, or how much further ahead of him the Doolittle Gang might get, he just couldn't ride off leaving a crippled old man and two women stuck in the mud.

"You've buried your supply wagon, old man," he said, his anger over the delay reflected in his tone. "Set your brake and get back there. We'll be shoveling mud at least until nightfall working it free." He pointed up at the sky, where thunderheads were quickly collecting. "And if I don't miss my guess, we'll be digging under a lot nastier conditions than these before the hour is out."

As he started to dismount, a small dog popped through the privacy beads at the mouth of the medicine wagon and joined the doctor and his wife on the bench seat. When the dog began barking, Morgan's horse widened his eyes and then shied away from the rig, nearly unseating his rider before Morgan had a chance to get his foot out of the stirrup. Remembering that he'd been unable to persuade

Amigo to get over his fear of dogs, even pint-sized little mutts like this one, Morgan reined the gelding up sharply.

"Lock that damn dog up!" he snapped at the old man. "We've got work to do!"

Then he climbed down off Amigo, grabbed the shovel that was lashed to the side of the wagon, and headed toward the cart. Zachariah joined him moments later, and set to work on the other side of the rig with his bare hands and a sugar scoop he'd removed from the back of the cart. A light mist had begun to fall by the time Morgan felt they'd dug enough to try using the medicine wagon to pull the cart out. Determined to get the task accomplished before a full-blown storm hit, he ordered the old man to the front of the rig to take control of the mules, and then he braced himself against the back of the medicine wagon. He would have to give the wagon a shove, then move quickly to get out of the way so he wouldn't be hit by the cart. Coiling himself into a push-and-run position, he shouted, "Now, old man! Go!"

The rig groaned for a moment as its big wooden wheels clung to the bank, and then it popped free, lurching up the incline with a surprising burst of acceleration. As Morgan was about to leap to the side, his boot slipped on the recently dampened mud and he went down on his knees. Before he could regain his footing, the rig slammed against the back of his head. In the next second, he felt as if a great wall of ice was surrounding his skull. And then he felt nothing.

*   *   *

When the marshal's big white hat came blowing down the road, tumbling end over end until it was out of sight, and he wasn't running along behind it, Zack figured something had gone awry. As he started for the back of the wagon, he spotted the lawman lying near the side of the road. He was sprawled out on his belly, arms spread, one leg bent at the knee and tucked beneath the other, looking like he'd been flung out with the bathwater. His head was turned to the side, his mouth was open, and his tongue listed at the edge of his bottom lip, ready to fall out at any moment.

Getting down to ground level with his thigh-high wooden leg was always a difficult task for Zack, and he knew that he was the least medically inclined of the three Pennys. So Zack turned to the back of the medicine wagon and knocked on the door. "Mariah! Come on out here. The marshal's had an accident."

Inside the wagon, Mariah was brushing the plaits from her jet-black hair until it hung like a curtain of the finest crushed velvet. She'd changed into a shrimp-pink cotton blouse and a dark brown jacket with matching skirt. The reason she'd stayed inside the wagon and out of sight during their forced departure from Bucksnort was the other change she'd made in her appearance. She'd taken a wad of cotton soaked in mineral oil and smoothed it over the exposed parts of her skin, removing all traces of the greasepaint which made her look more like a Kickapoo Indian. Now that her true, peachy complexion had been exposed, there was no telling what the arrogant marshal would do to her, no matter how effective or authentic her medicines might be. He might even jail her.

"Mariah, baby!" Zack called again. "This poor fool is out for the count, and looks to be hurt pretty bad. Get on out here."

She opened the door a crack. "I'm out of costume. What if he sees me like this?"

"I wouldn't worry too much about that, girl. This fellah looks like he's close to dead. Get on out here and see if you can't do something for him."

Her nursing instincts overriding her fear of being found out, Mariah climbed out of the back of the wagon and knelt down beside the lawman. After flipping him onto his back, she checked his pulse, noting that it was erratic, but strong, and then forced his auburn lashes apart. The whites of his eyes were jittery, and the deep green irises rolled up out of sight. In an effort to bring him around, Mariah slapped the lawman's cheek and said, "Marshal? Are you still in there?"

More than happy to repeat the procedure, she slapped him again, harder yet, but still he didn't respond. Morgan Slater was out about as cold as a man could get, and completely helpless. For one fleeting moment, Mariah wondered why they couldn't just leave him there in the mud. It would serve him right.

Instead, she leaned over the unconscious man and said, "You're not only a bastard, but a lucky one at that." Then she glanced up at her father. "Would you ask Oda to get me the smelling salts and our medical pouch?"

Zack limped off without another word, and as she awaited her father's return, Mariah slipped her hand beneath Slater's head. Feeling an irregular ridge as his scalp met her fingertips, she gently pushed against it. The spot felt a little softer than she thought it should. Concerned, Mariah eased his head back down to the ground, and her fingers came away bloody. She was staring at that hand when her father came hobbling back, with her dog, Daisy, bounding along beside him.

Zack dropped the bag on the ground. "How bad is he?"

"I don't know for sure." Mariah reached inside the pouch for a strip of clean white cotton to bind the marshal's wound. "But whatever hit him split his scalp open."

Oda lumbered up beside her husband then, and peered down at the fallen man. "Something split that thick-skulled head? Couldn't have happened to a nicer fellah."

Chuckling to herself, Mariah snapped a small glass vial apart, cradled the marshal's head in the crook of her arm, and waved the salts beneath his nose. He stirred slightly, and she did it again.

The first sensation to reach him was an intense chill. He was colder than he'd ever been in his entire life and could feel the few sparks of heat still left in his body flickering, then slowly dying, one by one. For some reason, he didn't really care. He was content to drift away on that frigid cloud. But then a new sensation swept over him, something bitter, a bright, hot odor that filled the inside of his head with tacks, and nails, and shards of glass. He shuddered violently, and then slipped back down into the sleepy comfort of his icy cave.

Mariah watched the marshal's eyelids flutter and then grow still. Glancing up at her father, she said, "He's worse than I thought. He's going to need a lot more care than I can give him out here."

Speaking in her usual drowsy manner, Oda made her own observation. "You know how serious a bump on the head can look at first. I bet he'll be up in no time."

Again Mariah parted the marshal's auburn lashes. "I don't think so. Take a look at those eyes."

Both Oda and her husband peered down at the injured man. Zack chuckled at the sight. "He looks just like that big yellow dog of yours did the day he tangled with our mule a few years back. Remember him?"

"You mean Cain?" Mariah thought back to her childhood and her very first pet. She'd been sure that the mule had killed her precious dog, what with his brown eyes rolled back into his head and his tongue hanging out, but Cain had surprised her by leaping to his feet a few minutes after the incident, and running off as if nothing had ever happened. She laughed at the memory. "I guess the marshal does look a little like Cain now that you mention it. Even his tongue's hanging out."

"Not only looks like him," Oda said. "The way this fellah struts around flapping that ornery tongue of his, he and that dog could be twins when it comes to just plain raising Cain."

Chuckling to herself over the recollections of why they'd chosen such a name for the dog, Mariah continued to sweep the salts across the marshal's upper lip as she playfully said, "Come on, Cain the Second. Wake up!"

He stirred again, tasting something vile. The horrid, bitter odor had returned. Through the pain inside his head he heard voices, words too vague and fuzzy to understand except for the one: *Cain*. Cain this and Cain that, he thought he heard them say. That loathsome smell reached his nostrils again, this time permeating his brain and burning the backs of his eyeballs, jolting him to wide-eyed consciousness.

"Take it easy," Mariah said, pinning the marshal's shoulders to the ground. "You've had a little accident."

His blurred gaze darted to the woman, and then beyond her to a pair of vague figures who stood staring down at him. The trio might have been wooden statues for all they meant to him. "What—what happened? Who are you?"

Mariah shot a curious gaze to her father as she spoke to the lawman. "We're the Penny family. Who are you?"

He opened his mouth to speak before he realized he didn't know what to say. It was a ridiculous state to be in—confused, here in body, but not in mind. He knew his name. Of course he knew his name. It was . . . hell, he didn't know. He sighed, straining to remember, knowing the answers were lying there in the folds of his injured brain, not knowing how to reach them.

He made another effort, and became enraged at his lack of instant success. Any damn fool knew his own name, any damn idiot at all. He tried harder. Everyone knew their name. *Everyone.* And his was . . .

2

". . . Cain?"

Yes, he thought. That had to be it. That was the word he kept hearing over and over as he clawed his way back to consciousness. These folks, whoever they were, had been calling him by name, trying to get him to wake up. Yes, of course, that was it—something that finally made sense. He said the name again, testing it, sounding a lot more confident than he felt. "My name is Cain."

Cain? Mariah thought incredulously. Was it possible the man didn't even know who he was? She bit back a smile. "That's your name all right, Cain. I guess you're not in as bad a shape as we first thought you were."

Zack and Oda exchanged puzzled glances, but kept their silence. As his daughter's amused gaze met his, Zack slowly nodded and gestured for her to continue talking with the marshal.

"What else do you remember?" she asked, expecting little as she saw the utter confusion in his eyes. "What about a last name? Do you know what that is?"

Of course he knew what a last name was, he thought. Did she think that he'd completely lost his mind? He knew a lot of things. For starters, he was lying alongside the road, one that looked familiar. He'd traveled this trail several times before, he was sure of it. Looking up at the sky to study the shapes and colors of the clouds, he could also claim knowledge of exactly when to expect the next downpour— *soon*.

What he didn't know was his own height, weight, or the color of his eyes. He saw that the woman peering down at him had violet eyes and black hair, and for all he knew, so did he. He glanced at his boots, knowing without question that his toes were pointing due south. Yes, he knew plenty. But he had no earthly idea what the full name of the man *inside* those damn boots could be.

"Cain," he said in a defeated whisper. "My name is Cain."

Mariah sat back on her heels, her expression now more than simply amused, and then looked at both her mother and father, giving them a quick wink. If a man ever deserved to be brought down a peg or two, it was this one. Besides that, he had cost them at least a hundred dollars by running the medicine show out of Bucksnort before it had even begun. He owed them that much in labor, if nothing else. And Zack could use some rest. As long as Slater's memory was faulty—and there was no way of telling how long that might be—he would be whoever they told him he was and do whatever they said . . . including, serving as a guinea pig for Mariah to test her new nostrums.

As she contemplated the perfect name for the lawman to go along with her perfect plans for him, a glint of gold at the edge of his vest caught Mariah's eye. When she recognized the object poking out from beneath the rawhide as his U.S. marshal's badge, her grin widened. Perfect. Not only had she found him a name, but another way to test his memory as well.

Biting her lip to keep from snickering, Mariah said, "Your name is . . . Law. Cain Law."

Law? He rolled the surname around in his mind, seeking a comfortable slot, a ring of truth. Law. It felt right and sounded right, too. It fit him as well as his broke-in boots.

Gripped with a kind of savage joy, sure that his complete memory would return now, Cain bolted upright, forgetting about the low, throbbing ache at the back of his head. Lightning flashes went off inside his skull, scalding his brain with their brilliant light. His body went rigid, and he collapsed against the rain-soaked roadway. And then, once again, nothing. Merciful, cold, nothing.

The rain started up again, this time in earnest. Oda and Zack fashioned a litter out of a canvas flap from the tent they lived in while on the road, and then

Mariah helped them carry the marshal to the medicine wagon. Several aborted attempts and strained muscles later, they finally managed to heft the lawman's 200-odd pounds into the rig. Once inside, they unceremoniously dumped him on Mariah's bed. Then they went up the road a short distance, searching for a place to stay for the next day or two.

Before long, Oda spotted a wide flat spot not far off the trail, and they decided to set up camp there. As he did during inclement weather or whenever he feared the family's safety might be at risk, Zack butted the rear opening of the tent against the back of the wagon, creating a two-room home where privacy was maintained, but help was within shouting distance. Tonight Mariah would sleep in the tent with her father and mother instead of in her bed in the medicine wagon. If the lawman should awaken or need further assistance, at least one of the Pennys would hear him.

The A-shaped tent was large enough to contain at least a dozen adults comfortably, and in fact, had been used on occasion to house the medicine show during surprise snowstorms and downpours. A little sheepherder's stove, its cylindrical black chimney stack sprouting through an opening at the side of the tent, served as both fireplace and grill. Amid intermittent raindrops splattering against the cloth roof above her, Daisy trotted up beside the stove, plopped her muddy body down on the canvas floor, and then stretched out to warm herself.

Hobbling to the center of the room, Zack hung a

lantern from a strap dangling down for that purpose, and lit it. Then he turned to his family, his concern reflected in his haggard features, and said, "I'd be handing both you gals some mighty tall talk if I didn't admit that I'm a mite worried about keeping the marshal around. Now that we got the poor fellah cleaned up and into one of his own flannel shirts, maybe we ought to wait for the weather to clear and just dump him at the side of the road somewheres along the way."

Mariah laughed. "And waste all those big muscles? Didn't you notice the size of that man's shoulders?"

"Ayuh, and I plainly did, young lady. That's exactly what I'm a-worried about. That young fellah could squash the lot of us flatter than one of the missus's griddle cakes with just a short thump of his fist."

Oda, who was fanning the fire, cast a sleepy-eyed gaze in her husband's direction and furrowed her brow, but kept her comments to herself.

"It'll be all right, Dad," Mariah said, referring to him with a rarely used term. She tried never to call Zack or Oda by anything other than their given names due to the confusion it could cause during a show. "Really it will, and besides—I've thought of one more way we could use him." She hadn't figured on mentioning her further plans for the lawman, but now it seemed prudent to do so. She leaned in close to both Zack and Oda, making sure their "guest" wouldn't overhear. "I'm about ready to test a few new recipes. I thought I'd let the marshal be the first to try them."

Zack rolled his eyes, and Oda groaned.

"It's not such a crazy idea. Some of the new things I'm working on require a different kind of testing, that's all." She paused, wondering how to explain herself without actually mentioning the secret nostrum she'd been developing of late. One mention of the term "love potion," and her very protective father would send her recipe and her plans for the future up in smoke.

She would have to nudge him a little by dangling one of his fondest dreams under his nose. "I want to keep what I'm working on a secret a while longer, if you don't mind, but I can tell you part of my plans. If this nostrum turns out to be as special as I think it is, we'll finally see one of our products advertised in the pages of *Godey's Lady's Book*—maybe even in the *Bloomingdale Brothers' Catalog* along with Lydia E. Pinkham's Vegetable Compound!"

Zack's whistle was long and low. As before, Oda only groaned.

Sure that her father's endorsement was no longer a problem, Mariah turned to her mother. "It isn't so hard to believe that this nostrum will be popular enough to wind up in a national magazine. Lydia Pinkham must have started out with something like that, and look how big her company got. What's wrong with using the marshal a little to help us on our way—or have you taken a shine to the man?"

"Humph! That'll be the day." Oda turned to her husband. "I'm with Mariah. We might as well get our money's worth out of the man for as long as we can."

Zack rubbed the sparse whiskers on his chin, as he

pondered this. "All right, then, but Mariah, listen up. You can't let yourself forget who he is and what he might do should you poison him or something. He is a U.S. marshal, you know, and one day, he's bound to remember that."

Mariah laughed. "Don't worry—even though I'd like to, I promise I won't poison him. Besides, how can testing my new products on an injured man be against the law? I'm only trying to cure him."

"I hope he sees it that way when he wakes up. Which reminds me—when he does come around, I think we ought to tell him who he really is. I'm not sure calling the man Cain Law instead of the name his dear mother gave him is gonna bode so well for us once his memory returns."

"But we can't do that! Don't you see?" Afraid the lawman might wake up and overhear them, Mariah lowered her voice. "If we tell him he's a U.S. marshal and give him his true name, he'd probably attach our wagon and make us take him back to wherever he came from. We'd lose the whole show season for sure!"

"She's right, Zachariah." Oda, never one to waste a lot of words, wiped her hands on a towel and shot a wary glance toward the back door of the medicine wagon. "There's only one thing we got to worry about if we keep him with us, and that's her." She pointed a pudgy finger at her daughter.

Knowing exactly what his wife was referring to, Zack sighed. "That's something else we got to think about, baby. What if you can't fend the man off, should he take it in his head to have carnival ideas about you the way that crazy Buck Christman did a while back?"

"That's *carnal* ideas, Dad."

"Carnal, carnival—it don't make much difference what you call it if'n he takes it in his head to pin you down and have his way with you, now does it?"

Mariah thought back to the pawings she'd endured while Buck was in their employ, the constant hassles she and Zack had put up with until they'd decided keeping the banjo player with the troupe simply wasn't worth the trouble. Those memories, coupled with the possible results her potion might bring, almost made Mariah change her impulsive plans for the marshal. Then an extraordinarily simple solution struck her.

"I have it!" she said, louder than was wise under the circumstances. Whispering again, she went on. "As long as he doesn't know who he is or what his past was all about, it's up to us to tell him, isn't it?"

Zack gave her an uneasy nod. "Ayuh."

"Then why not make him a blood relative?" She paused, trying to think of the perfect family connection, one that would keep the marshal at arm's length but would also prove the potency of her love potion. A cousin, perhaps. Yes! If a man like Slater were to take a liking to her, if he could accept her as his kin and even show a little more interest in her than he ought to, that would be proof enough that her potion worked!

"Why don't we make him my good old cousin, Cain, who joined us to learn the business. How do you like it?"

Zack pursed his thin lips and frowned.

Oda shook her head, grumbling to herself.

"It'll work," Mariah insisted, addressing her mother. "We'll just tell him he belongs to your brother Thomas. He's believed everything else. Why not that?"

Oda stiffened at the mention of her family.

Sliding his arm across her shoulders, Zack gave his wife a little squeeze as he said to Mariah, "Go on."

"There's nothing to go on about. If he's my cousin, he'll just naturally have to leave me be."

Zack glanced at Oda. "That gonna be all right with you?"

She shrugged. "I expect."

Zack gave her a short nod, and sighed in surrender. He never denied Mariah anything if he could possibly help it. "I reckon it might just work at that, but you'd best understand that I'm a-leaving the care and feeding of that man up to you, young lady. If he don't fit in or makes more trouble than he's worth, we'll just be getting rid of him any ole way we have to. Agreed?"

Mariah beamed. "Agreed. Mother?"

"Agreed. Now that we got that all settled, I'd like to get out of these wet clothes." Oda cocked her thumb, inviting her husband and daughter to give her some privacy.

Zack headed for the entrance of the tent. "I'll go on outside and secure that sorrel for the night. Guess while I'm at it I'd best check the saddlebags to make sure I found all the marshaling papers that fellah had on him." He reached into his shirt pocket, withdrew the shiny badge, and tossed it to his wife. "Find a good place to hide this, will you, woman?" Then he stepped out through the flap and into the tail end of the latest cloudburst.

Alerted by the sudden blast of cold air, Daisy got up from her warm bed, yawned loudly, then shook herself off and trotted out the flap behind Zack.

Mariah started up the back steps of the medicine wagon. "I'm going to check on the marsh—" She corrected herself, "—dear Cousin Cain to see if he needs any more salve or a fresh bandage."

"Careful in there." Oda warned her daughter before Mariah disappeared from her sight.

Once inside the wagon, Mariah stood very still in the darkness, listening to the lawman breathe, and picked out his strong masculine scent in the normally floral aroma of her tiny quarters. Although the wooden walls stretched to accommodate a ceiling of just over six feet, the actual bed of the wagon was ten feet long, the width not quite seven, and every inch of space had to be used in the most efficient manner possible.

A narrow aisle only wide enough to allow one person to pass split the room in half. On one side, the wall was a checkerboard of shelving fashioned with high "thresholds" to keep the contents from toppling down to the floorboards as the wagon bounced from town to town. These shelves were laden with Kickapoo Wizard Oil, Princess Tanacoa's Special Vegetable Compound, Sagwa Worm Syrup, and every manner of salve and tonic imaginable.

Across from the medical supplies, Mariah's narrow

bed filled just over six feet of wall space. The area beneath it served as storage for the kettles, vats, ingredients, and empty bottles used in the preparation of the medicines. The remaining space between the bed and the back wall was taken up by a built-in combination dresser/water closet.

Mariah lit a candle sitting in a saucer on top of the dresser and glanced down at her new "cousin." His head was butted up against the back wall of the wagon, and his feet were pressed against her dresser. The marshal's big body wasn't so much lying on her bed as filling it, consuming every square inch of a space she'd always thought of as quite adequate, until now. That he was a man of the law, added to the fact that no other man had ever known the softness of her mattress, made the sight startling, if not downright . . . arresting.

Stimulated by the thought and all it implied, Mariah moved on down the narrow aisle, and then eased her hip onto the edge of the railing which supported the mattress. Finally, she thought, grumbling to herself, a man between her sheets, and look who it turned out to be! A self-righteous, arrogant marshal who would just as soon hang her as bed her. It was yet another obstacle for her potion to overcome in order to gain the fame it so richly deserved. To get this mean-spirited, hardheaded bastard to so much as smile at her would be testimony enough to sell her product worldwide!

The lawman stirred then, groaning noisily, painfully. Mariah brushed her hand across his forehead. He was warm, but not hot or feverish. She took his pulse. It was strong and regular. She slid farther up the railing, nudging his big body aside with her right knee and thigh as she moved, and when she was able to reach his head, she carefully lifted him off of her pillow and removed the bandage. The linen came away fairly clean, suggesting that he had stopped bleeding. He began to moan as she laid him back down on her pillow, tossing his head from side to side, and Mariah caught his face between her hands to keep him from thrashing about and splitting the wound open again.

"Take it easy," she whispered, staring down at him as he quieted, really looking at him for the first time. The marshal was not what she would call a handsome man. He was masculine, certainly, virile and powerful, but too cruel of mouth and narrow of thought for her to consider him attractive. Although he looked to be less than ten years her senior, he bore the ruts of a deep and unrelenting anger beneath his high cheekbones, and the fine lines etched into his brow suggested that he was a man who never went out of his way to smile, much less laugh. Even his otherwise classic and aristocratic nose looked angry, the smooth, straight lines marred by a few knots and bumps, evidence of his many fights.

Mariah remembered the way he'd spoken to her and her family back in Bucksnort. Cain Law had an evil look about him, a malevolence of eye and viciousness of tongue to be feared by both men and women alike. What would he do when he regained his memory? What manner of vengeance would he seek against the Pennys for fooling him so blatantly?

Suddenly questioning her plans to use this man, she worried not for herself but for her family.

When she started to rise up from the railing, the marshal's hand suddenly shot up from his side, encircling her wrist. Then, before she could break free or even cry out, he jerked her back down onto the edge of the bed.

His green eyes frantic with uncertainty, he said, "What do you think you're doing?"

Mariah opened her mouth, but all she could manage at first was a tiny gasp of surprise. She'd been aggravated by this man since she'd first laid eyes on him, but now she knew a little fear—and it was mind-chilling. She gulped and then said, "Why Cain, honey, it's just me . . . Cousin Mariah. Now let go of my arm. You're hurting me."

Although he continued to hold her, something rang familiar in her words. Cain. Yes, now he remembered. That was his name: Cain Law. Yes. And this was his . . . *cousin*? "Did you say we're related?"

Mariah offered a sweet, innocent grin along with a coquettish nod. "First cousins on my mama's side. Now be a good boy and turn me loose." Her confidence growing as his faded, she jerked out of his grasp. "I swear if you aren't acting like a madman, Cousin Cain. That wagon must have plum rolled over your fool head instead of up against it."

He chuckled a little, but he wasn't really listening to her prattle. Cain was studying this woman who claimed to be his kin, trying to understand why she didn't look the least bit familiar to him. "First cousins, huh? Then you're Mariah Law?"

"Mariah Penny. I told you, we're related on my mother's side. You belong to her brother, Thomas Law. Well," she said, amending the story with a dollop of truth. "That is, you belonged to him until he was killed at the battle of Vicksburg some twenty or so years ago."

The War Between the States. Yes, he'd heard of that. He knew the battle had pitted Confederate soldier against Union soldier, brother against brother in some cases, but that was all he knew. He had no recollection of his father, or the name Thomas Law. Christ! Where had his mind gone?

"I—I'm so confused," he said, closing his eyes. "I don't know who I am or what I'm saying. I hope you're not offended, but to tell the truth . . . I don't even remember you."

Mariah smiled. "No offense taken. I'm here to help you in any way that I can. Just ask me anything, and if I know the answers, I'll fill in the blanks."

Overwhelmed with gratitude and the first sense of hope he'd had since the accident, Cain reached out blindly and patted his cousin's knee. "Where are we?"

"In New Mexico Territory. We'll be heading for the Colorado border as soon as the weather clears." She removed his hand from her knee, surprised by the burst of warmth it had generated there. "Maybe you ought to go back to sleep now and ask your questions later. You've had quite a blow to the head, you know."

But Cain didn't want to sleep. At least, not until he could make a little better sense of his surroundings— hell, of *himself*. If all this was true, and he really had no cause to doubt any of Mariah's claims, why couldn't he remember any of it? Why couldn't he remember her?

Or . . . did he? Cain peered into her unusual eyes, knowing instantly that, yes, he had gazed into them before. They were beautiful, exotic eyes, but the name Mariah didn't sound the least bit familiar.

He glanced around the inside of the wagon, his attention snagging on the rows of medicine bottles. These he recognized for what they were in an instant, and something about them disturbed him. But that was all they told him.

His stomach rumbled, and Cain suddenly realized he had no idea how long it had been since he'd last eaten. *What* had he eaten, and why couldn't he remember even that much? Panic raced through his veins, riding the coattails of his suddenly raging pulse, and he struggled into a sitting position.

Mariah tried to caution him. "Don't try to move yet!"

But it was too late. Cain was sitting up, grinding his teeth against the blinding pain and terrific ache at the back of his skull. "Food," he said thickly. "Would you please get me some food?"

"Sure." But she hesitated. "Will you be all right if I leave you alone? You won't try to get out of bed, will you?"

If he could have, Cain would simply have shaken his head, but he couldn't manage the task. Instead, he whispered, "I'll be fine. Just get me some food. And coffee, too."

"Coming right up."

As Mariah rose and started for the door, she could hear Daisy barking through the thin wooden walls of the wagon and her father shouting for the animal to quiet. She descended the portable steps and walked into the tent, thinking of going outside to check on her pet, but Zack and the dog pushed through the opening flap at that moment, saving her the trouble.

"Get on over there," Zack said irritably, driving Daisy with the "toe" of his wooden leg. "Mariah—tie that danged mutt to the back of the wagon a while and see if she can't learn a lesson or two. Her yapping just run off the marshal's horse!"

Mariah put her finger to her lips. "Cousin Cain is finally awake!"

Zack's gaze shot to the back of the medicine wagon. "Is he now? Well, maybe you ought to stick your head in the door and tell him he don't have a horse no more. Dumber-than-dirt Daisy just seen to that. The minute that deucedly stupid dog of yours started yipping, the mar—Cain's sorrel took off like the devil was at his heels."

All the better as far as Mariah was concerned, and one less familiar object which might jar the marshal's memory. She whispered, "Maybe it's just as well." Then louder, "Cousin Cain is hungry. He sent me out here to get him some food."

Oda, who'd changed into a plain wool wrapper of gunmetal gray and now stood at the stove stirring a pot of leftover stew, said, "I just started warming supper. If he wants a hot meal and biscuits to go with it, he's just gonna have to wait a spell like the rest of us."

"How about coffee?"

"Ought to be done in a minute or so."

The rain started up again, pounding fat drops against the canvas roof. Deciding to use the noise of the sudden downpour to cloak a little family conference, Mariah motioned Zack to come join her and Oda over near the stove.

"I told Cain we're cousins and all, and he seemed to believe me." Keeping one eye on the wagon's back door, she asked her father, "Did you get time to look through his things before the horse ran off?"

"Ayuh." Zack reached into his back pocket and withdrew a gold pocket watch and a thin wallet which contained the marshal's identification papers. "Except for some extra clothes and his mess gear, this and a little better than two hundred dollars was all he had with him."

"Two hundred dollars?" Oda peered down into her husband's palm. "I'd say that about covers what he cost us back in Bucksnort."

Zack raised his eyebrows. "Now, missus—you know we can't think about taking his money. That'd be outright thieving, no question about it."

Oda remained firm. "He owes us. Ain't nothing wrong with taking what's rightfully ours."

"Mother's right about him owing us, Zack, and near as I can figure, it'll take a lot more than two hundred dollars to square things. Why, don't you remember what he said to me back in town? He's lucky I'm not a real Kickapoo, Comanche, or Apache—I might have scalped him right then and there!"

Zack hemmed and hawed, weighing his innate

honesty against the injustices done to his family. Instead of putting a complete kibosh on the idea of keeping the man's money, he said, "I suppose it wouldn't hurt to keep a little of that money, maybe fifty dollars or so, but I've got to tell you—it feels like it'd still be flat-out stealing. No other word for it."

"I didn't exactly say that we should *keep* his money, Zack." Mariah glanced at her mother, assuming she felt the same way. "Oda didn't mean that either. What I propose is that we *pretend* it's ours— get it?"

At her father's frown, she explained. "Just stuff those bills in your pocket and dole it out to him like you're doing him a big favor." She punched his arm playfully. "Use it to buy him some new clothes when we hit Pagosa Springs, offer him a few bucks to spend on himself in the mercantile, make him feel *beholding* to us. That ought to keep him under our thumbs!"

Zack's scrawny mustache formed a narrow crescent over his upper lip as he said, "Oh-h-h. Now I get you." He glanced at Oda, nudging her with his elbow. "That little girl of ours has really got herself a head on her shoulders, don't she?"

Oda chuckled and turned back to the stove. "Ain't no surprise about that. The girl has my brain. Her plan sounds fine to me. I like it."

Mariah gave Zack a triumphant smile, and then removed the watch from his hand. Surprised to find that a man like the marshal even owned such a finely crafted timepiece, she studied the delicately etched gold case and then flipped it open. Opposite the dials was a frame containing a cameo photograph of a fragile, golden-haired woman. Shocked to find the image of anyone so genteel in the lawman's possession, she showed it to her father and said, "Who do you suppose this is?"

Zack studied the photo a moment, and then shrugged. "Could be anyone. His mother, sister, intended . . . wife, even."

Oda whirled around, and the trio exchanged stunned glances, each one weighing the new evidence against their own conscience. None of them had considered that the lawman might have a family somewhere, a wife who might wonder what had happened to him.

After a long, uncomfortable moment, Zack said, "It's most likely his mother. He didn't hardly strike me as the marrying kind." Then he took the watch from Mariah and handed it to Oda along with the wallet. "Hide these away with his badge, missus."

Oda had just pushed the items inside her dress pocket, when Daisy started barking and straining at the rope securing her beneath the stairs at the back of the wagon.

Alarmed, all three Pennys turned in unison, and found the newest member of their family standing on the top step, hanging on to the door frame as if it were a life preserver.

Zack found his voice first. "How'ya doing, son? Mariah tells me you don't remember us much."

Cain slowly made his way down the stairs, swaying as he fought for control of his balance.

Zack met him halfway across the tent and offered his hand. "I'm your uncle, Zachariah Penny."

Feeling like a complete idiot, Cain accepted his greeting. "Sorry, sir, but I'm still having some trouble remembering things." He searched his brain for just the slightest memory of this kind-faced old man, but nothing registered. "People, too, I'm afraid."

"Well, I wouldn't fret none about it," Zack said with as much nonchalance as he could muster in the face of such outrageous lies. "Y'all haven't been with us but a couple of weeks now. I expect things will start coming back to you in bits and pieces 'fore long."

"I hope so." Cain's gaze shifted to the stove, where he saw a short woman nearly as wide as she was tall working over a large cast-iron kettle.

"Your aunt Oda," Zack said just before calling to her. "Supper about ready, missus?"

She turned, giving a slight nod to the lawman. "Soon. Good to see you up and about again, Cain."

"Thank you, ma'am. I wish I could be a little friendlier, but I just don't—"

"You aren't about to hurt my feelings any. Don't give it another thought."

Silently watching the exchange between Cain and her mother, Mariah felt a shiver of excitement skitter down her spine. The lawman seemed to fill the inside of the tent, not just with his bulk, as he had in her bed, but with his very presence, making Zack and Oda seem incredibly small to her. And when he spoke! Even though Cain was very confused, completely unsure of who or what he was, his voice still commanded the attention—and unquestioning obedience—of all those within earshot.

She thought back to Bucksnort and the way the marshal had taken the crowd away from her father even *before* he'd shown his badge. The man was a natural, a force to be reckoned with. The kind of man strangers believed in. Before, she'd been thinking only of testing her potion and getting him to do some of the physical work for her father. Now she saw a much broader use for the man and his talents.

"Why don't you sit a spell?" Zack said to Cain, pulling up a collapsible stool. "You really shouldn't even be out of bed yet."

"Thanks, but no. I can't rest until I know a little more about myself and how I came to be here. Would you mind telling me why I'm traveling with you folks, where I came from, and where we're headed?"

Zack hitched up his trousers, trying to make himself as tall as the tale he would have to tell. "Why, this is the Doc Zachariah Kickapoo Medicine Show. I thought you already knew that."

Medicine show? Cain recalled the bottles in the wagon, along with the fact that something about them disturbed him. "Have I been helping you out in some way, or—"

"Allow me," Mariah said, thinking of the perfect role for the lawman. Given the authority in his voice and his commanding physical presence, she was only surprised she hadn't thought of it sooner. With a genuine smile, she flashed her eyes and said, "Why, Cousin Cain—surely you remember how fast you were becoming the most popular feature of our show."

"I was?"

Zack lowered his voice to its most dramatic pitch as he said, "And profitable, too, son!"

"Oh, yes." Mariah clutched her bosom. "The money has simply been *rolling* in since you joined up with us."

Cain closed his eyes and rubbed them, as if that might help stir up the embers of his memory, but his past was as blank as his present. He sighed. "Sorry, but I just can't seem to remember."

Mariah grinned. "See if this helps."

She dashed past Cain, winking at her father on the way, ducked into the wagon, and grabbed the props she was looking for. Garments in hand, she bounded back down the steps and launched herself up on the stool Zack had offered the lawman. After settling the stovepipe hat on her head, she fastened Zack's cape at her throat and then whirled, whipping the black satin garment into a dramatic frenzy.

When she came to a halt, the slick material still undulating around her, Mariah spoke in a deep, theatrical voice. "You, Cousin Cain, are the *one*!" She pushed her ear forward with her hand. "What'd I say, y'all?"

"He's the one!" Zack said, falling into rhythm.

"That's right! And he's the *only*!"

"Ayuh! The one and only!"

Mariah threw her arms out at her sides and let her head fall back. "The one and only . . . *Brother Law*!"

"Can we hear it for Brother Law!" Zack cried. "Healer of the sick and infirmed!"

Cain was astounded by the revelations and the

manner in which they were delivered. Looking from
Mariah to Zack, and then to Oda, he clutched his
chest and said, "Christ in a whiskey barrel! Are you
trying to tell me that I'm some kind of a . . . a
preacher?"

3

Navajo River, Colorado
One week later

Mariah took a deep breath of crisp mountain air, loving the heady scent of pine which seemed to saturate her to her very soul. This was an atmosphere in which she thrived and blossomed, no matter what the state of her mind. She was happy to be out of New Mexico Territory, even though at this time of year, its usually drab landscape was fresh with yellow Perky Sues and arroyos edged in delicate white flowers from the Apache Plume shrub. But here in southern Colorado, the land gradually evolved into a panorama of tall timber, bushy piñon pines, and lush valleys and mountain slopes carpeted with the blooms of bright lavender columbines. She was, in a word, home. And here in the towns of Colorado, the Penny family would stay throughout the entire summer and a good part of the fall.

Moving at their usual snail's pace, the family still had a two-day journey ahead of them before they would reach Pagosa Springs, some twenty-five miles north of where they'd spent the night. There they would put on their first really "big" show of the season, and Mariah hoped to work Cain into the act.

So far, she hadn't had much of an opportunity to train him. Her new cousin had gotten dizzy, and then passed out again shortly after learning about his role as Brother Law. When he'd finally awakened the following morning, he'd been sick to his stomach, and his memory of even the previous twenty-four hours had been sketchy at best. Zack and Mariah had insisted that the injured man remain in her bed until his brain had a chance to heal itself. And there he'd stayed, lying on the mattress in the medicine wagon for the past five days as the troupe moved north, Daisy lying on the floor beside him—little traitor that she'd become.

Except for her dog's odd and very irritating behavior, this arrangement had worked out fine for Mariah. She'd begun her cousin's medical "therapy" immediately, sick stomach and all. Leaving him with a bottle of love potion she'd labeled #20, she'd instructed him to swallow one teaspoon upon awakening and another each night after supper. Now, a week later, he had just under half a bottle left, but she still had no idea if the potion was working. Perhaps, Mariah thought, she ought to double the dosage. Either that, or make the next bottle "double strength." He certainly seemed physically strong enough to handle more medicine.

This morning, Mariah thought Cain had awakened especially full of vigor and energy, bright-eyed and confident of his physical condition, if not his mental abilities. He was, for all purposes, a clean slate just waiting for her to inscribe the missing information. She planned to begin filling it the moment the medicine show pulled out of camp.

The troupe, including Cain, decided to split the mules from here on out, leaving one to draw the medicine wagon with Zack and Oda aboard, and the other to haul the supply cart. Cain had assured everyone that he was more than able to handle the second rig, and Mariah decided that it would serve two purposes if she were to ride beside him. First, she'd be there to take control of the cart if Cain should fall dizzy again. Second, and even more important, it was way past time for Brother Law's lessons to begin.

While Zack and Oda packed the tent, Mariah put the pots and pans they'd used for the breakfast meal into a storage slot at the back of the supply wagon, and then wandered down the gently sloping hillside to the river, where Cain was putting himself together for the journey. She found him at water's edge, wearing nothing but a clean pair of snug-fitting jeans and his boots. His back was to her, his hands busy adjusting the small mirror he'd propped between the branches of a young pine. On a lower, thicker branch, he'd set a tin cup filled with shaving foam.

Mariah continued to approach him from behind, gliding through the sweet spring grass on her moccasined feet as if she were nothing more than a gentle breeze. When she'd gotten as close to Cain as she dared without him catching her reflection in his mirror, she paused and watched while he lathered his face. His beard had grown thick and full over the past week, and if not for its deep rust color, she probably wouldn't have noticed that his hair was auburn, not dark brown as she'd first thought. It was particularly nice hair, coarse and wavy, a little longer, she thought, than he'd have worn it as a lawman, but not nearly long enough for his role as Brother Law. No, for that dramatic part, he would need to let those thick waves grow until they skimmed the tops of his shoulders, at the least.

Cain dipped the shaving brush back into the tin cup and swirled it vigorously, drawing her attention to his magnificent, broad shoulders. Mariah had never watched a half-naked man perform his ablutions before, or any man really, save for her father. She had to admit, the sight was stunning enough to take her breath away—in spite of what she knew, and disliked, about this particular man. She moved a little closer.

He tilted his head back and began to paint a thick coat of lather along his neck. His skin was smooth and dark, a nutmeg color which made him look healthy and robust, even though he'd just climbed out of his sickbed. She noticed a dusting of dark freckles along his shoulders and arms. Those and the way his thick muscles seemed to roll as he moved, bunching and expanding, drew her nearer and nearer, hypnotizing her. She welcomed the pull, felt a warmth wash over her, and even understood that it had been brought on by something she'd never experienced before—sexual desire.

Mariah knew that she would not be content until she actually put her hands on him; until she could feel those muscles bumping against the sensitive flesh of her palms. Of course she'd wondered about the goings-on between male and female from time to time, and even dreamed occasionally of what it might be like to one day have someone of her own, but Mariah had never been drawn to a man this way before or felt the urge to touch one so intimately. Had her potion somehow missed its mark and affected her instead of Cain?

She laughed to herself, casting off the ridiculous thought, transfixed by this "cousin" she both coveted and loathed. When she was but a whispered "Excuse me" away, she slowly raised both hands, hovering there above his magnificent body, until—

"What the—" Cain leapt to the side, wheeled around, and plowed his palms down the sides of his jeans, seeking, but not finding, the grips of his pistols. "Jesus, Mariah! What the hell are you trying to do? *Scare* my memory back?"

She laughed, the sound a low, throaty chortle. "Sorry, Cousin Cain. I just came on down to see how you're doing. Feeling all right?"

"Except for my pulse," he said, turning back to the mirror, "yes. I'm feeling pretty good."

Mariah had an idea that his pulse might have matched hers at that moment, but not for the same reasons. Hers was racing along on a flood of astonishment at those feelings of desire. But his startled reaction to her approach had jerked her out of her lusty musings and made her wonder about something else. How could she possibly be so drawn to this man, knowing what she knew about him? Had she begun to awaken sexually only to discover that she was an indiscriminate wanton, a woman capable of the most debased of matings?

In spite of these concerns, Mariah's gaze wandered to Cain's back again, and once more she fell under his spell.

What could be the harm in touching him? It wasn't as if he'd guess her thoughts—he didn't even know what his own thoughts were yet. And it might even serve as a kind of test to see how #20 was working.

Deciding it would be all right to allow this one indulgence, necessary even, Mariah brazenly reached out and let her fingers light on his right shoulder. The muscles stiffened beneath her touch for a moment, but then relaxed almost as quickly. As her senses tuned to his warmth and the slick, smooth way his skin melted against hers, she slowly dragged her hand across the expanse of his shoulders, squeezing here, rubbing there, allowing instinct to guide her. Aware only of the way his body felt below her fingertips, not of the man himself, Mariah gave a startled yelp when his voice came to her from over his shoulder.

"Mariah . . ." His voice was tight, guarded.

Her hands fell quickly to her sides, and when she

looked up, she found herself caught in his speculative gaze in the mirror.

"What were you doing to me just now?" he asked, still staring at her reflection.

"I, ah . . . was just making sure your injuries have all healed. Your shoulders were kinda banged up, you know. I wanted to make sure you're as well as you're letting on, that's all."

Cain frowned, then returned the mirror to its original position and picked up his razor.

"No, wait!" Mariah said as he touched the keen-edged instrument to his cheek. "Let me."

"Thanks for the offer, little cousin, but I'm really quite able to handle this chore myself."

"I'm sure you are, but I think we ought to try something different with you." She took the razor from his hand. "Ever wear a beard before?"

He thought hard for a minute, and then sighed. "I don't know."

"It doesn't matter. I think Brother Law should, and I know just the kind of beard that would be perfect for him." She glanced around the area, and then motioned for Cain to follow her to a nearby boulder. "Sit a spell," she said, pointing to the rock. "I'm gonna transform you into the kind of fellah even the devil himself would believe in."

Cain grumbled but straddled the boulder and offered her his lathered chin. Holding her at arm's length, he warned, "I may not know one hell of a lot about who I was or what kind of man I used to be, but I do know this—if you should happen to cut me, you'll wish you'd left me on the side of the road to fend for myself."

After slowly moistening her lips, Mariah lowered her eyelids to half-mast and pinned him with a purposely smoky gaze. "Why, Cousin Cain, darling. I could never do a thing like that to you. You're much too important to me."

As he glimpsed into the depths of those incredibly beautiful eyes, feeling things he knew he had no right to feel, Cain suddenly couldn't be sure if it was genuine concern or a touch of insanity that was staring back at him. A sliver of fear poked at his chest, a sensation he was certain he'd rarely, if ever, experienced when dealing with men, much less women. "Maybe—" He cleared his throat, surprised to find that he could hardly talk. "Maybe I ought to just go ahead and do this myself."

"Don't be silly." Then, without another word, she gripped his chin to steady his jaw and neck, and drew the razor up the length of his throat.

As she worked, with the scent of sandalwood and of Cain himself swirling around her, Mariah became aware of the sting of sexual desire once again. This time, actual heat, not warmth, mushroomed inside of her, spreading even to her extremities. Her hands moved over the planes of his face, slipping and sliding through the rich aromatic cream, tracing the high ridges of his cheekbones, then slithering down to the chiseled hollows below.

She imagined exploring the rest of his body this way, and a little shiver coursed up her spine, bringing with it another burst of heat. Why *now,* she wondered, and with *him* of all people? *He* was supposed to be feeling this way about *her*! And besides, shouldn't the attraction a woman felt for a man be more selective than this, more logical somehow? She glanced into Cain's eyes, pleased to find him studying her with at least as much intensity. Maybe, she thought with a modicum of surprise, logic didn't have a damn thing to do with it.

Cain held very still as she worked, acutely aware she was holding a razor near his throat. There was something reckless about her, and she still had a kind of crazed look in her eye. Had she noticed the desire he was feeling for her and decided to do something about her depraved cousin once and for all? He gulped, moving his Adam's apple, making it an easy target for her razor, and thought about pushing her away. That's when she leaned in closer, shaving beneath his nostrils, and all thoughts of escaping her touch evaporated as her two slender braids dangled against his bare chest, sweeping him like a pair of miniature brooms.

Cain glanced up, worried that she'd noticed yet another inappropriate reaction from him, and caught her gaze, along with the faint scent of cinnamon. Her breathing was rapid, certainly more rapid than he would have expected, and the violet color of her eyes had darkened almost to indigo blue. She looked as if she was flushed with excitement, maybe even a little . . .

No! That couldn't be the cause of her high color and all-around glow. They were cousins! What kind of a man was he to even think such a thing? She straightened abruptly then, breaking eye contact with him, and marched over to the tree, where he'd left a strip of toweling. When she returned and began to clean the remaining lather off of his skin, her breathing had slowed and her eyes were their usual color again. Had he imagined what he thought he'd seen?

Trying to look as casual and unruffled as possible, certainly far more than she felt, Mariah backed away from the lawman and studied the results of her efforts. She'd shaved him clean except for a strip of beard an inch and a half wide which ran from ear to ear, outlining the shape of his strong, angular jaw. Cleaned up, his eyes sparkling with vitality, Cain didn't look quite as harsh or cruel as he once had. In fact, if she were honest with herself, now that she'd taken a good look at him, she'd have to say that he wasn't a bad-looking man. But of course, she couldn't say it. And never would.

Aware suddenly that her cheeks were burning— and worse, that Cain had watched them catch fire— Mariah said, "I think that shave'll do you just fine. Have a look and see if you don't agree." She handed Cain the mirror she'd picked up with the toweling and rambled on while he examined his reflection. "I tried to make your beard look a little like the one Abraham Lincoln used to wear, you know? It looks real honest-like. I'm thinking once we get you the proper clothing, folks are just naturally gonna feel pretty much the same way about you as they did him. Like it?"

He shrugged, far more interested in—and confused by—her. "It'll do, I suppose."

"Good." Mariah lifted the hem of her skirt and turned toward the slope. "We'll be pulling out as soon as you're dressed and ready to go. Get a move on!" Then, her cheeks still burning, she started up the hill.

Cain watched her as she walked away, unable to tear his gaze from the rounded outline of her bottom. Oh, she was wearing a proper enough skirt all right, but the way her hips swayed left room for doubt as to whether she'd donned enough petticoats and bloomers or whatever in the hell it was she ought to have been wearing by way of underpinnings. More disturbing than that—he couldn't seem to stop himself from staring at her or imagining the woman beneath that proper clothing.

What the hell kind of a man *was* he, anyway? It seemed to him that he must have been a moral kind of fellah, or thoughts such as the ones he was having wouldn't have disturbed him so. But still, if he was so damn principled, how could he be having these feelings at all? Desire hadn't just tickled his loins at the thought of Mariah naked under that skirt, it had licked him from within, painfully swelling him beyond simple arousal. Lord, if he was this depraved now, what the hell kind of a man had he once been? The woman was his *cousin,* for Christ's sake.

Maybe, he thought, desperate for a reasonable explanation, the fever in his mind had taken control over his body as well. Or maybe more than his memory had been scrambled in the accident, maybe his very soul had been lost in the bargain. Hell, Cain didn't know. He only knew one, utterly appalling thing for sure right then. He'd been hard almost since the first moment her sensuous fingers had touched his shoulder.

Better than one hundred miles from the Penny encampment, most of the Doolittle Gang was settling in for the night at the ruins of an ancient Indian village. Gang leader and elder brother Billy Doolittle had discovered the dwellings the year before on an advance scouting trip of the area. Located just below the sheer, overhanging cliffs of a towering mesa some thirty miles west of Durango, the series of little "cave pueblos" made a perfect, nearly inaccessible hideout.

Billy leaned in close to the fire pit and flipped the venison steaks over to the other side, ducking as the lard he'd used to sweeten the skillet popped and sizzled all around him. He glanced up at his brother, Artemis, and said, "How you coming with them biscuits, dreamy-eyes?"

Although Artemis hated the name, any nickname in fact, he grinned at his older brother and continued pounding his fists into the sticky dough. "Can't tell for sure, Billy. You know I ain't got much know-how when it comes to cooking, but I think they could use some more flour."

"There's that word again: *think*. What have I told you about that, Artie-boy? If'n I wanted you to go thinking on your own, I'd have told you to do it."

"Sorry."

"I'll just bet you are." Billy stacked the steaks, one on top of another to make room in the skillet for the biscuits, and then snatched the bowl out of his brother's hands. As he spooned the dough into the hot grease, he sighed and said, "I guess you went and forgot about that cowlick sticking straight up on the top of your head, huh, boy?"

Artemis dropped his chin to his chest. "I ain't forgot."

"Then maybe you forgot why it's there." When the kid didn't comment, he offered a reminder. "It's your own personal dunce cap, a kind of natural signal that lets the rest of us normal folks in on the fact that you ain't quite all there. A built-in dunce cap for a dunce!" He laughed, and then as he thought about it, laughed some more.

Artemis laughed, too, as always, wanting desperately to fit in with the gang, even at his own expense. Besides, Billy was right about the cowlick. It did look like a dunce cap, and he was a little bit slow. Not that Artemis had been born with any kind of abnormality, including the cowlick. His wheat-brown hair, straight as string, had always combed down nice, even without the benefit of Pa's bear grease. Until the accident, anyway.

It had happened on the day of his eighth birthday when he went out to give the Doolittles' best brood mare, Irish, a little extra feed. He'd dumped a generous portion of flax and grain mixed with sweet molasses into her crib, and then started to return to the house. That was when he noticed a spot of blood on her right rear fetlock. He had bent down to pick her hoof up from the bedding straw, but it wasn't until he came to that he remembered that Irish didn't allow *anyone* to touch her while she was eating.

The result of that error was a crescent-shaped scar about the size of a horseshoe near the crown at the back of his head; a stubborn cowlick which rose up from the peak of that crescent like a flag; and a mind that wasn't endowed with nearly as much common sense as it would have been otherwise. Hence the nicknames: "Artie-boy," "dreamy-eyes," "dummy," on occasion; and of course, continual references to the "dunce cap" shaft of hair.

The names hurt, especially coming from his last living brother, but he always laughed along with him, sometimes louder than anyone else. If he didn't laugh, Artemis was afraid, one day he'd lose control and do the one thing he really wanted to do. And that was cry.

A gang member named Tate, who was sitting at the edge of the cliff, brought a spyglass to his eye. "Rider coming in!" he said loud enough for all to hear. "It's Tubbs."

"Well, it's about time." Billy turned the biscuits and then covered the pan with a huge, oversized lid. "I'm so hungry I could eat a skunk. Wave him over."

Artemis perked up immediately. Of all the gang members, including his own brother, Tubbs was the one he liked best. Although he couldn't exactly say that the man was nice to him, Tubbs was the only one who never made jokes about his shortcomings, and usually didn't even laugh when the others did. He was the best friend Artemis had ever had.

After Tubbs left his horse, as well as the stray sorrel he'd come across in Mancos Valley, in the care of another member of the six-man gang, Shorty, he hiked up to the site of the ruins. He strolled into camp, tossed a sack of supplies in through the open doorway of one of the block dwellings, and pulled a bottle of whiskey from the inside of his shirt.

"Fill me a cup, would you, Billy?" he said, handing the bottle to his leader. "It's been a long day. In fact, fill one for everyone. I picked up a piece of bad news."

William Doolittle didn't take orders from anyone, but something about this desperado always set his hairs on end and gave him pause. Tubbs had ridden with the gang for just three months now, and had participated in only one job, some three weeks ago: relieving the Texas Exchange in Durango of the meager contents of its safe.

It wasn't as if the man didn't have his strong points. He did his work quickly, quietly, and well. He wasn't squeamish about using his guns, or turning them on lawmen, boys, and if the occasion warranted it, women. And, as an extra plus, the man knew how to listen, rarely shooting off his mouth unless he had something really important to say.

Other than the annoying habit Tubbs had of staring at the ugly craters left behind on Billy's face from a vicious case of chicken pox, Billy really couldn't point a finger at anything the man did that was out of line. But Tubbs gave him the creeps anyway.

Anxious to hear what he had to say, Billy poured the whiskey into two tin cups, leaving the bottle to the others to fend for themselves. "Tate! Cletus! Get on over here," he called.

As the men took their places around the fire, Artemis shuffled up behind, grinning broadly and looking closer to thirteen than his eighteen years of age. "You want me here too, don't you, Billy?"

Tubbs's gaze flickered up to the young man. "Sit down and be quiet."

Over his brother's scowl, Artemis beamed, and said, "Don't mind if I do," and then flopped down between Cletus and Tate.

"I have some disturbing news that needs discussing," Tubbs began.

Billy called a halt to the announcement. "If it's that all-fired important, maybe we ought to call Shorty in on this. Them horses will be all right if we leave them on their own for an hour or so."

In that quiet, nonthreatening, but somehow dangerous way of his, Tubbs slowly lifted his gaze to Billy. "Apparently you've never laid eyes on any of the mountain cats that roam this mesa, or seen one drag down a full-grown bull elk. I don't know about you, mister, but I'm pretty fond of the horse I've got. I don't have a hankering to train another."

That was something else Billy hated—being contradicted or humiliated in front of his men. To cover, he said, "What I meant was that I figured we'd swap Artemis for Shorty—almost the same thing as leaving them on their own, wouldn't you say?"

Tubbs shrugged. "We can just as well talk to Shorty later as Artemis."

Billy tossed down a long drink of whiskey. Then he checked the biscuits and pulled the skillet from the fire. "Well, get on with it, then. Supper's cooked."

Tubbs held his cup of whiskey between both hands, staring at it a long moment before he said,

"While I was in Mancos getting supplies, I took it upon myself to send a wire to a friend of mine in Santa Fe. I didn't much care for his answer."

"You gave our position away to someone in Santa Fe?" Billy slammed his empty tin cup into the fire pit. "Hell, even the dummy knows better than that!"

Tubbs shot him a murderous look. "I *said* I wired a *friend.* I asked him had he heard anything about some trouble up Durango way." His gaze returned to the cup of whiskey.

Billy waited for the rest, and then waited some more. Finally, exasperated, he said, "And . . . ?"

"He had."

"Well, news travels fast. So what?"

"Not what," said Tubbs. "Who."

The hairs on Billy's neck felt stiffer than ever, strong enough to hold his collar at bay. In his agitation, he turned to Artemis. "Get my cup out of that fire pit, boy. See if you can't be of some use!"

Artemis kept his fascinated gaze on his hero as he blindly reached into the pit and removed his brother's cup. Barely aware he'd burned the tips of two fingers, he tossed it next to Billy's thigh, and then settled back to hear the rest of Tubbs's story.

After pouring himself another cup of whiskey, Billy took a deep swallow and said to Tubbs, "Well? Do I have to beat it out of you? What'd your friend hear?"

"That the law is a little *more* than interested in the fact that the Doolittle Gang is riding again."

Billy took another gulp of his drink. "So someone recognized one of the boys, huh?"

"I'd say that's a fair assumption. No one knows me

or Artemis, yet." Tubbs shot Billy a sarcastic smirk, his gaze lingering on his "leader's" scarred cheeks. "Must have been Tate or Cletus or Shorty, or even more likely, *you.* You've got a memorable face."

"Well, so what?" Billy said with a sneer. "They'll never find us up here, and they sure as hell won't be expecting us to drop back into Durango next month to rob the train. I don't see that we got much of a problem."

"No?" Tubbs's tone was a clear suggestion of trouble ahead.

"What is it you ain't telling me?" Billy asked, his agitation rising.

"They've put a hound dog on our trail. Ever hear of a fellah named Slater?"

Except for the bright red craters of his pockmarks, Billy went paper-white. "*Morgan* Slater, U.S. Marshal? That Slater?"

Tubbs nodded, and then smiled, his thin lips set in a grim line. "The one and only."

"Aw . . . *shit!*" Billy spit into the fire, but then lifted his brow a minute later. "Maybe that ain't such bad news after all." He grinned. "Least this way we know he's coming. That gives us a chance to come up with a plan to eliminate him 'fore he eliminates us!"

4

Pagosa Springs, Colorado

Cain felt like a trained monkey. All he lacked was a leash and a bellman's cap.

He sat at the edge of Mariah's bed, alone in the medicine wagon except for Daisy, and attempted to squash down a growing sense of failure. He'd tried to become what they expected him to be. God knew he'd endeavored to follow Mariah's guidance in an effort to become at least as proficient a Brother Law as he'd been before the accident, but it was no use. He was no showman, no hawker of tonics and nostrums, and all the training in the world wouldn't turn him into one. Hell, he didn't even believe in their "miracle cures" and medicines, and he was pretty sure the old Cain didn't either.

That was another problem. Here it was almost

three weeks since he'd cracked his skull, and still his life didn't make sense, no matter how hard the family tried to fill in the blanks. When he'd asked about his past, all he'd been told was that he'd joined the show just two weeks before the accident. Both of his parents were dead, and the rest of his immediate family was scattered. He'd come to the Pennys because he'd apparently had some "trouble" down the road, category unknown. They said he'd asked to become a member of the troupe in an effort to "start over again," whatever the hell that meant.

What kind of man had he been? he wondered for the umpteenth time. Why did nothing he saw or touched leap to the forefront of his mind as familiar or genuine? Cain thought back to his encounter with Mariah at the river a few days past. She'd startled him, sneaking up behind him the way she had, and he'd automatically reached for his guns. If they'd been there, he had a feeling, he would have drawn on her, no questions asked. It certainly had felt that way at the time. What could have driven him to such extremes?

Maybe he was a wanted man, his likeness etched on posters stretching across the nation, someone who had no choice but to shoot first and ask questions later. Christ, what if he had been an outlaw, a *killer*? How in God's name was he to protect himself should someone recognize him? According to Zack, he no longer owned the pistols he'd reached for at the river. Daisy had run off the horse carrying his saddlebags with his clothing and money inside.

And that brought up another curiosity. Cain was pretty sure he hadn't even liked dogs before the accident, and in fact, may have actually hated them. He glanced down at the floppy-eared mutt, wondering what it was that disturbed him so about the animal. The dog was snuggled against Cain's leg, her muzzle propped up on his thigh, snoring, content to share her warmth and unconditional love. Cain's hand automatically went to Daisy's head, and then skimmed down the length of her body, the silken fur rippling in the wake of his palm. He had no memory of ever having so much as petted a dog.

When in bloody blue *hell* would he dredge up more than shadowy hints about his former life? What if he never did remember the man he'd once been? Cain felt his gut roll into a tighter ball at the idea of remaining so helpless within himself, so utterly dependent on the Pennys. And then it struck him; the biggest puzzle of all. This *family*.

He'd fallen into a kind of routine, and yet still they seemed like strangers. Zack was helpful and kind, unwavering in his support and optimism for this mind-broken nephew of his, but there was nothing about him which seemed special or familiar to Cain, no sense of family bonds. Wouldn't he at least remember his own uncle?

And what about Oda? There were blood ties there, but no innate sense of kinship. And how could he *not* remember an otherwise proper woman who usually had a stogie poking out of her mouth? Mariah had explained that in the early days of the show, a customer had given Oda a cigar as a joke, and when she actually lit it, the gag went over so well with the audience, they kept it as part of the act. If that wasn't enough, every time he crossed Oda's path, the same dilemma came to mind without fail—jump over, or go around her? Given her height and width, it was an observation he would have made many times in the past, and yet the first time the thought struck him, he knew without question, it'd been fresh. As fresh and foreign to him as Oda's beautiful, exotic daughter.

Mariah was the most disturbing family member of all. Since the episode at the river, he'd gone out of his way to keep her out of sight and mind—two difficult, and at times, impossible, tasks to accomplish. He was attracted to her, this cousin of his, no way to deny it, but was the temptation he felt for her something new since the accident, or had it been building since he'd joined the troupe?

In either case, the attraction was as sick as it was sinful, a thing to be banished from his mind and body with all haste. But how in hell was he to cool the fire she ignited in him when she was always nearby?

Mariah had been at his side almost constantly over the past few weeks, tending his wounds, bringing his meals, and reminding him to take his daily dose of something that was supposed to strengthen and purify his blood—#20 tonic. He'd balked over taking the elixir at first, loath to try even a spoonful, but finally gave in and tried the stuff just to please Mariah. It had a heavy, oily taste, a bite which reminded him a little of rotgut whiskey, and just a hint of sweet honey which made the concoction slide down his throat slicker than rainwater. He'd almost puked it up in the same moment he'd swallowed the first dose—and hadn't touched a drop since.

Ah, but Daisy, God love her, seemed to love the stuff, and actually begged for her "treat" each morning and evening. Cain patted the dog's head, again amazed at the bond he'd developed with the little animal.

And that led him to another enigma. He was merely amazed by Daisy's new attachment, but Mariah was downright flabbergasted. She didn't like the way her dog went for him, Cain could tell, even though she hadn't said anything to indicate those feelings. Her incredible violet eyes gave her away every time she found Daisy cozied up alongside him. They would narrow for an instant, and then deepen to a rich shade somewhere between indigo blue and royal purple. Cain's pulse lurched at the image, and that brought him back to thoughts of the unholy attraction he felt for her.

Maybe it wasn't just her exotic beauty or the graceful way she moved that drew him to her. It most likely had nothing to do with her at all, he told himself. He'd probably just been too damn long without a woman. Cain didn't bother to search his mind for validation of that theory, for he knew without even trying that he'd come up empty. Besides, if he could just believe that he *had* been too damn long without female companionship, then he would have some excuse, no matter how feeble, for his less-than-cousinly feelings for Mariah.

Other than this depraved desire and the impression that he didn't quite belong to this family, Cain recognized one more disturbing thing about himself. Whenever he tried to dig deep inside to discover who and what he was, flashes of anger or something too ugly to face blocked his thoughts, driving him away from whatever answers lay within.

He knew only that he was burdened by a rage coiled deep in his gut, one he suspected he'd carried inside himself for a very long time, but that it had been muted somehow. The anger was still there, no doubt about it, but he sensed that it was more hollow now, less potent. Had the accident prompted this tenuous sense of peace? Or had joining the family shortly before it been the cause?

Mariah rapped at the back door then, opening it in the same moment. "Cain? You decent?"

He looked up to see her framed in the doorway, her long black hair bathed in sunshine, and felt an immediate tightening in his loins. Decent? Not by a long shot. "I'm dressed, if that's what you mean. Come on in."

She stumbled in through the doorway, wrestling with the packages in her arms, and then dumped them at the foot of the bed. "Zack just got back from town," she said breathlessly, then narrowed her eyes as she noticed how contented Daisy looked curled up in the lawman's lap. She picked up the dog and shooed her out the door, in spite of the animal's low growl of protest. "As I was saying: Zack bought a few things for your debut as Brother Law. Get up and try them on."

"I don't know, Mariah," Cain said even as he stood and began to unbutton his shirt. "I have a feeling the medicine show will do a lot better if 'Brother Law' stays locked up in this wagon. In all honesty, I think you'd have to agree."

Agreed, seconded, and carried, she thought to herself. The man was *not* working out the way she thought he would. But still hoping for a miracle, Mariah kept those concerns to herself and helped Cain out of his shirt.

Trying to help him out of his sour mood as well, she said, "Don't be so hard on yourself. You've probably just got a little case of stage fright. Everyone in the business gets a squirrelly stomach now and again, even after years and years of putting on shows. You'll do just fine."

Over his muttered doubts, Mariah tore open the smallest package and withdrew a white dress shirt. As she slipped the cuffs over his wrists and drew the garment up to his shoulders, she couldn't help but notice the way the silk fabric whispered against his naked skin and how the muscles of his back rippled as he shrugged into the new shirt. It reminded her of the way he'd looked down at the river a few days past, and Mariah found she had to turn away and pause a moment in order to catch her breath and her wits.

When she'd collected herself, she tore into the other package and handed Cain his new coat and hat. As he finished dressing, she gathered up the shredded paper and tossed it out the door.

"Well," Cain said a few moments later. "Here he stands. The one . . . the only . . . Brother Law—impostor extraordinaire!"

At the self-ridicule she clearly heard in those words, Mariah slowly turned to find Cain standing in the center of the aisle. His hands were clasped at his waist in pious, mock humility, his full mouth turned down in a grimace. A beam of morning light shone in through the back door to land on this fictitious cousin of hers, illuminating his features with an unnatural radiance.

Cain still wore his own boots and jeans, but with the addition of the gleaming white shirt, knee-length frock coat of fine black broadcloth, and flat-brimmed hat of charcoal felt, the man was positively dazzling. Mariah's throat went dry. Had she once thought of him as less than handsome?

At her look of consternation, Cain's already deep frown slid into a scowl. "Between this stupid hat and preacher's coat, I must look like an Amish farmer without a crop to plow."

Mariah shook her head. "No, no you don't. In fact, you look . . . great. Turn around."

"Seems like a waste of time, but all right."

Cain spun in a slow, careful circle, giving Mariah a clear view of the way the coat hugged him across his broad shoulders, then tapered in at the waist and hips. Zack had chosen precisely the correct size and cut for the lawman, and the fit was perfect.

When he'd completed the circle, again Cain linked his fingers at the waist, but this time, his expression was anything but humble. "I think by now it should be fairly obvious to us both—I'm not much good as Brother Law, and all the preacher clothing in the world isn't going to change that fact. Go ahead and say it. I simply won't do."

Mariah ignored his words and looked him over instead, beyond the new clothing and "honest Abe" beard, to discover that most of the harsh lines around his mouth had faded, and that his dark green eyes exuded none of their previous malevolence. He would more than "do," she thought, forgetting herself for a moment. In fact, he exuded a certain charisma, a forthright and upstanding facade, but at the same time, he fairly glistened with a frank sensuality that set her pulse to thundering and her heart racing to keep up with the flow.

"I—you look exactly the way you ought to, Cain." She swallowed hard. "And don't worry your head none about your part in the show. You'll do just fine. Why don't you go on out back now and preen your feathers for Zack and Oda. I have to get into my greasepaint and costume now."

"Not yet." His voice was soft, more of a croon than a growl. He sat back down on the mattress and patted the spot beside him. "Come here a minute."

"We don't really have time for yakking just now, Cousin Cain. Oda's fretting to get to town."

He captured her wrist and pulled her down beside him. "She can wait a little longer. We have to talk now."

Mariah raised her chin and looked him full in the face. His eyes weren't entirely green, she noticed, but shot through with shards of amber. Gemlike.

Although she was gawking at him, her lips parted and moist, Cain cleared his throat and went on. "I'm not ready to take part in this show, and I don't think I ever will be. I thought it best to let you know that before we head into town."

"Umm . . . really?" she managed to say, even though she'd become a creature of pure sensation, not logic. All she really cared about at that moment was the fact that their knees were touching. Actually, just the fabric of his jeans had brushed against her muslin skirt, but the heat generated in that brief contact was almost enough to put Mariah into a swoon. She laughed, the sound oddly girlish to her own ears. "You're much too hard on yourself, Cousin Cain. All you need is a little more rehearsal and—"

"What I need," he said, finishing her sentence with a candor that surprised him, "is to believe in the products."

"The products?" She blinked, trying to understand what he meant. "I don't follow you."

"I'm talking about your medicines. It seems to me that in order to perform as Brother Law, I should at least be able to *pretend* I like Kickapoo Wizard Oil."

She laughed again, this time sounding more like herself. "Is that what this is all about?"

He gave her an awkward shrug by way of an answer.

"Oh, Cousin Cain." She slapped his knee, and then left her hand to rest there. "You don't have to actually take any of our medicines if you don't want to—except, of course, for Number Twenty. You might want a dose of Zack's compound now and then for the black-draught effect, but other than that, you seem healthy enough without the rest."

At her touch, that familiar tightening grew to uncomfortable proportions. Cain lifted Mariah's hand from his knee and dropped it between their bodies. It was a snug fit; her knuckles pressed up against his thigh. The change of position didn't do much to relieve the tension coiled in his gut, but he went ahead with what he had to say. "Black draught. Isn't that just—"

"It's a purgative known to clean you out and then some. That's why Zachariah's Compound is so popular. We make it with black draught, Epsom salts, a little cake coloring, and a healthy dose of Zack's old moonshine. It's supposed to perk a body right up."

"Moonshine, huh?" He shook his head. "I think you just made my point for me, Mariah. I don't seem to have it in me to go around selling worthless 'medicine' to folks who barely have enough money to put shoes on their feet. I just can't hawk this . . . this glorified moonshine the way you want me to. I think it'd be best for us all if I, well, if maybe I just . . . you know."

She did. Cain didn't have to say the words. Mariah could almost finish the sentence for him. She saw it in his expression and in the nervous way he'd linked his fingers, tenting and flattening them over and over. He was thinking of parting company with the medicine show. Forever. And at that moment, Mariah didn't know which disturbed her the most: his low opinion of her family's business, or the fact he wanted to move on.

Calling her carefully prepared elixirs "glorified moonshine" brought out her fighting side, but the thought of Cain's leaving the show made her heart kind of freeze up and then resume beating with a vengeance, bumping against her ribs with what felt like enough force to crack them. Maybe, she reasoned, if she could explain her medicines to his liking, both of her problems would be solved.

Mariah reached across the aisle to take a tin of her father's Magic Corn Salve from the lower shelf. "Zack makes this ointment with collodion, camphor gum, sassafras root, and a couple other ingredients known only to him. More often than not, it works, but even when it doesn't actually help to remove the corn, it at least soothes the pain to a more bearable level."

"Selling me on the worthiness of your father's salve isn't going to—"

"Please," she said, cutting him off. "Let me finish what I have to say. I understand some of your doubts, especially if you've had occasion to run across a few of the less-than-honest operations roaming the countryside these days." She glanced at the tin of salve, and then tossed it in Cain's lap. "Did you know that better than half of the farmers who think they have corns have nothing wrong with their feet but dirt calluses from wearing boots with cracks and holes in them?"

"No, I can't say that I did know that."

Catching the sparkle in his eye and the levity in his voice, she relaxed and went on. "I don't mean to go into the whole spiel, but I do want you to understand how hard we try to be a legitimate troupe. A lot of traveling medicine shows *do* sell these poor farmers nothing but boiled-down soap wrapped up in little papers with a label glued to it. But if a fellow actually follows instructions—soak your feet for ten minutes and rub this bar of salve on the corn—well, hell, yes! He'd be cured for life!"

Laughing, Cain said, "Oh, Mariah; I wish you could see the color of your face right now. If you can just keep it that shade for a few more hours, you won't be needing your greasepaint today."

She blushed, deepening the rosy hue that swept over her cheeks. "I'm sorry for getting so worked up. I suppose the whole family has been a little defensive since we quit working for the Healy and Bigelow Kickapoo Indian Medicine Company and went off on our own. I'm not saying that organization is crooked exactly, but they have close to a hundred troupes touring the countryside in their name from here to the East Coast, and they can't watch over all of them. Let me just say that several of those operations are a little on the shady side. Perhaps you're confusing our show with one of theirs."

Cain really had no way of knowing what memories had prompted his distrust of Zack's medicine show, but Mariah's explanation seemed perfectly reasonable. Except for one little thing. His expression more of a smirk than anything, he touched her cheek as he said, "Don't you think smearing greasepaint all over your face and fooling the public into believing that you're a Kickapoo princess is just a little on the shady side?"

So proud was she of her business ethics, down to and including the small deception she practiced with her identity, Mariah would have answered that question in an instant at any other time. But she found she couldn't speak, not with Cain's fingers still brushing her cheek, heating her through and through. Was this a normal reaction? How could something so insignificant, the mere touch of his fingertips—the pads a little rough, yet somehow smooth and silky, too—affect her so intensely? Mariah almost swooned as she imagined those hands dipping lower, caressing her throat, then moving lower still to—no! She had to think, to clear her suddenly muddled brain, to *answer* Cain's accusation.

"M-most, ah . . ." Mariah drew in a breath and forced herself to concentrate. "Most all medicine shows feature some kind of Indian, and of course, the Healy and Bigelow shows swear they have the only authentic Kickapoos. I've never met a real Kickapoo Indian, and I don't think Mr. Bigelow did either. He just happened to like the way the name sounded. Why, even the Indian he started us out with a few years back was a Sioux who couldn't stand reservation life."

"But how can you call your medicine show authentic, when you're so obviously fooling the public?"

"It's not as bad as it sounds. We're just giving the customers what they want when I dress up as Princess Tanacoa. At least half the attraction to our show is the entertainment we provide. I'm just an actor being who the people want me to be, and as long as I don't sell phony or dangerous medicines, I don't see the harm."

Now that she'd fully explained the Penny operation, neither did Cain. Most of all, he knew for sure that he didn't really want to just pack up and leave the show. Not until he knew more about himself. And not until he knew more about her.

He replaced the tin of corn salve on the shelf. "I only know two things right now. One, I am confused, but only about myself. And two, if you'll still have me, I'd like to stay and be of some help to the show. Trouble is, even if I believe in these medicines, I know I'm simply not cut out to hawk them. Is there anything else I can do to be of some value?"

Mariah had been considering that very thing. She smiled. "All we really need, Cousin Cain, is for you to drive the mules and do the heavy chores that are so hard on Zack. During the show, you can mingle with the crowd and show them your muscles—you know, like a saloon bouncer."

"A bouncer?" He turned to her, finally allowing himself to look into those beautiful eyes. They were a rich violet color this morning, complimented by her soft apricot dress, and her lovely face was beaming with enthusiasm and something he couldn't identify. He may have solved his problem about how to help the family, but if he stayed on with them, how in *hell* would he ever get over this insane attraction for Mariah? Could he risk being around her any longer? He didn't know. "Are you sure I'd be worth the trouble as a bouncer?"

"Of course. We could really use someone to remove folks who put us in the same basket as the crooked medicine shows. You know, the kind that call us names and try to have us run out of town."

The way you did the day we met, she silently added.

Cain sighed with both resolution and defeat. He would stay and help them as long as they needed help—or as long as they'd *let* him stay. But he did have one other, very real concern, one he had to make Mariah aware of before anything was settled. "I'll do the best job I know how as the show's bouncer, but there is something else to consider before you make any firm plans that include me. I'm a little worried about what's going to happen when my memory returns."

Of course, Mariah had plenty of reason to fear that same thing. "Worried? Goodness me, whatever for?"

"I don't know exactly. It's just a feeling, I guess." Cain flattened his palm against his chest and raised his voice a notch. "There's something ugly in here, Mariah, something evil, and I don't want you or the family to be around me when it breaks loose. It might be better for you folks if I were to 'find' myself alone."

Mariah's stomach lurched. She knew some of the fears he spoke of, for she'd seen his mean side before—but evil? He'd been a lawman, on the side of right and good. How could Cain even think that he'd once been an evil man? He had to be misreading his gut.

But even as the denials spread through her mind, she remembered the look in his eye back in Bucksnort, the sheer malevolence radiating out from the depths of his soul. She dreaded the day his memory would return, all right—she was no fool. He would be mad as hell, and most of that anger would be directed at her. But then she thought of his leaving, of never seeing him again, and she dug in for a fight.

For the first time in her life, Mariah Penny had a man. Oh, not in every sense of the word, and since he thought he was her cousin, she would probably never know him any more intimately than she already did. But except for that one little detail, the kind of thing that went on between most husbands and wives, she had a man. One she could shape into exactly the kind of man she'd always dreamed of, for as long as his mind remained a blank. She would, Mariah decided, worry about his memory returning when that day came. In the meantime . . .

Mariah turned her brightest smile on Cain, took him by the hand, and rose up from the mattress. "You know what, Cousin Cain?"

Charmed by her brilliant smile, not to mention the cute little way she was tugging at him, Cain climbed to his feet. "What is it, princess?"

"You worry too much! You can fret all you want to about the little nasties you find inside you once your memory returns, but not before. In the meantime, I'd appreciate it if I didn't have to hear any more talk about you leaving. Why don't you go on outside now. There's a little job you can do for me while I get ready for the show." She pushed him toward the doorway.

Cain laughed as he said, "I believe in your medicines now, I swear I do, Mariah! But if what you've got in mind involves tasting a new variety of wizard oil, I'd just as soon pass on the job."

"No tasting, I promise. I just want you to help Oda gather some herbs and mold from the creek bottom while I dress. Later, I might let you in on another of our secret recipes." She paused and looked over her shoulder. "How'd you like to help me whip up a batch of Sagwa Worm Syrup tonight?"

At the foot of the steps, Cain made a face and clutched his stomach. "*Worm* syrup? You're going to market some kind of cure for earthworms?"

She rolled her eyes. "Sagwa Worm Syrup is for *people* with tapeworms. You've still got a lot to learn, Brother Law, but if you turn out to be a good enough helper, Oda might even put your name on the label." Chuckling to herself, Mariah pulled the door shut behind her.

Cain glanced toward the river, his thoughts suddenly dark. Oda was on her hands and knees—searching the banks, he supposed, for the herbs and mold Mariah had mentioned. He took a step toward her, and then balked. He didn't want to go down there. A voice in the back of his mind whispered, "You'll be helping the devil himself with his own brew!"

Cain shuddered, wondering where that bit of information had come from, and tried once again to start for the creek. His feet refused to move. He did not want to help Oda, and he would not let them put his name on any of their medicine labels.

Cain hadn't the foggiest notion of *why* he felt that way. He just did.

5

In spite of his reservations about the products, Cain came to care deeply for the Pennys over the next two weeks, and even began to think of them as his family. His memory had yet to return, but he'd come to terms with this new Cain Law, and even found a certain peace within himself.

The strange rage still lay coiled in his gut like a hibernating dragon, and every now and then, a little twinge warned him that it might just raise its ugly head again. But as the days went on, the awareness of this malicious thing inside himself faded to an occasional burst of unexplained irritation. Other than that, he felt a distinct calm, along with an almost delicious sense of peace.

Cain also began to make himself useful to the medicine show, although his contribution to the actual hawking and selling of wares remained nebulous, and at times, nonexistent. In the little burg of Pagosa Springs he turned out to be more of an interested observer than a bouncer. He supposed the real test of his worth would come in the larger towns such Durango or Denver.

In the meantime, not only did he help Mariah in the preparation of the medicines they would sell—including Sagwa Worm Syrup, *with* Brother Law's name on the label—but he also came up with an effective way to advertise the show as they traveled down the road to Durango. Without halting or even slowing the wagons, Cain would dig into a goatskin trunk filled with advertising circulars, grab a handful of the fliers, and leap off the wagon. Then, after tacking the circulars to fence posts and telegraph poles along the way, he'd leap back aboard the cart, laughing along with Mariah over how long or fast he'd had to run to catch up with her again.

Of course, every time that happened, Cain would have to turn away before he got too caught up in her infectious laughter or playful eyes. Before he forgot she was his cousin again.

That persistent little problem with Mariah was really the only difficulty Cain continued to stumble over in the face of all this newfound contentment, but once they arrived in Durango, he was pretty sure he'd come up with a plan to alleviate even that. All he need do was convince Zack to grant him a small loan. Then he would head on down Main Avenue to Tenth Street, where he was told the saloon business thrived. And he would go there alone.

＊   ＊   ＊

Far from wealthy, but comfortable financially, the Penny family always stayed in the best hotels available along the show route each year. When not selling their wares in the more cosmopolitan towns, Mariah always dressed and behaved like a proper young lady, and to avoid being recognized as Princess Tanacoa, she took the precaution of obscuring her features under oversized bonnets.

For that same reason, she pretty much stayed hidden in her room most of the time, and usually only ate in the hotel restaurant the first and last nights in town. In between, Zack and Oda brought her meals to her in her room. Mariah didn't mind the isolation too much, although the show season lasted anywhere from seven to ten months of the year. Because of this, she didn't get much chance to meet many people her own age, men in particular. But she really hadn't been interested in finding a man of her own before now. Before Cain.

All she'd ever really aspired to since she'd come of age was having one of her nostrums accepted by the general public on a nationwide basis, the way her idol had when she formed the Lydia E. Pinkham Medicine Company. If Lydia Pinkham could do it, by God, so could Mariah Penny. In fact, she'd written to Mrs. Pinkham on several occasions asking for a little business advice. So far, all she'd gotten in return for her trouble were a few letters which were nothing more than advertisements for the famous Pinkham Compound, but Mariah remained undaunted.

Now safely ensconced in her room at the Strater Hotel, she dropped down on the fluffy bed, testing the softness of the mattress. It was firm, but resilient—just the way she liked it. She breathed deeply, inhaling the rich aroma of crisp new fabrics and Belgian wool rugs, and then ran her fingers across the bedspread. Slick and cool to the touch, it was made of sea-green chintz embroidered with clusters of bright blue forget-me-nots, a match to the pair of curtains hanging in front of the only window in the room: a wide, floor-to-ceiling sheet of glass sectioned into four panes.

The bed itself, made of oiled walnut, sported a tall carved headboard with matching canopy, and beside it sat a small table and a Queen Anne chair upholstered in bloodred velvet. Across from it was a large walnut armoire with carved finials and dark wainscoting, and a matching washstand featuring a marble top and a huge mirror. Over by the window, a small desk and chair provided a comfortable place in which to jot letters on the hotel stationery.

First class all the way, Mariah thought to herself. She fantasized that she was the first guest to touch the chintz bedspread or to pour water into the porcelain washbowl. Given the newness of the hotel, that might even be possible, she realized. Mariah chuckled at the idea. What would the management think if they knew a fake Kickapoo Indian and her mongrel dog were the first occupants of room 222? They'd probably puff up like purple globefish and explode, she thought, laughing aloud at the image.

She glanced in the direction of Daisy, who'd been

smuggled into the hotel along with her mistress. The dog was lying on the floor near the door, her tiny black nose pushed up against the crack between the floor and the bottom edge of the door. Her little black ears were pointed at the ceiling in anticipation, and even the pert tuft of white fur between her ears seemed more peaklike than usual, as if alert, too.

Every now and then Daisy would whine, calling, Mariah supposed, for the new light of her life, Cain Law. The dog had completely attached herself to him the last few weeks, and nothing Mariah did could tear the little animal away from Cain's side, save for occasions like this where Daisy was locked away from him.

"You really are a little turncoat," Mariah said to her pet as she stashed beneath the bed the soft damask valise she used for transporting Daisy to and from her hotel room. "Don't come crying to me when the new love of your life leaves us. He will someday, you know." At those last words—at the very real truth of them—Mariah's heart skipped a beat. *Not yet,* she prayed, *please, not yet.*

Someone knocked at the door then. She leapt off the bed, and as she crossed the room, she heard her father's voice sound through the thick oak barrier.

"Mariah, baby—it's me and your mother. Let us in."

Mariah opened the door, and waved both Zack and Oda inside.

"Is your room this grand?" she asked them.

Zack whistled long and low as he took in the rich appointments. "Ayuh. I believe maybe the citizens of

Durango may have cause to lay claim to their town being the Denver of southern Colorado after all. This here hotel is evrah bit as first class as The Windsor in Denver, wouldn't you say, missus?"

Oda cast a glance around Mariah's room, and then shrugged. "I expect. Let's go eat."

To keep Daisy from running out into the hall to search for the new object of her devotion, Mariah kicked the door shut. "Where's Cain? Isn't he taking supper with us?"

Zack shot at uneasy glance at Oda. "Not tonight, honey. He, ah, decided to have a look around town instead."

"Whatever for?" Mariah shooed Daisy from underfoot, sending her to a corner of the room. "Couldn't he have waited until tomorrow and let us show him around?"

Zack hedged. "Ayuh . . . actually, no, baby. He was wanting to go in on his own so's he could have a little fun by hisself."

"Fun?" Mariah wrinkled her nose and looked at Oda. Her mother's expression, impassive as usual, seemed strange for a moment, but then that little hint that there was more than Zack let on faded away. Mariah turned back to her father, her eyes narrowed. "What kind of fun can a man whose pockets are turned inside out have in Durango?"

"He ain't exactly flat busted no more," Oda said, surprising both Mariah and her husband with this generous wealth of information.

"Why *not*?"

"'Cause of me," Zack said. "I gave him the 'loan'

of a little of his own money—about twenty bucks' worth."

"*What?* Why in all that's holy would you do a thing like that? We had him right where we wanted him—beholding to us."

"Oh, he's still beholding to us, baby, don't you worry your pretty head about it. He's beholding about another twenty bucks' worth is all."

"But . . . oh, I guess it doesn't really matter." It was, after all, *his* money. But, feeling a little jealous of Cain's freedom relative to her own, she had to ask, "What kind of fun is he planning to have in town that he can't have with us?"

"That ain't none of your concern, young lady." Zack turned to the door, bringing the discussion to a close. "Cain is a grown man. I'm sure he'll come up with a lot of ways to spend that money, and not a one of those ways is any of our business. Now why don't we all go downstairs and see what kind of chef this fancy establishment has in the kitchen?"

Mariah hung back, her arms crossed over her breasts. Zack didn't have to say another word for her to understand what he'd been hinting at. Cain would be spending his "loan" in the saloons and on the "erring sisters" so plentiful west of town and the railroad tracks near the area known as "poverty flats." She bristled at the thought of Cain cavorting with one of those women.

Oda contemplated her daughter a moment longer than usual, then waved a hand toward her husband, shooing him away in the same manner Mariah had banished Daisy. "Go on down and get us a table. I want a word with Mariah—alone."

Zack's brown eyes narrowed for an instant, but then he shrugged and said, "All right, but don't be too long."

"Don't worry, Zachariah. I've got a bigger appetite than you do." Then, making sure her cigar was snug in the usual corner of her mouth, Oda flatted her palms against his chest and practically shoved him out the door.

Oda stood rock-still for a long moment after her husband had gone, her back to her daughter, and when she finally turned to face her, there was an unusual softness to her blue eyes, and even a hint of sadness. "I ain't much good at this woman-to-woman kind of talking."

Mariah almost laughed out loud at the glaring understatement. She didn't, but nodded instead. "I've . . . noticed."

"What I can do, is see." Oda pinned her gaze on Mariah, to make her point as best she could. "I don't like what I see when you're with Cain. It don't look any better to me when you're just thinking about him, either."

Mariah's mouth dropped open. She hadn't been aware that Oda had even noticed she'd become a grown woman, much less went to the trouble to figure out what she was thinking. For the life of her, she couldn't think of a snappy retort, or even form the words to a denial. What she did do, much to her horror, was blush like a lace-covered, eyelash-batting society girl.

Oda squinted a knowing blue eye, the one directly above the butt of her fat stogie, and slowly shook her graying head. "Ain't nothing but bad gonna come from it, girl. I know what I'm talking about. Nothing but bad."

"Lord almighty, Mother," Mariah finally said, finding her voice, as well as a much higher pitch than normal. "I don't know what you could be talking about."

"You know. Even if you and I ain't had much opportunity to talk about such things, you know. And so does your 'cousin.'" She turned and slowly plodded to the door. "Mark my words," she said over her shoulder. "I know that marshal's gonna wind up hurting you if you keep after him this way. Hurting you something awful. You coming to supper?"

"I, ah—in a little bit." The color began to ebb from Mariah's cheeks as her embarrassment slowly gave way to resentment. While she and her mother were fairly close, they'd never been able to discuss intimate matters, and hadn't so much as ever flirted with a conversation concerning the relations between husband and wife. Even when Mariah had become a woman, Oda's information had been scant, just enough to keep her from thinking that she was dying, but not enough to offer the tiniest clue about the significant part menses would play in her life as a full-grown woman. What made Oda decide to offer such dire warnings about Cain, and at this late date of all times? Mariah might have welcomed this motherly advice when she was a girl of thirteen. But now? The subject was even more difficult to address than before. Much too difficult.

Working to suppress her jumbled emotions, Mariah bit the words off as she said, "You go on ahead. I need to do some thinking about all this. I'll be along later."

With a short nod, Oda opened the door and stepped out from the room. Before she closed it, she turned back to Mariah and repeated the phrase, "Mark my words." Then she was gone.

Resentment giving way to astonishment, Mariah numbly made her way to the window and drew back the sheer draperies. From her second-floor view, she looked out on the vacant lot across the street from the hotel at the corner of Main Avenue and Seventh Street. Frequently that lot was filled with Indian ponies, tepees, and Utes from the nearby reservation as they came to town to trade with the area merchants. Tomorrow, the Doc Zachariah Kickapoo Medicine Show would set up shop there, with Mariah as the "star" attraction.

She didn't feel like much of a star tonight, nor did the idea of disguising herself as Princess Tanacoa afford her any sense of security. Whether she welcomed her mother's observations and advice or not, Oda had seen through the Indian princess, beneath the daughter she'd borne, and caught a glimpse of something Mariah had been suspecting herself: that she was falling in love with Cain Law. Now, the time had come for her to face the world she'd created for both herself and the lawman the day she invented a new life for U.S. Marshal Morgan Slater.

She probably should have encouraged her mother

to talk more, but there was really no use in that. The only thing Mariah had ever learned when she questioned Oda was that her mother could be an extremely private woman, one whose life before she married Zack had apparently been difficult. She had also learned to recognize when her mother was approachable, and even more important, when she was not. So what had Oda really been trying to do today? Spoil the obvious good time Mariah was having with her new "cousin"? Wouldn't she want her only child to be happy, if only for a short time?

Perhaps Oda had been thinking ahead to the day when Cain's memory returned. There would be plenty to worry about then, for them all. But now? As far as Mariah was concerned, Cain was her man. She had, after all, gone out of her way to create him and make him into the kind of person he was today. She thought of the hours she'd worked with him, training him to meet her needs and the needs of her family. Of course he was hers, custom-made. He didn't need anyone else—or did he?

As Mariah thought of her man in the arms of a saloon girl and the reasons he might find comfort there, the blood rushed to her temples, making her feel a little dizzy. In the scheme of things, she hadn't thought to consider *his* needs, but of course he had them. All men had needs. But just the thought of another woman's hands on Cain, or worse, *his* hands on her, turned Mariah's stomach and dredged up something primitive and savage inside of her. Savage, *yes,* she realized, feeling more like Princess Tanacoa than she'd have believed possible. She would have to find a way to stop whatever he was up to now, and figure out how to help him assuage his needs later.

Her eyes glowing to their deep purple depths, Mariah glanced down at her clothing. She'd changed into a perfectly respectable two-piece dress of rust sateen trimmed with black lace and ribbon banding. Although her bonnet was oversized and outdated, it made her appearance more than suitable for public view—whether she chose to go downstairs to the hotel restaurant . . . or out into the streets of Durango.

Her plan taking shape, Mariah grabbed a small bag and stuffed a couple of bills inside it. Then she dashed out of her room.

Some thirty miles due west of the Strater Hotel, Billy Doolittle sat near the edge of a cliff overlooking the lush Mancos Valley. Just east of this rich expanse of bubbling creeks and verdant meadows lay the snow-capped La Plata Mountains. Beyond them, the town of Durango sat waiting like a ripe peach, one Billy could hardly wait to pluck.

He turned to Tubbs, who'd joined him and Artemis on watch, and said, "Taking the dummy with you on this job is just about the stupidest idea you've ever come up with." To prove his point, he glanced down the hillside a few feet to where Artemis sat out of earshot. The youngest Doolittle was hunkered down near a family of squirrels, giggling and talking to them as he offered bits of a stale biscuit to those brave enough to come near. "You want *that* numskull covering you if there's a shoot-out?"

Tubbs shrugged. "The kid likes animals. No harm there."

"There'll be a heap more than harm coming at you—hell, at all of us if'n I let you take that dunderhead into Durango."

"I don't happen to agree." Tubbs glanced down the hill and studied Artemis for a moment. "What if we just poke around a little to see if Slater's even showed up yet? Maybe he's already been and gone. If I can't take him out without drawing the law down on myself, then me and the kid'll head right back here so you can work up another plan."

Billy grumbled to himself a moment and then spat into a juniper bush. It really wasn't a bad plan at all, but he just hated the idea of Artemis riding off with Tubbs. "I still can't say it sounds like such a good idea. There's something about it I don't like."

"You don't have to like it. Just allow me to do it, and you know why? When the time comes to confront Slater, I want a fresh face with me, not someone who'll give him cause to draw those pistols."

Still grumbling, Billy muttered, "Artie's *face* may not give you away, but you watch—he'll think of something to do that'll louse everything up."

Tubbs chuckled softly. "It'll be all right. The kid listens to me." He might have added, "Even if he doesn't listen to you." But instead, he said, "Call him up here and tell him he's going with me. If we head out now, we can ride into Durango first thing in the morning."

"You might be right, at that," Billy admitted grudgingly. "But one other thing. How can you be so sure you'll recognize Slater? I thought you only seen him the one time."

"That's right. It was when I was playing poker at The Bucket in Denver. I watched him round up the Anro Gang that night. I'll know him when I see him. There's something about those green eyes a man don't quickly forget."

Billy nodded, and even though it was against his better judgment, he whistled and waved his brother toward them. As the kid scrambled up the hill, several of the squirrels scampered along behind him.

"Yeah, Billy?" Artemis said as he reached the crest, his usual bright grin in place.

"Got a job for you." Motioning for silence before his brother could begin an endless round of questions, Billy went on to explain. "I've decided to send you and Tubbs here into Durango on a—"

"*Durango?* By myself, just me and Tubbs?"

"Shut your stupid mouth and let me finish, or you won't be going nowheres but asshole over teakettle down the side of this here mountain!"

Artemis's head injury was at times a blessing. In his exuberance, all he really heard was that he was being sent on a job, a *real* job, and to Durango, of all places. His grin never faded as his brother sputtered and fumed. He just nodded rapidly, and said, "I'm all ears, Billy. Go on."

"As I was trying to say, you and Tubbs are gonna ride into Durango and have a look-see around. We want to know what Marshal Slater has been up to.

You and Tubbs might even have to take him out. Think you can handle a big job like that?"

Something inside Artemis must have busted loose. He was sure of it. His head felt twice as big as normal, and the pressure of keeping a wild whoop of joy inside himself had his eyes bulging. But he had to keep that elation inside at all costs. If he didn't know another thing, he knew that much. Why, if Billy were to witness another of his frivolous fits of the giggles, he'd kick his butt down the mountain for sure, and take the job away to boot. To make certain that didn't happen, Artemis pinched his own upper arm, and twisted the tender flesh until the urge to celebrate subsided. "I can handle the job just fine, Billy. When are we supposed to leave?"

From behind him, Tubbs supplied the answer. "Now, if your brother's done talking to you."

Artemis pinched himself again as he said, "Then I guess I'd best get to packing my saddlebags."

"Not so fast." Billy stepped up beside him. "Since I ain't riding along with you, I only got this one chance to make sure you understand what I expect, so listen up."

"I'm a-listening." *Boy*, was he listening! His ears had to be sticking up as big as a jackrabbit's, maybe even a mule's!

"This here's a dangerous job, one that affects the lot of us. You got to keep that thick head of yours on business and that big mouth of yours shut, understand?"

A secret mission! Artemis couldn't dim his luminous grin a second longer. "I understand, Billy, I do!"

"Wipe that stupid grin off your face, boy! You know what'll happen if you don't keep a serious face about you and your mind on business, don't you?"

Artemis saw the vicious look in his brother's eyes, the one he always dreaded because something awful usually went along with it. All the elation and excitement in his body turned to stone. "I know what you mean, Billy. I swear, this time, I do."

Tubbs nudged Artemis in the back with his elbow, but kept his cold gaze on Billy as he said, "I'll make sure he understands from here on out. See you in a few days. Let's go, kid."

After they'd walked several yards beyond the lookout point, Tubbs turned to Artemis and spoke low so only he could hear. "Say—you know that big sorrel I found a few weeks back?"

Artemis brightened a little at the mention of the horse. "Yeah."

"He seems to have taken a shine to you. How'd you like to ride him into Durango?"

"Me?" He whipped his head around, his eyes almost back to their full radiance. "You mean ride him like he was my own?"

"Just like you bought and paid for him."

Artemis grinned and scratched his head right near the cowlick. "Could I name him Big Red? That's what I been calling him when no one's around."

"Big Red sounds just fine, kid. Just fine."

Back at The Clipper, a "theater" gambling hall on Durango's saloon block, Cain propped his elbows against the pitted bar counter and continued to observe the assortment of female entertainers amongst the poker and faro tables. A perky blonde with bosom enough for two women caught his eye almost immediately, but then he noticed the single pink feather poking up through her frothy pile of platinum curls. The adornment reminded him of Indians. And that reminded him of Princess Tanacoa.

Shortly thereafter, every woman he glanced at seemed to feature some characteristic he could liken to one of Mariah's, which in turn made her an unsuitable choice as his companion for the evening. Hell, he could probably search all night and never find a woman in town he'd consider suitable.

Why had he even bothered to come here? he wondered as he drained his beer mug. He should have taken the twenty dollars and spent it on a new hat—one that didn't make him look like a preacher without a flock. It would sure as hell be wasted if he were to spend it on a woman.

Cain knew exactly who he wanted, and knew too that no substitute on earth would do. All the saloon girls in Durango rolled into one couldn't possibly satisfy the unholy craving that dogged him day and night. No one but his violet-eyed temptress of a cousin could do that, and she was completely off-limits. Maybe another beer would help ease the agony.

"Hey, barkeep!" he said, holding up his empty mug. "Send down another, will you?"

As he waited for the only relief he supposed he'd get this night, Cain glanced around the saloon again.

It was late afternoon, and a weekday at that, but The Clipper was damn near filled. Most of the customers were huddled around the gaming tables, but only a few of them were engaged in games of chance. Many simply appeared to be sharing a sip and talking politics, the focus of which was Grover Cleveland's chances of reelection in the race against the Republican, Benjamin Harrison.

One of the town leaders voiced his concerns about the newly revamped Republican party. Couldn't it still be as corrupt as it had been during the '84 elections? How could an honest voting man know? And say! shouted another. That reminds me—have you heard the latest rumors? That pushy female lawyer, Belva Lockwood, is thinking of running for president as the nominee for the Natural Equal Rights party— *again*! Have you ever heard of anything so outrageous? Hoots and a round of guffaws followed this declaration, and Cain lost interest in the conversation just as his beer arrived.

He wrapped his fingers around the handle of the glass mug, and then froze. The bartender's gaze was still on him, measuring him. Cain furrowed his brow as he said, "Is there some kind of problem, mister?"

"Oh, ah . . . no, sir." The bartender wiped his hands on his apron. "You look a little familiar, is all. You from around here?"

Of course, Cain didn't know. In fact, it struck him then that this stranger might know more than he did about his past. Careful not to reveal too much, he said, "I've passed through here a time or two. You remember me, do you?"

The man shrugged. "Not really." He stared at him a little longer, and then shook off a sudden tremor. "Must be mistaken. Forget I mentioned it."

A boy of about twelve pushed in through the doors and approached the bar then, scuffing his heels across the wood floor as he walked. Without glancing at the customer holding a beer, he stretched to his full five feet and said to the bartender, "Is there a man calls himself Brother Law in here?"

"Hell, son, how am I supposed to know the name—"

"I'm Cain Law. What is it?"

The boy turned wide eyes on him. "Are you *Brother* Law?"

"I am. What do you want?"

The boy looked him up and down, frowning at Cain's jeans and dark blue shirt. Only the flat-brimmed hat with the dead-level crown suggested a man of the clergy. The young man cocked his head sideways, squinting as he said, "You don't look much like a preacher."

"I never said I was a preacher. Now what the hell do you want?"

Duly impressed by the man's authoritative tone, the boy said, "A lady sent me to come find you."

Assuming the lad was referring to Oda, Cain set his beer on the bar and gave the youngster his full attention. "Did she say why she wants me?"

Looking from side to side, the boy lowered his voice. "I think something bad happened to her, but she didn't say what. Her eyes was real big and worried-like, but even then, them were the prettiest eyes I ever did see."

Cain leaned down, took the lad by the shoulders, and dragged him forward until their noses were practically touching. "What did she say to you and where is she?"

The boy's eyes widened further, and then he stuttered, "Sh-she's j-just up the s-street. Sh-she said to tell you to come help her out. S-said she was having some kind of a emergency."

6

Hiding in an alley just around the corner from Main Avenue, Mariah stole another peek down Tenth Street. There was still no sign of Cain or the boy.

She kicked the edge of the boardwalk. "There goes my last two bucks!" Sure she really *had* been robbed, Mariah slipped back between the buildings again. In the almost futile hope of finding Cain, she'd gone and paid a boy the outrageous sum of two whole dollars to go and look for her "cousin" by checking the twenty-some odd saloons in the "sporting" part of town. Although she had managed to catch sight of the boy popping in and out of a few of these establishments, it'd been a good long time since she'd last seen him. Had he taken her money and run? Mariah glanced around the corner again. This time she spotted both Cain and the kid as they burst through a pair of swinging doors not two blocks from where she stood.

Mariah quickly ducked back into the alley. In order to make her claims more believable, she pulled a few strands of long dark hair loose from her tight chignon, leaving them to dangle down from her temple, and then loosened the ribbons on her bonnet and knocked it slightly askew. She was debating whether to tear a couple of buttons off the bodice of her dress as the boy came running past the alley. He pointed at her, shouting something over his shoulder as he went by, and disappeared up the street. A few short moments later, Cain reached her.

"Mariah!" He stepped into the alley, his horrified gaze taking in her state of dishevelment. "Jesus—what happened?"

She parted her lips to deliver her prepared tale, when Cain took her into his arms, surprising the words right out of her mouth.

"Are you all right, honey?" he asked, pushing the oversized bonnet to the back of her head for a better look. He ran his fingers across her eyebrows and then down along her cheeks, checking for bruises. "What happened, princess? Did someone hurt you?"

There was something in the way he spoke, and even more so in the way he was looking at her, that disturbed Mariah enough to raise goose pimples on her arms. This was no time for nerves. She had him right where she wanted him, didn't she? Mariah shook off the sensations and went ahead with her plan. "Oh, Cousin Cain," she said, her features carefully twisted with worry. "I'm afraid I've gone and lost the twenty dollars I was supposed to use to buy supplies." She held up her empty bag. "Zack will be *so* disappointed in me. Whatever will I do?"

More concerned about her physical safety than anything so fleeting as currency, Cain's gaze scanned her again. "Who did this to you?"

"Some youngsters, ruffians, you know the kind." Mariah sniffled against a linen handkerchief she'd brought along for just that purpose. "I guess I let them get the best of me, and well . . . how they did it really doesn't matter, does it? They made off with my money, and now there will be hell for me to pay. Oh, Cain!" She squeezed out a tear. "What in all that's holy will I do?"

Dragging his thumb up Mariah's cheek, he brushed the little teardrop away. "You can stop worrying about that money, for starters." Without hesitation, Cain reached into his jeans pocket and withdrew what was left of his loan. After stuffing the bills inside her velvet handbag, he pulled her into his arms again. "There's a little better than nineteen dollars there— plenty to pay for the supplies. Now tell me exactly what those boys did to you."

Feeling a pinch of guilt, Mariah averted her eyes, looking instead at her velvet bag. She ought to have been happy, relieved at the least, to know that Cain hadn't yet bought himself a woman for the night. But another emotion seemed to be crowding those pleasurable sensations aside, one that felt a hell of a lot like remorse, or something close to it.

"Come on, princess," Cain whispered, trying to coax the details of her ordeal out of her. "I can't go after those ruffians and make them pay for what they've done if I don't know who they are and what-all they're guilty of."

Guilt. Now there was a word, perhaps the one which best described the way she was feeling at the moment. Good and guilty. Should she admit her hoax and beg for his mercy? What if he turned into the mean, hateful man he'd once been?

Mariah glanced up into his eyes. Hard as she tried, she could find no hint of Morgan Slater there. All she saw was Cain Law looking concerned, worried, maybe even a little bit anguished.

Lord, what had she been thinking of when she'd come up with this ruse? She'd prevented his buying a woman, that was for sure, but at what cost? When she had first sent for Cain, she'd expected his curiosity, certainly, perhaps even hoped he might be a little alarmed as well, but never had she imagined this response. His features were dark with outrage, those forest-green eyes reflecting something much deeper than concern. Had she not been passing herself off as his cousin, she might even have taken it for love. Was this reaction due in part to her #20 potion? He'd been taking it on a regular basis for over a month now, so that possibility certainly wasn't out of the question.

"Mariah, are you listening to me?" Cain gently shook her shoulders. "It can't be as bad as all that. Tell me what happened so I can help you."

Again there was deep concern in both his voice and his eyes. How could she have deceived this man, now or even in the beginning? Overwhelmed by a burgeoning sense of remorse, Mariah pushed out of his arms and turned away. "What's done is done," she said, eager to have the entire episode behind her. "I'd just as soon forget about it."

"Not on your life." Cain caught her shoulders and turned her to face him again. "I want to know if they hurt you, and I want to know *now.*"

"They didn't hurt me at all." Again she jerked out of his embrace, this time making her way to the boardwalk. "Please—can we just go? This isn't a good part of town for me to be seen in. Zack will have enough trouble securing a permit for the show tomorrow without having its 'star' parading down the wrong side of the street."

Cain couldn't argue against her logic, so he joined her on the boardwalk. She tucked the loose strands of her hair up under her bonnet and retied the ribbon, and then he took her by the arm and led her back to Main Avenue.

They walked in silence, passing only a few towns-folk, until they'd crossed Ninth Street, which was beyond the saloon district and the Bank of Durango. Cain slowed their steps as they reached the post office, and suggested they turn the problem over to the authorities. "Let's head on over to City Hall and see the sheriff before we go back to the hotel. He'll round up those boys, and maybe even get your money back before it gets dark."

"I can't go see the sheriff about this. As a Kickapoo princess, I'm not even supposed to be walking the streets of Durango between shows, and I don't want to tell him who I *really* am. In either case, he's *not*

going to be interested in my troubles, so let's just forget about the robbery, all right?"

"No, it's not all right." Cain remained adamant in
his convictions, determined to bring her assailants to
justice. "I still think we ought to just march right up
to the sheriff and report your attack."

"Well, we're not going to! You know as well as I
do that I can't afford to be recognized." Grumbling to
herself, Mariah glanced past the drugstore and
Gephart's General Outfitting Store to the four-story
Strater Hotel and beyond. It was supper hour, and
even though most of Durango's inhabitants were taking the late-afternoon meal with their families, she
had no desire to risk crossing paths with even one
upstanding citizen who might recognize her as
Princess Tanacoa tomorrow.

Then she remembered Zack and Oda. They were
waiting for her in the hotel dining room. Her
appetite had completely vanished, but she had to let
them know that she wouldn't be dining with them
after all.

Increasingly concerned about having their conversation overheard, Mariah tugged the sides of her bonnet as far forward as they would go, and lowered her
head. "We can't talk here any longer. Let's go down
to the train depot where we'll be out of sight of the
main roads."

Although he didn't understand the need for such
privacy, Cain said, "If it'll make you happy, then lead
the way."

As they resumed their walk, Mariah said in a low
voice, "When we get to the hotel, I'd appreciate it if

you'd take a minute to go into the restaurant. Zack and Oda are waiting for me. Would you please let them know that I've decided to take some air with you instead of joining them?" Then she added a caution: "And whatever you do, *don't* tell them about the robbery!"

The depot didn't afford quite the privacy Mariah had hoped it would, what with workmen—the very customers she'd hoped to avoid—still spilling out of the roundhouse and wandering through the train yard. So she and Cain walked beyond the town to the banks of the Animas River. There, halfway down the sloping river gorge, they settled themselves amongst the young willows which crowded the watercourse and surrounding hillsides. Directly across the Animas, above the white-capped rapids, the San Juan Smelter belched great puffs of smelly smoke into the Colorado skies, marring what otherwise would have been a magnificent view of the silvery San Juan Mountains.

Cain stared out at the raging waters, waiting for Mariah to explain herself, but after several moments of silence, he turned to her and said, "Why does everything have to be such a big secret with you, princess?"

"I told you. Folks like to believe I really am a Kickapoo Indian."

"I don't mean that." Cain reached over and pulled the tails of the black satin ribbons at her throat. Then he slipped the oversized bonnet from her head and tossed it atop the willows beside her. "I feel like you're always trying to hide yourself from me. Even back in town just now as you told me about the robbery, I sensed you were hiding something. What really happened, Mariah? You can tell me."

But she couldn't, of course. Her own guilt, and maybe even a little sorrow, swelled in her throat, making it difficult for her to breathe. Instead she hung her head.

"Don't do that." Cain removed the pair of hairpins securing her chignon at the nape of her neck, freeing her long tresses. "Hold your chin high and be proud of yourself, no matter what happened back there."

With the tightening in her throat growing to unbearable proportions, Mariah did as she was told. Billows of thick ebony hair fell over her back and shoulders, and a few locks found their way past her bosom to coil in her lap like shiny black serpents. "I already told you what happened—some ruffians stole my money. There's nothing more to tell."

"Yes there is," Cain said, his voice a gentle whisper. "Maybe I shouldn't be the one to do the telling, but did you know that you're simply the most beautiful woman I've ever seen?"

In spite of her inner turmoil, Mariah laughed. "How is that supposed to make me feel better? You don't even *remember* any other women!"

"Maybe not," he said, chuckling along with her. "But I do know this: I'm certain that I would have remembered knowing someone more beautiful than you. And I don't."

Mariah's heart leapt at those words, plummeted to the pit of her stomach, then raced back up again. She hadn't thought she'd ever hear such words—certainly not from Cain. Maybe tricking him out of his money had been the right thing to do after all, she thought with sudden satisfaction. If any woman deserved to be the object of these wonderful compliments coming from this magnificent man, it was her, not some cheap saloon girl who couldn't see past his wallet. And knowing that his declarations were probably prompted more by her love potion than by what he actually saw in her didn't make them any less splendid, either. In either case, *she* had coaxed them out of him.

Feeling better about herself, Mariah glanced in Cain's direction. He was still staring at her, looking at her the way he had in the alley, with no sign of condemnation or even a hint that he might consider her the slightest bit inferior to him. Mariah swallowed hard, but continued to bask in his open adoration. She loved seeing herself through Cain's eyes, for he looked on her simply as a woman, his opposite *and* his equal, in the most basic of ways. Cain saw Mariah as the woman she'd grown into, and saw her in a way no other man ever had, not even her devoted father.

Mariah finally looked away from him as she softly said, "Thanks for the lovely compliment, Cain. It means a lot to me, but I wasn't trying to do you out of a few kind words."

"Then what were you trying to do me out of?" He tugged on one of her long curls. "You didn't bring me all the way down here just to look at the river. Something's bothering you. What is it, princess? I'd like to help, if I can."

As the waters of the Animas roared around the boulders strewn throughout the river, the gurgling of the rapids lulled her into thinking maybe Cain *could* be of some help, even though most of her problems arose from the way she felt about him. Without meeting his gaze, she quietly asked, "Have you ever been in love?"

Cain considered the question a moment, plumbing the depths of his injured mind for some hint that his heart had once belonged to another, but he came up empty. "I don't know for sure, Mariah, but I don't think so."

Could the admission mean what she hoped it did? That the woman in his watchcase had meant nothing of a romantic nature to him? Mariah's pulse picked up a little speed. "Could you tell me what love means?"

"I'm not sure I know what you're asking, princess."

She could only explain by describing the way she was feeling about him at that moment. "I guess I'm wanting to know if it sometimes hurts you inside, and if it does, is it all right."

This all added up to one dismal fact, to Cain's way of thinking: Mariah was pining away for some lost love. He tried to shrug off his sharp sense of disappointment, but when he spoke, his voice came out sounding harsh. "I don't know the first thing about love. Why don't you ask your mother these questions? She's bound to be a bigger help than I am."

Mariah laughed. "Oda really is a wonderful person, but she is not the kind of mother a girl can talk to about such things. She almost fell over with apoplexy the day I asked her what these were for." She pointed to her breasts.

His gaze fell to the area she'd indicated, and Cain quickly looked away. "I don't want to talk about this anymore, Mariah. Maybe you can ask these questions of your father if your mother won't discuss them with you."

Chuckling again, she said, "That's a ridiculous idea. Zack is less interested in telling me about these love things than Oda is. I thought you said you and I could talk about anything."

"We can." Cain took a length of her loose hair, threading the silken strands between his fingers, and gave them another gentle tug. "But not about that. Talk like that makes me think of you in, shall we say, less-than-cousinly terms. A fellow could get himself hanged for having ideas about a family member as beautiful as you. Is that what you want for me?"

Loving not the words so much as what she heard behind them, Mariah smiled coyly as she said, "Of course not. That would be perfectly awful." Prompted by Cain's gentle fingers, which were weaving in and out of her hair, she inched closer to him. "It's been better than six years since a fellah's been jerked to Jesus here in Durango. I don't think I could stand it if you were the one to break that long dry spell."

She'd spoken the last sentence so quietly, that Cain had had to lean in toward Mariah to hear what she'd said. And that had brought his mouth within inches of hers. Hell—he had just been kidding when he said he could be sent to the gallows, but if anyone saw him now, he figured, they'd "jerk him to Jesus" on the spot for lusting after his own cousin.

Cain could almost feel the rough texture of the hemp circling his throat, but he couldn't seem to back away or stop gazing at those dusky, roseate lips. Would it really be so awful, he wondered, desperate for a taste of her, to indulge this shocking need? All he wanted was a kiss, he told himself, a brief sharing of the lips, nothing more. Would it really be such a crime—moral, legal, or otherwise?

Mariah watched Cain's changing expression, thinking he looked like he was about to say something, but when his lips parted, nothing came out but a short gasp of warm breath. He smelled of malt, probably from the beer he'd had at the saloon, but it wasn't an unpleasant aroma. Rather it beckoned her, drawing her closer to him. His eyes had darkened beyond the color of the forest, and taken on an odd but thrilling sheen, and his nostrils were slightly flared, as if he'd sprinted for a block or two.

At the more-than-pleasant sensations his very nearness brought out in her, Mariah found herself gripped by a surprising desire to run her fingers over the thick auburn hairs of his Lincoln beard, and to crush her mouth against his.

And why not? she mused, shocking herself. She'd often wondered if she had what it took to lure Cain into pulling her against his chest and kissing her until she couldn't breathe. But could she bear it if he rejected her, or suffer the consequences? At the thought of folding herself within the warmth of his strong arms, of feeling his hot, full lips on hers, Mariah began to feel light-headed, as if she were fading away with the rapidly setting sun. How on earth could she *ever* have thought of this man as less than irresistible?

The consequences of her actions be damned, Mariah leaned forward and offered her mouth to the lawman she'd at one time hated enough to deceive.

7

It wouldn't be right to kiss Mariah, Cain knew, but he found himself slipping one arm around her waist and the other across her shoulders, preparing for something that could never take place. It was wrong, so terribly wrong. He wouldn't go through with what he had in mind. He couldn't.

But he did.

The very instant Mariah leaned forward and lightly brushed her slick, satin lips across his mouth, Cain realized that nothing could have kept him from her. He met those dusky lips, kissing her softly at first, sweetly, staying within the bounds of decency, stretched as those limits might be. All he need do was remain in complete control of himself, or at least pretend that he was, and he would be able to keep this unholy desire in check.

But he didn't.

As Mariah began to respond to his lingering kisses, parting her lips tentatively, and then her teeth with a virginal coyness that nearly drove him over the edge of sanity, Cain forged ahead, engaging her tongue in a ritual as primal as mating itself. She tore her lips from his at the onset of this display of lust, eyes and mouth both wide with surprise, and then dove back in, eager for the other revelations which might lay in store. And Cain was only too happy to provide them.

She was new at this, maybe even a complete apprentice, and the thought that his might be the first lips to have caressed hers filled him with an exquisite sense of power, made him feel reckless. He continued to kiss her, pressing against her breasts and hips until they were practically lying down, the willows a lush, deep mattress which shielded them from the world outside. Cain's hands, both tangled in Mariah's long raven tresses, wandered across her back, fingered her ribs and collarbone, and then went to her breasts.

Somewhere in that brief moment of allowing his hands to roam beyond the boundaries of decency, Cain finally realized his folly.

He pushed away from her, rolled to his side, and then stumbled to his feet, turning his back to her. "Jesus, I—I don't know what to say. Sorry isn't nearly a good enough apology for what I just did. Forgive me if you can." Then he staggered off toward the river, his legs sluggish under the increased weight of his arousal—and his conscience.

Mariah didn't breathe a word in reply. In fact, she

couldn't breathe at all. She lay in the willows as if struck by lightning, too stunned to speak or move, and watched as Cain made his way down to the riverbank. When he hunkered down at river's edge and began to splash the icy waters of the Animas against his face, his words of apology finally sank in. He was sorry? Whatever for? For giving her the most wonderful experience of her life? Mariah's lips were still tingling, and the rest of her body was so remarkably alive with sensation, she felt almost omnipotent. As long as she lived, she knew she would never forget the way his mouth had fit against hers, a perfect match. How could Cain even think of blaming himself for something she'd so blatantly instigated? And why did there have to be blame at all?

Without bothering to smooth her tousled hair or straighten her skirts, Mariah jumped to her feet and hurried down to the riverbank. Cain was still dousing himself with ice-cold water as she crept up behind him and said, "Why do you feel you must apologize to me?"

He'd been thinking that the only way he was going to cool this raging fever within would be to throw himself into the frigid river, clothing and all. When he heard Mariah's voice, and the message she brought, he nearly did fall in, freezing the lust right out of his body.

After balancing himself, he finger-combed his damp hair, then stood up to face Mariah. Cain saw no censure in her eyes, no mortification or shame in her expression, but he repeated his apology anyway.

"I wanted you to know how really sorry I am for taking advantage of you like that. I acted like a vile, disgusting animal, and there isn't an excuse in the world good enough for me to justify my actions. All I can do now is promise that it won't happen again." *Even if I have to leave you to make sure I keep that promise.*

Mariah, still reeling with the newfound sensations, was much too distracted to understand why their embrace had disturbed him so. Quite innocently, she said, "I don't see what you're so upset about. Whatever did we do that's so all-fired disgusting, anyway?"

"Jesus, Mariah! I may have forgotten my entire past, but I do remember that it isn't exactly good manners to go around kissing my female cousins and putting my hands where they don't belong—and on a *first* cousin, at that!" He closed his eyes. "I ought to be horsewhipped for even thinking of you in that way."

His cousin. Lord almighty! In her haste to sample the forbidden delights this man possessed, Mariah had completely forgotten about that aspect of their relationship. No wonder he was so remorseful! She was willing to do almost anything to ease Cain's mind—except tell him how wickedly the Penny family had deceived him.

Instead, she offered him the second-best thing: the secret of #20 potion.

Laughing breezily, she said, "It's me who owes you an apology, Cousin Cain. I have a feeling that my new recipe is what's making you act all spunky around me, not some nasty side to your nature."

Cain would have grabbed at any excuse to absolve himself of this crime, but he was pretty sure where this was leading. "What new recipe is that?"

"The tonic I've been having you take twice a day in order to strengthen your blood."

"What about it?"

"Well, truth is, it's not exactly a simple spring tonic. It's a little something I mixed up special to sell by mail order once I got the kinks worked out of it. I didn't think you'd mind too much, so I decided to test it on you. It's a . . . love potion." She gave him a sheepish grin. "Looks like it works, doesn't it?"

She waited for some kind of response from Cain, but he didn't answer right away, or even look as relieved as Mariah expected him to be. In fact, he looked downright angry. After a nervous chuckle which came out sounding strangled, Mariah went on. "I wouldn't lie about thing like this, Cousin Cain, if that's what you're thinking. Why, in that second batch alone, I dropped in twice the ginseng I usually do, and even added a little myrtle root bark for good measure. As powerful as that potion is, I'm surprised you've been able to remain a gentleman as long as you have."

"Oh, really?" His words were sharp with sarcasm, devoid of any hint of amusement. "I think it's time I let you in a little surprise of my own."

Mariah didn't like the look in his eyes, the glitter of a quiet rage rising up from those emerald depths. She was almost afraid to hear his answer. "You have a surprise, too? For me?"

"Yes, dear cousin. For you. I swallowed one"—he

held up a forefinger—"count it, *one* teaspoon of that medicine, and no more."

"B-but you've gone through better than two bottles of Number Twenty! Surely you didn't just pour it out."

Guilt muting his anger, Cain subdued his tone as he admitted his chicanery. "Not exactly. I managed to find someone who likes the stuff, so I've been feeding it to her."

"You've been giving the love potion to my *mother*?"

In spite of his raging emotions, Cain found himself wanting to laugh at the thought of unsuspecting Oda drinking down a daily dose of love potion—with slow-moving Zack on the receiving end of her amorous attentions.

"No, Mariah, not your mother," he said, catching his breath. "Daisy."

"My dog?" She gasped and clutched her bosom. "You've been feeding that concoction to my sweet little Daisy?"

He shrugged. "I couldn't see any harm in it. She loves it, and actually sits up on her hind legs to beg for her dose each morning and night."

Mariah wasn't at all happy about the idea of her precious little dog imbibing all those roots and herbs. She ought to lecture Cain about the danger he'd put the animal in by messing with her diet, but she couldn't help bursting out in laughter instead.

Cain grumbled under his breath as he said, "I don't see what's so damn funny about any of this."

"Oh, but I do!" Still laughing, Mariah leaned

against his broad shoulder for support. "Daisy's been getting all google-eyed whenever you're around, and she's the kind that never, but *never* cottons to strangers." After another burst of laughter, she admitted, "Why, I was beginning to get a little upset about the way you'd 'stolen' my Daisy away from me, and here all the time, it was just my potion. It does work!"

Cain peeled her fingers off his arm, and then took her by the shoulders. "I wouldn't waste your time patting yourself on the back or worrying about that dog, Mariah. You're better off concerning yourself about me."

"You? But—"

"Daisy drank the potion. That means I don't have a damn excuse in hell for my behavior."

So stunned was Mariah by this declaration, and what it might mean, she could offer nothing more than a blank look by way of response.

Cain filled in those blanks, making sure she understood. "That's why I apologized to you earlier, and apologize still. I want you, damn it, and I want you in a way no cousin has a right to. Even with your limited understanding of these things, you must have some idea of what I mean by that."

Mariah thought back to the way his body had pressed against hers in the willows, the heat and urgency in him, and there was suddenly no doubt in her mind what it meant when Cain said he wanted her. She shivered from head to toe, and then moistened her lips. "Yes. I think that now I do understand."

"Then you'll also understand that it's become a problem I'm going to have to deal with real soon. If I can't, I'll have to move on." Cain took her by the hand, accepting her shocked silence as censure, and began walking up the hill to where she'd left her bonnet, pulling her alongside him. "We'd better get you fixed up now, and then head back to the hotel. It's getting dark."

Late the following morning, Tubbs and Artemis rode into Durango, refreshed from the night they'd spent tucked away in the ponderosa pines just outside of town. They came in from the west, curving around to the north with the trail along the Animas River, and reached the town limits at a wide street called The Boulevard. From there, Tubbs, who'd learned the layout of the town when the Doolittle Gang had bungled their attempt to relieve the Bank of Durango of its assets, led his partner down Fifth Street to Main Avenue, where most of the town's businesses were located. They'd just turned the corner at the Denver & Rio Grande Depot, when Artemis spotted a commotion on the corner of Seventh Street.

Wild just to *be* in Durango, and with his hero, of all people, Artemis could hardly stay still in the saddle. When he twisted sideways to face Tubbs, he nearly toppled off his horse as he asked, "What do you suppose is going on up there?"

Tubbs squinted. The last time he'd been in town, there'd been a small group of tepees set up on that

spot, Utes in town to do a little trading. It was a good
cover for robbing the bank, or so Billy Doolittle had
foolishly thought. As they drew closer, Tubbs realized
that this time it wasn't an Indian encampment at all,
but a group of townsfolk crowded around a white
wagon trimmed with bright red and blue paint. "It's
nothing," he said. "Just one of those traveling
medicine shows."

"No kidding?" Artemis whipped his head around.
"Is it one of them real Indian medicine shows with
doctors and magic elixirs and such? And what about
music? I love music!"

"I expect it is, kid, but it ain't none of our concern." Dismissing the entire subject, Tubbs concentrated on the reason they'd come to Durango in the
first place. He decided to head straight to Tenth
Street and the gambling halls—the place he would
most likely run across Marshal Slater—and urged his
mount into an easy lope, encouraging the kid to do
the same.

Artemis hesitated, calling after him. "Hey! Wait up
a minute, would you? Can't we stop at the show for a
little bit?"

Slowing his mount until the two were riding side
by side again, Tubbs muttered, "Oh, for Christ's sake,
kid. We got work to do in this town. I don't have time
for that kind of nonsense."

If he thought it would have done any good,
Artemis would have dropped to his knees and kissed
the man's boots. Instead, he implored, "Please,
Tubbs. I've always wanted to go to a medicine show,
but Pa never would take us—said he could brew all

the tonic we'd ever need right there in his still. The one time I asked Billy to go, he just laughed at me."

Although Tubbs doubted the kid had intentionally mentioned his brother's cruel ways in order to get his sympathy, it did persuade him. "Oh, hell, why not."

Artemis let out a whoop, startling Big Red so badly, the sorrel almost dumped him.

"Remember what I said about that mouth of yours, kid!" Tubbs had his hands full controlling his own mount. "We'll stop for ten minutes. No more."

A low fence surrounded the usually vacant lot, and as the pair dismounted and tied their horses to its top railing, Artemis apologized. "Sorry I shot off my mouth like that. I'm trying not to get so danged excited, really. It just drives Billy crazy when I get to hooting 'n' hollering."

Tubbs broke into a rare smile. "No problem, kid. Now get on up there and see what it is you just got to see." He checked his watch. "Don't forget—ten minutes."

"Aren't you going with me?"

"I'll be close by." Again he glanced at his watch. "Nine minutes and fifty seconds, kid. Don't waste it talking to me."

Without another word or even so much as a thank-you, Artemis vaulted over the fence and joined the crowd. It didn't take him long to wriggle his wiry body past the farmers and women who were blocking his view, and in less than ten of those precious seconds, he had a spot at the head of the crowd. A tall skinny man was playing the banjo and singing "God Bless America," while a short woman with a cigar butt poking out of the corner of her mouth pounded on a tom-tom.

Artemis clapped along with the beat, swinging his hips to the rhythm. When the other members of the audience turned to stare at him, he grinned and exaggerated his movements as if he were a part of the entertainment.

Then the music abruptly stopped, leaving Artemis as a kind of one-man band, and an Indian princess stepped out through the back door of the wagon. Artemis froze in mid-clap, his hands held high as if in surrender when the woman came into view. She was without a doubt the most incredible and fascinating creature he'd ever seen. Forgetting to think his actions through, he stepped forward beyond the boundaries drawn for the crowd, and greeted her.

"Morning, ma'am," he said as he yanked his hat from his head and squashed it flat beneath his armpit. "You're just about the prettiest thing I ever did see."

Mariah was generally prepared for almost anything from her audience, for in the medicine-show business, anything could and did happen, but this grinning young man took her completely off guard. She glanced at Zack, who seemed to be as surprised as she, and then back at the young man. Before she could ask him to step back behind the boundary, he started talking again, this time fingering one of her braids as he spoke.

"Are you a real live Kickapoo Indian? I didn't think there was such a thing!"

As Mariah tried to think of a way to ease the man back into the crowd, Cain looked up from his post at the head of the wagon and noticed her dilemma. He'd been scanning the audience in his role as Brother Law the Bouncer, looking for agitators who'd already stopped by the saloons for a belt of confidence, or self-righteous citizens thinking of discrediting the Penny troupe. When he saw the young man at Mariah's side and her clear discomfort in his presence, Cain started in her direction.

As he bulldozed his way through the crowd, liking the way he felt, the sense of authority that went with his new role, it occurred to Cain that the youth might be one of the ruffians who'd accosted Mariah the night before. Incensed by the idea, when he reached the young man, he grabbed him by the arm, pulling him up short, and said to Mariah, "Is this one of the little thieves who knocked you around last night?"

Stunned by the hint of Morgan Slater she saw in his eyes, as well as by his incorrect assumption, Mariah stuttered as she said, "N-no!"

The twitter in Mariah's voice only served to confirm Cain's suspicions. She was frightened, and after what had happened to her, he supposed she had a right to be. His anger growing, Cain tightened his grip on the young man's arm. "You miserable little son of a bitch—what'd you do with the money you stole from her?"

Artemis turned white, and his heart began to beat double time. "I don't know what you're talking about, mister! I swear I don't!"

Mariah pleaded with Cain. "Leave him be! He didn't do it."

But Cain's gaze didn't even flicker her way. "Take a good long look at him, princess. I think he did."

"Oh, please stop, mister," Artemis said. "I don't know what you're talking about! You got to let me go."

Every eye in the crowd was on them by now. Soon the audience would break up and leave, Mariah figured, or worse, the sheriff would intervene. There was nothing to do but tell the truth. She tugged on Cain's jacket, keeping her voice low but firm as she said, "Turn him loose! There *was* no robbery. I made it all up."

Cain loosened his grip, but kept hold of his captive as he turned to her. "You don't have to lie about this, Mariah. If he's—"

"I lied yesterday, *not* today. Now let him go. We're losing our audience."

Cain glanced around him, noticing the uneasy expressions on the women and the concern on the faces of their men. He released his hold, and the young man slipped and nearly fell in his haste to get away.

Eager to get past this and on with the show, Mariah faced Cain and said, "I know you have questions, but you'll have to let me explain later."

"Damn right I've got questions."

"And they deserve answers, but right now, we've got a show to do." She took a dark bottle of medicine from the large white buckskin pouch she carried. "You frightened that poor fellow half out of his mind, and we've got to do something to make it right. Take this to him and tell him we're sorry. If this doesn't satisfy him, tell him to see us after the show."

At the fringe of the crowd, Tubbs waited until he was sure the preacher's attention had been diverted. Then he approached Artemis, who was hunched over the fence, holding his belly as if it might explode at any moment. "What was that all about?" he asked, noticing that the man in the frock coat was on the move again. "For a minute there I thought you were about to get yourself arrested."

"Me too," Artemis said, taking short breaths, praying the cramps would ease up. "I don't know exactly what I done wrong. I swear I don't."

The man in the frock coat was heading in their direction. Tubbs put his face right against Artemis's. "God damn it, kid—maybe Billy's right and you are a dunce. You musta done something to bring this fellah down on us. What is he, anyway? Some kind of lawman?"

Artemis shrugged, struggling against the urge to cry. He'd never meant to make such a mess of things in front of his hero. Couldn't he ever do anything right?

Cain approached then, offering his apologies. "Sorry if I shook you up, son. Are you all right?"

His gaze darting from the big stranger to Tubbs, Artemis straightened and rubbed his stomach. "I just got a little bellyache. Ah, that's why I was thinking of getting some medicine. That's all I wanted, mister. I didn't do nothing else but look to get some o' that tonic. I swear it's true."

Cain nodded. "I know it is. I thought you were someone else for a minute. I made a little mistake, so I'd like you to have this with our compliments." He offered the bottle of wizard oil, and then turned, acknowledging the other man. "I'm sure we can round one up for you too, if you'd like."

Tubbs had been listening to the man speak, wondering what it was about him that made his skin crawl, but until he faced him and saw the intensity in those brilliant green eyes, he hadn't known what it was. Now that he did, his blood ran cold.

"The kid ain't no friend of mine," Tubbs said as coolly as possible, fighting the urge to reach for his guns. "I saw him hanging over the railing and come by to see if he needed some help. You part of the medicine show?"

Cain offered his hand. "I'm Brother Law. I try to keep things smooth and peaceful-like while the show's playing." After shaking Tubbs's hand, he turned back to the young man. "I have to get back to work now. Just let me know if there's anything else I can do to make it up to you."

Feeling bolder, absolved of his unnamed crime, Artemis tugged his jeans up. "Now that you mention it, I would like to take a crack at that banjo, and maybe even beat on them drums a little bit. I love music."

There was something in the way the kid spoke, some little hint of naïveté or simplicity of mind that didn't quite fit with his years, but Cain was too preoccupied by thoughts of what Mariah had confessed to sort it out. "I suppose if you're still around when the show's over, it'd be all right."

Artemis gulped down the urge to holler his joy. Though it was a struggle to remain calm, he said,

"Thank you kindly, Brother Law. I just might do that."

Waiting until well after "Brother Law" had touched the flat brim of his hat and disappeared into the crowd, Tubbs motioned for Artemis to remain propped up against the fence. Then, keeping his voice low, he said, "You know who that was, kid?"

Artemis scratched his head, bouncing his cowlick as if it were on springs. "A preacher of some kind, I guess."

"If he's a preacher, I'm the sheriff of Durango." Tubbs held his index finger near his mouth, making sure Artemis understood the warning. "Keep your yap shut over this, kid, but he ain't even close to being a preacher—that's Morgan Slater, U.S. Marshal."

Artemis nearly fell backwards over the low fence.

Tubbs reached out and caught him. "Get a grip on yourself, kid, or I swear to God—I'll shoot you down right where you stand."

Artemis had no doubt that he'd do it, even though he was a kinder sort than Billy or the rest of the gang. So he took a deep breath and worked at collecting himself before he dared to speak again. "If he's, you know, who you say he is, then why's he dressed up like a preacher-man?"

"Because he's one clever son of a bitch, that's why, and keep your voice down!" Tubbs fingered the grip on one of his pistols. "Who's gonna be looking for a marshal traveling with a medicine show? Why, he can keep watch on the whole damn town in that disguise and get the drop on the lot of us before we even know what hits us!"

Artemis shuddered at the thought. "Then let's get the hell out of here!"

Still trying to keep a low profile, Tubbs resisted the urge to bury his fist in Artemis's gut. "Our *job,* kid, is to find Slater and then take him out. Remember?" At Artemis's nod, he continued. "Well, we've found him. Now we have to work up a plan to take him out. Are you with me?"

Afraid of being left out just as he was let in, Artemis nodded. "I like doing my job, Tubbs, I swear I do. I just got to know one thing."

"What?" Tubbs asked.

"Just exactly what does it mean when you fellahs say we got to 'take him out'?"

As the show drew to a close, Mariah left the few stragglers to Oda, who only really enjoyed selling the medicines and collecting the money, and then turned her attention to the other side of the wagon. Zack and Cain were talking with the young man who'd put her in such a sensitive situation. Because of *him,* she'd had to tell Cain at least part of the truth about her deception yesterday. Sooner or later, he'd want to know the rest, and since she had yet to come up with a good enough explanation, she could only hope he would wait until later to interrogate her.

As it was, Mariah could barely think past his parting words of yesterday. Cain was attracted to her and he hadn't even been medicated into feeling that way.

The knowledge that her potion had nothing to do with his ardor boggled her mind, but what it did to her body was twice as calamitous. And she loved the feeling. How could she keep him feeling that way about her? As long as he thought of himself as her cousin, he'd never come to her that way again, never bestow one of those hot kisses on her. She would have to think of something, anything, to keep him with the show a little while longer. Anything, of course, but tell him who he was. If she did that, Cain would be gone in a flash, and she'd probably wind up in jail.

As she considered a way to explain herself, Mariah became aware of banjo music in the background, not the hesitant tunes usually plunked out by Zack's less-than-skillful fingers, but a rousing—and rather perfectly executed—rendition of "Oh, Susanna." As she glanced toward the men to see who was playing, she noticed that Cain was heading her way. Time was up.

"There you are," he said as he reached her. "Now what was it you were trying to tell me earlier? You weren't robbed after all?"

Mariah automatically began to back away, rounding the corner of the wagon toward the safety of her mother.

"Come on, Mariah. No more lies," he demanded, following her. "I've a right to know what happened and why. Out with it."

Feeling trapped, she glanced behind her. Oda was selling Zachariah's Special Spring Tonic to a couple of farmers, and behind them, a long line had formed. The fact that customers needed her attention bought Mariah a little more time to come up with a story.

"All right. We'll talk," she said, her voice low,

secretive. "You deserve to hear the truth, but not here, and not around these folks. I'm sure I don't have to tell you why."

Although he hated the idea of being put off again, Cain agreed. "When and where?"

"How about after supper, in my room at the hotel? That way I won't have to go sneaking up and down the hallways."

Again Cain agreed. "I'll be there—but this time, princess, you'd better be prepared to tell the truth. *All* of it."

8

It was a good thing Artemis had worn his pullover-style shirt, because otherwise he'd have busted his buttons and left a trail of them all the way down Main Avenue. Not only was he *early* for his meeting with Tubbs, but he'd secured a position with the medicine show as planned. *Two* jobs done right in *one* day! Glory be, was there no end to all this new-found happiness?

Repeating his instructions to himself as he entered the area of Durango known as "poverty flats," he said to himself, "Down Tenth to the first saloon on the right past the railroad tracks." Sure that he'd found his destination, Artemis glanced up at the nameplate nailed to the wooden building. Although it listed severely, looking as if it might come loose and splash into the mud puddle in front of the threshold of the establishment, he was able to match the letters to the ones Tubbs had written down for him. *Fat Alice's Saloon and Entertainment Palace.*

Enormously pleased with himself, Artemis stepped inside the saloon and scanned the tables for his "partner." The place was dingy and dusty, but practically deserted, making it easy for him to find Tubbs. He was seated, his back to the wall, at a table in the far corner where lighting was almost nonexistent. Filled with pride to think that he'd finally gotten the hang of this outlaw business, Artemis marched over to the table, dragged out a chair across from his best friend, and plopped down on it.

Eyeing the liquor bottle just inches from Tubbs's left hand, Artemis puffed up his chest and said, "Give me a shot of that there whiskey, would you?"

"I'd sooner give you a pop in the mouth, kid. You have trouble controlling yourself sober. Damned if I'm going to turn you loose with a bellyful of rotgut."

His lungs deflating along with his sense of importance, Artemis said in a small voice, "A sarsaparilla'd be just fine."

"In a little while, kid. First tell me how it went with the show—and keep your voice down."

Artemis perked up some at that. "It went great!" At Tubbs's glare, he lowered his voice to a whisper. "The old man, Zack his name is, said I could play banjo in the show as long as I didn't expect much by way of pay. I said, no, I just like playing music anywheres I get the chance, and that my pa used to let me play the mouth organ or the spoons, and sometimes even the fiddle when we—"

"Get to the point, kid."

"Sure, Tubbs. Point is, I did like you said. Told 'em my name is Artemis, just plain old Artemis with no other name behind it, and they didn't even care about that. Zack says I'm hired for as long as the show's in Durango and maybe even longer, when they go all the way to Denver!"

"What'd I say about whispering!" Tubbs practically shouted. "And just for the record—we don't give a good goddamn about your new job past Durango. Understand?"

"Sure." As eager to please as ever, Artemis dropped into his usual subservient manner. "I didn't mean to get you all upset, Tubbs. I just wanted you to know what a good job I did of fooling them medicine-show people."

"I'm more interested in the job you did fooling Slater. How'd he take on about you joining the show?"

Artemis shrugged. "Didn't hardly talk to him at all. I guess he don't mind a bit." Knowing now that he and Tubbs had been sent to Durango for the express purpose of killing the marshal, he fought a shudder as he said, "You ain't expecting me to go taking him out, are you?"

Tubbs looked long and hard at Artemis. "I don't know how we're going to take care of him yet, but if I can't get to him, I might have to give the job to you. Think you can do it?"

"I—I don't know, Tubbs." Hearing his partner's muttered oath, Artemis kept his head low and his gaze pinned to his lap. "Don't be mad at me. I ain't never done murder before, is all. I don't know how to do it."

Tubbs took a swallow of whiskey and exhaled loudly. "I'm not mad, kid. I guess I'm a little edgy, what with finding the 'preacher' and trying to think of a way to get at him."

"Me, too." Artemis shuddered, again reminded of exactly what that entailed, and then laughed nervously. "I'm strung up tighter than a horse thief."

"You won't be for long, kid." He winked. "I got a little surprise for you, a kind of reward for doing such a good job with the medicine show."

Artemis's eyes widened, but he managed to keep his voice low as he said, "A reward . . . for *me*? What is it?"

Tubbs cocked his thumb toward the bar, and then leaned across the table. His eyes gleaming wickedly, he said, "They got a one-room crib behind the bar here. That red-haired whore over there is gonna meet us back there in that room and see if she can't help us get rid of that edgy feeling."

"You mean you got a woman for you *and* me?" At Tubbs's nod, Artemis clutched his chest, where his heart was trying to hammer its way through. Glory be! How could he ever live through all this happiness? Or was he living in a dream?

After a supper of roast beef and fried oysters which her father had brought to her room, Mariah settled Daisy into a corner with a bowlful of scraps from the meal and then combed out the knot of hair at the nape of her neck. Cain would be here soon, and she'd pared her options down to just one: a near-truth that would either bring him closer to her, or drive him away. If only she had more time to discuss the changes she was going to have to make in her plans with her mother and father, then maybe—

Zack! She should at least inform Zack about *what* she planned to do, if not why. What if Cain went directly to him after talking to her? Would her father stick to the original script, or back her up?

Thinking of dashing across the hall to her parents' room, Mariah quickly tied a blue satin ribbon around the bulk of her hair and then hurried to the door. She was too late. As she reached for the knob, Cain knocked, announcing himself.

Mariah swung the door wide and gestured for him to enter. "Hurry up and come in before someone sees you."

Cain frowned as he stepped across the threshold. "Don't make this sound any more sordid than it already is, princess."

He flipped his Brother Law hat onto a brass hook near the door, and released the button at the waist of his frock coat, ready to get down to business. Then he turned toward Mariah. She'd moved over by the window, offering her trim silhouette in profile. She was wearing a sky-blue dress with a royal-blue velvet bodice—colors that turned her eyes to a rich shade of amethyst—and she'd tied her hair loosely with a blue satin ribbon, which left it to spill down her back.

He forced himself to turn away from the alluring sight, but before he could speak, Daisy scampered up to him and began rubbing her head against his boot.

"Daisy," Mariah said, her tone a clear command. "Go lie down."

The little dog ignored her mistress's direction and continued to rub against Cain, rolling her big brown eyes up at him in adoration.

He gruffly said, "Go on, Daisy. Lie down." She tucked her tail between her legs, but did as he asked. His voice still carrying that commanding tone, Cain said to Mariah, "Let's get that robbery business out of the way. Then I think we'd better talk about finding a replacement for me in the medicine show."

Mariah, who'd been doing a little pouting of her own over the way her dog continued to worship Cain, whirled on him, eyes flashing with panic. "But you can't leave—we need you."

"We'll talk about the robbery first." His tone brooked no argument.

"Oh . . . all right." She came closer to where Cain stood. "I made up the story about being robbed because Zack told me about the loan he gave you. I wanted the money back."

"Then why the big story? Why didn't you just ask me for the twenty dollars if it meant that much to you?"

"I—I was afraid you'd want to know why I needed it." She lowered her gaze. "I was embarrassed, and didn't know how to ask you."

Cain softened his attitude, along with the rigid rules he'd set for himself. He'd sworn that he wouldn't put his hands on her or touch her in any

way during this discussion, but he found himself closing the distance between them, and then taking her
shoulders in his hands. "Look at me, princess. We've
been able to talk about darn near anything until now.
Why should you be embarrassed if the family's a little
low on money? Hell, I don't have a dime to my name
that isn't given to me by Zack. If anyone should feel
embarrassed, it's me."

Mariah knew then that she could proceed as
planned. She'd tell him almost all of it, and let the
chips fall where they may. She inched closer to Cain,
leaning forward until her bodice brushed against the
fabric of his coat. Then she looked up into his green
eyes, seeking warmth and understanding there, and
said, "This family is as flush as it's ever been. We
don't need your money."

"Then why, Mariah? Why—"

"I didn't want you to have it, that's why. I—" She
bit down on her bottom lip, shaking off a sudden
attack of nerves, and then let the story fairly tumble
out of her. "I did it because I couldn't stand the
thought of you spending your time or your money on
one of those cheap saloon girls."

Not fully understanding, Cain laughed. "Christ in a
whiskey barrel—is that what this is all about? Me
having a little fun with a sporting woman?"

"It's not about you and one of those girls, Cain."
She moistened her lips. "It's about us. I can't stand
the idea of you kissing anyone but me."

He groaned. It was bad enough that he'd fallen for
her, his very own cousin, but to have gotten her to
thinking that there could be something between them

was truly unforgivable. "Jesus, Mariah. I never meant to lead you on or make you think it'd be all right for us to carry on with one another. It's wrong, and all the rationalizations in the world won't make it right. That's why I have to leave the show."

"No, you don't!" Mariah slipped her arms beneath his coat, then wound them around his waist and clung to him, determined to have her own way. "You don't understand how it *really* is, Cain. There's something we didn't tell you after the accident, something we should have told you, but didn't because we figured life would be easier for us all this way. We were wrong."

"This is what's wrong." He gripped her wrists and took her hands off of his body. "And nothing you can say is going to make it right between us."

"We're not *blood* cousins, Cain. Doesn't that make things all right?"

As her message sank in, Cain absently entwined her fingers with his. "Exactly what do you mean by that, Mariah? And I want the truth."

"We're not honest-to-God cousins because Thomas Law isn't your natural father. Your mother was a widow with a young son when she married Oda's brother. You were that son, so you see? We don't share any blood."

He wanted to believe her—God, how he wanted to believe her. "You don't know how much I'd like to accept that story, princess, but if it's really the truth, why'd you bother to lie to me in the first place?"

"Because of the last banjo player we hired." At least this part of the story was true. "He, ah, well, he was always trying to, you know, get at me. You hadn't been with us long, and even though you hadn't tried anything yourself, Zack thought as long as you couldn't remember us, he might as well let you think we were blood relatives to make things a little easier for me. That's really all there is to it."

At last, something that made sense. But what if the sincerity in her beautiful eyes was faked? Even if it wasn't, what was he to do now? If he went after that which he wanted so badly, if he were to take Mariah into his arms right now and kiss her until they were both crazy from wanting one another, what then? She was, after all, still his cousin, if only in the vaguest sense of the word. Surely if he were to stay on with the show, his behavior around Mariah would be subject to the family's censure.

Whether a relationship between them would be sanctioned, Cain couldn't guess. He couldn't even think about that until he was one hundred percent sure she hadn't lied to him again. Beyond these few thoughts, he was incapable of reasoning things out— especially not with Mariah looking up at him, her beautiful eyes filled with expectancy and, God help him, a fair amount of desire. Not here and not now. He firmly set her away from him, spinning on his heel as he said, "I hope you understand what I have to do now."

Mariah tried to reach the door before Cain, but his longer stride outdistanced her. Without stopping for his hat, he opened the door and stepped across the threshold. "I think I ought to have a little talk with Zack and Oda. Is there any reason that I shouldn't?"

"Not really," she said, sighing with defeat. "I told you the truth, and I expect that they will, too. Ah, but I do think it'd be best if you didn't tell them why I let you know we're not really cousins. You know, don't mention . . . us."

Cain nodded once, sharply. "Go back to your room, Mariah. You and I will talk more tomorrow."

Mariah closed her door behind him, wishing she could jump into his back pocket in order to overhear whatever happened in her parents' room. She leaned back against the wall, whispering a silent prayer that Zack would confirm her story, and then thought back to the things she'd said to Cain. She'd hoped for a little more excitement from him when she told him they weren't related, even if he did feel that he had to rush out and confirm her story. She'd longed to see a glimmer of exhilaration in his eyes, and even just a hint of the love she felt for him. Maybe, she dared to hope, she would see those things when Cain returned.

The minutes ticked by—five, ten, fifteen. Mariah waited impatiently, crossing to the wall her room shared with her parents' to press her ear against the damask wallpaper. She repeated this step over and over, but no matter how many times she listened, the most she could hear were a few muffled chuckles. A good sign, she supposed, but what was taking Cain so long to return to her? Or did he even plan to return? Lord, what if Zack had stuck to the script, and Cain was packing up his things as he'd threatened to do! At the thought, Mariah could stand the wait no longer. She crept out into the hallway and tiptoed over to the room next door. Carefully pressing her ear just below the brass numbers 223, she picked out her mother's voice.

"... why else would she tell Cain such a thing?"

Then came Zack's voice, more heated than Mariah had heard it in a long time. "Could be a lot of reasons!"

"Humph. Ain't but one I can think of."

Her father was shouting now. "If you're so danged sure that she and that miserable 'cousin' of hers are up to no good, why don't we just march over to her room and ask her about it once and for all?"

"*We* ain't gonna do anything!" A rare, protective tone, almost defiant. Then, quieter, "Ain't no place for you in a talk like that."

Zack's voice came again, so hot and so angry, the volume alone gave Mariah the chills. He never raised his voice like that, not even with the mules. "Why not, woman? Because I'm not her real father? Is that what you were going to say?" His voice was quivering now. "I ain't got no real rights when it comes down to the business of her life, is that it?"

"Oh, Zachariah, don't be such a fool. You know I'd never bring that up. Who her daddy is ain't got a thing to do with it. It's that temper of yours when Mariah and men are the subject that's got me in a fret."

Mariah heard her mother's voice drone on, but the rest of Oda's words were lost in the sudden roar that filled her mind. Sickened, shocked, numb in some places, much too sensitive in others, she rolled away from the door and flattened her back against the plaster wall. What did it all mean? Had her entire life been a lie?

She felt sick. She had to get away, back to the safety of her room, but she couldn't seem to make her legs move. Bracing herself against the wall, she made ready to push against it and launch herself toward her own door, but in that moment she heard someone coming up the stairs. A minute later Cain rounded the landing and came on down the hallway.

Not now! She couldn't face him. Not now. Mariah pushed away from the door, stumbling over her own feet.

"Mariah?" Cain noticed the odd look in her eyes as he drew closer, the kind of glazed panic in her expression. "What's wrong, princess?"

Tears rolled down her cheeks, and she opened her mouth to speak, but before she could get any words out, the door to room 223 opened, and Zack stood staring out at her.

"Mariah?" he said. "What the— You're crying! What's happened to you, baby?"

Baby? Mariah's head was buzzing. She repeated what she'd heard, hoping above all hope that he would deny Oda's words. That he would make everything all right again. "Am I really your baby, Dad? Or has it all been a lie?"

Zack seemed to wilt against the door frame, his good leg buckling along with the wooden one. He sighed, a long, miserable sound that took every drop of breath from his body. When at last he spoke, his voice was cracked, sounding much older than his years. "You been eavesdropping on your ma and me? That it?"

Oda squeezed herself between her husband and the door. "What's going on out here? What's the matter with Mariah?"

Looking from Oda to Zack and then to Cain, who appeared to be completely baffled, all Mariah could think to do was turn on her heel and run to the end of the hallway. Pausing at the landing, she took only a moment to look back at her mother and Zack. Then, deliberately avoiding eye contact with Cain, she fled down the staircase, and into the night.

9

At the other end of town, Artemis trudged down the middle of Main Avenue, denying himself one of Durango's biggest claims to fame—full boardwalks throughout the town and electric arc lights to illuminate them after dark. He stumbled over a particularly fresh pile of horse manure, coating his boots, but he didn't take a second's notice of the mess. Nothing mattered to him right then except what had happened in the back room at Fat Alice's Saloon.

He'd been enormously excited at first, swollen up bigger than a mule when Pearl, she said her name was, stripped off her fancy dress and stretched out on that sagging mattress. Hell, Artemis had never even seen a naked woman before, much less bedded one, and just the thought that this Pearl was gonna let him put his hands anywhere he wanted to on her nice

plump body nearly had him coming undone in his
pants before he'd been in the room two minutes! Of
course, all that was before Tubbs took his turn.

Pearl made the mistake of asking Tubbs how he
wanted his fun, and then called him lover-boy. Tubbs
slapped that Pearl right across her painted-up mouth
and told her he wasn't paying her to talk. Before he
did anything else, he turned and grinned at Artemis,
telling him, "Watch this and see if you can't learn a
thing or two, kid." Then he tore off his trousers and
climbed on top of her without so much as a "pardon
me, ma'am."

Since he'd never seen anything quite like that
before either, Artemis watched them for a while,
randy as a goat and still feeling big as a mule. But
then he glanced beyond the sweating bodies to Pearl's
face. Her indifferent gaze was fastened on the ceiling,
and her mouth, untouched by Tubbs's lips, was still
perfectly painted, but at the same time pinched and
drawn, as if she might be uncomfortable or something. That's when Artemis noticed her hands were
filled with the soiled sheets beneath her, drawn into
tight little fists.

By the time his hero had finished with Pearl,
Artemis's excitement had evaporated, and in its place
he felt nothing but disgust and a deep sadness. All he
wanted to do was leave, disappear into the night, and
pretend none of this had happened. Tubbs didn't
understand that at all. He laughed at him, sounding a
little like Billy as he told him that it was about time he
learned to be a man. Tubbs kept on laughing, saying
that he might as well take both turns with the girl

since *one* of them didn't seem to have the heart for such work, and that's when Artemis turned and bolted from the room.

Far as he knew, Tubbs would probably laugh all night long over that one, Artemis thought as he slipped in through the back door of Naegelin's Livery. Well, he could laugh all he wanted to if it made him happy, but there were just some things Artemis couldn't do. Treating a delicate little female like that was one of them.

And he was pretty sure that killing a man for no good reason he could think of was another. It wasn't just that he didn't know how to do murder; he didn't want to learn how, either. If it turned out that Tubbs gave him the job of taking out the marshal, Artemis didn't know what he was gonna do. He only knew that if he couldn't bring himself to do the deed, Tubbs wouldn't just laugh about it. There'd be hell to pay.

More troubled than he could remember being in his entire life, Artemis climbed under the medicine wagon and burrowed himself in the used bedding straw beneath it to hide himself from the world. Then he dropped into a fitful sleep.

Cain, Zack, and Oda stood in the hallway on the second floor of the Strater Hotel, staring at one another, a trio of mutes shocked into silence. Cain finally broke the silence by saying, "I'm sure what happened here between you folks is none of my business, but why don't you let me be the one to go after Mariah."

"Isn't your place, that's why," Zack said defiantly. "This family's had a mighty tall skeleton hiding in the back of the closet for too long now. Them bones been a-rattling around trying to get out in the light for nigh onto twenty years."

Oda, her expression as unreadable as ever, stared hard at her husband. "Buried is where they belong and where they should have stayed."

"Well, whether we like it or not, they ain't buried no more. Them bones have risen up sure as Lazarus now, woman, and there ain't a thing we can do about it but pull together and go look for our girl."

Cain stepped between them, facing Zack. "I still think I ought to be the one to go after her. I have a pretty good idea where she might be, and I'm afraid it might be awfully tough going for you, especially at night."

Zack's face fell. "I guess I ain't much of a tracker at that."

"But I am, and I'm damn good at it." Cain paused, wondering where in the hell that bit of information had come from, knowing, somehow, that it was true. With a simple nod, he started for the stairs.

As he'd guessed he would, Cain found Mariah down by the Animas River. She was sitting amongst the willows almost in the exact same spot as yesterday, her eyes wet with tears. When he approached her, she glanced up at him, acknowledging his presence. Then she turned her silent gaze back out to the roiling waters, silvery and shimmering in the near-darkness. Cain sat down beside her, giving her the only thing he could at that moment: some quiet time to sort through her feelings.

When she finally broke the silence, Mariah spoke in a voice husky with emotion. "The Spanish named this river *el Rio de las Animas Perdidas*. It means 'the river of lost souls.' That's how I feel right now, Cain. A lost soul with no one I can trust . . . and no one to love."

He moved closer to her and eased his arm across her trembling shoulders. Then he did what little he could to comfort her. "I don't know what happened with you and your parents tonight, but no matter how bad it is, remember you have me, princess: dear old Cousin Cain."

The remark drew a tiny chuckle from her, but no reply.

"And, of course, you have much more than me. Even if you've had a fight, you still have a mother and father who love you very much."

"A father?" Mariah whipped her head around to meet his gaze. "But you're so wrong, so very, very wrong. I *lost* my father tonight, Cain. Did you know that?" As he shook his head she explained. "I snuck up to their door to see how things were going with you and Zack, when I overheard them talking. Zack mentioned that he wasn't my real father."

"Oh, Mariah." Because he didn't know what else to do, Cain squeezed her shoulder. "I'm sorry. I didn't know."

"Neither did I until tonight." She looked back out on the river, fresh tears spilling over her eyelids.

Reaching over to brush the moisture from her cheeks, Cain softly said, "I'm sure this has been a real shock to you, princess, but Zack and Oda were pretty shook up, too, the last time I saw them."

Mariah didn't have any trouble believing that. She could still see the shock rippling across Oda's normally calm features. Her mother was upset all right, but Mariah suspected it was only because she'd been found out. Which reminded her of her own deception. Almost afraid to hear the answer, she asked, "Did all of this come up when you went to see Zack?"

"I suppose it must have, but not in my presence. Zack just admitted that you and I aren't blood cousins after all, and then Oda asked me to leave them alone. I went downstairs to get a newspaper, and when I came back . . . well, you know what happened after that."

Knowing that Zack had backed her up, and in front of Oda, brought Mariah little comfort. All she could think about was her parents' duplicity. "Yes," she said. "I sure as hell do know what happened after that."

"Oh, come on now, princess. It's not really so bad as all that, is it?"

Something hot twisted in her chest, burning her, and she fought against the pain, wanting only to keep the anger. "They've lied to me all these years, Cain. I feel so betrayed, I don't know if I can ever forgive them. But I don't really expect you to understand."

"Not understand? *Me?* Try living in the boots I've been wearing these past few weeks. If you really want to experience that 'lost soul' feeling, why not climb inside my head for a while?"

"It's not the same thing," she said, speaking without thinking.

"It sure as hell *feels* the same to me. Didn't you just tell me not two hours ago that Thomas Law wasn't my natural father?"

Mariah gasped. "Oh! Well, yes, but—"

"No buts about it. I'd say it's not only exactly the same thing as what happened to you, but it's also as ironic as hell!"

Lord, how could things have gotten so completely crazy that the story she'd made up about him turned out to be true about her? What could she possibly say to make him understand? She gave it one last try. "The difference between us is that I always thought I knew who I was. Now . . . I'm not so sure anymore. And I don't know if I'll ever be sure about who I am again."

"I still don't see a difference. You know a hell of a lot more about yourself right this minute than I know about me. One of the biggest things you're not considering is that no matter what Zack and Oda may have done or how they deceived you, you know that they both love you very much." His mood suddenly reflective, pensive, he took his arm from her shoulders and draped it across his knees. "And another thing—if you should choose to, you can reach out for that love anytime you want it."

Mariah was crying again, this time as much for him as for herself. "I'm sorry. I didn't mean to bring up your memory problem or your missing past."

"Don't be sorry—learn from it."

Mariah wiped her tears and then glanced at Cain.

He was staring out at the river the way she had, his look as dark as the approaching night. "What do you mean, 'learn'?"

"Learn to appreciate the fact that you know who at least one of your parents is," he said, quietly. "I have absolutely no memory of mine. You can tell me anything you want to about Thomas and Mary Law, but they mean nothing to me—understand? Nothing. I can't bring up an image of them, I can't hear their voices, and I can't touch them. If there is a lost soul sitting down here tonight, it's me, princess, not you."

Cain was right, utterly and appallingly right, and it was all because of her and the lies she'd told him. Just what she needed, Mariah thought: guilt on top of heartbreak.

Too disoriented to sort through her feelings any longer, she jumped to her feet and ran toward the Animas. She had no intention of jumping in the water, or actually any idea about where she was going. She only knew that she had to run away, to escape from the present and the past.

Cain only saw that Mariah was running headlong toward the river. He tore after her, catching her as she reached the water's edge, then spun her around and into his arms. "Mariah, please stop and think about what you're doing!"

"Let me go!" she said, fighting him. "I just want everyone to leave me alone—including you."

"That's not going to happen." He held her firmly. "It may not seem like it now, but back there at the hotel are people who want to hold you, to love you. We all do."

"And which people are those, Cain?" Mariah stopped struggling against his powerful arms and challenged him instead with her gaze and her words. "Zack, a man I can no longer trust? Oda, a woman it seems I know next to nothing about? Or maybe you're referring to yourself. How *do* you feel about me, Cain?"

She caught him off guard. "Christ, what a question, Mariah. I care one hell of a lot. You know that I do. I, ah . . ." But he couldn't say the words he suspected she wanted to hear, or even identify the emotions battling within his chest. Something was holding him back, an ugly, malignant thing he'd carried with him for a very long time. Whatever it was, it was too deep to unearth now, too big.

When he looked into Mariah's eyes and saw the pain and despair shining through her tears, he did the next best thing he could think of. The only thing he could do. Cain lifted her up on her toes, fully capturing her lips and her body with his own, and showed her the way he felt.

The kiss he'd stolen the previous afternoon had been thrilling and exciting, passionate in its own way, but now that the moral restraints on indulging in such intimacies had been tossed aside, Cain's lust for Mariah knew no boundaries. He couldn't seem to stop kissing her, couldn't keep his hands from caressing her soft skin or plunging into her thick, dark tresses.

Mariah went wild in response, encouraging him past those previous limits, all but begging him for the experience of tasting everything he had to offer. She was ripe with a refreshingly candid desire, and so very, very . . . vulnerable.

If not for that final thought, and the reminder of how fragile her emotions were at this time, Cain was sure they'd have been lost to one another for the balance of the evening, victims of a passion that would not be denied. As it was, he managed to release her, and abruptly set her away from him.

His voice much deeper than normal, his throat tight, Cain said, "That ought to give you some idea how I feel about you."

Mariah was breathless. Her lips were on fire, and her entire body felt as if it were electrified. Strangest of all, her anguish had been muted somehow, and now she felt like laughing—no, giggling like a giddy little child. Containing the urge, she looked up at Cain with a shy smile as she said, "I appreciate your setting me straight about that. And by the way—you 'feel' pretty good."

Returning her grin, he admitted, "So do you." Then, worried that he might give in to the impulse to take her back into his arms, Cain dug into the pocket of his shirt. As he withdrew a blue satin ribbon, one he was certain she'd lost as she raced away from the hotel, he said, "I found this lying on the railroad tracks. Maybe you'd like to use it to tie up your hair."

She glanced at the ribbon, and then at Cain. "We're going back to the Strater now?"

"I think we'd better. We can't even begin to figure out what's going on between us until you get yourself straightened out with Oda and Zack. It wouldn't be fair to anybody otherwise. Especially you."

For a moment, Mariah was afraid that she might burst into tears again. Not because she perceived his suggestion as a rejection, but because he was right. No matter how badly she wanted to stay right here with Cain, she had to return to the hotel and get her life back to some kind of order. And to do that, she would have to sever or mend her ties to the couple who referred to themselves as her parents.

It wasn't easy, but Cain smuggled a hatless, slightly disheveled Mariah back into the hotel without anyone noticing her. Then he left her in the company of her parents and went off to his own room, giving the Pennys as much privacy as the situation warranted.

Mariah wished he hadn't been so noble. As she looked at Zack sitting stiff-backed on the edge of the bed, and at Oda, who appeared to be sulking at the desk, Mariah could have used a friend about now. She fidgeted in the Queen Anne chair, crossing and uncrossing her legs a dozen times over, nibbling at her fingernails, and fiddling with the velvet buttons on the bodice of her dress, but she couldn't seem to ask even one of the millions of questions she'd thought of while sitting by the river.

Zack finally broke the ice. He nodded toward Mariah as he said, "I expect you're all in a fret trying to figure out why your ma and I never owned up to the fact that I ain't your natural pa."

But you are my father—you are! Mariah didn't say the words but nodded solemnly.

Zack glanced at his wife. "Your ma and I talked

it over while Cain was out looking for you, and we think it'd be best if you and Oda work this out alone."

Mariah's gaze darted over to where her mother sat. Her head was bowed, and she stared at the floral pattern in the rug as if hypnotized. She looked especially tired, droopy, and even her mouth, devoid of the usual cigar, sagged slightly at the corner where her stogie normally fit.

Mariah looked back at her father and said, "Thank you."

With more difficulty than usual, he got to his feet and limped toward the door. "I'll be back a little later. You two take it good and slow. . . . Listen to one another." Then he was gone.

The room remained silent even after both women knew Zack was out of earshot. Tiring of waiting for her mother to begin her explanation, Mariah forced the issue by saying, "Who is my real father?"

Oda's head jerked up at this question as if she'd been doused with cold water. Since she had little left to hide, she simply said, "Patrick O'Conner, but he went by the name Storm."

The fine hairs on Mariah's arms stood up, and a tremor racked her spine. To hear the name, to suddenly be told, "No, you're not a Penny, but an O'Conner," filled her with a sense of the unreal, as if she were struggling to awaken from a nightmare.

Oda, who recognized no such reaction in her daughter, went on to say, "Since I'm a Fitzgerald by birth, I guess that makes you about as Irish as a girl can get."

Mariah snapped out of her fugue enough to recognize that the tone her mother had taken was the one she always used when she figured she'd done about all the talking she had to. But she wasn't about to let her mother off the hook that easily. "Tell me about him. Were you two married? Is he dead? What happened?"

Oda's gaze fell back down to the rug, and she began twisting the hanky she held in her hands. "I, ah . . . ain't much good at this kind of talk."

"It doesn't matter to me how good you are at it, just do it, please."

Still unable to look her daughter in the eye, Oda let her mind wander back to the past. "Storm and Zachariah was good friends since the war, when Zachariah got his leg shot off and Storm saved his life. They pretty much did everything together after that, and both signed up as scouts for the wagon train my folks was with. We got as far as Stonewall Valley before the family went on without me."

Oda never spoke of her own parents, and in fact, was so adamantly opposed to questions about them, Mariah assumed they'd died horrible deaths while crossing the country as homesteaders. Risking her mother's wrath, she said, "Tell me about the Fitzgeralds before you go on."

Surprised by the question, Oda's gaze shot to her daughter. "Ain't much to tell. It was me, ma and pa, and my two little brothers, Mike and Jimmy."

"Did . . . did something happen to them on the trail? Are they dead?"

Oda shrugged. "They're only dead to me as far's I know."

"But—"

"I can't explain about them without talking about Storm first. Besides, isn't he the one you want to know about?"

"Yes," Mariah said in a bare whisper, promising herself not to interrupt her mother again until she'd run out of story.

Again averting her gaze, Oda went on. "I never saw a man as handsome as Storm before or since. He had thick black hair like yours, and the most gorgeous blue eyes I've ever seen on a man or a woman. I was sixteen during the crossing, didn't know nothing about men and their ways, and just kinda followed him around like I was a stray puppy looking for a handout." She paused, not sure how to proceed. "To this day, I think it's 'cause I was the only girl of age with the wagon train that weren't taken, but whatever the reason, both Zachariah and Storm were kind of sweet on me."

Her mother paused again, chuckling softly to herself, and Mariah prompted her to continue by saying, "You had your pick of the two, but chose Storm, is that it?"

Oda nodded. "I don't know if 'chose' is the right word, but once Storm put his hands on me, once he . . ." As Oda's words trailed off, she absently brushed her fingers across her lips.

Mariah's cheeks heated as she imagined the roguish Irishman touching her mother's hair, kissing her, and in that instant, she thought of Cain, of the electricity in his touch and the way he made her feel. Had Oda been drawn to this man she called Storm in the same way? Not sure whether she felt repulsed or sympathetic, Mariah quickly said, "And then what happened?"

"Then . . . well, next thing I knew, you were on the way, and I was shunned by my family."

Making a fairly easy guess, Mariah said, "You and Storm weren't married when I came along?"

"Not then or ever." Oda sighed heavily. "Soon's he found out about my troubles, he took off so fast, he raised a dust cloud that pretty near covered up the sun. Sure darkened my day, anyways. I thought many times afterwards, that might be how Patrick got that nickname, Storm."

Mariah thought of Cain riding off that way, of the day when his memory would return, and was again struck by the similarities between herself and her mother when it came to men. She wanted to laugh, cry, shout, and scream, all at the same time, but she did none of those things. Instead she grew cold inside, numb against the pain.

"Because of me, you lost the man you loved and your family. You must have hated the sight of me the day I was born."

Oda's head snapped back, looking as if she'd been slapped. "I never hated you. Not for one minute."

Mariah went on as if her mother had never spoken. "Tell me about the Fitzgeralds. Where are they now?"

Oda had dreaded this question. "The Fitzgeralds is a mighty stubborn bunch, I'll warn you about that right now in case you ever get it in your head to go find them. Once they disowned me the way they did, I knew they'd never let me back in. They ain't gonna want to let you in either."

"Of course not. Nobody wants to claim a bastard."

"That ain't true, young lady! Your father, Zachariah, God love him, was there to pick up the pieces of my busted heart, and offered to make a decent woman of me again. When he married me, he claimed you."

"And you, of course, were all too happy to marry him."

"Yes, I was." Oda raised her chin. "Ain't never had a day's regret about it, neither. Zachariah has always been a good husband to me, and a wonderful father to you. From the minute you was born, he thought of you as his own. It was him named you. He came up with Mariah because it rhymed with his name. I thought it was right clever, and fittin' too."

Clever maybe, but Mariah wasn't sure about the rest. She had yet to shake that deep sense of betrayal, but she did feel a certain empathy with Oda. As she asked the final question which continued to nag her, even though she was pretty sure she knew the answer, her tone was less accusing, softer than it had been. "Why didn't you ever tell me any of this before now?"

This time Oda looked her daughter right in the eye. "'Cause of Zachariah. I told you, he thought of you as his own from the day you arrived. Later, when it looked like we weren't going to be blessed with a child of our own, I think he forgot you weren't his. I couldn't take that away from him."

If the door hadn't opened at that moment, Mariah might have burst into tears.

"Everything all right in here, ladies?" Zack said, sticking his head into the room.

Oda looked to her daughter, clearly giving her the floor.

Mariah slowly rose from the chair, swallowing her tears before she could say, "Things are fine, Zack. Come on in."

As he limped into the room, Mariah met him halfway and threw her arms around his shoulders. "I have to leave now," she whispered in his ear. Then she stepped away from him.

Turning to his wife, he asked, "Everything okay, woman?"

Oda, a little wobbly in the voice, said, "She needs to go to her room and be by herself for a while."

Zack stopped Mariah before she left, and said, "Don't think too small of me or Oda, baby. She had a hard time of it a while back."

Mariah took his hand for a moment and squeezed. "She had you the minute things got rough. How bad could it have been?"

His face coloring all the way to his hairline, he said, "I've always figured she got the short end of the stick, with me being a one-legged fellah and all, but I do believe that there's someone for everyone, Mariah. Oda and I are about a perfect match. Can't think of another woman who'd want me, or a man that'd put up with her. I know the good side of that woman, and so do you. See if you can't find it in yourself to forgive her, if there's even anything to forgive."

"I'll have to think about it some more, Dad." The familial term had rolled off her tongue automatically, and Mariah realized with sudden clarity that Zachariah Penny would always be her father. And that she would always love him, no matter how many lies he'd told, or whom her mother had been with at the moment of her conception. She put her arms around his neck and soundly kissed his cheek. "I love you, Dad. I always will."

His throat tight, he whispered, "And I love you, baby. Good night."

Mariah continued down the hall to her room, but the minute she heard the latch click into place on her father's door, she reversed her direction and tiptoed to room 226. With no hesitation, she tapped lightly on the door.

A few moments later, Cain opened it. "Mariah! Is everything all right?"

Anxious not to be seen by Zack, Oda, or any other hotel guest as she entered his room, Mariah ignored the question and swept by Cain, pushing the door shut behind them. Only the small lamp on his bed table was lit, giving off a soft, beckoning glow. The bedspread and blankets were pulled back, the *Durango Herald* was strewn across the exposed flannel sheets, and the pillows were mussed.

Cain caught Mariah's hand, turned her to face him, and studied her expression. If anything had changed since they'd parted, it didn't look as if it had been for the good. The sadness in her eyes had increased and perhaps deepened into sorrow. "Your coming here

isn't a good idea, Mariah. I thought we decided that
down at the river."

"Yes, we did," she said. "But it isn't every night a
girl finds out that she's a bastard."

"Christ, is that what—"

"Shush. I don't want to talk about it right now."
And she didn't. She just wanted to look at Cain. God,
but he was incredibly handsome in the shadowy lighting. Mariah thought she'd never seen *anything* that
looked as good to her as this man did at this moment.
His thick auburn hair was rumpled and had grown to
an appealing length over the past few weeks. He was
in jeans and stocking feet, but in his haste to answer
her knock, he'd thrown on his shirt without bothering
to button it. Parted down the center because of the
oversight, it offered a seductive glimpse of his sleek
skin and chiseled muscles.

Mariah impulsively drove her fingers into that convenient slot, forcing the edges of the material wide
apart, and slid her hands along his naked skin to his
back. Then she met his surprised gaze with a smoldering look of her own, and said, "I don't care *what*
we agreed on down at the river. I need you. And I
need you now."

10

Mariah's hands on his body, the curiosity in her touch, were at once heaven and hell, but Cain denied himself the satisfaction of responding, and concentrated only on the despair he saw in her eyes. "Don't test me, princess," he said thickly. "I'm only human, you know."

"This isn't a test, and I don't know what you mean when you say you're only human. Why don't you show me?" She slid closer to Cain and brought her hips up tight against his. "Show me the way you feel like you did down at the river."

Along with the challenge, Mariah threw her head back, exposing the silky column of her neck. Cain took a good long look at that inviting sight, an even longer glimpse of the woman beneath the invitation, and said, "All right, princess. If that's what you want, I will."

He took her into his arms then, nearly sweeping her off of her feet, and drew her to him so gently, and so very tenderly, for a moment she thought she'd imagined the gesture. Then he began to kiss her, again gentle in his touch, starting with her forehead. He moved downward from there, bestowing her eyelids with tiny little kisses, and finally went on to her mouth, barely skimming her lips with his in a gesture more caress than kiss. Then he tucked her head against his chest beneath his chin, folding her tighter in his arms, and began to rock her, slowly swaying her to the beat of his heart.

After several minutes, Cain leaned back, lifted her chin with his index finger, and stared into her eyes. They were wet again, but the despair was gone. He smiled as he quietly said, "That's how I feel about you, princess. I hope now you finally understand how much you mean to me."

Tears were everywhere—in her throat, her eyes, and running down her cheeks—but Mariah didn't feel the least bit sad. If she felt anything at that moment, it was confusion. She didn't know what she thought about anything—not Cain, not Zack or Oda, and not even herself. Suddenly eager for a little solitude, she sniffed back her tears and whispered, "I guess I ought to go back to my room now."

Cain took her by the elbow and steered her to the door. "I think you'll find that a good night's sleep is what you need most. In the morning, your head will be clearer and you'll have a fresher outlook on things."

As he pulled open the door, Mariah turned to him, eyes dry now, but wide with alarm. "Wait a minute!"

"Now what?"

"You're not sending me away because you, ah . . ." She bit her lip, trying to find the right words. "You didn't borrow any more money from Zack, did you?"

The next morning Cain was still laughing over Mariah's parting words. Apparently she hadn't quite understood how much he cared for her, or how difficult it had been for him to turn her away. Once she got her problems with Zack and Oda worked out, he intended to make damn sure she knew what he was about, in no uncertain terms.

Cain thought back to the shy way Mariah had glanced at him earlier in the morning when he'd stopped by her room to collect his hat. Clutching her robe at her throat, her hair mussed, eyes languid with sleep, she'd looked so warm and cuddly, it was all he could do to form the words "good morning" instead of just barging right in on her. Oh, yes, he thought, his blood heating: She'd know exactly how he felt about her before the week was out. And it wouldn't be a minute too soon.

Whistling as he stepped into the livery and up to the medicine wagon, Cain opened his jacket, withdrew Daisy, and set her down on the scattered straw littering the main aisle of the stables. "You go on over in the corner and get your business out of the way, you raggedy-eared mutt, and then we'll get this show on the road." But she didn't move. Instead, she sat up, rolling her big brown eyes at Cain in complete adoration, and propped her little white feet right in front of her nose. "Begging isn't going to do you a damn bit of good, Daisy. Your love potion days are over. Now skedaddle!" He clapped his hands, and the animal fell to all fours and ran off.

Cain had just started up the walkway to get the mules, when the little dog began barking frantically. Then a frightened voice cried out from beneath the wagon.

"Help! Help me! Get it off of me!"

Cain dropped to his knees to see Daisy attacking a man who was curled into a fetal position. She was circling him like a band of Indians, occasionally dipping in and out of the perimeters she'd drawn in order to nip at his back, buttocks, and shoulders.

"Daisy! No!" Cain shouted. "Bad dog!"

Artemis, who was still half-asleep, wasn't exactly sure what was after him—a dog, a coyote, or even a wolf! He swung out blindly, protecting himself, and connected with a ball of fur. The animal yelped once and then ran from the barn, howling all the way.

"Daisy!" Cain said as she scampered off. "Come back here!" But she didn't even slow down. She disappeared around the corner and shot toward Main Avenue. Assuming that the dog was headed back to the hotel and her mistress, Cain bent over and looked under the wagon again. His new assistant was still curled into a ball. "You can come on out now. She's gone."

Artemis, more afraid of this man than he'd been of the dog, slowly wormed his way out from under his shelter for the night. As he stood up, he brushed the bits of straw and dirt off of his clothing and then dragged his hands along the sides of his head to smooth his hair.

Cain looked him up and down, frowning as he said, "You told Zack you had a place to stay. Is this it?"

"Oh, n-no, sir. I just wanted to be here first thing in the morning." He spit out a shaft of straw he'd somehow sucked into his mouth during the night. "I didn't want to be late for the show my first day on the job!"

"I think we'd rather have you late than looking like a basketful of week-old wash." He studied the young man's head and the odd little tuft of hair sticking up like a warrior's feather. "You got a comb?"

Artemis colored, and then his mouth fell into a sheepish grin. "A comb ain't gonna fix what you're looking at. That there's my natural dunce cap."

Cain walked around to the back of the young man, noticing the scar and the way the hair grew at its crest, and continued on around him until they were face-to-face again. "I see you have a little problem with that cowlick back there, but why in hell would you call it a dunce cap? Do you like making fun of yourself that way?"

Artemis couldn't have fibbed to this great legend of the law even if he'd had a story prepared. Through teeth that were chattering so much he could barely talk, he said, "A-ain't my idea." He chuckled nervously. "M-my b-brother says it's a dunce cap 'cause I'm so danged stupid most times." At this news, the marshal's expression grew even sterner than it already was. Artemis had heard plenty about this lawman, all of it bad, so he quickly said, "'C-course, it's all right with me i-if you want to call me a dunce, t-too. I'm used to it."

"Well, I'm not." Muttering to himself, Cain opened the padlock at the back of the wagon and stepped inside. When he came back out, he was carrying the straight-edged razor Mariah used to keep his Lincoln beard trimmed. Opening the instrument to reveal the blade, he said, "Turn around, son."

Why? Artemis wondered. So the man wouldn't have to look into his eyes as he carved him up? Did he know Artemis was a Doolittle? That was it—he knew. He knew! Grabbing his throat as he backed away, Artemis blurted out, "I ain't done nothing wrong, M-Marshal! Weren't m-me what done any of it, I swear!"

Mariah, who'd just stepped inside the barn, froze. Had she heard right? Had their new employee just referred to Cain by his former title?

Cain froze too, a sudden headache the cause of his immobility. Something the young man had said disturbed him, but what was it? Everything had gone kind of fuzzy on him, yet he could feel that the answers were there, so close, on the tip of his brain if not on his tongue. How could he reach out to decipher them? Maybe if he tried a little harder, really tried this time.

"Cain!" Mariah called his name, horrified to think what his reaction might be. Which man would turn to her? The one who consumed her thoughts day and night, or the lawman?

The sound of Mariah's voice, along with the panic

in her tone, broke Cain's concentration. He glanced down at the razor in his hand, and then at the young man still clutching his throat. Laughing at the sight this combination must have presented to her, he said, "I'm just about to give your new assistant a little trim. What did you think I was going to do—slit his throat?"

It was Cain. *Her* Cain. Breathing a sigh of relief, Mariah continued on into the barn. "What I think doesn't matter, but you really should have let Artemis know what you were planning to do to him."

Cain shifted his gaze from Mariah to the young man. He did look frightened, as if he expected some physical harm, rather than the simple haircut Cain had in mind. Had this brother Artemis mentioned been as cruel to his body as he'd been to his mind? Cain chose his words carefully and spoke softly, "I'm trying to help you, son, not hurt you. Now turn around."

Artemis's knees were knocking something terrible, but since the lawman had given him a direct order, and he couldn't think what else to do anyway, Artemis spun on his heel and stood shaking. An enormous hand touched his shoulder, the fingers bigger than any he'd ever felt, and then moved up to his head. Artemis squeezed his eyes shut, waiting for the pain, but all at once, those big hands returned to his shoulders and turned him back around. When he opened his eyes, he was staring into the lawman's face again.

"There," Cain said, flinging the shaft of hair to the ground. "Now you don't have that dunce cap on your head anymore. A grown man shouldn't run around thinking he's a dunce."

A grown man? Artemis backed away, uncomfortable being in such close proximity to the lawman, and then thought about what he'd said. No one had ever called him a man before, much less a grown-up. And no one had ever thought to cut off that dunce cap, either. Artemis reached up, feeling the spot, and found it smooth, merely a small extension of his scar.

Why was this Slater fellow being so nice to him? Was it just another of the marshal's clever tricks? *He knows I'm a Doolittle, he does!* Artemis backed toward the stalls, nearly falling over his own feet in his haste to put some distance between himself and the lawman.

Cain, already turning away from the young man, didn't notice the sudden movement, but Mariah did.

As Cain ducked back inside the wagon to replace the razor, she moved closer to her new assistant. Although the "danger" had passed, Artemis still looked frightened, as if he might even faint. He hadn't been so afraid of the razor after all, she suddenly realized, but of the man! And the fact that Artemis had referred to Cain as "Marshal" meant that he knew that Brother Law was Morgan Slater. Why had he waited until now to even mention the fact? And why was he so afraid of him?

Cain climbed down from the wagon then, and Mariah's heart lurched. Artemis may have been frightened of this man, but now, she was terrified. What if this new assistant of hers should refer to Cain as a marshal again? And what if the next time, Cain heard it and understood who he was? She had to have a private talk with Artemis. And soon.

"Did you find Daisy?" Cain asked as he came up alongside her.

"Daisy? You took her with you when you stopped by my room this morning."

"Yes, but . . ." Cain paused to glance over at Artemis. "She got upset when I brought her into the barn, and ran off. I thought she'd gone back to the hotel."

Mariah groaned. "This town has an ordinance prohibiting dogs from running loose, and the sheriff generally doesn't have another thing to do but go around looking for strays. She's probably in jail."

Cain laughed, sure she was kidding. "Oh, come on. She must be back at the hotel."

"No, Cain. She's not."

Artemis spoke up. "I'll go get her, Miss Princess. It was me scared her off."

She glanced at the young man, seeing the perfect opportunity for a little discussion. "Why don't we get her together? I'll probably need someone along with me to convince the sheriff that I really do own that dog, anyway."

"Now wait a minute," Cain said, piqued. "I thought you couldn't afford to be seen by the sheriff!"

Mariah gave him a sheepish grin. "I didn't want to report that 'robbery,' remember? I doubt he'll recognize me as Princess Tanacoa, in any case. Besides," she said, adding the final inducement for Cain to stay behind, "Zack is waiting on the corner of Seventh for you to bring up the medicine wagon. Artemis and I shouldn't have any trouble with the sheriff. Zack got permits for everyone, including Daisy."

"Me, too, Princess?" Artemis asked.

She corrected him as they walked out of the barn. "Please call me Mariah, and yes, we got a permit for you too."

Walking backwards so he could see the beautiful woman buried deep inside the large black bonnet, Artemis said, "Hey! I thought you was really a Kickapoo Indian! What happened to your face?"

Mariah's smile was indulgent but calculated as she explained the necessity of posing as an Indian. By the time they'd reached the steps of City Hall, Artemis not only seemed to understand, but had sworn on his mother's grave never to divulge her secret, and Mariah was pretty sure she'd gained a lifelong fan.

Once inside the cavernous building, they were shown to a bench just outside the sheriff's open door and told they would be called when he finished his interview with a reporter from the *Durango Herald*. From this vantage point, Artemis could hear almost every word of the conversation going on inside the office, but he was far too interested in the gorgeous creature sitting beside him to pay too much attention to what they were discussing. At first.

Just as he opened his mouth to ask the princess if she ever planned to marry, Artemis distinctly heard a voice from inside the sheriff's office say, "I don't know why you want to keep running stories about a couple of bank robberies that happened damn near two months ago. That Doolittle Gang is probably all the way to Kansas by now."

Unable to stop himself, Artemis gasped, and then smashed his head flat against the wall.

"What's wrong?" Mariah asked, alarmed by the fear she saw in his eyes.

"N-nothing, ma'am. J-just a little gas." He squeezed his eyes shut, hoping he had enough strength to hang on tight to his seat, for if he let go, he was pretty sure he'd bolt right out the front door.

Suspecting that his anxiety had something to do with the conversation in the other room, Mariah cocked her head toward the doorway. A man she assumed to be the sheriff was talking.

"Why don't you newspaper types concentrate on the real troubles we got around here with them god-dang Utes?"

"Because the Indian Rights Association frowns on that sort of journalism. Now back to the subject, Horace. I'm on deadline and just have a couple of questions left. Would you mind answering them?" A pause, and then the same voice: "We understand that this U.S. marshal, Morgan Slater, is supposed to be tracking the Doolittle Gang. Is there any truth to the rumor that he was killed by them?"

Mariah's heart practically stopped, and beside her, Artemis gasped again.

"I don't know where you got that information," the sheriff replied, "but if he's dead, the law don't know about it. He is overdue checking in, I'll give you that, but I'll also give you twenty-to-one odds that he's sniffing them out as we speak. There's no one like

Morgan Slater when it comes to getting his man. He'll turn up soon, and when he does, he'll have a Doolittle clutched in each fist!"

Mariah's heart started again, racing in double time. Dear God! She'd never considered that he might have been on an assignment when they crossed paths. If so, she and her family may unwittingly have put Cain in danger. What if this Doolittle Gang were to come across him here or on the trail, and recognize him? Surely there'd be a confrontation of some kind, but in Cain's state of mind, he probably wouldn't know them, much less be able to defend himself. Had the deception she'd practiced left him helpless, an easy target for the outlaws?

Mariah's mouth went dry as she imagined the dangers which might lay ahead, and beside her, Artemis began to tremble. He seemed as disturbed by all this as she was. Why?

As the conversation in the office segued into words of praise over the way the sheriff kept order in Durango, Mariah leaned in close to Artemis and whispered, "All right. I want the truth, and I want it now. I know you're aware that Cain is Marshal Slater. What does he have on you?"

Artemis's eyes bulged and his windpipe closed up, making it difficult to talk. But that was all right, because he couldn't think of what to say or do anyway. Mariah had frightened him half to death with such a direct question, and for the life of him, he couldn't imagine what Tubbs or Billy would expect him to answer. Because he couldn't think what else to do, Artemis made a kind of choking sound, and then shrugged her off.

The ploy didn't work.

"Come on, Artemis—are you wanted by the law?"

"Oh, n-no, ma'am. I sure ain't. Not yet, anyways."

"Not yet? What does that mean?"

Artemis squeezed his eyes shut and his bottom lip began to tremble as he tried to think of how to get out of yet another trap he'd gotten himself into.

Seeing his distress, Mariah persisted, using a more gentle, nurturing tone. "You don't have to worry about me. I promise not to tell anyone what you know, especially not Cain. He, ah—" She paused, thinking up a logical excuse for his new name. "He's doing a special job right now and he doesn't want anyone to know who he is."

Didn't he already know that! Artemis began trembling again, sweating too, as he tried to think of what to say.

Still trying to reassure him, Mariah smiled and offered her hand. "You can trust me, Artemis—remember? All I want from you is your promise that you'll keep what you know about Cain to yourself. You mustn't let on to anyone, especially not him, that you know who he really is. Is that a deal?"

That was it? Just keep his mouth shut and do the same job Tubbs wanted him to do? It almost seemed too easy. Hardly understanding what had just happened, Artemis accepted her handshake. "D-deal."

"Just one other thing," Mariah said, raising her voice. "What do you know about this Doolittle Gang?"

"H-holy shi—ucks, Miss Mariah!" Artemis lurched

forward, nearly falling off the bench. "W-why d'you want to ask a question like that?"

The fear was still shining in his eyes, brighter than ever, and his complexion had taken on a waxy sheen. What on earth was this young man so frightened of? "I just want to know who they are, Artemis, that's all. Have you seen them? Would you recognize them if they were to come to town?"

Artemis couldn't take any more. He got to his feet, in spite of the fact that his legs had turned all quivery, and shot a fast glance toward the front door. He imagined himself running through that door, running and never stopping. Not for Tubbs. And not for Billy. He was leaning in that direction, thinking of launching himself, when the sheriff came out of his office.

"You folks want to see me?" he asked Artemis.

Mariah rose, gesturing for Artemis to join her, and then smiled up at the sheriff. "We're with the medicine show. I lost my dog a little while ago. It seems my brother here accidentally let her get away while he was giving her a bath." She batted her long black lashes. "I need to find her right away. We've got a show to put on."

"I'd be delighted to help, ma'am." Then he showed Mariah and her "brother" into his office. There he explained all the ramifications of Ordinance #7—including instructions to kill any bitch in heat found loose in the town of Durango. After that, he levied a small fine, collected Daisy from the group of animals he'd impounded the day before and that morning, and bid them good day.

Through it all, Artemis remained quiet and subdued, his thoughts scattered. He knew he probably ought to run right over to the hotel on Tenth Street and inform Tubbs about his conversation with Mariah and what he'd overheard in the sheriff's office. Especially because he had noticed Wanted posters in the police station with Billy's picture glaring out from them. But if he did that, he would jeopardize his new job with the medicine show. And Tubbs wouldn't like that any better than the news he brought.

Glory be! What was a fellah supposed to do? He'd be in a world of trouble no matter what he did. When he added those woes to the fact that he couldn't even remember the questions he was supposed to be asking the marshal, well, hell—Artemis figured he might as well start digging his own grave, 'cause he was sure to be lying belly-up before this day was over!

Later that night, after an exceptionally profitable show, Mariah, who'd yet to sit down to a fine meal in Durango, decided to risk a public appearance, and joined Zack, Oda, and Cain at a window table in the hotel restaurant. The Strater boasted of its fine cuisine, offering items such as bluepoint oysters and a variety of French sauces to garnish a long menu of meats and vegetables. Staring out at Main Avenue through the windows, Mariah absently picked at her favorite supper in the world: fried chicken with corn fritters smothered in honey. She'd worked herself into a dreadful headache, what with worrying about

Cain and the danger she'd put him in. If that wasn't enough, every time she looked at Oda, she remembered that Zachariah wasn't her father, but that some man she'd never met had claim to that title. This little complication distracted her so much during the show, she'd accidentally sold a male customer a bottle of remedy for "the female complaint" when he'd ordered Zack's Special Spring Tonic.

Now she couldn't even concentrate on her food. Both Zack and Cain were busy shoveling down mounds of browned potatoes and chunks of the biggest steaks she'd ever seen, and Oda was intent on her slab of ham. The three of them were far too caught up in assuaging their appetites to take notice of the fact that she'd completely lost hers.

She knew that no matter how hard she worked on her problems, none of them would simply fade away. Oh, she supposed she would get over the deception practiced by her parents in time, but Cain was another matter entirely. Soon he would revert to Morgan Slater and walk out of her life forever. She couldn't prevent it. Not with the sheriff of Durango actively searching for him. Not with Artemis and his penchant for talking without thinking. And not with Cain's habit of reading the newspaper in the evening before turning in. She couldn't buy up all the papers in town each and every day! Sooner or later—and now she was sure it would be sooner—all the lies would come crashing down on her, breaking her heart in the process.

There was nothing to do but admit that part, too. For days now, Mariah couldn't seem to lose the almost sick feeling that churned in her belly when Cain was near, or the ache in her chest when he was not. She'd even swallowed a little of her own Special Vegetable Compound, hoping to straighten herself out, but it hadn't worked. She supposed she'd known all along that it wouldn't.

Until last night, she'd been unable to put a name to her malady. But then Cain had taken her in his arms, holding her the way she supposed a lover might, and she knew for certain what ailed her. She loved Cain Law, loved him as she'd never dreamed of loving anyone. Now she stood on the threshold of losing that chance at love before she ever got to express it to him or herself.

Mariah glanced across the table, catching his gaze as he washed part of his meal down with a long swallow of beer. He winked at her and smiled, then fell back to the business of finishing his meal. She loved him enough, Mariah realized then, to ensure his safety by coming right out and telling him who he was and why he'd been on the trail to Durango.

Would he turn his back on her after that? Probably, but that would be better than witnessing his murder. She had no choice but to tell him, and tonight was as good a time as any.

Mariah dipped her finger into the honey on her plate and brought it to her mouth. She slowly licked it from her finger as she considered how best to explain why she'd done what she'd done. Cain would be mad, of course, but he had admitted in his room just last night how much he'd come to care for her. Was it enough? Maybe she could talk him into taking her with him when he moved on!

Her heart raced at the idea of spending the rest of her life with the man she loved. Once she explained everything to his satisfaction, she told herself, there would really be no reason for him to leave her behind, save perhaps the little problem between her and her parents. That seemed to be important to him, but if she were to show him that she'd patched things up with them, there would be nothing to keep her and Cain apart!

She'd noticed that he was staring at her from across the table, his green eyes practically glowing in that odd way she found so exciting. His eyes were pinned to her mouth, and Mariah realized she was still licking the honey off of her finger, still rolling her tongue in circles, seeking the very last drop. Yes, she decided then and there. She would do it. She would tell him who he was and beg him to take her away with him. She would do anything if it would keep Cain looking at her like that for the rest of her life. Anything at all.

Breaking into a broad grin, Mariah turned to Oda, who was sitting beside her, gave her a big, noisy kiss, and said, "You're just about the most wonderful mother in the world!"

If Oda had been puffing her usual cigar, it would have dropped out from between her lips and landed with a splat in the middle of her mashed potatoes. Her mouth still agape, she glanced across the table to where her husband sat, her brows high with surprise. Zack, normally unflappable under any circumstances, was a mirror image of his wife's stunned expression.

Cain, not exactly sure what was happening, cleared his throat.

Shifting her attention to her father, Mariah said, "And Zack is not only the best father in the world, but he runs the best medicine show this country has ever seen! Why, hiring Artemis as a musician was an inspiration! He really knows what he's doing with the banjo."

Zack, still visibly surprised, agreed. "Ayuh, he does, at that. Why, it seems that boy can play almost any musical instrument you hand him, and any tune as long as he's heard it before. A natural, the kid is. Just a born natural."

Mariah beamed, knowing the show could go on without her. "I think it'd be a good idea to keep him around for a while. He's just plain good for business, not to mention an extra pair of strong hands. Wouldn't you say so, Mother?"

Oda stared at her daughter a long moment, sure something was afoot but baffled as to what that something might be. "Oh, I suppose he's all right."

Satisfied she wouldn't be leaving her parents in the lurch, Mariah glanced across the table at Cain again. His reaction was even better than she'd hoped. He was smiling at her, a bright, open grin with just a hint of sensuality, an expression which suggested that as far as he was concerned, the barriers had fallen.

Mariah returned the smile triumphantly. Tonight would be the night, all right. Tonight would be a time for truth . . . and love.

And time was a-wasting.

Without another moment's hesitation, Mariah gathered her untouched chicken into a napkin and excused herself from the table.

11

Artemis gnawed on what was left of his thumbnail as Tubbs paced in their cramped room at the Last Stop Hotel. He was having trouble explaining about the medicine show and Marshal Slater, Lord if he wasn't, and any minute now, he expected Tubbs to turn on him, call him viler names than Billy had ever thought of, and then maybe even shoot him.

But Tubbs surprised him by saying, "That clever son of a bitch! So as far as you know, Slater has stayed in disguise and hasn't even made contact with Sheriff Black?"

His confidence building, Artemis smoothed the sides of his hair, hoping to draw attention to his new haircut, and said, "Nope, but I did."

"You did what?"

Artemis hadn't meant to mention the episode at

City Hall, but now it seemed a rather important bit of information. At least part of it, anyway. Still preening, he quickly relayed the story about the lost dog. "While I was waiting in the sheriff's office for him to go get Daisy, I took a look around, and what do you think I spied?"

"Get on with it, kid."

"A Wanted poster of the Doolittle Gang. There was a likeness of Billy, and Shorty, and Tate, and a whole lot of words beneath that." He didn't mention that Mariah had deciphered those words as he added, "Most of what it said was a description of Cletus."

"Damn!" Tubbs punched the rough-hewn wall, driving several minute slivers into the tight skin around his knuckles. "Cletus should already be in place up at Silverton, poking around for information about the next big gold shipment to Durango." He shook his head. "Nothing we can do about that poster now but hope it ain't reached Silverton, and that if it has, no one's noticed him. Billy and the rest will be heading for Needle Creek in a day or two, and then there'll be no turning back."

This was the first Artemis had heard that Billy was changing locations. "What's at Needle Creek?"

Tubbs, busy wondering if he ought to send a wire to Cletus warning him about the poster, and trying to figure out exactly how to word the message in a code only Cletus would understand, thoughtlessly said, "That's where we're going to dynamite the train to stop it."

"We're going to blow up a train?" Artemis was

absolutely incredulous. "Won't someone get hurt that way?"

Sorry now that he'd mentioned it, Tubbs brushed him off. "We're going to blow up the tracks, kid, not the train. No one's going to get hurt, so forget about it. What else have you learned? Did Slater tell you when he figures on leaving the medicine show?"

Artemis scratched his head, still trying to draw attention to the fact he no longer wore a dunce cap, but Tubbs was interested only in answers. Trouble was, Artemis had forgotten to ask the questions. Backed into a corner, he did what he'd done earlier: lied to his hero. He never would have thought himself capable of it just a few weeks ago, but Tubbs hadn't called him names or slapped a woman around in front of him before then, either.

With a surprising amount of ease, Artemis shrugged and said, "He ain't planning to leave for a while yet, leastways not until after we take the medicine show to Silverton. He'll most—"

"Silverton!" Tubbs grabbed Artemis by the collar of his shirt. "Slater's going to Silverton?"

His eyes bugging out of his head, Artemis nodded rapidly. "Well, sure he is. We got a show to put on."

"Why the hell didn't you tell me that the minute you walked into this room?"

"I—I d-didn't figure it was too important where the show went, Tubbs! We ain't taking the train for a week or so yet."

"The train! Morgan Slater is taking the goddamn train to Silverton and you didn't think it was important enough to mention!" Enraged, Tubbs didn't just shake Artemis this time. He threw him against the wall. "Maybe Billy's right about you after all."

Momentarily stunned, Artemis staggered a few steps to the left, then listed to the right. "Sorry, Tubbs," was all he could say as he shook his head to try and clear it.

"You'll be a lot more than sorry if you mess up like that again." But as he considered it, suddenly the thought of finding the marshal aboard the train didn't sound so bad. In fact, Tubbs couldn't think of a simpler way to take Slater out than kicking his ass down into one of the steep, rocky gorges between Durango and Silverton.

A few hours later in room 226 at the Strater Hotel, Cain tossed and turned between his flannel sheets. He was having another nightmare—actually, the same nightmare he'd had three nights running, a terrifying scenario in which he was both hunter and quarry. A group of nameless, faceless men bore down on him, driving him farther and farther into a box canyon from which there was no escape. He turned on them, the hunter now, and reached for pistols that were no longer strapped to his thighs. His heart hammered loudly against the walls of his chest and sweat popped out along his brow, running down into his eyes, blinding him. He was trapped! Cain could no longer see his tormentors, but they were coming after him, the sharp retorts of their weapons exploding all around him. *Bang! Bang! Tap! Tap . . . tap.*

Cain abruptly sat up in bed, suddenly aware that

the sound he heard was someone knocking at his door. Groggy and disoriented, his pulse still racing, he lit the small lamp on the bed table and climbed out of bed. Tugging his jeans up over his hips as he hurried across the room, Cain held his waistband together with one hand and opened the door with the other.

Squinting into the hallway, with its blinding lights, he said, "Mariah? What the hell . . . ?"

Without waiting for an invitation, she brushed past him and pushed the door shut behind her. Cain quickly turned away from her and hastily buttoned his jeans, but not before she caught a glimpse of the shock of auburn coils at his groin. Mariah shivered at the sight, wondering when or if he would initiate something in that area of their relationship.

Shirtless, but with his pants decently fastened, Cain turned back to Mariah. She was dressed in a voluminous robe of soft white cotton, her long black hair spilling over one shoulder like a river at midnight, that flow barely contained by a purple satin ribbon. Her eyes, captivating as always, were alight with a curious glow; a far, far better dream than the one he'd been having. Cain cleared his throat. "Is something wrong, princess?"

"It's, ah, Daisy."

He glanced down at her arms, finally noticing that she was carrying her dog. The little mutt's tongue was hanging out, and she wore a big purple bow between her ears which matched the shade of Mariah's ribbon. "Is she sick?"

"Umm, not exactly. She ate most of my chicken

dinner and now she can't sleep." Mariah gave him a shy smile. "But I think she'd forget all about her tummy ache if you'd just talk to her a while."

Cain could think of a thousand things he wanted to do at the moment, and talking wasn't anywhere near the top of the list, especially not to a dog. Daring to believe that Mariah's visit meant what he hoped it did, he returned her smile. "She must have something awfully important on her mind if it can't wait until tomorrow."

"Important, yes. She, ah . . ." Cain was moving closer to her, the soft glow of the lamp casting shadows on his smooth, naked torso. Suddenly Mariah's prepared speech faded, growing vague and insignificant in her mind. "She's—"

"Daisy doesn't have a thing to say to me, does she?"

Mariah shrugged. "Not really. I just brought her with me so I'd have an excuse for being out in the hallway."

His hope evolved into reality. Mariah had come to him because she couldn't stay away any longer. Because it was time for her to show him how much she cared. Desire lapped at his loins as Cain snatched Daisy from Mariah's arms, marched over to his bed, and picked up one of his two pillows. He continued to the corner of the room nearest the door, where he dropped the pillow to the floor and settled Daisy onto it.

As he turned back toward Mariah, Cain checked the clock on his dresser. "It's after midnight. What took you so long?"

A little warning went off at the incongruous statement, but Mariah stumbled along, still searching for the right words to explain how she'd tricked him into thinking he was Cain Law. "I, ah, didn't mean to disturb your rest. Maybe I ought to just go back to my room."

"Oh, no you don't." Cain stepped between her and the door. "A woman doesn't come waltzing into a man's room wearing nothing but her nightclothes just to deliver a dog. You have something to tell me. I suggest you get on with it."

The lamp's soft glow hit him full on the torso, highlighting his chiseled muscles and the rigid outline of his chest. How was she supposed to think with him standing there half-naked, looking so very, very seductive? Mariah swallowed hard, forcing herself to remember the things she'd planned to say. She'd come to tell him who he was, to possibly even save his life; yes, that was it. Her mind back to the business at hand, she said, "I have something really important to tell you, something that may change the way you feel about me forever—"

"Of course it will change the way we feel about each other, sweetheart, but those changes will be for the good." Cain opened his arms, and then whispered, "Come here."

Another unexpected statement, this one even more incongruous than the last, and delivered in such a smoldering way, Mariah's legs began to tremble. Did he think she'd come to offer herself to him? Did he want her? Mariah shook off a tremor of excitement at the idea, knowing she'd never be able to proceed if she allowed herself to be drawn into his warm embrace.

She closed her eyes against the invitation, her ears against the sensual caress of his voice, and said, "Let me finish, Cain. Before we can talk about the real reason I'm here, I thought you might like to know that things are just fine between me and my mother."

She'd even gone to the trouble of meeting his terms. Cain smiled. "I'm way ahead of you, princess. Don't think I didn't notice how hard you were trying at supper to patch things up, or how delighted Oda looked."

She blushed, feeling just a pinch of guilt. "I've done a lot of thinking since supper about some other things, too. I—I came here because I have . . . something to tell you."

"I know you do, and I have a pretty good idea what that something is."

Mariah's eyes went wide with panic. "You . . . do?"

"But of course I do." He started for her.

Mariah turned her back to Cain, afraid to look him in the eye. Lord! How long had he known? Since Artemis had called him "Marshal" in the barn? If so, why had he kept his silence? Or was he testing her, waiting to see how far she'd go—waiting for her to *hang* herself? She could feel him behind her now, so close that his hot breath grazed her shoulder.

"All right," she said quietly, her back still to him. "So now you know. What are you going to do about it?"

Cain laughed and bought his hands to her shoulders, lightly squeezing her. "What do you think I ought to do?"

Strangle her? He moved his hands then, sliding them beneath her hair, and slowly fit them around her throat. For a terrifying moment, Mariah thought he might just do it. But then he lowered his head, to nibble the side of her neck. "Maybe I should have said, 'What would you like me to do?'" he whispered.

She nearly forgot both the question and the answer. Cain's touch had rendered her every bit the amnesiac he was, but she somehow managed to say, "Ah . . . forgive me?"

"Forgive you? For what? Having the strength and courage to come to me tonight?" Although he wasn't sure why she insisted on acting so coy, Cain couldn't wait a minute longer to take Mariah into his arms. He spun her around, gathered her against his naked chest, and buried his face against her hair. She smelled of fresh soap and roses laced with just a tang of cinnamon, an intoxicating, mind-scrambling scent he was sure he'd never get enough of. Tearing himself away from that aromatic cloud of jet-black hair, he tilted her chin, forcing her to look into his eyes.

"You didn't come here at midnight just to let me know how well you're getting along with your mother, or to ask me to forgive you for anything. I was under the impression you had something important to tell me." Certain he knew what that something was, Cain winked as he said, "I'm ready to discuss it, if you are, princess."

He didn't know. Or did he? Mariah's confusion was complete. Hoping to clear things up, she said, "I'm ready, too."

Lost in her eyes, Cain noticed they were shimmering in that beguiling shade somewhere between indigo blue and deep purple, but also that they were blinking up at him as if she had no idea what was happening. Taking control, and responsibility for the next move as well, he pulled Mariah up tight against his hips and whispered from deep in his throat, "Maybe it'd be easier on us both if *I* begin this conversation."

Realizing for certain where his assumptions had led him, Mariah drew her elbows up between their bodies, bracing herself against him. But the gesture did nothing to discourage Cain. He smiled as he dragged the pad of his thumb along her jaw and then down the side of her neck to the hollow of her throat, caressing her there in big, soft strokes. Mariah's thoughts faded away again as she felt a delicious heat spreading throughout her breasts—and below.

Cain noticed the blush staining her throat and cheeks. He chuckled. "Are you warm, princess?"

His voice, low and husky, was like a velvet croon, more kindling to the fire growing within. Mariah didn't answer his question. She couldn't speak.

Reading the answer in her eyes, Cain tore the ribbon from her hair, then freed the pearl buttons fastening the front of her robe. As he slowly removed the garment from her arms and shoulders, letting it slide from his fingers to the floor, he softly said, "Better now?"

Mariah still couldn't find her tongue, could barely think, but she did realize that she was standing in Cain's room wearing nothing but her plain muslin Mother Hubbard gown—and not a heck of a lot beneath it. Nervously chewing her lower lip, she said, "I—I came here to tell you something."

Again, Cain took the lead. "I know you did, princess. Why don't we 'talk' where we'll be more comfortable."

It wasn't a question. He took Mariah's hand in his and led her to the rumpled bed. Then he sat at the edge of the mattress and pulled her down beside him. "Now just what is it you're so eager to tell me about?" As he spoke, he fingered the bit of lace at the throat of her nighty, and then began undoing the buttons there.

Mariah tried not to think about what he was doing, but instead about what she'd come here to say. Morgan Slater. That was it. She was supposed to tell him he was Morgan Slater, and then beg him to forgive her and take her away with him. Should she come right out with it, or ease into the conversation slowly?

Cain's hand slid inside her nighty then, skimming her soft breasts. Everywhere he touched, her skin burned and rippled, and when his thumbs brushed her nipples, the pleasure he brought her was so sharp, so unexpected, she thought she would die from the sheer agony of it all. Oh, God! Did he know what he was doing to her? Mariah sucked in her breath, and her eyes fluttered to a close.

"Easy, princess," she heard Cain whisper, his voice

darker and richer than she had ever heard it before. "Maybe you ought to lie back."

She felt weak, short of breath, and much too warm to think, so when he coaxed her down to his pillow, Mariah didn't protest. She was grateful for the opportunity to relax a moment and the chance to gather her wits so she could move on with her plan.

As she struggled to arrange her thoughts, Mariah felt the mattress sag. In the next instant, Cain was lying beside her, his hands skimming across her body again. Before she could speak or even open her eyes, his mouth was on hers, his tongue busy parting her teeth. The kiss he bestowed now was different from all the others, more insistent and demanding, hotter somehow. How was she to think, much less carry on any kind of lucid conversation, under these conditions?

"Cain," she said, the sound muffled against his lips. "Wait a minute."

"Talking too fast for you, am I?" He grinned and kissed the tip of her nose. "We'll go as slow as you like."

Mariah's throat suddenly went dry, and her mouth fell open in mute understanding. There would be no more talking in this room tonight, at least no discussion of any consequence. She would either have to succumb to his advances, or leave—and leave now.

But she couldn't, not yet. Mariah had often wondered about the actual mating of men and women, especially since she'd crossed paths with Cain, but to actually do it? To just let it happen? Should she? Could she?

She moistened her lips, preparing either to speak or kiss him back—Mariah was no longer sure what her intentions were—but before the decision could be made, Cain's big hands were on her again. He gathered her nightgown in his fists and then rolled it up and over her head in one quick movement, leaving her nude except for her thin cotton drawers.

Embarrassed, shocked, but still curious, Mariah's eyes flew open. Cain was looking at her, his expression filled with appreciation. His eyes had turned to an impossibly dark shade of green. The color made him look more animalistic than usual, dangerous somehow, and suddenly—a lot more like Morgan Slater.

Fear tripped up the base of Mariah's spine even as a sudden warmth bloomed low in her tummy, terrifying and thrilling her beyond belief. Whatever was happening here, this was *not* the time to remind Cain of who and what he really was.

"Jesus, you're beautiful," he whispered as he moved lower to nuzzle her throat. "Definitely the most beautiful woman I've ever seen." Cain looked up to meet Mariah's gaze, and then lowered his voice to a low growl. "Definitely."

Tears of joy stung her eyes, but this was not the time for crying, either. This was a time for discovery. Cain continued to scatter kisses, his lips following the path his big hands had blazed, and when his thumbs rasped across her nipples, drawing a cry from her, his mouth immediately went to her breasts, soothing and arousing their dusky tips into hard little nubs.

Just when she thought she could stand the pleasure of his touch there no longer, Mariah realized that Cain's hands were on the move again, and had reached down to roll her drawers over her hips. He paused briefly, drinking in the sight of her, and then tossed the undergarment aside.

"Hey, here I am doing all the talking," he said, his voice dark, husky. "Do you mind, or have you got a thing or two to say?"

Mariah could barely think, much less know what to say or do next. Her lashes fluttered to her cheeks as she whispered, "You seem to have a lot more information on the subject than I do."

She heard Cain's hoarse laughter, but after that, she was lost in a whirlwind of sensation. Cain's fingers skimmed the apron of ebony curls at her groin, whisking lightly from side to side, building the frustration and need inside of her until Mariah thought she'd go mad.

She knew she couldn't stand it any longer, but before she could voice her distress, Cain forged a path between her legs, coaxing her willing thighs apart. Then his fingers dipped beneath her dark curls and began caressing her most intimate self. Mariah gasped, cried out with astonishment at the electrifying sensations, and squeezed her legs tight with the shock of it all.

"It's all right, princess," Cain whispered huskily as he tore off his jeans. "Open up to me, honey."

If she was to stop him at all, Mariah sensed, it would have to be now. She could do it by demanding that he let her up, or even by simply saying, "You're not Cain Law, your name is Morgan Slater," or maybe, "Ever hear of a fellow called Morgan Slater?" Either of those statements would probably stop him, she figured.

But she didn't do it. The pleasure Cain's touch brought her was agony, but the void she felt when he moved away from her was utter torture. Mariah closed her eyes and inched her legs apart, willing herself to relax. In the next moment Cain eased his way between her thighs, sliding along her cleft, searching for the perfect complement to himself. When he found it and made an attempt to gain entrance, Mariah cried out in pain, gripped the brass rails on the headboard, and went rigid.

"Easy, honey," he said, working to keep his voice calm and soothing, nonthreatening. "Don't be afraid. I'll try something else." Her throaty response to that was garbled and wary, so Cain reached up and peeled her hands off of the headboard, kissing each of her fingers before drawing them down around to his hips. "Guide me, princess. Let me know if you want me to go faster or slower."

As uncertain now as she was aroused, Mariah gave him a tentative nod. This time when Cain eased himself back between her thighs, he slid down along the damp grooves of her body, carefully slipping back and forth, but making no attempt to penetrate her. Mariah's fingernails dug into his buttocks as her fervor grew, and she spurred him on, her previous doubts forgotten. Higher and higher he urged her to some unnamed peak, until at last her spine arched and she tumbled over the precipice, bucking and twisting against Cain's groin.

As the surprising spasms shooting through her body began to subside, Mariah sucked in her breath and let it out in a long, satisfied sigh. Chuckling softly to herself, she glanced into Cain's eyes, gauging his reaction to her uncivilized responses. She saw no hint of censure in his eyes, but instead, a crooked grin. Returning that grin, though hers was more shy than sensual, Mariah whispered, "I don't know why I was so, you know, nervous. Th-that was absolutely the most wonderful thing that's ever happened to me."

"That," he pointed out, "was just the beginning."

It was then Mariah noticed that other than the crooked grin, Cain's features were rigid and intense, reflecting none of her newfound feelings of satisfaction and contentment. She moved her hands along his body, discovering that everywhere she touched, he was rock-hard; not just the part of him that remained sandwiched between her legs, but hard from his shoulders, to his arms, to his thighs and buttocks. Every square inch of Cain seemed to be made of steel.

Before she knew what he was up to, he took her bottom into his hands, shifted his hips, and gently pushed against her. Mariah stiffened against the onslaught, but Cain continued to work his way inside of her, murmuring words of encouragement against her hair, angling himself one, two, three different ways in each new attempt to break down the walls that stood between him and complete, utter possession of her.

Finally, when she thought she could no longer stand it, with one resolute thrust the final barrier suddenly gave way. Cain drove deep inside of her, filling her so completely, Mariah wasn't sure she would survive. She was trapped beneath a prison of solid muscle, a willing captive perhaps, but a captive, nonetheless.

Firmly embedded in Mariah, Cain forced himself to remain still, shuddering slightly as he said in a voice gritty with emotion, "Jesus, princess. You feel so, so—Jesus." Again he shuddered. "You're mine now," he said, nostrils flaring, breathing rapid. "Do you understand what that means? You're mine."

Before she could answer, he came down on her mouth, the kiss more a primal branding than anything else. And then Cain began to move again, slowly at first, thrusting his hips against hers, driving in and out of her with that rigid, steel-like shaft; yet incredibly enough, instead of pain, she felt herself responding all over again.

He was flame and she was fuel, made to be swept up, engulfed, and then consumed by this man's passion. He drove her upward and onward, climbing those same high peaks again, and then, incredibly enough, beyond them to newer, more rewarding heights. Pleasure mushroomed inside of her, radiating an exquisite satisfaction throughout her entire body as Cain's thrusts grew in intensity and speed. Then she was lost, incinerated in a mad rush of passion, her cries merging with his groans into one grand proclamation.

Later, as Mariah swam through the maze of pulsating pleasure, she discovered that she was truly lost, profoundly affected by what she'd given up of herself—and even more by what she'd gained. She'd never thought of human copulation as anything but an act, a mere meeting of bodies seeking gratification, but now she knew it to be a much deeper experience than mere physical pleasure. She felt inexorably tied to Cain, and knew without question that she would feel that way for the rest of her life.

They were still joined below the waist, his arms wrapped protectively around her, his head buried in the pillow beside her. His breathing was labored and uneven, his skin damp to the touch, and all because of her. Because of what Cain Law felt for her.

Would Morgan Slater feel the same way? she suddenly wondered, her thoughts returning to the reason she'd come to his room in the first place. How could she possibly risk giving all this up now by even hinting at his true identity? He might became so angry at the way she'd used and tricked him that his anger couldn't be cooled, and God help her then.

A sudden memory of the woman pictured in his watchcase flashed into Mariah's mind. How convenient of her, she thought, berating herself, to have forgotten that woman until now; especially should she turn out to be Slater's wife as Zack had suggested. Mariah shuddered at the thought, and at the prospect of how Cain would react if that were the case. As Morgan Slater he would never forgive her for tricking him, or for the intimacies they'd just shared. She'd lose him forever. Mariah's lip quivered, and in spite of her struggles against them, the tears began to fall.

It was a long time before Cain recognized those faraway sounds for what they were: weeping. He was in a fog of passion, basking in a new and utterly satisfying realization. He had no actual memory of love-making in the past, even though he knew instinctively that he'd done this before at least several times over, and probably with many different women. But he needed no clear memories of the past to realize that he'd never made love with such savage abandon before, or with such intense pleasure.

Mariah was without question the perfect complement to him. In spite of the fact that nothing had changed where his memory was concerned, he felt whole again for the first time since he'd awakened on that muddy road with no recollection of who he was.

When Mariah's soft sobs finally did reach his ears, Cain lifted his head from the pillow and gazed down on her. "Oh, princess," he whispered, his heart breaking. "I never meant to hurt you. You have to believe that I didn't want to hurt you, but I only did what had to be done. If there had been any other way, if I could have—"

"It's not that," she said. "Honest, it isn't. It did hurt at first, and it was more . . . violent than I thought it'd be, but I'm all right now."

He licked the moisture from her cheeks. "If you're all right, then why the tears?"

Both happy and sad, enraptured but frightened, Mariah's throat ached, making it difficult for her to speak. "I—I guess because everything is so surprising, so new, and so . . . Is it always like this between a man and a woman? So intense and, well, wonderful?"

Cain considered the question a moment, and then shook his head. "I honestly don't know, princess. I just know that it's never been like that for me before."

"But how can you know for sure when you can't even remember your life past two months ago?"

"I just *know.*" He traced the curve of her cheek with his fingertip. "You'll have to trust me on this, but I know."

Suddenly feeling shy, and on the verge of tears again, Mariah turned away from Cain and rolled onto her side. He immediately fit himself against her body, from the nape of her neck to her bottom and down to her toes, and then wrapped his arms around her and laid his head upon the thick blanket of her hair. As she snuggled deeper into his embrace, Mariah glanced over to the doorway and saw that Daisy was curled on her pillow, sound asleep. The soft rhythm of the little dog's snoring suddenly filled the otherwise quiet room.

Chuckling to herself, Mariah said, "I think Daisy has just run out of questions for you."

Cain lifted his head enough to see into the corner. "It's just lucky for her she's cute as the dickens and of some use to the show, or I'd run her out of this room."

For Mariah, Daisy's worth was the unconditional love she offered. Whether she ever "danced" along with Princess Tanacoa again was inconsequential.

Frowning, she said, "'Lucky for her' . . . 'some use to the show'? What do you mean by that?"

Shrugging, Cain ran his fingers through her hair, loving the feel of it, the smell. "Just that all animals should be of some practical use. I always wanted a dog when I was a kid, but my old man wouldn't let me have one, no matter how hard I begged." Mariah stiffened in his embrace, but Cain went on, unaware that he was speaking of a past they both had thought was lost to him. "My mother died when I was born, and I guess my old man thought he had to raise me twice as hard to make up for the loss. He had a rule about the kind of animals we were allowed to have on the farm. Every animal had to be productive in some way and capable of earning its keep. In other words, if it could plow a field, pull a wagon, or fill our bellies at night, we could own it. Otherwise . . ."

The words drifted off with his thoughts as Cain's memory suddenly filled with images of his father. The first impression that came to him was a face vague and watery, with no identifying features. The man's name didn't accompany this memory, nor was the background of a barn with its surrounding fields distinct enough to identify, but he was sure that he'd lived on this farm during some period of his life, with the man whose face was slowly coming into focus.

His features were bold, this nameless father of his, the general shape of his face oblong, but the remarkable thing about him was the absence of curves. All his features seemed chiseled in straight lines and sharp angles. Even his hair, bright orange in color, grew straight up from the top of his forehead, broom-like in appearance. His father. And beside him, Cain was begging for the privilege of owning a dog, a use-less plea to a man who had no use for anything frivolous or intangible. Not even love.

Cain sighed, gaining just a bit of insight into him-self, understanding better why he had so much diffi-culty naming the emotions burgeoning in his chest for Mariah, and even why he had such mixed feelings for little Daisy. The dog had been the first to worm her way into his heart after the accident, yet he'd been reluctant to so much as touch her in the beginning. Now he knew why.

"Did you hear what I just said!" He was in shock, struck by the significance of the revelations. "I remembered something from my childhood, and I know what my father looked like!"

Mariah had heard all right. Her heart hadn't beat once since he'd first uttered the words "my old man." She was just glad that he couldn't see the fear in her eyes as she swallowed hard and said, "I heard you. It made me kind of feel sad. A dog shouldn't be lumped in with farm animals. A dog is someone to love, and someone who'll love you back . . ." She paused a moment, thinking of the depth of her deception where Cain was concerned, and then quickly added, "No matter what you do or how you may have wronged them."

He shrugged. "I wouldn't know about that. I never was able to persuade my father to let me have a pet."

"I've always had a dog to love. Daisy's been with me for seven years now. Before her, I had a big yellow

Labrador mix who used to drag me around by the diapers. He was a hell-raising dog, always into something or tearing something to shreds, so we named him—" She cut herself off before she said the name, Cain, and began to laugh. Once she started, she couldn't seem to stop.

Cain, who couldn't see Mariah's face or even begin to fathom what had set her off, tapped her shoulder. "What's so damn funny?"

She doubled over at his words, her laughter nearly hysterical, and inadvertently rubbed her bottom against Cain's groin. Suddenly, memories, dogs, and the past were of no concern to either of them. Mariah's chuckles faded and quickly turned to sighs as she became aware of an insistent pressure prodding her from behind. Those sighs became moans when Cain's hands slid down her belly to the apex of her thighs. By the time he rolled her over onto her back and fit himself between her legs, Mariah's past was as blank as his. And Cain was a name that belonged only to her man.

After that they dozed off, sleeping in each other's arms for nearly two hours, and as he awakened, Cain's vague memories of his red-haired, practical father prompted thoughts of Zack and a few of the things Mariah had said in haste down at the river. He shook her lightly to awaken her, and asked, "When you first came here tonight you only mentioned Oda. Did the other thing you wanted to talk about have something to do with your father?"

Mariah yawned, stretching languidly against the warm flannel sheet as she said, "Things are fine with me and Zack. He's the only father I've ever had, or wanted."

Cain kissed her forehead, and then because he couldn't resist them, her swollen lips. "And it doesn't bother you that you don't know your real father?"

Clinging to his beard, Mariah took the time to kiss him back, responding with an amount of vigor equal to his before she answered him. "A 'real' father need only meet two requirements as far as I'm concerned. He must love me, and be there to protect me. Zack has never failed me in either way."

Although he was deeply touched by Mariah's declaration, Cain felt a disturbance deep in his gut, a definite rumbling from that malignant dragon within. Something in her words, something about fathers and their children, about love and being there for them, collided inside him, filling him with dread and more than a little twinge of sadness. Of all the things his father taught him, he knew instinctively that loving wasn't one of them. Perhaps that was the memory which prompted these uneasy feelings. Cain held Mariah tighter, closer.

Far too immersed in the pleasures of the present to allow the past to burden him further this night, he shook all those troublesome sensations aside and cupped one of Mariah's breasts in his hand. "What do you think Zack, and even Oda, are going to think about this?" He squeezed, pinching her nipple lightly. "If you recall, they did go out of their way to make sure this sort of thing wouldn't happen, by lying to me about our 'blood' relationship."

Mariah smiled up at him, so in love at that

moment, she thought her heart would burst. "I think it'd be best if we didn't tell Zack and Oda about us just now." Feeling bolder than she ever imagined she would, Mariah reached down beneath the sheets. Finding what she sought, and finding it firm and throbbing, she filled her palm with it, and said in a low voice, "A thing like this belongs between us and no one else."

Cain sucked in his breath, unable to speak for a moment, and then let it out through a groan. "A thing like that belongs between something all right. Would you like me to show you where?"

12

The following night at about eleven, with Daisy tucked into her arms, Mariah crept down the hallway to Cain's room. Everything had been going smoothly. Her plan to keep Cain in the dark about his real identity was working, up to and including keeping him away from the newspaper article about the Doolittle Gang.

Earlier that evening, Mariah had given Artemis the nineteen dollars Cain had returned to her, and then her "partner in crime," as she'd come to think of the young man, bought every copy of the *Durango Herald* the minute they arrived back at the hotel. After that, he fled into the night to dispose of them down in poverty flats. Cain, apparently not too disappointed he'd missed buying his nightly copy, decided to go to his room to rest rather than search any farther than the lobby for a newspaper.

Smiling as she realized how much she had to do with his state of exhaustion, Mariah knocked softly at Cain's door. When it opened, she said, "It's Daisy again. She misses you, and thought of a few more things she'd like to talk to you about."

With a husky chuckle, Cain swung the door wide. "Do come in. I was just thinking about how much I miss her."

At just after ten the next night, Mariah hurried down the hallway again, this time sans dog. As she reached up to knock on Cain's door, it suddenly opened. He stood in the entryway, nude from the waist up.

"What took you so long?" he asked thickly.

Her eyes twinkling with mirth, Mariah batted her lashes and said, "I only stopped by to say good night. I've decided to stay in my own room this evening and maybe get a little rest. I've been kind of tired lately, and—"

"Get in here." Cain took her by the hand and pulled her into his room. Then he kicked the door shut behind them.

Down the hall a few feet, the door to room 223 softly clicked to a close at almost the exact same moment.

The Penny family prided themselves on the manner in which they manufactured their medicines, taking special care to always use the freshest, most authentic ingredients available. Even their own brand of wizard oil was made largely from its working properties:

camphor, ammonia, chloroform, sassafras, cloves, and turpentine. Many of their contemporaries made wizard oil with up to seventy percent alcohol as its main ingredient, but the Pennys added just enough for preservation. As for the other medicines, nothing but pure mineral water would do as the base liquid for these recipes.

Although their travels took them to almost every corner of the Southwest, no matter which route they chose to follow each year the Pennys always began their show season in the town of Pagosa Springs. There the family not only manufactured as much medicine as they could carry, but filled two large barrels from the geysers which bubbled over near the bathhouses in the little town. They occasionally sold this mineral water as is, but more often than not, they kept it in reserve to use in replenishing their supply of elixirs.

Now that their stay in Durango was almost at an end, one barrel of mineral water was empty, and the second was just over half-full. This afternoon, two days before they would board the train to Silverton, was not a show day, but a time to refill the water barrels at Trimble Springs, a fashionable hot springs resort some nine miles north of town.

Mariah, in particular, was looking forward to a visit to Trimble Springs, for the family usually stopped in long enough for each of them to take a soothing hot mineral bath. After three consecutive nights in Cain's bed, parts of her felt almost raw, while others ached from her unusual exertions. Smiling to herself as she recalled the events that had given her such an assortment of aches and pains, Mariah tightened the rope which secured the water barrels in the supply cart and then walked to the back of the medicine wagon.

"Need any help in there?" she said.

Zack appeared at the back door, then carefully made his way down the stairs. "Got her all buttoned up, baby. Is the supply cart ready to go?"

Mariah nodded, watching as Oda stepped from the back of the wagon and plodded down the stairs after her husband. Then she said, "All that's left is hitching up the mules. Where's Cain? I thought that was supposed to be his job."

Zack spun on his good leg and began to head toward the stable. "He borrowed another twenty bucks to go into town. I can take care of the mules this one time."

Mariah froze in her tracks. Cain in town? And with twenty dollars? If not for the last three nights they'd shared, her top priority might have been wondering what he intended to do with the money, but her first thought now was of his safety. And of her heart if any harm should befall him. What if the members of the Doolittle Gang came across him?

Hurrying to catch up with her father, she asked, "Did Cain mention where in town he was going, or what he needed the money for?"

"No, baby, and I didn't ask him." Zack turned and fixed his brown eyes on his daughter. "It ain't none of my business—or yourn. I thought your ma and I had a long talk with you about that man. I still ain't too happy that you went and told him he weren't your true and natural cousin."

From behind Mariah, Oda said, "Neither am I."

"Oh, you two." Mariah tried to laugh them off. "I told you it was an accident when I let it slip out about him not being my real cousin, but there's no reason to worry about Cain. He treats me just fine. I am a little concerned about him going to town alone, though. What if someone should recognize him?"

Zack shrugged. "He's got Artemis with him. They'll be all right."

Although Mariah didn't think much of the kid as a bodyguard, at least he knew whom to watch for around Cain. He'd been every bit as interested as she in the Wanted poster featuring the Doolittles—maybe more. Glancing at the rig, she said, "Is there anything else I can do to help get this show on the road?"

Zack kept a skeptical eye on his daughter, but started down the main aisle. "Why don't you and your mother get them mules brushed and in their traces. I promised Artemis I'd saddle up his horse for him. He has a hankering to go to Trimble Springs with us."

"He has a hankering for just about everything that comes his way!" Mariah laughed, thinking about what a sweet but frightened young man Artemis was as she picked her way through the scattered straw to where the leather goods were hanging on a large wooden peg.

Just then, Zack's voice called out from the other end of the aisle.

"Lord almighty! You two get on down here. Quick!"

Mariah dropped the traces where she stood and raced to meet her father. He was standing in front of the last stall, his mouth agape.

"Take a look at that horse, baby." Waiting until his wife had joined them, he said, "I believe that Artemis must have 'found' this sorrel. Don't he look like the one that belonged to our dear cousin Cain?"

Mariah peered into the murky stall. "It does look like it's the same horse."

Zack grabbed the horse's halter, steadying him, and then brushed the animal's flaxen forelock aside. "Ayuh. Look at those markings on his forehead. A perfect three-point star with a comet-tail blaze. That's about the last thing I noticed before this here gelding run off on me. It's the marshal's horse all right. Question is—if he ain't seen him already, what's Cain gonna do when he does? Might just be enough to jar the man's memory loose."

Feeling off balance, Mariah grabbed the stall and leaned against it. "We have to think of something, and fast."

"How about this?" Oda pushed her way between Zack and her daughter, glanced briefly in Mariah's direction, and then looked up at her husband. "I think it's time we tell Cain who he is, cut our losses, and get the hell out of town."

Mariah whirled on her. "No! We can't risk it. What if he wants to press charges or something? We could all wind up in jail."

"Now, baby," Zack said. "I don't think he'd go and do a thing like that, not after the good way we've been a-treating him and all. He might get in a bit of a fret over the way we done him at first, but I expect he'll just rant a little, then pack up and be on his way."

Not if she could help it! Mariah wouldn't allow this to happen—not now. She turned to her father, and pleaded with him. "Please listen to me, Dad. I think it's really important that we keep him with us as Cain Law for as long as we can. Besides, I've never known anyone like him, never—" She cut herself off just short of revealing too much. "I've never had any man treat me as kindly, except for you. I really don't see any harm in keeping him around a little longer."

"I do," said Oda.

Concerned by the knowing look in her mother's eye, but much too short on time to do anything but continue to plead her case, Mariah said, "Cain will probably cause us more harm and a lot more trouble than any of us ever imagined if we tell him who he is now. I say we stick to our story." Then she turned back to her father, making one final effort. "If I can think of something to do with this horse before Cain gets back, will you promise to let things go on the way they are?"

Zack tucked his chin up against his throat and stared down at his daughter in surprise. "What's got you in such a state? You haven't gone and let yourself get all google-eyed over that man, have you?"

"Oh, Dad," she said, purposely using that term. "For heaven's sake, no. I'm just afraid he'll come back before you two give me a chance to do something about this horse!" From behind her, Mariah could swear she heard Oda muttering under her breath.

Zack scratched his head. "I don't know."

"Well, I do," Mariah said, unlatching the stall. "And I wish you'd just promise to leave things be."

Because he still couldn't say no to Mariah, Zack slowly nodded his head. "All right, missy, but just you watch yourself around that man. He tries anything a'tall, you come running to me, hear?"

"Thanks, Dad, I will. Now why don't you and Oda go get those mules ready." She blew him a kiss and then stepped inside the stall.

"You go ahead, Zachariah," said Oda. "I'm gonna stay and help Mariah." Once her husband was out of earshot, she leaned across the waist-high door and whispered, "I seen you in the hallway last night."

Mariah sucked in a breath of air stale with urine and animal droppings. Turning to face her mother, her movements slow, deliberate, she said, "I, ah, couldn't sleep, so I took a little walk."

"I also seen where you went on that walk. Right into the marshal's room."

With her mother's gaze boring into her, there was no way in hell that Mariah could deny the obvious. She lowered her gaze. "All right, I did go to his room, but I— Oh, my God! Did you tell Zack?"

"What do you think?" Oda smirked. "He'd a' been screeching like a scalded cat by now if he knew what I knew."

Although she was relieved, Mariah knew by the look in her mother's eyes that she only had a temporary reprieve. "Are you planning to tell him?"

"That depends on you. If you go to your father and say that you've changed your mind, and that you think it's time we sent the marshal on his way, then he'll never know a thing about what's been going on with you and that man."

Tears stung the backs of her eyes and Mariah stared at her mother. "I can't do that. I love Cain."

"Love." Oda grumbled to herself, and then to Mariah. "Love ain't nothing but trouble. Haven't you learned that much from me here lately?"

Mariah's smile was ironic as she softly said, "I never learned a thing about men and their ways from you. I had to find out about them pretty much the same way you did, I guess." At those words, Oda did something Mariah had never seen her do: She began to cry. Sick at heart, Mariah rushed to the stall door, put her arms around her mother, and said, "Oh, please stop, Mother. I don't want to hurt you, but I can't stand the idea of having to send Cain away. Can't you understand? Try to remember how it was with you and . . . Storm."

Sniffing back her tears, Oda gripped her daughter's arms. "That's exactly why I want you to stop seeing Cain. He'll be nothing but trouble for you. Nothing but heartache and trouble!"

"No, no!" Mariah released her mother and backed deeper into the stall. "What I have with Cain isn't the same!"

"No," Oda whispered. "I suppose it isn't. It's worse, because you are living a lie. The marshal doesn't know yet who he is, but when he does—"

"You think I don't know that? Of course I do, but

what if this is all I ever have? What if I never feel this way about another man as long as I live?"

Oda stared at her, measuring her with sad blue eyes, but she didn't say a word.

Feeling her mother's empathy, if not her approval, Mariah went on. "I don't mean to belittle or slight the way you feel about Zack, but can you tell me you felt the exact same way about Storm?"

Oda blushed, her normally robust complexion darkening to an almost purple hue. "No, I can't. It weren't the same," she quietly said.

"Then you do understand!" Mariah stepped forward to take her mother's hands. "What I feel for Cain is at least what you had with Storm, and maybe a little of what you have with Zack—it could even be both, I don't know for sure."

"Mariah . . . it's all a lie."

"Yes, it is, but I don't intend to do a damn thing about that until I absolutely have to." At the thought, she trembled from head to toe. "Just tell me the honest truth: Could you or would you have given up either man, your lover or your husband?"

Oda looked at her daughter, staring long and hard as fresh tears rolled down her cheeks. "It don't matter what I did, or what I think now. You can't have Cain for much longer. He's bound to remember who he is someday soon, and then he's going to wind up hurting you. Hurting you real bad."

Mariah couldn't help but concede that much. It was the truth. "Maybe he will, but it's my hurt and my heart that will have to suffer. I'm willing to take that risk for as long as Cain wants me. Please,

Mother, I beg you—keep what you know to yourself, and help me figure out what to do with this horse."

Oda, wishing to hell she'd brought a cigar with her, wiped her hand across her mouth in an effort to still the sudden trembling there. Then she dried her cheeks and leveled her pale blue eyes on her daughter. "We might get rid of this here horse the easiest by just taking him to the edge of town and turning him loose."

Mariah now believed that nothing on earth would be able to drag what Oda knew about Mariah and Cain from her, and that drew a wealth of emotions from her. She threw her arms around her mother, hugging and squeezing her, mingling tears, memories, and their very hearts.

Then, swallowing the lump in her throat, Mariah smiled and said, "Thanks for everything." She glanced at the horse, wiping her eyes as she studied the animal's flaxen mane and tail. "I'm afraid if we turn him loose, he'll just find his way back here again, and we'd still have the same problem. We need to figure out a way to disguise him."

"You mean like put a hat and coat on him and call him Brother Law the Second?"

"Something like that, I suppose," Mariah said, laughing through the remnants of her tears. "But I think it'd work better if we were to figure out a way to color his mane and tail. Maybe if we dye it with a little ash from the blacksmith's fire! What do you think?"

"Dyeing sounds good, but I never seen no sorrel with a black mane and tail. Ought to be red."

Red. But where to get red dye, and right this minute? The more Mariah thought about keeping Cain's past a secret from him, the more sure she became that she could pull it off. After all, day after tomorrow they'd be on the train to Silverton, a sleepy little mountain town where they would all be safe and no one would recognize Cain as Slater. Durango's sheriff and the infamous Doolittle Gang posed the only danger she could think of, and so far, none of them had come forward to identify him.

If her luck could just hold out for another thirty-six hours, long enough to get out of Durango, Cain would be hers—maybe, she dared to hope, forever.

"I have it," Mariah said, struck with inspiration. "I believe that Colorado is the Spanish word for color-ful, and for a very good reason!"

"Ah." Oda nodded in understanding. The color of Colorado's soil ran the gamut from light chestnut to rich terra-cotta, and the hillsides around Durango leaned toward a deep rust color. Once an item of clothing was stained with this soil, it never came clean again. Oda broke into a rare grin. "You think-ing we ought to give that horse a little mud bath?"

Mariah matched her mother's grin. "I'll just go get us a bucket."

Cain knew exactly what he planned to do with at least half, if not all, of the twenty dollars as he stepped across the threshold of Gephart's General Outfitting Store. He was going to buy himself a new hat, something that suited him better than the ridiculously pious Brother Law skimmer he'd been wearing of late, something closer to the kind of hat he assumed he had been wearing the day he'd been injured.

Maybe, Cain figured, if he could start dressing more like himself, he'd begin to feel more like himself, and thereby remember exactly who he was. It was suddenly very important to him to remember everything from the past, because until he did, he wouldn't be free to offer himself completely to Mariah, the way he should have before he let her into his room that first night, the night the memories of his father had come flooding back.

Sure that the day his entire memory would return was near, Cain fought his way through the crowded little store which advertised everything "from soup to nuts," and went toward the rear, where the clothing was on display. Dogging his footsteps, Artemis labored to keep up with him as he continued firing an endless round of questions.

"What about after we get to Silverton, Cain? You gonna stay with the medicine show when it moves on north?"

"How many times are you going to ask me that same question, son? I already told you I don't know." His attention caught by a table piled high with leather goods, he absently added, "I suppose I'll stay on with the show as long as they'll have me."

"Oh, yeah, that's right." Artemis gulped and dragged his hand across his brow, sure he was sweating. Why couldn't he keep the questions he was supposed to ask the marshal straight in his mind, or hell, even remember half of them? If he wasn't careful, he was going to do what he usually did when given even the smallest of jobs: mess up.

Cain fingered the French calf cigar case he had picked up from the table, and popped the snap, opening it. The case was lined with red satin, the nickel frame embroidered with wildflowers. Cain chuckled to himself, imagining Oda's expression should he present her with such a gift, and decided the $1.45 price tag would be worth her look of surprise.

He turned to Artemis, handing him the cigar case, and said, "Would you mind holding this for me so I can go try on a few hats?"

"I sure can. Whatever you want." Artemis grabbed the case, cradling it in his palm as if it were made of eggshells, and began to wander around the store as Cain disappeared down an aisle filled with children's clothing and stacks of shoes.

Cain spotted the men's hats displayed against the back wall, but as he started in that direction, the women's millinery section to the left of them caught his eye—specifically, a lavender-and-black hat topped with a pair of frothy lemon-colored ostrich tips.

His original mission forgotten, Cain took the bonnet from its wooden perch and turned it on his fist. It was a leghorn shade hat made of chantilly net and finished with shiny black beads, elegant satin ribbons, and the eye-catching yellow feathers. Without even closing his eyes, Cain could see the bonnet nestled in Mariah's ebony hair, and then he imagined her strutting proudly down Main Avenue the way every other woman in town did.

Without so much as batting an eye at the outrageous $14.65 price, Cain asked the clerk to box the hat for him. Then, down to less than five dollars, he looked around the store for Artemis. He found him practically drooling over a harmonica he'd picked out from a collection of musical instruments.

"Find a good one, did you?" Cain asked as he approached him.

Artemis's eyes were as big as the tambourine he'd just returned to the shelf. "Look at how this mouth organ shines! It must be made of pure silver!"

Cain took the instrument from the kid and read the engraving on the side. "It's a Richter from Germany, and although the plates are brass, the thing does have silver covers. Good eye, Artemis." Cain turned it over and read the price-tag. "Eighty-five cents. You have expensive taste. You going to buy it?"

"Buy it?" Such a thought had never occurred to him. Now that it had, Artemis began to laugh. "Oh, glory be, no. Billy don't ever let me carry no money around."

"Billy? Who's that?"

Artemis knew then that he'd finally gone and done it: He'd messed up worse than ever. His throat closed up on him and something began to squirm in his gut. "Ah, B-Billy's my b-brother."

Cain frowned as he stared at Artemis. The kid had turned white, and his hands, including the one which still held the harmonica, were shaking. Even though the day had warmed to a comfortable 77 degrees, Artemis looked as if he'd just climbed out of a snow cave.

"I don't think I'd be wrong if I were to guess that your brother is not a very nice man. Does he beat you, son?"

Not sure how he even got into this conversation, much less how to get out of it, Artemis rolled his eyes. When he opened his mouth to speak, to deny at least the beating part, the only thing that came out was a strangled, gurgling sound.

As he saw the terror in the young man's eyes, Cain's temper snapped. "Where is this brother of yours, Artemis? I think maybe I ought to go have a little talk with him."

"Oh, God, no! God in heaven, no, no, no! You can't do that!" Just the thought of the marshal confronting Billy prompted Artemis to do something he'd worked and worked at training himself not to do in public. He began to cry.

"Take it easy, son." Cain moved up close to Artemis in an effort to shield him from curious or amused customers. "I'm not much of a family man, but I do know this isn't the way brothers should feel about one another. What does Billy do to keep you so afraid of him?"

Artemis squeezed his eyes shut, hard, hoping the act might wring every drop of moisture from them as he tried to figure out what to do next. How could things have turned so badly on him? What had he done to make it all go so wrong? This wasn't how things were supposed to go—the marshal wasn't supposed to be asking *him* questions! In spite of his efforts, several tears escaped through his puckered lids and ran down his cheeks.

Feeling at least partly responsible for Artemis's distress—he had, after all, backed him into a corner with all the questions about his brother—Cain patted his trembling shoulder. "Forget I mentioned Billy, Artemis, but if you ever change your mind and you do want me to have a talk with him, all you have to do is ask. Understand?"

Artemis blew his nose on the sleeve of his shirt. "Yes, sir!" he said between hiccups.

Cain took the harmonica from the young man's hand, and then impulsively reached over and grabbed a two-dollar sheepskin banjo off the shelf. There were, he decided then and there, worse things than not remembering who had raised you. Sometimes *knowing* was harder to live with.

Keeping his voice calm and compassionate, Cain smiled at Artemis as he said, "I figure anyone who can play music the way you do ought to have his own instruments. Consider these as a little gift for being such a good helper."

Didn't it just figure. No sooner had Artemis finally capped his well than along came Cain to blow the lid off again. Tears spilled down his cheeks before he could even think to slam his eyelids shut, and he began bawling like an orphaned calf. A squeaky "Thanks" was all he could manage to say before Cain spun on his heel and headed for the cash register. After lagging behind awhile so he could wipe his nose and his tears on his cleaner shirtsleeve, Artemis flashed a grin as broad as Cain's shoulders. Then he followed his new hero out of the store.

*   *   *

Mariah and Oda had just finished "bathing" the horse and cleaning their hands when Cain and Artemis returned from their mysterious trip to town. As they strolled in through the wide back entrance to the barn, Mariah could see that Artemis was beaming.

"Look what Cain got for me at the outfitter's store!" He held up the harmonica in one hand and the banjo in the other. "They're mine and no one else's . . . forever!"

"Put them in the back of the medicine wagon," Cain said as he quickly tucked the hatbox under the bench seat of the supply cart. "I think we've held up this trip to the hot springs long enough."

As Artemis disappeared around the back of the wagon, Cain approached Oda. "This is for you," he said, handing her the cigar case. "It's just a little something to thank you for putting up with me the last few weeks."

It was a good thing she hadn't lit a new cigar yet, or it would have fallen from her surprised mouth into the bedding straw and most likely set fire to the barn. She looked from Cain to the cigar case and over to her daughter. Her mouth twisting into an almost bashful grin, she said, "That's pretty fancy. You sure it's for me?"

He pinched her cheek. "I'm sure. Now what can I do to get things moving around here?"

From behind him, Mariah said, "You can help me finish hitching the mule to the supply cart."

Careful to appear businesslike and cousinly, Cain kept his voice brisk as he said, "Right away."

As he reached under the animal's belly to pull the harness strap up tight, Mariah leaned against the wooden seat and eyed the package Cain had placed there. "What's in the box?" she asked, more than a bit curious after witnessing his generosity with both Artemis and her mother.

Cain wanted to wait until he and Mariah were alone before he gave her the bonnet, so he only lied a little as he said, "I bought myself a hat."

"Oh." The word was barely audible. Mariah hadn't really expected Cain to be out buying gifts for her, and she was most certainly happy to see that he'd spent his twenty dollars on tangible goods rather than on a few moments with a wild saloon girl, but still, she couldn't help feeling a few pricks of disappointment. In fact, she was so distracted by the thought that Cain had slighted her, Mariah forgot to take Artemis aside as she'd planned, to let him know what she'd done to disguise the horse. And why. When the young man's voice cried out from the other end of the stable, Mariah was as startled as anyone.

"Hey! Somebody's been messing around with Big Red!"

13

Mariah hadn't known she had it in her to move so fast, but when she heard what Artemis had to say, and realized that all their work might have been for naught, she practically flew down to the stall. She found him gawking at the big sorrel.

"Hush," she whispered as she approached him, very aware that Cain was not far behind her. "I don't know where you got this horse, but I do know it doesn't belong to you. Marshal Slater lost one just like this a while back."

"Holy shi— Y-you sure it's his?"

"Sure enough that we can't take any chances. I thought I was doing you a favor by disguising it. He'll hang you for sure if he thinks you're a horse thief."

Artemis peeked over her shoulder to see the marshal bearing down on him. "B-but T-Tubbs found it, not me!"

"It doesn't matter *who* found it, Artemis."

"Found what?" Cain wanted to know as he approached them.

Mariah gave a little jump. "Oh, ah—it's nothing." Realizing that Artemis was incapable of coming up with a reasonable story, she turned to Cain and flashed him a bright smile. "He forgot that he asked my dad to groom Big Red for him. Ah, Zack found a stone bruise when he was cleaning his hooves."

"Th-that's right," Artemis said, proud of himself for understanding what Mariah was trying to do. "I'm gonna stay right here and soak Big Red's foot so he'll be all better."

The mud bath she'd given the animal had included his three white socks. Mariah narrowed her gaze toward Artemis as she said, "I don't think that will help much. In fact, he could be a problem on the show circuit. You might want to consider leaving him behind and getting a new horse in Silverton."

Artemis didn't know what he should agree to at this point, but the thought of saying good-bye to the horse filled him with sadness. "I'll think on it some."

Cain, who hadn't missed the way the young man's expression fell, stepped forward. "Why don't you let me take a look at him. Maybe it's not as bad as we think."

"Ah, no!" Mariah splayed her fingers against Cain's broad chest, and then whispered under her breath, "I think he'd feel better about it if we let him care for the horse himself."

Artemis sensed that things were taking a turn for the worse. He quickly ducked around the gate, catching the latch behind him, and then made a great show of examining one of Big Red's hooves.

"Just holler if you need any help," Cain said, leaning across the stall door.

At the sound of his previous master's voice, Amigo raised his ears and nickered softly.

The call stirred something at the back of Cain's mind. He looked in at the horse, cocking his head and wondering what it was about the animal that seemed so familiar. The sorrel nickered again, this time tossing his brick-red mane. "Easy, big fellow. You think you know me?"

"Ah, Cain?" Mariah, said, tugging on his sleeve. "Zack needs your help with the mules, remember? Artemis has things under control here."

"You're right." Speaking louder, he said, "Don't hesitate to call me if you want some help, son."

As Artemis glanced back to say thank you, he saw Cain reach across the opening and rub Big Red's forelock. When he brought his hand away, particles of dark red dirt rained down on Artemis's head, and the marshal's fingers were streaked with mud. Feeling like his Adam's apple had swollen to twice its size, Artemis rolled his eyes toward his new hero, and gulped.

Mariah, who'd also noticed the mess, held her breath.

Cain stared down at his hand, shook his head, and then said to Artemis, "Maybe you ought to groom that animal again while you're at it, son. Looks to me like he's been out rolling in the mud."

*   *   *

Less than an hour later, the troupe, minus Artemis and his "crippled" horse, were well on their way out of Durango. The sky looked multilayered, teal-colored below the noonday sun, followed by a royal blue-black strip, with a pale periwinkle-blue tint hugging the horizon. Ahead of the medicine wagon and supply cart, the San Juan mountain range loomed in the distance, one red-cliffed mountain peak rising above another to what seemed like infinity.

Cain waited until they'd gotten beyond the edge of town to point at the box wedged between his and Mariah's feet. "Why don't you have a peek at my new hat?"

Mariah, who'd been marveling at the way the verdant tips of the giant ponderosa pines seemed to fringe the spacious blue sky overhead, leaned down and picked up the box. She casually flipped the lid off and glanced inside, expecting to see another version of the big white hat that he'd lost near Bucksnort. Instead, her gaze met a luscious confection of lavender lace, black satin, and lemon-colored plumes.

Momentarily stunned, she finally said, "W-wherever did you get such a lovely bonnet, and . . . whose is it?"

Slowing the mule so he could observe her full reaction, Cain said, "I bought it for you, princess. Do you like it?"

"Oh, Cain—oh, Lord." Mariah lifted the hat from its nest of wadded paper as if it were some great treasure. "It's absolutely the most beautiful thing I've ever seen."

"Put it on. I can't wait to see it on you."

Mariah gazed at the bonnet, guiltily chewing the inside of her lip. She didn't deserve such a gift. She knew Cain's finances well enough to realize that buying the bonnet had made it impossible for him to replace the preacher's hat he abhorred with something more suitable.

She lowered the frothy bonnet back into the box. "You'll never know how much this means to me, but I can't accept such a gift."

"Why not?"

"For one thing," she said, gazing longingly at the hat, "as Princess Tanacoa, I can't even wear this in most towns, and certainly not often enough to warrant the expense. You have to take it back."

"Not on your life. We're heading for Silverton day after tomorrow, right?"

"Yes, but—"

"I can't think of anything I'd rather do than escort you in that hat out of the Strater Hotel and down Main Avenue the morning we leave to catch the train. You'll not only be the most beautiful woman walking the streets of Durango, but the most fashionable. By God, if you don't wear that hat for me, I will."

He hadn't laughed after he said those final words, because he meant them. She mattered to him. Up until that moment, Mariah thought she'd fully understood what love meant. Now she realized she hadn't even gone below the surface of it. Love was more than a warm feeling in the pit of her belly whenever Cain touched her, and much more intense than the lurch her heart made each time he came into view. Love was all-powerful and all-consuming.

That was how she felt about Cain, and whether he felt that way about her didn't matter at the moment. The kind of love she had for this man stripped her to the bone, exposed her raw and bare, yet strangely enough, made her proud to be so naked to the world. She wanted to stand up and shout "I love you," longed to hear her voice echo the phrase through the majestic pines. She mouthed the words, but didn't say them. She knew they were best left in her mind.

Filled with a kind of love she'd never dreamed she could feel, and with a deepening, ever-stronger sense of belonging to this man, she loosened the ribbons on her serviceable black bonnet, removed it, and tossed it into the back of the supply wagon. Then she fit the new hat to her head, swiveled toward Cain, and asked, "How does it look on me?"

Cain whistled long and low. Without benefit of a mirror, she'd set the bonnet on her head at a slight angle—certainly more of one than the designer had in mind, he suspected—and the effect was startling. The bright colors were perfect for her, the yellow in particular, which accentuated the shiny ebony of Mariah's hair and startling amethyst shade of her eyes. The thing he liked best, though, was the sauciness of the hat and the way it made her look: irascible, mischievous, and even a little bit naughty.

Since he had firsthand knowledge of how downright naughty Mariah could be, Cain's voice dropped to a low growl as he said, "It's a damn good thing your parents are just ahead of us. That's how good you look to me right now." He patted the seat beside him. "Move a little closer."

There was barely enough from for the two of them as it was, but Mariah snuggled herself up tighter against his thigh and looped her arm through his. "Better?"

"As better as things can get for now, I suppose." He gazed into her eyes, gripped with a savage and possessive kind of joy. God, but she was beautiful, Cain thought, proud to call her his own. And then just as suddenly, it occurred to him that it was possible he didn't have the right to think of her in that way. Or the freedom.

"Is something wrong?" Mariah asked, seeing his changed expression. "You suddenly look so . . . so unhappy."

Cain transferred both reins to one hand, freeing himself to slide an arm across Mariah's shoulders. "I'm not exactly unhappy, princess. Unworthy, is what I was thinking."

"Of what?"

"Of you." He kissed the tip of her nose. "You deserve so much more than I can give you right now."

"But—but that's ridiculous! You've given me so much already, made me feel so . . ." She blushed and let the sentence die in her throat. "I'm perfectly content the way things are."

"I appreciate the sentiments, Mariah, but I'm talking about the future."

And to continue with talk like that, wouldn't he just naturally want to bring up the past? Not if Mariah could help it. She forced a laugh. "Please, Cain. I really don't want to think or talk about the future. I like things the way they are right now. Don't spoil our lovely drive."

He glanced ahead at the small dust cloud traveling down the road in front of them, picking out the bright red door at the back of the medicine wagon. Zack and Oda wouldn't much care for the way things were right now, lovely drive or not. No self-respecting family would. He'd promised himself he would have this talk with Mariah, and have it he would. "The last thing I want to do is spoil the day, but it's time we talked about the future, princess. Our future together."

Had he said *our* future? What exactly did he mean by that? Surely nothing so permanent or extraordinary as—

"I'm talking about . . . marriage." There. He'd finally said the words he should have said three nights ago. Feeling reckless, he continued. "And, eventually, I expect you'll want a family somewhere down the road."

Beside him, her heart thundering, Mariah nearly swooned. Having accepted the situation as impossible from the beginning, she had never allowed herself so much as a small daydream about this moment. Now that it was here, she didn't know whether to shout her joy from the highest Rocky mountain, or throw herself from it in despair. She wanted nothing more than to be his wife, but Cain couldn't marry her. Not as Cain Law, a man who didn't exist, and not even as Morgan Slater, a man who'd most likely been claimed long ago by the woman in the watchcase.

Aware only of Mariah's pensive silence, not her distress, Cain went on. "I do realize that before we can make any firm plans, I've got to get the mysteries of my past cleared up. Wouldn't you agree?" Cain glanced at her, noticing a peculiar glaze to her normally bright eyes. "Mariah? Are you with me?"

Her tongue, feeling twisted and fluttery in her mouth, couldn't seem to choose the correct words to form a sentence. Mariah didn't know what to say. She smiled at Cain, her expression a little tight, a little too animated, and gave him a jaunty nod instead.

Determined to get at the truth about his past, Cain didn't notice anything amiss in Mariah's reaction. He was filled with the fire of self-discovery. "Something's gnawing at me inside, and until I get it out, until I truly know who I am, I can never be completely yours. I thought it might help if we start with my childhood. I know that my father Thomas had red hair and wouldn't let me have a dog. What can you add to that?"

Guilt was weighing Mariah down, but for this question, she had an answer that was nothing less than the truth. "I don't know your father or any of my mother's other brothers. Her family shunned her when they discovered she was expecting me. I've never met any of them."

"Jesus. I'm sorry, princess. I forgot about that."

"You've forgotten a lot of things since you were injured, and that's why we shouldn't be talking about the future."

"I don't follow you, princess."

"How can it be any plainer?" she said, speaking

out of the pain in her heart instead of the logic of her mind. "For all we know, you already have a wife! You don't have any business proposing to me."

Cain laughed. "That's ridiculous. Wouldn't your family know if I was married?"

"I—ah . . ." She paused to take a long breath, trying to clear her mind and resume the role she'd chosen to play. "I—I told you already that you weren't very communicative about your past when you joined the show. We know virtually nothing about you before that."

His mouth fell open, not so much at her words, but at the ominous ring in them. "And you think it's possible? You believe that maybe I do have . . . someone else somewhere?"

Thoughts of the woman in the locket again filled Mariah's head, and she knew she couldn't lie to him about that, no matter how hard she tried. She looked away and offered a tiny shrug.

Christ in a whiskey barrel. Was it possible? Is that what he felt clawing his gut, fighting to rise to the surface of his consciousness? A woman he'd forgotten somewhere along the way? A wife! Surely he'd have had some sense of her, some little twinge of guilt about her—if not now, certainly on the night he'd made Mariah his own.

Then, as if beckoned by those thoughts, the woman appeared in his mind: blond, petite, fragile. He squeezed his eyes against her image, but it only grew stronger. Robin's-egg blue eyes, skin so fair it was nearly translucent. And frail. She was very, very frail. His wife? Or someone else? He called to the woman in his mind, thinking that her name might automatically form on his lips, but she faded away, folding herself back into the dark cloak of his forgotten past.

Shaken in ways he couldn't begin to fathom, Cain's movements were deliberate as he removed his arm from Mariah's shoulder and took the reins in both hands. All ten of his fingers were trembling, he noticed, even though this section of road was relatively smooth.

In a voice as stiff as his suddenly rigid spine, he said, "I guess talking about a future together was pretty presumptuous of me, now that I think about it. Besides"—he managed a small chuckle, trying to put her at ease—"you have big plans for a future in the business world. I expect if you're looking to throw in with anyone, it'll be a lawyer or a doctor when you get to New York."

He may as well have said, "Now that I think about it, I believe I do have a wife waiting for me somewhere." Tears burned her eyes, but Mariah refused to let them fall. Hadn't she brought this on herself? "Massachusetts," she whispered.

She'd spoken so softly, Cain hadn't quite heard the word. "What?"

"Massachusetts," she said, firming up the timbre of her voice along with her conscience. She may not have had the guts or whatever it took to tell Cain who he was and what he'd been, but Mariah had to make certain he knew that she didn't expect a future with him. It was one thing for her to dream that he'd never regain his memory and be hers forever, but quite another to drag *him* into that fantasy.

"The Lydia E. Pinkham Medicine Company is in Lynn, Massachusetts. If I'm going to catch the eye of a lawyer, I suppose it'll have to be one of those Harvard fellows from Boston."

"Right. Harvard." Cain laughed, the sound hollow, and wondered how things had gotten so completely turned around.

While the members of the Penny troupe were filling their barrels with mineral water from Trimble Springs, Artemis brought Tubbs into Naegelin's stables. He pointed out what Mariah had done to the stray he'd found running loose on the range.

"Jesus, kid," Tubbs said, fingering the animal's once flaxen mane. "How'd she get his hair this color?"

Artemis laughed. "She and her ma rubbed mud on him, and when me and Cain got back from the store, Big Red was red all over."

"And you really do think he belongs to the marshal?"

"The marshal?" Artemis scratched his head. "Oh, you mean Cain?"

"That man is Morgan Slater, a United States marshal, and don't you forget it again for one minute." Concerned that Artemis was no longer concentrating on his job, Tubbs grabbed him by the collar and shook him. "Well? Is this the marshal's horse, or not?"

"Is, I think. Is." Tubbs released his shirt and gestured for him to go on. Speaking rapidly, Artemis related all that he knew. "Big Red started talking to him like they was old friends the minute he first seen him, and Cain—the marshal—was kinda staring back at him with one of them 'ain't we met somewheres before' looks. Sure enough seemed like this was his horse to me. It give me the creeps, the way Big Red carried on, I kin tell you that."

The idea gave Tubbs a lot more than the creeps. It confused the hell out of him. "Why would the woman want to keep the identity of this horse a secret from the sheriff? I thought he was using their medicine show as a cover, and that they knew he was a U.S. marshal."

There were too many questions and too many facts coming way too fast for Artemis. He scratched his head and truthfully answered the statements he understood. "Miss Mariah said she wouldn't tell Cain about the horse because he'd hang me as a horse thief if he found out Big Red was his. She likes me, and gave me money to buy all the newspapers every day, too."

"The newspapers, kid? Why do you do that?"

"Cause of Cai—the marshal. She don't want him reading stories about us."

"*Us?*" The veins in Tubbs's neck bulged. "Which 'us' are you talking about."

Artemis began to back away, but he wasn't nearly fast enough. Tubbs caught up with him and dragged him into the empty stall next to Big Red's.

"Answer me, kid, and do it now, or I swear this will be the last breath you ever draw."

"Us, the Doolittles, but she don't know who we are. I swear she don't, Tubbs. Let me go!"

He did, but he kept his body directly in front of Artemis, blocking his escape route. "What *does* she know about the Doolittles, kid? Take your time and repeat her exact words, if you can."

Artemis let his breath out on the tail end of a shudder. "She just knows what we heard in the sheriff's office, I guess—that Marshal Slater is tracking the Doolittles and that some folks thinks they might have killed him. She ain't never said another thing about them to me. Just to keep my eye out for anyone who might want to hurt Cain."

Sorry now that he'd sent the final confirmation wires to both Silverton and Mancos, Tubbs smashed his right fist into his left palm. The wheels of the plan were too far in motion to stop them now, and he had no real proof that their lives or the job were in jeopardy, but still; this business with the horse, along with the Indian princess and her newspapers, gave him more than a little cause for concern.

Speaking calmly, choosing his words carefully, he said, "Sorry if I got a little rough, kid, but we can't take the chance of something ruining our job now, can we?"

Artemis shook his head.

"Then tell me a little more about this princess. Is she working with the marshal, you think?"

Artemis had never thought of that before, so he had to consider the possibility a while before he answered. "Don't know, Tubbs. Like I said, all she asked me was did I know what the Doolittles looked like, and then told me to make sure they didn't go sneaking up on Cai—on the marshal when he weren't looking."

"That sounds to me like she *is* working with him!"

Again, Artemis had to shrug. "I don't see how she could be. She's a girl. What could she be doing for him?"

Tubbs, who'd ridden with Quantrill during the war, was very aware of how useful and effective a woman could be when put to work in the name of the law. He'd had more than one narrow escape from Pinkerton's female operatives. And he wasn't in the mood for any more. "Why'd she want the newspapers?"

"So the marshal wouldn't go reading about himself getting killed, I guess. She didn't say."

Tubbs stared at the kid a long moment, piecing together all the information he'd been given, trying every which way to make it fit into a pattern he could understand, but no matter how he looked at it, he always wound up with more questions than answers. There were just some things, he decided, he'd have to find out for himself.

"Here's what you're going to do, kid," Tubbs said, staring him right in the eye. "First, you've got to sell that horse. Go to Naegelin, tell him you're desperate for money and have to sell him today. Be sure you get rid of him before those show folks get back to town, understand?"

Although he hated the idea of parting with his high-stepping friend, Artemis nodded. "Sell Big Red. Got it."

"Then comes the important part." He moved closer, taking Artemis by the lobe of his ear. "I want you to listen real good from here on out, kid, because

we can't take any more chances around the marshal
or that princess. You listening?"

Artemis nodded carefully, but rapidly.

"Good. Tell me a little more about that Indian
princess. What room is she in at the hotel, and when
do you expect her to come back?"

By the time the Penny troupe returned from
Trimble Springs, it was late in the evening. After all
four of them had taken long, private mineral baths,
they had decided to partake of their supper at the
resort. Though she hadn't felt particularly festive,
Mariah had even worn her new hat into the small but
fashionable restaurant, drawing oohs and ahhs from
both Zack and Oda.

Now back at the Strater, all Mariah wanted to do
was go to the privacy of her room and sleep. She said
good night to Cain in the hallway in full view of both
her parents, and then slipped into her room. That was
when a sudden sense of danger came over her, a feeling that she wasn't entirely alone. She quickly lit the
small lantern on her dresser and glanced around the
room. She was the only occupant, but she couldn't
shake the feeling that something was amiss.

With only a soft glow illuminating the corners, she
slowly strolled around her room. Nothing appeared to
be out of place, and the windows were closed tight,
yet still she felt a deep sense of violation, of invasion.
She tore open the drawers of the dresser and stared
down at her clothing. Everything was neatly folded,
all there as far as she could tell, and yet . . .

Since Mariah had been a small child, she'd always taken extra care in folding and stacking her handkerchiefs, piling one atop another like a perfect wedge of seven-layer cake. Now her confection of hankies was decidedly lopsided, the corners mussed and twisted. She never would have left them in such a state.

She heard something then, a squeak or a whimper, and turned this way and that before realizing that the sound had come from under her bed. *Daisy!* Mariah hurried across the room, fell to her knees, and lifted the coverlet. Her little dog was huddled into a ball, and shaking like a bowlful of tapioca.

"Oh, sweetheart. Come here." Mariah opened her arms, and the little dog raced to her. Once she examined the animal and found her unharmed, she gathered Daisy against her bosom and began to rock back and forth on her heels.

Someone had been in her room, of that she had almost no doubt. Someone who'd frightened Daisy half to death, riffled through her drawers, and did God knew what else. Although Mariah's first impulse was to race from her room and into Cain's arms, she forced herself to remain still. If Cain, or even her parents, knew what she suspected, the first thing they'd do was call in the law. The sheriff would then recognize Cain as Morgan Slater. And that would bring her fantasy of a life with him to a complete and utter end.

Besides, she thought, rationalizing her decision from every angle she could think of—what if she were mistaken? Something else could have frightened Daisy enough to send her hiding under the bed. A gunshot, a clap of thunder, loud voices—any of those

things, even though Mariah had heard none of them
herself. As for her dresser and the disorderly pile of
handkerchiefs, she supposed she could have mussed
them up herself and not noticed. After all, the only
thing she really paid any attention to these days was
Cain, was it not?

Mariah laughed to herself, forcing a lighter mood.
She'd probably jumped to conclusions by assuming
that an intruder had gone through her things. Why
would anyone be interested in anything Mariah Penny
or Princess Tanacoa owned in the first place? It didn't
make sense. She had no jewelry, no exorbitant
amount of money, nothing of any value to warrant a
search of her room.

After taking Daisy for a short walk outside, she
decided to keep her suspicions to herself. It wasn't as
if she was in any danger, especially if she took a few
simple precautions over the next two nights. And
once they got to Silverton, everything would be all
right again—including the rift she'd felt between Cain
and her since his talk about their "future."

But as she wedged the Queen Anne chair up under
the doorknob, securing her room for the night, something in her gut told Mariah that she was a fool.

14

Two days later, Tubbs sat on the edge of his sagging mattress at the Last Stop Hotel, going over the final plans with Artemis. Within the hour, they would both board the Denver & Rio Grande for the trip to Silverton, and once they were on the train, their contact would have to be kept to a minimum.

"Then you want me to sit with the marshal?" Artemis asked.

"Close by will be good enough. Just so you don't have any trouble finding him when I give the signal to bring him back to the last car. Remember what you're supposed to do?"

Nodding, Artemis said, "You're gonna signal that you're ready for me to bring the marshal back to you by bumping into me when you walk by."

"And why is it so important for you to choose your seat carefully?"

"'Cause you can't bump into me unless I'm sitting on the aisle."

"Good. Real good. Then what do you do?"

"Then I tell him I got something to say to him that needs to be said real private-like. He gets up and follows me to the car, where you'll be waiting on the step outside the door." Tubbs hadn't explained things any further than that, but Artemis remembered what they'd talked about when they'd first found Cain in Durango. Worried about the life of his new friend and hero, he said, "Er, w-what happens after I bring him to you? Can't we just talk to him a little?"

"No, Artemis, we can't. You know we got to take him out, and you know why."

He hung his head. "I . . . guess so."

Tubbs noticed that the kid's lip was trembling, and he decided against informing him about the newest amendment to the plan: the fact that he'd decided to take the princess out right along with the marshal. Even though he hadn't found a damn thing in her room to tie her to Slater or the marshal's office, he didn't like the way the odds were stacked. Just the fact that it looked as if the woman was in cahoots with Slater was good enough for Tubbs.

Getting rid of her would be a simple task if he could get Artemis's full cooperation. First the marshal, then the girl. One, two, over the side and into the gorge. Robbing the train was a chancy enough proposition without taking any unnecessary risks. And leaving Princess Tanacoa, or whoever in the hell she was, alive was too much of a gamble.

He grinned at the kid. "How does the plan sound so far, Artemis?"

He looked up at Tubbs, then back down at his lap. He was far from happy over the idea of taking Cain out, but much too frightened of Tubbs and his brother to allow his doubts to show. It was a struggle, but Artemis smiled as he said, "Sounds good. Anything else you want me to do?"

Relaxing a little, Tubbs said, "Now that you mention it, there is. Once the marshal's gone over the side, I want you to go back to where he was sitting and tell the princess that he wants to see her. Send her out to me. I'll still be waiting on the step."

Artemis gasped. "You ain't gonna take her out too, are you?"

"No, kid, of course not. I just want to have a little talk with her. Understand?"

Pretty sure that he did understand, Artemis faked a coughing fit to cover a sudden attack of the shivers. He wasn't real smart, he knew, and he wasn't real good at figuring, reading, and sometimes just plain thinking. But when he did know something, he knew it. Period. And right now, he knew without a doubt that Tubbs planned to murder his two best friends in the world. Murder them, and then sit back and laugh about it the next time the gang gathered around a campfire.

Tubbs slapped the kid's back, thinking he was coughing because he'd swallowed wrong. "You'd best get on down to the depot now. I imagine that 'Brother Law' is wondering why in hell you aren't down there helping him load up the medicine show."

*　　　*　　　*

If Tubbs wasn't right about another thing, he was right about that. When Artemis strolled into the train yard, he saw that Cain had enlisted the aid of a couple of railroad men to load the supply cart onto a flatbed car.

"Need any help?" he asked.

"I sure do—it's about time you showed up." Cain studied the young man, noticing how pinched and drawn he looked, particularly around the mouth. "Are you feeling all right this morning?"

"Oh, sure. It just took me a while to get packed up, is all." He held up a tattered valise. "What should I do with this?"

Cain took it and tossed it inside the medicine wagon. "Get on up with the mules. I'll secure the door, and when I holler, you can start things rolling up the ramp." As Cain reached for the door, Mariah suddenly came up from behind him.

"Morning," she said, setting her dog inside on the floor of the wagon. "Just give me a minute to pour a bowl of water for Daisy, then you can lock up."

Feeling nervous and awkward, the exact same way he'd been feeling around Mariah since their trip to the hot springs, Cain stepped back out of her way. They'd been polite strangers for the last two days, friendly and smiling, but wary and distant beneath the surface. God, how he missed being with the real Mariah, laughing with her . . . touching her. Cain wanted to rip off her proper little homespun velvet traveling suit, peel open the royal purple jersey, and reclaim the

woman inside. Maybe even, he thought with a surprising recklessness, stake a claim to her heart.

Mariah closed the door and fastened the catch.
"There," she said, turning to face Cain. "She ought to
be just fine for the next five hours."

"Maybe *she* will, but I won't be. Will you?" Before
she could answer, he took Mariah's hand and led her
around to the side of the medicine wagon. There,
where their privacy was far from ensured, but fewer
prying eyes could find them, Cain reached up and
adjusted the bonnet he'd bought for her until it set at
the naughty little tilt he adored. "I think it's time we
had another little talk, princess. Now, before we
board that train."

Mariah shook off the little tremors his touch sent
through her and forced herself to instead remember
their last discussion. "It won't do any good to talk
about the past, Cain, and I can't allow myself to think
of the future. It wouldn't be fair to either of us."

"I'm not interested in the past or the future right
now. All I care about, Mariah, is you, and here, and
now. I've missed you so much." His arms ached to
hold her, to reach out and crush her to his chest,
but for propriety's sake, Cain kept his hands at his
sides. His fists were closed tight, rigid with self-
restraint. "I just about went crazy hoping you
would come to my room last night. When you
didn't show, I thought about breaking down the
door to your room."

She shivered as a response blossomed in her heart,
then tickled her spine and ran all the way down to her
toes. "B-but I thought . . . after what you said on the

way to Trimble Springs, I didn't think you wanted me to come around anymore."

"Oh, I wanted you, princess." Fighting the almost unbearable urge to drag her into his arms, Cain's knuckles went white with the exertion. "And I want you still. Do you have any idea how much?"

"Want, yes," she said, her breathing shallower, faster. "But wanting and having are two different things. What about that someone you remembered as we talked? I know you were thinking about her. I could see her in your eyes."

The urge to comfort her was almost as acute as the urge to claim her, but Cain did neither as he waited for a small group of travelers to pass by. When he spoke again, his voice was low, cracking with emotion. "There is no other woman for me but you. If there were"—he thumped his chest—"I'd know it in here."

"Who was she, Cain?" Mariah persisted, wanting to believe him, knowing he would dodge the issue if she let him. "Who did you remember?"

"I don't know." Cain wanted it to be the truth so badly. He didn't want to know the name of the woman in his mind, or where she might have fit into his past life. He only wanted Mariah. "I've done little but try to call up the memory of a wife or sweetheart the past two days, and I just can't do it. I really don't know who that woman was, but she can't have been too important in my life, or I'd have remembered who she was by now. I just know that's true. I want you to know it, too."

There was something more. Mariah knew Cain well enough to sense that there was something more, but the relief that he would be hers again, for at least a few more days and nights, was so sweet.

She looked into Cain's intense green eyes and the world seemed to grind to a halt. The clouds froze in the sky, birds forgot to sing, and even the steady *hiss, hiss, hiss* of the nearby locomotive faded to a faint buzz. There was only Mariah and Cain.

He had yet to put so much as one finger on her, but Mariah could almost feel his touch, taste his kiss as he stared down at her mouth with abject longing. Her bosom heaving with frustration, Mariah absently moistened her lips in an effort to relieve the sudden aching there. It only made her want him more. So much more, that she now found herself thinking of shaming her family's good name by throwing herself into Cain's arms in a public train yard. She actually took a step toward him, but then she heard Zack's voice calling her. The voice of reason.

"Mariah! Over here!"

Bright spots of color stained her cheeks as she realized what she'd been thinking of doing, and she turned toward the depot in time to see her father round the corner.

"We need your help, baby," Zack said, panting as he limped up to meet her. "Go join your ma on the train. She's trying to hang on to a pair of them fancy new 'conversation' seats for the four of us, and you know her—she's a mite timid when it comes to standing her ground with strangers. She's in car three thirty-four."

With a final glance at Cain, one that held as much promise as longing, she said, "I'm on my way."

As it turned out, Mariah's help hadn't been needed. Oda had done just fine hanging on to the seats. Sitting two abreast, the women faced the north and Silverton, while the men, after they boarded the train, sat opposite them, riding backwards.

The seats were bench style, comfortable enough, but situated so close together that the men had to sit with their legs apart to afford enough room for the knees of the ladies. Zack just popped the hinge on his wooden leg, giving Oda plenty of room to stretch her stubby legs, but Cain, being thick of thigh, had a harder time making room for Mariah's knees between his legs without bringing them into contact with his body. A difficult task, but one he enjoyed immensely.

Once the whistle blew and locomotives got under way—one forward, one aft—Zack did most of the talking, centering on the topic most near and dear to his heart: ways to make the medicine show better and more profitable.

"And I was thinking," he said, "that we ought to get a little more use out of Artemis. I'll bet he could play as many as five instruments at one time if we was to figure out a way to get everything attached to him."

Desperate to find something to take her mind off the way Cain was looking at her, Mariah leapt into the conversation. "Artemis does a pretty fair job of bringing them in with just the banjo and harmonica going at the same time. Are you sure you want to try and turn him into a one-man band? It doesn't take much to get that poor kid rattled, you know."

Zack glanced ahead two rows of seats to where the young man sat. Artemis was twisting and turning, peering out of one window and then another, craning his neck in every direction so as not to miss anything, and just generally looking like he'd never been on a train before. Zack's smile was warm as he realized that he'd gradually come to think of the young man as a part of the family—in a way, as the son he and Oda never had.

"Maybe you're right, baby," he said. "I'll ask Artemis whether he wants to add any more instruments, and leave the decision up to him. I expect I ought to ask him if he even wants to go on with us. It's possible he won't stay past Silverton, now that I think on it. Might be that he's got family around these parts."

Cain, who'd been intent on Mariah and the way she swayed with the gentle rhythm of the train as it slowly gathered steam, forced his attention to Zack. "I don't know about any other family, but Artemis has mentioned a brother Billy to me." As he recalled the incident in the outfitter's store, something else struck him. "I don't think it'd bother Artemis too much to leave that part of his family behind, but the name sure sounds familiar to me. Did I have a brother Billy, too, by any chance?"

Mariah and her father exchanged glances, and Zack, the patriarch, took the responsibility of yet another lie. "Ah, no, Cain, I'm afraid not. You were an only child . . . just like our Mariah." He gave her a warm smile, and then went on with his plans for the show. "I've been thinking about changing your part, too, baby. We've about wore little ole Princess Tanacoa to the ground."

"I thought I was doing just fine." Mariah glanced at Oda, seeking a little support, and noticed that her mother had fallen asleep.

"It ain't that you can't do the job," Zack said. "I was just thinking maybe we ought to try something new, maybe an act like that Princess Lotus Blossom and her blasted Tiger Fat cure. Why, she reels in the suckers with that spiel faster than she can count the money."

"And she's as crooked as Daisy's hind legs, too— don't forget that." Mariah looked at Cain, which was a mistake. His expression had hardly changed since their talk at the depot, and was still incendiary enough to melt the buttons on her bodice. She clasped her knees together tightly, careful not to brush against his legs, and quietly said to her father, "I think one Princess Lotus Blossom is quite enough."

"But that's just my point, baby. Don't you see?" Zack was far too caught up in the creation of a new show to notice that his wife was softly snoring, or that his daughter and Cain were so intent on each other, he might as well have been playing to an empty hall. He went on, his enthusiasm increasing as he visualized the new act.

"Why, there must be hundreds of Kickapoo Indian shows, maybe even *thousands*!" He lowered his voice. "And each one of them has an Indian princess or a medicine man. Ah, but if we was to dress Mariah up in a Chinese mandarin robe, put her hair in one long braid down her back and maybe add some silk veils—you know, kinda wrap her up like a cocoon— why, she could just as well be a princess from China as a Kickapoo Indian." He tapped his index finger against his forehead. "Ayuh. That and a grease stick with a little more of a yellow cast to it, and I believe it'd work at that. What do you say?" He elbowed Cain in the ribs. "Can't you see Mariah done up that way?"

He certainly could, but Cain doubted he and Zack were picturing the same "princess." His Mariah was naked, her body shimmering through gossamer scarves as silken as her skin. At the image, desire flared in him, and Cain dropped his arms in his lap, hoping the gesture would hide his growing ardor, if not cool it. Through a throat so tight it barely allowed the passage of air, he said, "Sounds like it might bring 'em in all right. What do you think, princess?"

Taken off guard—for she, too, had been distracted with other thoughts—Mariah accidentally brushed her knee against the inside of Cain's thigh. The train chattered over a rough section of track, vibrating her body from head to toe, and Mariah forgot what they'd been talking about. "Ah, whatever Zack decides will be best for the show. I never question his judgment."

"Oh, I ain't quite decided yet, baby." Zack went on, verbalizing a few other ideas, oblivious to the fact that neither of them was listening to him any longer.

As her father's voice droned on, Mariah's eyes met with Cain's and locked. In that split second, she knew precisely what he was thinking and how he was feeling. She drew in a long breath as the train's whistle sounded, and the grind of the laboring engines filled her ears, merging with the sudden roar of her own pulse. Straining under the arduous task of climbing high into the San Juan Mountains, the locomotives chugged and steamed, building pressure in an almost perfect imitation of the way her own body was reacting to Cain and the gentle, rhythmic rocking of the railroad car.

Cain restlessly shifted his hips and then took the frock coat from the seat beside him. After carefully folding the garment, he draped it across his lap. Then, with much difficulty, he tore his gaze from Mariah, turned toward Zack, and made several comments about the suggestions he'd come up with to improve the show.

They went on this way for two hours, the incessant *clack, clack, clack* of the train growing in intensity, gathering momentum, fueling both Cain and Mariah almost beyond endurance. By the time the cars had passed through Rockwood and climbed to where the rails spread out along a narrow, rocky shelf blasted out of the side of the granite mountain, Oda had awakened, her features pinched, her complexion leaning toward green.

Reaching for her new cigar case, she said, "Take me outside, Zachariah. I ain't going to last much longer."

She didn't have to ask twice. Used to her motion sickness, Zack locked the hinge in his wooden leg, leapt up from his seat, and pulled Oda up alongside him. "We'll see you two a ways down the track," he said. Then he and Oda moved up the aisle toward the front of the train.

Cain waited until they'd left the car before asking Mariah, "What was that all about?"

"Oda gets sick when she rides the train. Especially with all the twisting and turning now that we've climbed into the mountains. She and Zack will probably spend the next three hours the way they usually do: riding up front on the platform behind the tender."

Three hours, he thought to himself. Three impossibly long hours. How would he be able to sit through those interminable minutes across from Mariah, feeling her legs nudging his, remembering the way she'd moved beneath him and called out his name just a few nights ago? Cain didn't know if there was a word for the way he was feeling—"aroused" didn't come close in intensity—but he did know that the next few hours were going to seem like three weeks if he couldn't think of a way to distract himself. And soon. But how could he, with Mariah sitting there looking so damned tempting?

Seeking a few distractions of her own, she was staring out the window at the incredible scenery, the tall timber and snowcapped peaks looking down on the rapidly moving Animas so far below. The train rounded a sharp bend, and Mariah swayed like a gentle wave, her knees rubbing against Cain's, the river lapping the beach. She closed her eyes and sucked in her breath, thrilled to have had even that small contact with the man she loved—the man who was almost, but not quite, hers. Never to be completely hers.

The train twisted around another bend, the car rattling and lurching from side to side, and this time, it was Cain's knees crossing the boundaries. His voice low, he said, "This is one hell of a train ride, princess. Is it always this . . . this stimulating?"

She nodded, both torturing and thrilling herself by keeping her gaze locked into his. "I think," she said a little breathlessly, "it has something to do with the narrow gauge of the tracks. It kind of exaggerates the movements."

His nostrils flared. "It sure as hell exaggerates something."

"Yes." Her voice was but a whisper. "I would say that it does."

Desire rippled down Cain's spine, shooting sparks to every sensitive spot in his body, a few of those sparks landing in places he'd hadn't realized before could be erotically charged. How could he not respond to Mariah? The way she was looking at him was enough to put him over the edge. Her eyes were languid, heavily lidded, the dark amethyst color barely visible beneath her sooty lashes, and her moist lips were slightly parted, offering several tantalizing glimpses of her tongue.

Knowing only that he had to make an attempt to be with her, Cain leaned forward in his seat, capturing Mariah's legs between his knees, and said, "I've been watching that mind of yours working for as long as I can stand it. A 'penny' for your thoughts, Miss Penny."

Across the aisle and down two rows, Artemis was in the midst of a rousing game of paper-scissors-rock with the youngster sitting next to him. He'd just slapped his palms together twice and balled his fist to form a rock, when something crashed against his shoulder, nearly knocking him off his seat.

"Hey!" He looked up at the clumsy passenger.

"Beg pardon," Tubbs said, barely glancing in the kid's direction.

"Oh, ah, th-that's all right." The words had come automatically, and Artemis had even turned back to the boy to resume their game, before the significance of what had just happened sank into his mind. It was time! Lord almighty! It was *time.*

Swallowing the sting of bile, Artemis said to the youngster, "I, ah, got to get some air now. Maybe we can play more later." Then he rose from his seat with shaking legs, and made his way toward the back of the train.

Cain continued to coax Mariah. "Just a few words, princess, a little hint about what you're thinking right now. That's all I want."

"Is it?" She blushed as the words left her mouth, feeling ridiculously shy. But Mariah didn't let the attack of nerves stop her. She went on. "I was just thinking how much fun it'd be to, ah . . ." Adjusting her skirts so the passengers across from them couldn't see, Mariah nudged his calf with the toe of her boot, then let it drift up his leg to the knee. ". . . raise a little Cain."

His entire system seemed to shut down, but somehow, Cain found the strength to lift the coat from his lap. After offering Mariah a glimpse of his obvious discomfort, he let the garment settle back over his groin. "Haven't I mentioned that in my past life I used to be a mind reader?"

The word "No," came out as a soft groan, and then Mariah's eyes rolled to a close as she understood the power she had over this man. And the power that he had over her.

Cain only understood that he could no longer just sit there watching her changing expressions and the way she squirmed in her seat. He had a feeling, as he noticed her breasts rising and falling beneath the velvet jersey, that she couldn't just sit there much longer, either. Her eyes were too languid, too seductive.

The train took another sharp bend then, lurching violently, and pitched Mariah forward, nearly flinging her off of her seat. Cain automatically reached out to her, preventing the fall, and in the process caught her at the bust. He held her that way many moments longer than necessary, the pads of his thumbs caressing her rigid nipples through the velvet jersey, and then finally released her. Mariah's features were tense as she fell back against her seat, her lips parted in ecstasy.

"Christ in a whiskey barrel," Cain said, beside himself with lust as he gazed at her expression. "You're about to, ah . . . without me, aren't you?"

Mariah laughed from deep in her throat, then dragged in a breath and let it out on a long shudder. "Uh . . . huh."

"Jesus." Cain's whole body went rock-hard, his blood thundering through his veins. "I can't take any more of this, princess. Not one more minute."

Leaning forward in his seat, he shrugged into his Brother Law coat, stood up, and buttoned it at the waist. Then he reached for Mariah's hand and tugged her to her feet. "They added a parlor car with private compartments near the back of this train. We're going to go find us an empty one if I have to empty it myself!"

Outside on the step of the last car, Artemis leaned his elbows against the rail and cautiously peered down the sheer face of the rocky cliffs which supported the railroad tracks. The Animas River raged through the gorge below, wide and strong, but since he was gazing at it from hundreds of feet above, to Artemis it looked like a small trickle—and even more like a slender, watery grave that would soon claim his new best friend, Cain Law.

Even though the two men were alone, Tubbs talked out of the corner of his mouth, his gaze directed away from the kid as he said, "What happened to the old man and woman? I didn't see them."

Still staring at the water, Artemis shrugged. "I don't know. I didn't see them leave their seats."

"Maybe they went to one of the parlor cars for a better place to sit."

"No. I was with Zack when he bought the tickets. He didn't pay extra for no parlor seats. I expect they're just taking a walk somewheres."

Tubbs stayed quiet for a few minutes, checking the landscape ahead until he was satisfied with the deadly drop below. Then he glanced at Artemis and said,

"Go get him, kid. Tell Slater anything you want to, as long as it's not the truth. Just get his ass back here, and get it here now."

The first two compartments Cain opened—and had to mutter apologies into—contained well-heeled families seeking privacy with their small children. The third housed a group of four businessmen. When he opened the next, and found it empty, he pulled Mariah inside and slammed the door behind them.

"What if the conductor comes by?" she asked, apparently more concerned about the fact that they hadn't paid for the special accommodations than she was about privacy. "We don't have tickets to be in here."

"The last thing I'm worried about right now is a damn ticket." He glanced around the small compartment. It had the same bench-seating for four as the other cars, a small aisle between the two pairs, and a window overlooking the deep gorge below. Best of all, it had a door. When Cain discovered that the door had no lock, he turned to Mariah and held out his hand. "Give me one of your shoes."

She was wearing a pair of scalloped high-topped boots made of kid leather, but it took less than a minute for her to unfasten the buttons and drop one boot into his waiting palm.

Cain hunkered down and wedged the toe of her boot under the door, slamming the heel of his palm against the back of the shoe until he was certain that no amount of force from the other side of the door would jar it loose. Then he stood up and turned to face Mariah. She was standing with her back against the window, a self-conscious grin wobbling the corners of her mouth. She was breathing heavily, gripping the edge of the velvet window curtain for balance.

From the corner of his eye, Cain could see that she'd tossed her second boot onto one of the bench seats. Along with her drawers.

"It looks like you're in as big a hurry as I am, princess," he said. "That's good, because I've got a feeling this isn't going to take too long."

He popped the buttons on his jeans as he crossed the short distance between them, and shoved the pants down to his knees when he reached her. He lifted her off of her feet and pressed her against the window, pinning her there, and raised her skirts up to her waist, filling his palms with gobs of purple homespun. Then he filled Mariah.

Artemis raced up and down the aisle of each car, frantic after the first pass through the entire train. There was still no sign of Cain or Mariah. It was like a nightmare, a feeling that they'd somehow been transported to another train and another time. Was it possible? Could they have just disappeared?

Each time he reached the front of the train, he found Zack and Oda standing out by the coal car. In the last car, Tubbs waited like a starving vulture. But still no Cain. No Mariah. By the third pass through the cars, in his panic, Artemis didn't recognize *any-*

one, not even the boy he'd been playing paper-scissors-rock with. Glory be! Where could they have gone to?

The glass cold against her naked bottom, Mariah groaned as Cain thrust into her. Within seconds, the searing passion of her man became more than enough compensation for any heat loss she might have endured, and she welcomed all that he had to offer, giving herself up to him with complete abandon. She wanted to hang on to the exquisite sensations as long as possible, to indulge her senses with every heated inch of him. But because of that intense passion, along with the way the train rattled against her spine, she exploded almost instantly.

Cain was certain he'd done little more than drive into Mariah—two or three short thrusts, he figured in the misty reasoning of runaway passion—before she arched her back and began to buck against him, moaning her pleasure in high-pitched, staccato cries. The strong contractions of her body sent Cain hurtling toward that same point of no return in the very next instant. His knees buckled with the force of the first impact, nearly sending them both to the floor, and he gripped the burgundy velvet curtains for balance, tearing them from the wall. Only a pair of gold satin pulls and tassels were left of the window drapes, and Cain clung to those cords, somehow remaining upright.

And then he felt himself coming; coming, laughing, and, hell, maybe even crying in a heated rush of

such intensity that he feared he might black out.
Mariah erupted a second time, crying his name
aloud in the throes of her pleasure, and from somewhere within him came a sudden impulse, a primitive urge to arch his back and cut loose with a howl.
He was a savage now, a beast, a madman whose
throat strained to release a primal roar; but still
vaguely aware of their surroundings and the need
for relative quiet, he managed to restrain at least
that urge.

When he was spent, Cain fell against Mariah, burrowing through her hair until his mouth met the satin
of her moist skin. His teeth gently nipping her neck,
he drew in a long, shaky breath. Then, his voice
husky with the kind of emotion he knew he'd never
experienced before, he said, "God, but I love you,
Mariah. I'll love you forever."

Tubbs's cheeks puffed out, coloring a little as he
glared at Artemis and said, "They didn't up and
throw *themselves* off the train, kid! They have to be
here somewhere!"

His chin quivering, Artemis sniffled. "But I looked
everywhere! I'm telling you, they ain't on the train no
more."

Tubbs grabbed him by the shirt collar and pushed
him until his head was sticking out over the black
iron safety railing at the back of the car. "We don't
have the time for your nonsense, Artie. We've got to
take care of business, and we've got to do it now. You
ready to talk sense?"

The air current generated by the speed of the locomotive was cold, icy against Artemis's skin, but that wasn't what got his knees to knocking and his hands to shaking. The view did that all by itself. Tubbs had leaned him out over the railing on the inside curve of the rails. Dead ahead, he could see a tight bend in the tracks, a turn around the mountainside which would leave precious little room between the jagged rocks and his head—if any.

Artemis nodded rapidly. "Yes! Yes!"

Tubbs pulled him back inside the railing. "Good thinking, kid. Now here's what we're gonna do, and this time, you do it exactly the way I say. Are you with me?"

"Y-yes, sir. I am."

"Good." Tubbs pulled up the waist of his trousers and adjusted the angle of his guns. "You and I are gonna search this train from one end to the other—together. You just walk on ahead of me, pretending like you don't know me, and I'll let you know when to stop or if I want you to check a compartment door."

"Check a door?" Artemis scratched his head. "Why would I go do that?"

Tubbs grabbed him by his shirtsleeves. "Didn't you check the private compartments?"

"Ah, no, sir, I didn't."

"Why in hell *not*?"

Artemis backed away. "Well, because like I told you, I was with Zack when he bought all the tickets. Weren't none of them special, just plain seats."

Tubbs cuffed him alongside the head. "Didn't it ever occur to you that someone *else* might have tickets for a private compartment—a lawman or two, for

example, someone who might even invite a U.S. marshal in for a little visit to that compartment?"

Artemis looked to the heavens for the answer. "I—
no, sir, I'm afraid I didn't think about that."

Tubbs gave the kid a push toward the door. "It's a
damn good thing *one* of us thought of it. Head for the
parlor car with the private compartments, Artie boy.
We're gonna go get us a marshal."

15

Once he reached the correct parlor car, Artemis tested the door to several compartments, and to his horror, found passengers inside each room. He glanced down the hallway to where Tubbs stood watching, and used a mortified expression to plead for permission to quit pestering these strangers. The look he got in return brooked no argument. Tubbs gestured for him to try the next compartment.

When Artemis turned the knob to door 4, and then pushed, nothing happened. He pushed a little harder. Still nothing. He knocked. "Hello? Anybody in there?"

Inside the room, Mariah's hat, hairpins, and purple jersey had joined her lone shoe and drawers on the bench seat. Cain was in the midst of removing her camisole as the knock sounded on the door and

Artemis called out Cain's name. He froze, his palm resting on one of her breasts.

"That sounds like Artemis," he whispered. "What in the hell do you suppose he's up to?"

Mariah, her nipples more erect now with the fear of discovery than from Cain's touch, whispered back, "I don't know, but I think it's him for sure. Who could he be looking for in a parlor car?"

As if in answer, Artemis's voice called through the thin wooden door once again. "Cain? You in there?"

Muttering an oath under his breath, Cain weighed the consequences of answering Artemis against those of ignoring him. Mariah did not hesitate to offer her opinion. She shook her head violently, whipping the loose strands of her thick ebony hair around her shoulders. Then she placed her finger on her swollen lips. Cain grinned, agreeing with her, and sealed their bargain with a gentle kiss. And then kissed her again.

"This is the conductor," came a loud voice a few moments later. "Is someone in there?"

Cain broke away from Mariah and crept toward the door. Carefully pressing his ear against the wood, he heard the conductor speaking to someone—Artemis, he assumed.

". . . and no one has purchased a ticket for this compartment. It's possible that there has been some kind of leak in the roof, and the door is merely swollen shut. Thanks for bringing it to my attention."

Then Cain heard a harsh, angry voice he didn't recognize.

"Can't we just break the damn thing down?"

"Whatever for? As I already mentioned, no one is in there, and no one has the right to be." The conductor's voice was disdainful, clearly irritated to have been dragged into a discussion with such coarse passengers. "Our arrival in Silverton will be soon enough for the maintenance crew to see to the problem. May I show you gentlemen back to your seats now?"

Muttered grumbles were followed by retreating footfalls, but Cain continued to listen until only the soft *clack, clack, clack* of the wheels against the rails met his ears. Since there was really no other explanation he could think of, he assumed that Artemis had been recruited by another passenger to help sneak him into the high-priced seats.

Laughing to himself at the thought, Cain turned back to Mariah. She was standing against the window, looking like a wild Gypsy, half-angel, half-devil, her skirts mussed, ankles and petticoats exposed. Her hair was a mass of uncivilized waves and curls; her full breasts heaved, straining against the pink satin laces of her French cambric camisole.

"Now where were we, my wild little angel?" Cain asked in a husky voice.

Her smile coy, Mariah let her fingers flutter down into the valley between her breasts. "I believe you were busy taking advantage of the view."

With just over an hour remaining of the journey, Artemis slowly made his way back to his original seat. Tubbs had kept him all the way at the back of the train on the outer step of the last car for nearly an hour, lecturing him about how damn smart that Marshal Slater could be, and warning him over and over again not to let his guard down for a minute when he was around him.

Artemis could hardly believe that Cain and this evil lawman were one and the same man. And yet Tubbs, a man he respected if no longer revered, seemed certain that he was. He insisted that Cain, in all his cleverness, had indeed been in the "stuck" compartment, huddling in that room with Mariah and at least one other lawman or railroad official. Planning, Tubbs had gone so far as to suggest ways to foil the Doolittle Gang should they decide to attack the Denver & Rio Grande.

Artemis didn't believe it for a minute. He didn't want to. He'd thought and thought, trying to come up with the truth about Cain, but the more he thought about it, the more his head hurt. By the time Tubbs sent him back to his seat, he had a headache searing the scar by his cowlick, which made him feel as if he'd been branded with a hot iron.

When Artemis finally stepped back into car 334, he almost yelped with surprise to find that the entire medicine show troupe had returned to their seats. Approaching them tentatively, he said, "Where in tarnation have all you folks been? I been looking high and low for the lot of you."

Zack smiled up at the young man and patted his hand. "Now Artemis, not one hour ago you came out to check on me and the missus for about the tenth time, and for the tenth time I told you—we were staying put until the train passed by Elk Park and the hardest part of the trip was behind us. What's wrong with your memory, son? The train ride shake it out of you?"

Artemis grinned and blushed. "Nah. I remember talking to you just fine." He looked at the lawman from under hooded eyes. "But I sure ain't seen Cain and Mariah anywheres around for a spell."

Mariah waved him off. "We've been walking from car to car, taking in the sights. I don't know why you didn't see us. We saw you."

"Me?"

"Yes, Artemis." She laughed, shaking a finger at him. "Cain and I were just coming from some parlor seats we'd 'borrowed,' when we saw you and another fellow talking to the conductor. What were you up to? Trying to sneak inside one of the compartments?"

Artemis beamed. If she'd seen him in the aisle with the conductor, that meant Tubbs had been wrong about Cain and Mariah having secret meetings in the private room. Dead wrong. He smiled and lied through his teeth. "Yep. I thought we'd take a little ride in them fancy seats a spell all right. The conductor didn't think it was such a good idea. If you folks will excuse me, I reckon I'll just go sit with the common folk where I belong, and have myself another little game of paper-scissors-rock."

Buried deep in the heart of the San Juans, surrounded by thick forests and waterfalls spilling down along the steep mountain slopes, the small town of Silverton sat in a lush green valley shaped much like a bowl. The only access to it from the south had been by foot or horseback until 1882, when the Denver and Rio Grande Railroad Company blasted its way through forty-five miles of rocky mountain terrain.

Some citizens fought the invasion of the outside world, citing the inevitable arrival of fortune-tellers, beggars of the "professional class," and any other number of undesirables, parasites all. Other townsfolk loved the idea of welcoming new blood to their little burg, and actively campaigned to recruit them through newspaper ads and well-thought-out ordinances.

The Penny family was fortunate in that the sheriff of Silverton happened to side with the more far-sighted citizens. Permits for a week's worth of medicine shows were not only reasonably priced, but happily offered as well.

Having gotten that part of their business out of the way the afternoon they arrived, the troupe checked into Silverton's finest hotel, The Grand. After settling themselves in their rooms, they walked a few doors down Greene Street to the St. Julien restaurant for a little French cuisine. By supper's end, everyone was too exhausted to do anything other than retire to their respective rooms for the night.

Thirty minutes after they had bid one another good evening, the door to Cain's room opened. Finding himself alone in the hallway, he crept down the Oriental runner in search of Mariah. His room, Cain had reasoned, was straight across from Zack and Oda's, while hers was a discreet two doors down, surely the more desirable location for a little tryst.

Mariah couldn't have agreed more.

Shortly after that, Artemis stuck his head out the door of his room, checking the hallway to make certain it was clear. Satisfied that it was, he darted toward the stairs. Then, following Tubbs's directions to the letter, he headed into the night and on to Silverton's notorious Blair Street, the rougher part of town.

As he waited for the kid to show, Tubbs sat at a corner table in Mattie's Place and dealt himself another hand of stud poker. He was in a foul mood. When he glanced up and saw Artemis creep into the saloon and then nervously look in his direction, Tubbs was pretty sure that his mood wasn't about to get any better. He waved the kid over.

"What took you so damn long?" Tubbs demanded even before the kid pulled out a chair. "I've been waiting for you for over an hour!"

Artemis blinked, his eyes smarting from the heavy cloud of smoke which hung over the room, and eased his skinny frame onto a wobbly three-legged chair. "We was at supper. Zack paid, so I figured you wouldn't mind." Over a sudden roar from the crowd as the piano player sat down and began to pound the ivories, he raised his voice. "You ever had gravy called Bernadette, or wait a minute—I think maybe it was Bernasel. I don't know, something like—"

"My patience is at an end, kid." Tubbs leaned across the table, the cards he'd been holding crumpled into a ball. "Did you take care of business?

That's all we need to think about. Business. Don't forget it again."

Artemis gulped. "Yes, sir. And yes, I did. The marshal's room is right smack next door to mine. He's in room seventeen, and I'm in fifteen. You planning to get yourself a room at The Grand, too?"

"No, kid. I'm put up at a hotel around the corner with Cletus. We're just fine."

Artemis craned his neck this way and that. "Say—where is Cletus?"

"Laying low, kid. Just like all of us should be."

"Yeah, but you should do it at The Grand." Artemis smacked his own forehead. "Glory be, Tubbs! You should see the room I got! Why, there's velvet curtains fancier than most folks got clothes, some fuzzy red wallpaper that feels like petting a dog backwards, and a bed I swear is made of cotton balls! You fellahs ought to get yourselves a room over there."

His mood considerably brighter, Tubbs didn't interrupt the kid's dissertation to remind him that it would be a very poor idea to put Cletus in the same hotel with the marshal, or to tell him that he planned to slip into room 17 sometime during the night. It was best, Tubbs decided, if Artemis didn't know any more than he had to. And he definitely didn't need to know that by morning, Morgan Slater would be lying on his own bed of "cotton balls," those fancy velvet curtains flapping a farewell to his cold, dead body.

An hour or so before dawn, as the wide Colorado sky began to loosen its grip on the night, Tubbs got up from his post just inside the door of room 17, and stretched. He'd been sitting there for hours, listening and waiting for the marshal's return, but all had been as quiet as a graveyard.

Because it was much too chancy for him to stick around until the sun came up, he knew he couldn't wait any longer to be on his way. Gritting his teeth as he thought about his continued failure to finish off the marshal, Tubbs let himself out of the room and stole away into what was left of the night.

As the light of dawn slowly trickled into her room, Mariah stretched, burrowing deeper beneath the blankets, and then snuggled into the crook of Cain's arm.

Silverton. They'd finally reached Silverton, with no further mishaps. Now, it looked as if everything would be all right. She glanced at Cain's sleeping face, thinking that soon she would have to trim that Brother Law beard again; it was getting a little shaggy. Then Mariah sighed and snuggled even closer to him.

She loved him. Lord, how she loved him. Had she bothered to tell him how much yet? Mariah thought back to the night before, trying to remember exactly what she'd said and when, but the entire evening was a blur of passion, pleasure, and contentment. She fingered one of Cain's nipples, still amazed at how very much like her own body his could be, at how quickly even this part of him hardened and grew erect.

"Careful what you ask for, princess . . ."

Cain's voice was husky with sleep, and it stirred her almost as much as his touch did. She reached lower beneath the covers. "Or I might get it? Is that what you were about to say?"

Leaning up on his elbow, a thick lock of his auburn hair dipping low over one eye, he gave her a crooked grin as he said, "Do you really think you can handle it? Maybe your eyes have gotten bigger than your—" He interrupted himself as he saw that a narrow beam of sunlight had turned the hairs on his arm to a pale rust color. "Christ in a whiskey barrel—it's morning! Your parents will be out and about soon."

"Oh, my God! I forgot all about them!"

Cain threw back the covers and leapt out of bed, gasping as the cold mountain air slapped at his naked body. At over 9,000 feet, Silverton's altitude offered some damn frigid mornings, even in early summer.

Mariah laughed at his antics as he dressed, amused as she watched him hop from one foot to the other in an effort to warm himself. She hadn't had the chance to inspect him in such an exposed state before, but now that she did, she decided the view had definitely been worth the wait.

She loved his body almost as much as she loved him—especially his nude backside. It was nice and round and heavily muscled, a perfect thing for her to hang on to whenever the ride got too rough. Mariah blushed at the memory of one of those rougher "rides," amazed that she could still have such a response after all they'd been to each other of late.

Cain fit his hat onto his head. "See you at break-fast," he whispered as he opened the door and peered out into the hallway. Then he was gone.

Mariah sank back against her pillow, loath to climb out of the bed, so rich with his scent. She thought of how pious and proper he'd looked in his frock coat and preacher's hat as he slipped out of her room, then of how very irreverent and wicked the man beneath the Brother Law costume could be.

It was time, she decided, to buy the man she loved a little present, something to replace that ugly skimmer. He would most certainly appreciate the thought; Cain hated that hat as much as she loved the lovely bonnet he'd bought for her.

Her mind made up, Mariah decided to stop by her parents' room and borrow another twenty dollars from Zack's dwindling purse. Then, later in the morning, but before the troupe had to prepare for their opening performance, she would take him to Sherwin & Houghton's General Merchandise store.

Mariah smiled. The hat would be her first gift to him, another little way for her to say "I love you," just in case the actual words hadn't yet fallen from her lips.

After a hearty breakfast of ham, eggs, and plate-sized flapjacks, the troupe split up. Zack and Artemis went to the livery to groom the mules, and Oda went back to her room to mend a few loose beads in the Princess Tanacoa costume. This left Mariah with the free time she needed to do a little shopping.

Smiling secretly as she and Cain strolled down Greene Street, Mariah drew in a deep breath of crisp mountain air. "Don't you just love Silverton?"

Cain thought it was funny that she mentioned that subject. He had just been dwelling on the little pocket town—in fact, thinking about it almost nonstop since early this morning. Even though none of the landmarks, the hotels, or public buildings looked particularly familiar to him, he knew without question that he'd been there before. More disturbing, his gut told him that for some reason, Silverton had once been a very important part of his life.

"Cain? Are you listening to me?"

"Sure, princess. I was just trying to figure out if I've ever been here before."

A cold little finger seemed to tap at the back of her neck, but Mariah shrugged the sensation off. She would let nothing spoil what she and Cain had together now. Nothing. "This is probably your first visit here. You'd remember a place like Silverton if you'd been here before. Why, it even has a bowling alley!"

"A bowling alley?" He rolled the words on his tongue as if tasting them, trying to understand what they meant. "I—I don't think I know what that is."

"You mean you've never heard of bowling before?"

"I've heard the word, but I don't know what it is. Things like that have happened to me a lot since the accident. I know a word, but not what it means."

"Then let me help with this one. There's a small building around the corner with a couple of wooden alleyways inside. You throw a heavy rubber ball at a number of wooden bottles, and hope that you can knock them all down. A young boy at the other end of the alley sets the bottles back up, and then rolls your ball back down to you so you can try again. That's all there is to it. It's just a silly little game."

Silly, yes. Bowling sounded like a real waste of time to Cain, and yet something about the word continued to disturb him. He seriously doubted that he had ever tried to play the game. Maybe Virginia had been the one who liked to visit the bowling alley. She was awfully fond of games. *Virginia?*

A sudden, sharp pain shot through Cain's head. He stopped in his tracks, his boots scraping against the boardwalk in front of the livery. At almost the same moment Virginia's name had sprung into his thoughts, the image of the mysterious blond woman had come to mind. Was she Virginia? If so, what part had she played in his life before Mariah?

Sick to think what the memories might mean, Cain closed his eyes and mind against the answers—answers he now knew were there waiting for him to call them up, waiting patiently like old friends . . . or bitter, dangerous enemies. Yes, finally he knew something, and knew it without question. If he wanted to, he had it within his grasp to figure out who and what he was. If he wanted to.

"Cain, my God—is something wrong?"

He could feel Mariah tugging at his sleeve, saw that she was worried about him, but he couldn't speak or think past the stunning revelations in his mind. He felt helpless—the day he was born he hadn't been this helpless—and even worse . . . scared. Jesus, but he was scared. What would Mariah do if she knew what he'd discovered? How would she react? Would she realize, as he did, that those answers might just mean the end of what they had together?

The end of his time with Mariah. No, no. He couldn't think of it. He wouldn't. If Cain didn't know another thing right then, he did realize that he'd never been happier in his life than he was with her. Never.

"Cain, please," Mariah said, her voice quivering. "What's wrong? You're making me nervous."

He had to touch her, had to feel that which was real to him. Then he would be himself again. Cain put his arms around Mariah, hugging her tight for a long moment, propriety be damned. When he released her, his voice was hoarse as he said, "I'm all right. I just felt a little nauseous for a minute."

"You're sick?" Her hand automatically went to his forehead. His skin was cool—almost too cool. "The store is on the corner of Thirteenth Street just a few feet ahead, darling. Do you feel well enough to go on, or would you rather go back to the hotel?"

"I'm fine." He assured her by wrapping his arm around her waist and coaxing her forward. "Let's go on."

But as far as Mariah could see, Cain looked anything but fine. He was unnaturally pale, and a network of tiny wrinkles she'd never seen before webbed the corners of his eyes and his mouth. The cold finger at the back of her neck grew icy, insistent, but Mariah refused to acknowledge it. She centered her thoughts on Cain.

As they stepped down from the boardwalk to cross the alley, Mariah heard the chatter of youngsters. She glanced in the direction of the voices, and saw that two young girls were playing jack-straws in the dirt.

One of them, a child of around five who lacked her front teeth but more than made up for the deficit with a riot of flaming red curls, looked up at Cain and broke into a huge grin. "Hi, Daddy."

Mariah's first impulse was to laugh, but she put her palm over her mouth and shifted her attention to the second youngster, a girl of around seven who was busy chiding the little redhead.

"Don't pay any attention to Amelia," said the younger girl's friend. "She thinks every man she sees is her daddy!"

"Do *not*!"

"Do too!"

And so the conversation continued, until Mariah had to turn away to release her laughter. She glanced around to see how Cain was taking to "instant fatherhood," only to discover that he was no longer beside her. When she turned all the way around, she saw that he was back up on the board-walk, leaning against the post with both hands pressed against his temples. He looked as if he was about to pass out.

Mariah rushed to his side. "Oh, Cain! You *are* sick. Let's go find a doctor."

He heard her voice, but it seemed far, far away, belonged to another lifetime . . . another woman. The image of something bright burned into his brain, and as it came into focus, he realized that it was the badge of a United States marshal. The badge of Morgan Slater. His badge.

"Cain, please—you're scaring me!" Mariah grabbed the sleeve of his shirt, tugging at it, and his hands fell away from his face. He straightened his spine, but continued to use the post for support.

She expected to see that he'd gone even paler, to perhaps find a measure of pain in his expression, but the haggard, hateful features that looked on her instead turned that icy finger at her neck into a hand. And then wrapped it around her throat.

His fury bigger than both of them, he clenched his fists at his sides, and said, "God in heaven, Mariah! How could you have done this to me?"

Her world went black, filling with terrible gloom. She took a backward step, her voice quivering. "Done what?"

More images now, rolling though his mind like some hideous fireball. The medicine show. Bucksnort. This band of lying, thieving—

"What's wrong?" Tears built up in her throat, making her voice wobbly. "Please, Cain. What's happened?"

"Cain? Who the hell is *that*?"

"Oh, God!" Mariah took a few more backward steps, this time stumbling and nearly falling. "Oh . . . *God.*"

"You *lied* to me." His features were black with rage. "You stole my *life,* you . . . you bitch!"

"Oh, b-but I never meant—"

Morgan wrapped his strong fingers around her arms, hauling her up close. "What in God's name were you thinking? How could you have done this to me?"

"Please—please let me go. Y-you're hurting me."

Her voice was pitiful, a wail, but still Morgan's hands squeezed. His rage knew no bounds. He wanted to shake her, crush the very life from her lying, cheating body, and most frightening and irrational of all . . . kiss her until she begged for mercy.

Even more furious now—with himself as well as her—Morgan abruptly released Mariah and flung her away from him. "Get out of my sight!"

She didn't move. Tears rolled down her cheeks and her chin quivered, but she made no move to save herself.

Morgan seethed with anger. He couldn't deal with her now, not with her betrayal, and not with his rage over that terrible treachery. Even worse, he could no longer trust himself, didn't know what he might be capable of doing to her at that moment.

Protecting them both the only way he could, Morgan advanced on Mariah, his voice harsh, gritty. "If you care just a little bit about your worthless hide, even this much"—he held two of his shaking fingers not a quarter of an inch apart, and stuck them in her face—"do us both a favor and run. Do it now. Run, god damn it! *Run!*"

Tears pouring down her face, Mariah whirled around and flew along the boardwalk, her new hat flying off her head to roll end over end along the muddy street, black hair tumbling down over her shoulders, streaming out behind her like the silken tails of a child's kite.

Morgan didn't allow himself the satisfaction of watching her flight for long. He had other business to tend to, another life to remember. First he needed to calm down, to bank this raging inferno inside, but how? If he were a drinking man, he'd have fortified himself; a smoker, he'd have rolled a cigarette. But he was a— Hell, he didn't know *who* or what he was anymore.

He took several long, cool breaths, pumping oxygen into his overheated system. Then finally, slowly, he turned on his heel and woodenly marched back to the alley.

Morgan stood there staring at the children for several long moments, watching them play their game as he continued to calm himself, struggling at the same time to fit the pieces of his missing life together. Then, when he was finally ready, he hunkered down in front of the little red-haired girl.

Arms outstretched, Morgan quietly said, "Hi, Amelia. Come say hello to your daddy."

16

Her legs were shaking so badly, Mariah didn't know how she managed to move, much less run, but she made it to the end of the block and turned onto Twelfth Street. She stood there trembling like a cornered rabbit for a few moments, gathering her wits, and then finally dared a peek down the boardwalk to where she'd left Cain.

He was kneeling in the alley, his arms wrapped around the little red-haired girl. Before Mariah could grasp the full significance of this display, he rose and lifted the girl onto his broad shoulders. Then he headed up Thirteenth Street, away from where Mariah was huddled in the shadow of the livery. Unable to stop herself, she began to follow them.

Oblivious of the shoppers she stumbled across, of the censuring gasps from the fine ladies of

Silverton as they noticed her dishevelment, Mariah dashed to the corner of Thirteenth and Greene, and peeked around the building to see Cain approaching a little white house at the end of the block. It was a relatively plain home, no gingerbread at the windows or gables, and yet the yard was well-tended, the walkway swept and tidy—clearly the dominion of a woman.

Mariah's heart slowed to a dull thud in her breast, and then turned to stone as the door to that orderly little home opened. She caught a glimpse of a slight blond woman—one who looked a great deal like the photograph she'd seen in Cain's watchcase. After exchanging a brief embrace with the woman, Cain carried the little girl across the threshold. Then the house swallowed him up, taking him away from Mariah. Forever.

Oda had just folded the repaired costume and set it aside, when the door to her room burst open.

"Oh, Mother!" The words came out on a sob. "It's happened!"

She knew. Somewhere in her motherly breast, Oda knew exactly what had happened, but when she crossed the room and closed the door behind her trembling daughter, she just glanced at her and calmly asked, "What happened, baby? Are you all right?"

"Oh, I'm fine," she said sarcastically. "Just fine." The dam burst then, robbing Mariah of the ability to speak or even think. Crumbling inside, she flung herself toward her mother's bed and threw herself upon the mattress.

Because she hated confrontations of any kind, Oda's first impulse was to run and get Zack. He would know how to calm their hysterical girl better than she could. She moved toward the door, but at the last second changed her mind. She was certain that Cain had had at least a little to do with Mariah's collapse, and Zack wouldn't know what to do or say to help his daughter, short of going after the marshal with his shotgun.

Numbly going about the task herself, Oda dragged a spindle-backed chair up beside the bed and waited until Mariah's sobs had subsided a little before she spoke. "What is it, baby? Did Cain's memory come back?"

"He . . . knows." Her voice was a shattered whisper, garbled with tears. "Cain knows . . . everything."

"I expect he's pretty upset about it, too, huh?"

"Upset?" She laughed, the sound frantic, heart-wrenching. "He was definitely upset, to say the least."

"Well . . ." Oda sighed heavily. "It ain't like we weren't expecting it, you know."

"Oh, Mother, you don't know the half of it." She began weeping again, her throat and heart aching so badly, she expected to split apart at any moment. "There's a child," she said, picturing the little red-haired girl.

"Did you say there's a . . ." Oda almost strangled trying to get the word out. "a . . . *child*?"

"Yes—yes!" Mariah's sobs increased, the flow so fierce, she had to bury her face in the pillow to keep from drowning in tears.

"Oh, Lord." Oda was crying now, talking more to herself than her daughter. "I knew this would happen. I knew it the minute you set eyes on that good-for-nothing lawman. Saw it every time you looked google-eyed at him, too."

She thought back to the night she'd told her daughter about her own conception, to Mariah's stiff formality toward her ever since that night, and then hurled a few of Mariah's own words back in her face. "Answer me this, young lady—do you hate it? Do you hate that baby the way you think I hated you?"

As the meaning of Oda's words finally sank in, Mariah slowly lifted her head from the pillow and stared at her mother as if seeing her for the first time. "You think that I'm going to have . . . Cain's baby?"

Oda blushed as her gaze fell to Mariah's lap. "Ain't you?"

"No." But she suddenly wished she was, and knew one other, even more important thing: If she were carrying Cain's child, she'd love it more than life itself. Mariah swung her legs over the side of the mattress and threw her arms around her mother. "I'm sorry. I'm so very, very sorry about the things I said to you back in Durango."

Oda, none too good at this emotional business, tried to get away with a few pats to Mariah's back, but that brief contact was her undoing. She wrapped her stubby arms around her daughter's shoulders, squeezing her tight, embracing her the way she hadn't done since Mariah was a small child.

"I told you that I never hated you, girl, and I

meant it. I guess now you understand what I was saying." Speaking through her tears, Oda wiped her nose and went on. "I ain't gonna hate that babe of yours, neither. I'm a Penny now, not a Fitzgerald. You and your baby are staying with this family for the rest of your life, if'n you take a notion that's what you want."

Both laughing and weeping, Mariah released her mother and held her at arm's length. "As far as I can tell, I'm not in a family way, but knowing how you'd feel if I was, knowing that you'd . . ." Mariah started to cry again. "The child I was telling you about was in the alley, a little girl we happened across on the way to the store. I think she might be Cain's daughter."

"Oh . . . goodness."

Mariah swallowed her tears, determined to keep them down. "That was almost as big a shock as the rest. He nearly went crazy when he remembered who he was, yelling at me, calling me names." She closed her mind and ears to the memory.

Oda, still seeking ways to comfort her, said, "We knew this might happen. We knew anything was possible when we decided to keep the marshal with us. That's why I didn't want you to fall in love with him."

"I know." Mariah hung her head. "I just never thought it would *hurt* so much to lose him. I never thought . . . I guess I somehow hoped that he'd never remember who he was, that he'd only have memories of me." She collapsed against the flattened pillow, awash in fresh tears despite her determination to keep them inside.

Because she didn't know of any other way to help

at this point, Oda reached over and patted Mariah's back for several minutes. Finally her daughter's tears ebbed and her sobs became intermittent, punctuated by miserable little hiccups. Feeling that the worst was over, Oda sat back in her chair. Then someone knocked at the door.

Her mothering instincts stronger than ever, she leapt to her feet. "You stay put, baby. I'll go get rid of whoever that is." When she opened the door, Oda knew in an instant that the worst had only begun— and that there'd be no easy way to get rid of the angry lawman whose bulk filled the entryway.

"Excuse me for disturbing you, *ma'am,*" Morgan said, his tone bitter. "I'll try not to take more than a moment of your time. May I come in?" The question was purely rhetorical, for Morgan had no intention of giving her a choice. He pushed the door open, and after stepping past the speechless woman, slammed it to a close.

The lawman's fury entered the room with him, and Oda bristled in self-defense. She saw it all in his eyes: the frustration, the rage, the burning need for vengeance. Preparing herself for the fight, a mother bear protecting her cub, she stretched to her full five feet and issued a warning. "You so much as lay one finger on me or Mariah, and we'll scream bloody murder so damn loud, even the sheriff down in Durango will hear us."

Morgan almost laughed. He didn't. He snarled instead as he said, "Don't worry. I have no intention of touching either of you." His gaze flickered briefly to where Mariah still lay on the bed. She had yet to lift her head or acknowledge his presence. "I've come for my things."

"Your . . . things?"

Morgan glowered at her. "Yes, Oda. You know what I want: my *badge,* my *guns,* my *wallet*! Those will do for starters, until I can remember what else your thieving family might have stolen off of me."

Oda puffed up her bosom. "You got no call—"

"Save your breath," he said deliberately, the warning unmistakable. "Just get my things, and get them now. You're in enough trouble as it is without adding any more charges to the list."

Swallowing hard, Oda glanced at the bed. Mariah was sitting on the edge of the mattress now, busy drying her tears. She looked pale, defenseless, utterly vulnerable. "Your things ain't here. They're in the supply cart. I can't leave Mariah alone right now, and she's—"

"I'd be happy to stay here with her, ma'am. In fact, I have a few questions for her." Before Oda could voice her concern, Morgan saw it in her eyes. "I'm the law, remember? I didn't come here to hurt anyone. I came here for a little justice—not that your family knows the meaning of the word. Now go get my things!"

Oda remained uneasy. How could they ever have been so foolish as to cross a man such as this? Her gaze darted to Mariah and she raised her eyebrows.

"It's all right, Mother." Mariah's voice was weary, resigned. "Go ahead. I'll be all right."

Oda hardened her expression as her gaze shifted back to the lawman. She marched over to the door and opened it, but before going through it, she reached into her dress pocket and withdrew the silver cigar case he had given her back in Durango. Looking over her shoulder, her blue eyes narrowed, she dropped the case on a nearby dresser.

Before she left, Oda also dropped one final warning. "If you hurt that girl in any way while I'm gone, you bastard, you won't find a rock big enough to crawl under to get safe from me." Then she slammed the door behind her.

"Amazing," Morgan said with a shake of his head. He started toward Mariah. "I have to hand it to this family: You're the most amazing bunch of liars and thieves I've run across in a long time. Your mother is actually indignant—threatening *me*, for Christ's sake! Why, I could haul her and the lot of you off to jail on so many charges, not a one of you would ever see the light of day again."

Mariah sighed heavily, but had no words to defend either herself or her parents.

He stood at the foot of the bed, his fingers gripping the bedpost. "If it wouldn't trouble you too much," he began, venom tipping each word, "I'd like to know why in the hell you didn't tell me who I was right after the accident."

His wrath washed over her like a lava spill, shrinking her body, her worth, and Mariah had to get up from the bed to feel whole again. Smoothing her hair as she walked over to the window, she made a silent vow to be truthful with him from here on out—for the sake of her own dignity, if not his. "You cost us better than one hundred dollars in sales. So we decided to make it up with your labor. Besides, we were afraid you'd make us take you back to Santa Fe for medical attention if we told you who you were. A delay like that would have ruined our whole show season."

He laughed bitterly. "Far better to ruin a man's life, I suppose. Is that it?"

"Cain, we never—"

"Morgan." He ground his teeth as he spoke. "My name is Morgan. I'll thank you to use it—or better yet, try calling me *Marshal Slater.*"

She couldn't look at him any longer. Not as Cain Law, Marshal Slater, or Morgan . . . the father. Mariah turned away from him as she solicited the one answer she feared the most. "She—that little girl playing jack-straws in the alley—she was your daughter?"

Her voice was so soft—like the whisper of an angel, Morgan thought—he could barely hear her. He toughened himself against the sound. "Yes."

The word came out sounding like a hiss, and it may as well have been, for Mariah could swear she felt the fangs of a deadly serpent sink into her heart. She'd guessed as much, but to hear it confirmed from his lips, to know for certain that the man she loved had a daughter, struck her like a fatal blow. The fact that he most surely had a pretty blond wife to go along with that child was too devastating to even think about.

At Mariah's silence, Morgan moved up behind her. "How could you have kept my girl from me that way, or let all these weeks go by without her so much as getting a wire from me? She thinks I forgot all about her! Doesn't that bother you at least a little?"

"Of course it does!" She whirled on him, grief-stricken for them both. "It never occurred to me, or any of us, that you might have been a family man. I didn't know—how could I?"

"You knew all you had to." His expression darkened, as did his tone. "You knew my name. And you deliberately chose to keep it from me."

There was no real way to deny that, or to rationalize the decision they'd made, and again, Mariah had to turn away from him, away from the terrible disappointment she saw in those hard green eyes.

She looked out the window to the mountains beyond. A great bank of dark black clouds had gathered there, one of those instant mountain storms that hadn't been there just moments before, and she could feel the temperature falling, plummeting along with her pulse. It would rain soon, maybe even snow, deluging the area with thunder and lightning. Mariah thought for one crazy moment of rushing headlong into the violence of that storm, of forcing herself to be pummeled and punished for the terrible sins she'd committed against the man she loved.

Cain—she continued to think of him by that name—stood close behind her, waiting, she supposed, for more answers. Mariah felt as if she'd been turned inside out, emptied of words, of thoughts, of emotions. She quietly said the only thing left to her: "I'm sorry for everything. Terribly sorry."

Sorry, he thought to himself. As if such a tiny word could wipe away even one of her cruel, heartless lies. It made him furious to think that Mariah had been the mastermind behind this betrayal. She'd altered his life without permission, reshaped his very soul, and never once thought to seek his consent.

Morgan was furious, yes, but even worse, he felt profoundly bereft. And he had more than just an idea of why he felt that way. He and Mariah would never again share what they once had, never again have that special something he'd never had with Virginia or any other woman—that special something he'd spent his entire life avoiding at all costs. Until Mariah had tricked him. Until Mariah.

Morgan studied her trembling shoulders, his gaze lingering at the mass of unruly dark hair spilling down to below her waist. Desire came alive in him, hot and urgent, and for the first time, painful as well. Morgan didn't know how it was possible after what he'd discovered today, but God help him, he wanted her still—wanted her so badly, it was all he could do to keep from taking her that instant. In fact, he couldn't remember ever wanting her more.

Again his gaze fell to her shoulders, and he was surprised to find his fickle hands hovering there, poised and ready to plunge into that river of thick ebony waves—to do that, or to take her by the throat and squeeze until he could squeeze no more.

Had he regained his memory only to discover that he'd gone completely mad? What kind of a man had he become during that period of forgetfulness? He sure as hell wasn't Cain Law any longer, but he hadn't quite returned to the old Morgan Slater, either. He just plain didn't know who the hell he was anymore. Morgan only knew that if he continued to stand there thinking about how much he once cared, how he wanted her still, he really would go mad.

To protect himself against those feelings, he dwelled on the anger. Then he called up a few memories of what her lies had wrought.

"Jesus, Mariah." The sound of his own voice was sharp and harsh, more venomous than he'd intended, but Morgan forged ahead, using that tone to help insulate himself against her charms. "You must really be proud of your little charade. You did such a good job, you even tricked me into proposing marriage."

She turned on him at this, eyes ablaze. "That was never my intention! The last thing in the world I ever expected, or wanted from you, was marriage. The proposal was your idea, and yours alone!"

She'd never, but never, looked more beautiful than she did at that moment, and he knew that no amount of dredging through his memories of Mariah would ever change that opinion. She was a beautiful, desirable . . . liar. "Nice try, but I know a conniving female when I see one. You did everything you could to push me into marrying you—up to and including that vile-tasting love potion you concocted for me!"

"What?" A sudden jolt of anger drove her onward. "If you aren't the most arrogant, conceited—"

"It must have seemed like a good idea at the time, having a lawman in the family—someone who couldn't lock you and your crooked operation up once his memory returned. Nice plan, Mariah. Too bad it didn't work. Too bad you had to make such a 'personal' sacrifice for nothing."

Even in her anger, Mariah recognized the incongruous word. "'Sacrifice'? What are you talking about?"

He leaned in close, his eyes glittering with a rage that touched her soul. "Why else would you have let me . . . *spoil* you the way I did, if you weren't trying to trick me into marriage?"

Mariah drew in a sharp breath, and lowered her gaze from his all-knowing eyes. *Because I loved you,* she thought. *Because I knew all along we'd only have a short time together, and I wanted it all. Everything a man and woman could experience together, I wanted with you. The future didn't matter to me.* But she said nothing. She let her chin fall until it touched her chest.

Morgan hated her posture, the defeat in the set of her shoulders, but the wounds to his soul were too fresh, and Mariah's betrayal too grave, for him to douse the flames of his anger. "Were you and your thieving family so intent on looking legitimate that as a little insurance you all gathered around and decided to offer a sacrificial virgin?"

Mariah's lid blew. Every last drop of remorse or shame evaporated as the fire in her blood surged to the forefront. "You dirty . . . rotten . . . *bastard*!" And with that, she took a swing at him.

Morgan caught her hand in midair. "Careful, little *princess*! I doubt you want to add 'assault on an officer of the law' to the charges against you." Still gripping her wrist, he pulled her up close. "I'm not quite through with my interrogation. Tell me about that name, Cain Law. Where the hell did you come up with that?"

Mariah wrenched her arm loose and took a backward step. Her voice a whisper, just this side of smug, she said, "Remember I told you about that big yellow dog I had as a kid?" She paused dramatically, gratified to see a flicker of understanding in his dark green eyes. "That dog was always in trouble or raising some kind of Cain or another, so we named him Cain. You reminded us a lot of that dog."

"You named me after a goddamn dog?"

She tossed her head back, flipping a few ebony waves over her shoulder. "I don't know what we could have been thinking of, insulting our dog that way. We always liked him."

A new kind of rage charged through Morgan at her flip comments, a kind he'd never felt before. But he didn't stop to examine it. "In that case, I suppose naming me after your dog was a pretty appropriate thing to do. You folks did kind of turn me into your own trained pet, didn't you? 'Cain do this, Cain do that.' My little performances must have been worth a few laughs, if nothing else."

On the defense again, Mariah lashed out at him. "You had at least a little of it coming, you miserable bastard! You treated us like dirt back in Bucksnort, as if we were no better than common thieves!"

"Looks like I was right, doesn't it?"

This time, Mariah whipped her arm around so fast, Morgan never saw it coming. Her open palm cracked against his cheek, the sound ringing in his ears long after he'd grabbed her wrists and jerked her off of her feet. "Damn you, Mariah! Damn you for the lying, thieving bitch that you are! How could you have cared at all and still done any of this to me? *How?*"

Her knees buckled, and she hung there by her wrists, suspended only by his grip. Mariah's throat went dry and the tears began to fall. Her bottom lip wobbling, she said in a choked whisper, "Oh, Cain—I never wanted this to happen. I really *am* sorry."

The door opened then, and Zack crossed the threshold, with Oda directly behind him. It took only an instant for him to see that the marshal had Mariah by the wrists, and that she was crying.

"Here's your things, Marshal," he said, crossing the room. "You get your hands off my girl, and you get 'em off now! She ain't the one done you wrong, anyways. I am."

Brought to his senses not by Zack's words alone, but by his protective tone, Morgan released Mariah and turned to the old man. "You've all done wrong, and every one of you knows it."

Oda, bristling like a banty hen, stepped in front of her husband as the marshal approached them. "Don't matter what we done in the past! You promised not to hurt our girl if I left you alone with her—you *promised*!"

"I didn't hurt her—certainly not as much as this family has wounded me." Done with talk, Morgan reclaimed his badge and studied it for a moment, wondering how he ever could have forgotten this, the most significant part of his life. Then he pinned the gold star to his shirt beneath the Brother Law coat.

After taking his gun belt from Zack's outstretched

hands, he fastened it around his waist, lifted the Colt from the holster, and spun the chamber to make sure it was still loaded. He gave the old man a narrow gaze as he asked, "What about my hat and jacket?"

"Your hat blew away like we told you, and your horse run off with your saddlebags. I expect your jacket was inside one of them."

Morgan was none too pleased to realize that he'd have to wear his Brother Law garb a little longer. "And my wallet? I know Amigo didn't run off with that."

Amigo? As he recalled his missing horse, something disturbed him other than the fact that the animal had taken off for parts unknown. There was something else there, a little sliver of memory at the back of his mind, but before he could work it up to examine it, the old man dropped the wallet into his hand, along with his gold watch.

Morgan stared at the timepiece a long moment, and then quickly counted the money. When he came up better than a hundred dollars short of what he knew he'd had with him, he said to Zack, "Where's the rest of my money, old man?"

Zack shrugged. "Went for your expenses, mostly. I bought you them clothes you're wearing, and don't forget—you borreyed twenty bucks not once, but twice." He glanced beyond the sheriff to Mariah. "You still got the twenty dollars you asked for this morning?"

After snatching her reticule off the bed, she hurried forward, pulling the bills from her bag. Mariah handed the money to the marshal, careful not to touch him. "I only borrowed it to buy you a new hat so you wouldn't have to wear the skimmer except at show time. We didn't quite make it to the store, if you'll remember."

Morgan didn't look at her as he took the money. He didn't dare. "What about the twenty dollars you took from me in Durango? Where'd that go?"

"Oh . . . that." She backed away from him. "Your expenses, mostly."

Morgan turned on his heel, his expression incredulous. "What kind of expenses could you have incurred on my behalf?"

Her gaze darted to both Zack and Oda in a plea for help, but before they could come to her aid, Mariah remembered the vow she'd made to herself. She raised her chin high and told him the truth. "I gave the money to Artemis. He used it to buy up all the newspapers in the hotel the last two days we were in Durango. He must still have part of it left."

"He did . . . what?" Morgan glanced at Zack, and the old man nodded, the confirmation offered along with a grim expression. Looking back at Mariah, Morgan went on. "Why in hell did you make him do a thing like that?"

"I knew you liked to read the paper each day. I accidentally found out that the *Herald* was planning to run a story or two about the Doolittle Gang and the marshal who was after them. Since you were that marshal, I thought it'd be in the best interests of the medicine show if you didn't read about it."

The Doolittles! Christ in a whiskey barrel! They'd completely slipped his mind. "The hell with the show's best interests! Do you have any idea the danger you could have put me in by not telling me about that gang of thieves?"

Alarmed by the depth of anger flashing in his dark eyes, Mariah backed another few steps toward the window. "I did think of the danger, so I had Artemis help me keep a lookout for the Doolittles. I'd have told you about them if either of us had spotted one of them."

"You, spot one of the Doolittles?" He laughed bitterly. "Now there's a hell of an idea. I guess it takes one to know one."

The marshal's tone had gotten so vicious and hateful, Zack decided it was time for a little interference. "That'll about do it, Marshal Slater. I know you're a mite upset, but you got no call to holler at my girl that way. 'Tain't fittin' and 'tain't right."

"I don't mind explaining, Dad." Mariah's gaze flickered from her father to Cain. "The day I went to collect Daisy from the sheriff, Artemis and I saw a Wanted poster for the Doolittle Gang. We studied the pictures, and figured we could recognize them if they were in the area."

Artemis. The Doolittles. Again he had that feeling that there was something more, a small fact which in this case could make all the difference between life or death. His own. Then it came to him. A name . . . *Billy!* Was that the reason the young man had quivered and quaked that day in the outfitter's store? Could the brother of Artemis be *that* Billy? It didn't seem likely, and yet there was some connection there. He was sure of it.

Morgan headed for the door, stopping to pause by the dresser. He stared down at the silver cigar case, a deep sense of anger along with a fair amount of regret stinging him from within. He glanced at Oda and gave her a sharp nod.

Then, toughening his voice, he said, "Don't try to leave town—any of you—until I say you can. That"—he swept an authoritative finger at the Penny family—"is a direct order from the United States Marshal's Office. I suggest you obey it."

Then he headed for the stables.

17

Artemis sat with his back against the stall door, his arms snugged up tight over his head. Another clap of thunder rolled through the little town, ending this time with a particularly sharp bang. Artemis hated storms. Not the rain, sleet, or snow so much, but the accompanying uproar from the skies and brilliant flashes of light; omens all, to his way of thinking, of the end of the world.

It had been a very strange day all around, now that he thought of it. First, Oda racing—she who usually wobbled, racing!—into the livery, then huddling with Zack, whispering privately. After that, the pair of them rummaging through the supply wagon, and then hurrying out the door, on the run as before.

Now this. Artemis looked up to see Cain stalking down the length of the barn, coming right at him. His stride was determined, almost angry. What in tarnation was going on around here?

"Get up, Artemis. We have to have a little talk." Morgan glanced around, spotted an empty stall, and directed the young man to follow him into it. "I have a few questions." Remembering Artemis's strange behavior at Naegelin's Livery, he decided to begin there. "Let's start back in Durango with that horse you left behind."

Artemis gasped. He'd always known the marshal would recognize his own horse—hell, any man worth his own salt would! Why had he ever let Mariah convince him otherwise? "Th-that weren't my idea. Not a bit of it."

"What wasn't your idea?"

"The part about rubbing that red Colorado mud all over his pretty silver mane and tail so's you wouldn't recognize him. Mariah and her ma done that. I said, don't know why you're bothering with that mess, ladies, that fellah's gonna know it's his own horse no matter what you do. But no, they wouldn't listen to dumb ole Artemis. Nuh-uh."

Until then, it hadn't occurred to Morgan that the horse in Durango might have been Amigo. He'd simply been wondering about something he had overheard that day—something about a man named Tubbs. His fists closed, but he managed to keep his voice on an even keel. "What did you do with my horse, Artemis? Did you sell him?"

"Yep." Delighted that the questions continued to be so easy, he laughed and gave a carefree shrug. "Mr. Naegelin at the livery bought Big Red. Gonna rent

him out, I expect, but I'm sure he'll sell him back to
you if you've a mind to go fetch him."

His fists tightened further. "He's going to use him,
stone bruise and all?"

Artemis laughed. "Mariah made that stone bruise
business up so you'd leave me and Big Red behind.
Ain't nothing wrong with him that a good bath won't
fix."

So Mariah and Artemis were working together.
Had Billy Doolittle been involved somehow as well?
Morgan tabled that thought, too confused over his
feelings for Mariah to consider it just yet, and went
on to the next question.

Morgan figured Mariah and her family must have
sold Amigo right out from under his nose to keep him
from remembering the horse, along with his former
life. His voice grew deceptively soft as he went on.
"Where did you get that sorrel in the first place? Did
someone sell him to you?"

Lulled into a sense of security by the previous nonthreatening questions, Artemis automatically answered
without thinking it through. "No, but I never stole him,
if that's what you're a-thinking. Tubbs found him wandering around in Mancos Valley and just plain give him
to me. He likes me."

That name again. "Tubbs? Just exactly who is that,
son?"

Artemis's eyes bugged out as he realized the enor-
mity of his mistake. "Ah, Tubbs, well, he's just a
friend. Nobody special."

"Was he on the train to Silverton with us?"

The pressure behind his eyeballs grew intense as

Artemis tried to think of what to do, what to say. He opened his mouth, but only a small croak came out.

"I'm going to assume that he was." A frown creased the bridge of Morgan's nose as he studied the nervous young man. How much information had the Pennys shared with Artemis? Everything? He decided to bluff. "Mariah told me that you know I'm a United States marshal."

Artemis nodded rapidly, terrified of where this might lead. "Yes, sir, I do know that, but she told me you was working on a special job and that you didn't want anyone to know who you was. I ain't told a soul that you ain't really Brother Law. Honest." Pushing his luck, he tapped the marshal's frock coat. "That's a real smart disguise you got there, too. Nobody'd ever think there'd be a marshal hiding in preacher's costume."

Until that point, Morgan had figured that when he finished with Artemis, he'd stop by the store for a new hat and coat, then pay a visit to the barber for a shave and haircut. Now the young man had inadvertently handed him a reason to continue awhile as Brother Cain Law. "I'd appreciate it if you keep that information to yourself, Artemis. In fact, that's an order from the marshal's office."

Artemis instinctively saluted. "Yes, sir."

"I'm pleased to know you understand the need for secrecy. I hope you will understand this as well: I have a few more questions, and if you don't want to wind up in jail, you'll have to answer them now— with the truth."

Again Artemis nodded, this time his bulging eyes desperately looking for an avenue of escape.

"Why were you trying to find me on the train? I heard you knock on the door of my compartment and call my name."

"You mean you *was* in there the whole time?"

"Yes." A vivid picture of why he'd been inside that compartment suddenly loomed in Morgan's mind, and he had to struggle against the memory as he continued to interrogate the young man. "Who was outside that cabin with you? Was it this Tubbs person? I heard his voice, so don't lie to me."

Tears sprang into Artemis's eyes, and in the next moment another clap of thunder cracked overhead, rattling the timbers on the roof of the barn. He fell to his knees, sobbing. "Please don't ask me no more questions, and please don't put me in jail. I didn't do nothing wrong! Glory be, I swear I didn't!"

Rain hurled itself against the structure, slamming into the wood with torrential force. Nervous horses nickered to one another, and mules brayed. Above the din, Morgan heard Artemis sobbing, telling him with his expression even more than he'd asked of him. The young man had been with this Tubbs, whoever in the hell that was, and he hadn't been up to any good.

Morgan thought back to Durango and the day Artemis first joined the troupe. He'd been talking with a man when Morgan approached him with the free bottle of tonic, a man who'd insisted that Artemis was a stranger to him—a man, it now occurred to Morgan, who'd been wearing a sheepskin coat exactly like the one he'd lost along with Amigo. That man had to be Tubbs; Morgan would have staked his reputation as the best tracker west of the Mississippi on it.

Hunkering down to the young man's level, Morgan got right to business. "Tell me about your brother Billy, Artemis. I'd love to know just everything about him."

Artemis's bowels cramped up good and tight over that, knotting into a thousand balls the size of fists. He had to lie to Cain, he *had* to, or he'd be paying in hell for the rest of his life. "A-ain't nothing to tell about Billy. Nothing you'd want to know, anyways." Artemis tossed in a crumb of truth, making himself feel a little better. "Billy's a mean, ornery sort, and I don't like him one bit. I try to stay away from him, I do."

"I can certainly understand that." Morgan kept his tone calm, almost soothing. "Please tell me this, son—is Billy here in Silverton?"

Thrilled to be in a position of telling the truth once again, Artemis giggled as he said, "No, sir, he sure ain't. I don't know where he is." Artemis had sure enough forgotten the name of the place Billy, Shorty, and Tate were going to be waiting tomorrow when the train came by. Then he thought of another truth, and a rather urgent one at that. "Is that about it, Cain? I got to go do a squat something awful."

Tubbs prowled the inside of his hotel room like a restless cougar, occasionally glancing out the window to stare down at the sodden streets below. Every time he thought he finally had things right, something else went wrong. Now this business with the marshal asking the kid questions. Too many questions. He should have shot the son of a bitch the minute he laid eyes on him in Durango, and been done with it.

Artemis kept a furtive eye on Tubbs as he paced. He didn't know if he'd done a good thing or a bad thing by coming here, but it was turning into one hell of a strange day. First all those upsetting questions from Cain, and now Tubbs grilling him the same way.

Why couldn't everybody just leave him the hell alone? If all that questioning wasn't bad enough, after he got away from the marshal, he'd gotten soaked clean through to the skin when he lit out of the barn. Now he was cold, shivering right down to his toenails.

Tubbs stopped pacing. "By the way, kid—are you a hundred percent sure you had the right room number for the marshal?"

"Yes, sir. Like I told you before—he's in room seventeen. I know it's true, I swear."

"All right, all right. I guess he just sacked out somewhere else last night." As he considered the possibilities of where Slater might have been instead of his own room, Tubbs scratched his head. "What about the girl from the medicine show?"

"Miss Mariah?"

"Yeah, her. Are she and the marshal sweet on each other, by any chance?"

Artemis considered the question, wondering if maybe this wasn't an area in which it'd be all right to tell the truth. "Maybe . . . could be . . . I don't know for sure. Why? You thinking of courting Miss Mariah yourself?"

Tubbs stared at the kid, shaking his head. "No-o-o. If you could just keep your mind on business for a change, you might have figured out that I am trying my damnedest to . . . *find a way to get at that goddamn marshal so I can take him out!*"

Tubbs's angry voice reverberated throughout the room, filling Artemis's head with the echo of his rage. "Sorry," he said timidly. "I think, yes. They're sweet on each other."

"Thank you, kid. I wish you'd have told me that last night. They're probably bunking together. What room is the girl in?"

"I think she stays in room twenty-two. Why?"

"Because, Artemis." His face was red, almost purple with frustration. "It's high time I caught up with that sneaky son of a bitch of a marshal. If I have do it by catching the bastard with his pants down, then I will. One way or another, before this night is through, Morgan Slater will be one dead son of a bitch, or I'll know the reason why!"

Lord almighty! If he hadn't gone and done it again! He'd messed up. Now it looked like his foolishness might just cost his new best friend his life. Should he warn Cain? Was there a way to do it without jeopardizing his own well-being?

After Artemis ran out of the barn, Morgan went straight to the sheriff's office to inform him that reports of his death had been greatly exaggerated. He hadn't gotten as much information as he'd hoped to out of Artemis, but Morgan knew that the young man

was scared, frightened half out of his wits by something . . . or someone. Morgan still had a strong
hunch that whatever had Artemis so skittish would
eventually lead directly to the Doolittle Gang.

Sure that he was on the right track, he sent a wire
to Durango, informing the sheriff there of his where-
abouts and requesting an update on the Doolittle file.
Then at mid-afternoon, Morgan joined the medicine
show just as the first performance was getting under
way.

The rain had let up, but the streets were muddy,
dotted with puddles and small lakes whose surfaces
were coated with thin layers of crinkled ice. He
slipped easily into his previous role as Brother Law
the Bouncer, and perused the crowd for undesirables—even though, near as he could figure, most of
the undesirables in Silverton were taking part in the
medicine show.

When at last the performance ended, uneventfully
but successfully, Morgan gathered the Penny family
and Artemis at the back of the wagon. Directing the
bulk of his remarks to Zack, the easiest person for
him to deal with, Morgan quietly said, "Since you fine
folks saw fit to make me a member of this medicine
show, I've decided to stay on with you as Brother
Law for a little longer."

Artemis clapped his hands, drawing frowns from
all three Pennys.

"Understand," Morgan went on, "that I'm staying
with the show strictly to have further use of my
Brother Law disguise. I want to keep Marshal Slater
laying low until I find out what's been going on in my,

ah, 'absence.'" His gaze flickered to Mariah, then quickly returned to her father. "You might also want to know that I've checked out of the hotel. I have family here, and I'll be staying with them until I leave Silverton."

"Glory be!" Artemis could barely contain himself, so happy was he to hear this information. Now he didn't have to worry about whether he should or shouldn't warn the marshal about Tubbs's plans for him! Now he could sleep soundly, knowing that for one more night—the last night that mattered, since they would board the train in the morning—his hero would be safe, no matter how many hotel rooms Tubbs checked.

Morgan noticed the young man's high color and the general glaze that had lacquered his eyes. "Is something wrong, Artemis? You look like you might be a little upset."

"Oh, no, sir. I ain't a bit upset. I didn't know you had kin in Silverton, is all. I'd be right proud to meet 'em."

"I'm afraid, given the circumstances, that's not possible. I do expect you to keep the information about my family to yourself, however. And by the way—that's another order."

He saluted. "Yes, sir!"

Morgan's attention returned to the Pennys. "That goes for all of you."

That night, as Mariah thought back over the day, she didn't know which had been worse: listening to

Cain speak to her family in such clipped, businesslike tones, or hearing him talk about his own family so casually, and learning that he'd be living with them from here on out. It had been one thing to see him hold his little girl, but to imagine him with his wife, to know that they were cuddling in bed together the way she and Cain had cuddled just last night, was too much to bear. All she wanted to do was sleep. Sleep and forget.

With that in mind, Mariah turned in early. She tossed and turned for hours, nightmares and watery images drifting in and out of her thoughts in a continuous parade. Remembered moments with Cain always ended cruelly as visions of him alongside his wife nudged them aside. She thought she heard a noise as she pictured the petite blonde in his arms— metal against metal, a rattle—and wondered briefly if she hadn't just listened in on the sound of her own heart breaking into a million pieces. A beam of light skipped across her face shortly after that—a brief warming from the sun, she illogically decided. Then she caught his scent.

The unmistakable odor of male perspiration drifted under her nostrils. The scent of a stranger. By the time Mariah realized that someone had broken into her room, it was too late to scream, or even to blink. A meaty hand clamped over her mouth as the man fell across her breasts, crushing her to the mattress.

Tubbs touched the cold blade of his knife to her throat as he said, "Make one little sound, and it'll be the last one you ever make, sweetheart."

At the sound of the man's voice, Daisy rose up

from her spot near the foot of the bed, arched her back, and began barking in a kind of half-yip, half-growl. All four legs stiff, she hopped forward, making several threatening lunges toward the man who'd attacked her mistress. On her last lunge, Tubbs reached out, snatched her up by the scruff of the neck, and flung her toward the wall.

Daisy's sharp yelp of pain was followed by a patter of tiny feet as she scurried under the bed, where Mariah knew she would now stay, huddled and frightened.

"Where the hell is Marshal Slater?" Tubbs demanded, his tone deadly. As he spoke, he took the hand that had been at her mouth and wound a length of her hair up tight in his fist, controlling the movement of her head.

Mariah's eyes grew huge, straining to get a clearer look at the man's features, but it was too dark. He'd referred to Cain as Marshal Slater. Was the man a part of the infamous Doolittle Gang? Gooseflesh broke out on her scalp.

"You got trouble with your hearing?" He twisted the wad of hair up tight against her skull.

"I—I don't know where he is." Even though she could pinpoint the precise location of the house on Thirteenth Street, she could not allow an animal like this to terrorize Cain's family or hurt the man she loved. "I guess he's in his own room."

"Guess again, sweetheart. I just came from room seventeen—*empty* room seventeen." The tip of the knife pressed against her flesh, piercing it.

Mariah stiffened as she felt a drop of blood roll

down the side of her neck. "I'm telling you the truth! I don't know where he is."

"I don't believe you, sugar." Tubbs licked his lips. "I heard that you and the marshal have gotten mighty cozy. Don't make me ask you about him again, sweetie."

"B-but, honestly—I don't know." Her eyes more used to the darkness, at last she saw her attacker. His features were unfamiliar to her—he wasn't one of the men she'd seen on the Wanted poster—but his expression was not. He meant business. And would kill her if necessary. Mariah's mouth went dry, but somehow, she managed to go on. "We, ah, had a fight this morning. I don't know when he'll be back."

"A fight." Damned if it didn't just figure with the way his luck had been running of late. With a short, angry laugh, Tubbs considered his next move. There was only one option left to him, and it really wasn't a bad one at that. After all, he'd planned to take the woman out right along with the marshal anyway.

Tubbs released her hair. "You want to live to see another day, you'll do exactly what I tell you, and you'll do it quietly, so not even the cockroaches will hear you. Understand?"

She gulped. "Yes."

"Get up." He rose, lit the lamp, and stood back just far enough for her to climb out of bed. "Now get dressed."

"D-dressed? But—"

"You're disturbing the cockroaches, sweetheart." He turned the knife over in his palm, catching her eye with the glint of steel. "Just shut your mouth and get dressed. We're going for a little walk."

She had no choice. Her legs wobbly, Mariah got up, crossed over to the freestanding closet, and took out a dress. Without turning to look at him, she whispered, "Would you mind stepping outside while I change?"

"I would mind one hell of a lot, sweetie. Now get a move on."

Keeping an eye on the door, Tubbs watched Mariah struggle into her petticoats without removing her nightgown or robe. When she finally had to slip out of the garments long enough to don her chemise and dress, he caught a glimpse of her naked back through her curtain of long black hair.

After she'd buttoned the bodice to the throat, Mariah turned back to the man. His eyes were luminous, filled with a particularly chilling kind of lewdness—a look that left no doubt as to his thoughts, or his intentions. Her fists automatically curled and her spine went rigid.

Tubbs laughed at her reaction. "Don't worry, sweetie. Not with Slater unaccounted for." He winked. "Maybe later. Just the two of us." He brandished the knife. "Fix your hair, and put on some shoes and a hat. We have to be on our way."

Mariah wound her hair into a sloppy knot at the top of her head and pinned it there. She slipped on her low-topped boots and reached for the only hat she had left: the deep, black bonnet which hid most of her features.

Then she bent over, automatically reaching for her nighty and robe, but straightened, instead. Always tidy to a fault, she figured if she were to leave her garments strewn about the room, when her mother and father eventually came to check on her, they would be more likely to figure out that she hadn't left of her own accord.

"Listen up, and listen good," Tubbs said as he moved closer. "Don't look at anybody and don't talk to anybody once we leave this room. Not so much as a peep from you, or"—he slipped the knife, handle first, up inside the sleeve of his sheepskin coat, palming the blade—"I'll whip this out and stick it in your gut so fast, you won't know what hit you. Understand?"

Mariah nodded, her heart in her throat.

"Good. I'd hate to have to carve up a fine specimen like you." Then he opened the door, took her by the arm, and dragged her out into the hallway.

As he reached back to pull the door closed, Daisy shot through the opening and dashed down the hall. Before Tubbs could react, she disappeared around the corner, her tail raised high like a flag. He laughed and clucked his tongue. "Sorry about that, sweetie. I hope a coyote don't get your little dog. She'd make a mighty fine snack. Just like you."

He wrapped his arm around her waist. "We're just gonna walk out of here like a pair of old married folks, understand?"

She nodded, and he hauled her down the hall and out into the frigid night air.

18

The rest of the family had been in bed for hours, but Morgan was too restless for sleep, his mind far too busy trying to put his life back in order to give him the slumber he needed. And he was brooding, nursing his wounds.

Why not? The Penny family hadn't merely stolen his former life away, but the new one as well. Mariah had created a life for him which included her and all they had shared, only to cruelly snatch that away, too! His loss, near as Morgan could figure, was not only painful, but twofold.

During the many weeks of his recuperation from the accident, bits and pieces of the past had sprinkled down from his memory, filtered through his brain, and settled back into place. Yet even now that he'd returned to himself, there were still a lot of missing pieces, chunks of his life that he simply could not account for. Or, perhaps, would not.

Maybe, Morgan thought with a heavy sigh, he couldn't remember certain details because they were no longer important. In fact, many things had become less significant to him of late. Things like the burning need to bring justice to a disorderly world; the "hunt" when he was on the trail of a desperado; the anger he once felt inside, and the way he'd practically nurtured those feelings of anger in order to keep them alive.

Suddenly Morgan realized that the rage of long ago was gone, that the ugly serpent which had stoked his gut with a fiery and unrelenting anger roamed no more.

He suspected he had Mariah to thank for that. In fact, he had many things to thank her for, but the number fell short of the list of crimes she'd committed against him. Way short. Morgan stared at the roaring fire, hoping it might somehow burn the image of Mariah from his mind, her taste from his lips, the feel of her satiny skin from his fingertips.

If he could just do that—lose the memory of Mariah as easily as he had lost his days and nights with Virginia—he might experience a little peace of mind for the first time in his life, perhaps even gain a sense of well-being. Oh, but it all seemed so futile, so impossible, so . . . very, very painful.

More restless now than before, Morgan stared intently at the blue-tipped flames, still trying to scorch a clean path in his mind, but he continued to see Mariah's beautiful face. He listened to the crackles and pops hissing out from the stone hearth, but instead heard Mariah's dulcet voice— along with Daisy's mournful howl.

Startled by the unexpected intrusion, Morgan cocked his head toward the window. Had he merely imagined he heard the tiny dog? As if in answer, the sound came again. Daisy? Maybe it was a skulking coyote, a lone wolf, or even another dog. It certainly couldn't be Daisy, now that he thought of it. Mariah was much too solicitous where her little pet was concerned to let her run wild at night, particularly at such a late hour.

Again his gaze fell on the fire, and again, he tried to burn the memory of Mariah from his mind. The barking suddenly became louder and closer. More alarmed this time, Morgan turned back toward the window and listened intently. Along with the dog's yowls, he could hear one of the neighbors shouting at the animal to shut up. Then the dog yelped, a high-pitched squeal suggesting that someone had thrown an object, and hit the mark. After a few moments of relative quiet, the howling resumed, louder still.

Morgan pushed himself out of the rocking chair, tugged on his coat and hat, and went outside to investigate. At the end of Thirteenth Street, toward Greene, he saw a little blob no bigger than a jackrabbit sitting in the middle of the road.

"Daisy?"

Morgan whistled and called her name again, louder this time. The little dog jumped straight up in the air, and then came running, her tiny paws slipping and sliding out from under her as she hit several small patches of ice along the way. Just before she reached Morgan, she planted her feet and then bounced into the air, hurling herself into his arms. Her tiny nails dug into his chest as she burrowed beneath his jacket, and when her head emerged near his throat, she started to whine and lick his chin.

"Take it easy, Daisy," Morgan said, comforting her as best he could. "How come you're out running loose at this hour?" He glanced toward Greene Street, half expecting to see Mariah dashing around the corner, but there wasn't a soul in sight. Obviously the little dog had escaped from her mistress somehow, and come looking for him.

Knowing that Mariah would be frantic over her missing pet, Morgan decided to take her back to the hotel immediately. Even though it was after midnight, he rationalized that he was honor-bound to do that much for the animal. No matter that he would be confronting Mariah in the middle of the night, or that she would most surely be in her nightclothes, her hair hanging loose and mussed, her body warm from sleep . . .

No matter! He would simply toughen himself against her charms during his walk to the hotel. Get a firm grip on himself and remember that in spite of his mutinous body, he still wanted more than anything else to throttle her.

By the time he reached Mariah's room and softly tapped on the door, Morgan was feeling tough, impregnable, and even a little magnanimous. When she didn't answer after a few minutes, he rapped a little harder, and then tested the knob. It turned, so he let himself in.

The lamp was lit, showing him in an instant that she was gone. He'd just covered a good bit of the town and most surely would have seen at least a glimpse of her if she were out looking for Daisy. Where could she be?

Morgan was considering the inconvenience he might cause the Pennys should he disturb them at this hour, when he noticed Mariah's nightclothes strewn across the rug. That, plus her rumpled bed, raised his natural curiosity as a lawman. Mariah had been nothing less than neat around him, so she'd obviously been in a hurry when she left.

Deciding her absence warranted a further investigation, he set Daisy on the bed and then hurried out to the hallway. He wavered at Zack and Oda's door a moment, and then impulsively crossed the hall to room 15 instead. Morgan tapped lightly so as not to awaken the Pennys, and then tapped again.

He heard Artemis stirring, and as he waited to be let inside the room, he recognized the irony in Daisy's midnight sojourn. If Mariah hadn't conspired for him to take her love potion, and if he hadn't parried that conspiracy by feeding the elixir to the little dog, Daisy never would have become fond of him or come looking for him tonight. And Mariah would be—where the hell could she be? And who, if anyone, was she with?

By the time the door finally opened, Morgan's thoughts had turned dark. Without a word, he shoved the young man out of the way and pushed the door shut behind them. Then he yanked Artemis to the center of the room with him, where there would be less chance of them being overheard. Speaking in a quiet hiss, he said, "I want some answers, son, and I want them now. Exactly what is Mariah up to, and who is she with?"

"Huh?" Artemis blinked up at the lawman, his mind a muddled blur.

"I was just in her room, and she's not there. You know what?" Morgan jabbed his index finger against Artemis's shoulder. "I think you might know where she went."

"M-me? But I don't know what she—" Artemis gasped, chopping his own sentence in half. Holy shit! He'd been so worried about Tubbs taking out the marshal, he forgot that his partner had been fixing to take both the marshal *and* his little female deputy out when they were all on the train. How could he not have remembered such an important fact!

"Out with it, son! Is she working with you and this Tubbs person? What's going on?"

Artemis had been walking the fence which lay between right and wrong for too long, struggling with the harrowing trail much too often of late. He should have known that one day soon he would be falling to one side or another, even if it meant hurting himself in the process. Refusing for once to consider the consequences to himself, Artemis took a blind step. "I think she's probably with Tubbs."

Morgan went white with rage. Tubbs, the man who'd stolen his horse? The man who wore his jacket? Now this Tubbs had taken possession of his woman as well? Half out of his mind with both jealousy and fury, Morgan bunched the collar of Artemis's long flannel underwear into one strong fist, and lifted him to his toes. "What the hell is she doing with him?"

"I think—" He began to cry. "Lord almighty! I don't know for sure."

"Can you guess? Make a guess!"

"I—I can't with you a-squeezing the life outta me!"

Morgan released his hold and Artemis crumpled to the floor. "Go ahead, son. I'm listening."

Big fat tears fell down his cheeks now, but Artemis didn't bother to wipe them away. He kept his gaze trained on the marshal and the huge Colt "peacemaker" strapped to his thigh. "I—I don't know why Tubbs wanted Miss Mariah for sure, but I think he mighta forced her to go with him."

"You mean he kidnapped her?"

"Could be. I think . . . yes."

"Christ!" Morgan spun in a slow circle, trying to make some kind of sense of Artemis's explanation, but he couldn't. "Why would this Tubbs be so interested in Mariah?"

He'd survived the fall, and it felt really good to be off that fence at last. Artemis decided to tell the marshal everything he knew. Everything. "I expect 'cause o' her working for you and all, and Tubbs getting so danged mad. He's been trying to take you out since we got to Durango!"

"Take me out? As in *kill* me?"

"Yes, sir. I thought he was gonna bust a gut when we couldn't find you on the train, 'cause he meant to fling you down into the gorge between Durango and Silverton. He tried to get you again last night, but you never come to your room, and he waited and waited, getting madder and madder—"

Morgan grabbed Artemis's collar again, this time pulling him up to his feet. "Slow down, son. Go back to the part about Mariah. Did I hear you say that she's working for me?"

"Ain't she?"

Morgan shook his head. "If anything, I've been working for her."

"B-but, Tubbs said she was one o' them female deputies. Said you and her was locked in that train compartment with someone from the railroad company, and that you was all planning ways to bust up the gang."

"The 'gang,' Artemis?"

His eyes rolled to the back of his head, and a sharp pain stabbed at his gut.

Morgan slapped Artemis on both cheeks. "Don't pass out on me now, son. Talk to me. Tell me about this gang."

"It—it's the Doolittle Gang." His voice was a squeaky wheel. "We're the Doolittles."

Lecturing himself for not following his instincts a little sooner, Morgan said, "Your brother Billy, he's . . . ?"

"A Doolittle. That's right, Marshal." Strange. The confession hadn't felt near as bad as he thought it would. And the marshal hadn't tried to shoot him yet either. "I'm Artemis Doolittle, but I ain't never gone on a job before. I swear I ain't done much wrong."

Morgan wasn't listening. He was too busy trying to

determine exactly what kind of danger Mariah might be in—especially now that he knew Billy Doolittle was involved. "This morning in the barn, you told me that your brother was not in Silverton. The truth, Artemis: Is he here now?"

Relief kept growing in him, filling him with a mad kind of elation. "No, sir. I told you the truth in the barn, and I'm a-telling it to you now. Billy ain't nowheres near here."

"All right, I believe you. Now what about Mariah? You say this Tubbs thinks she's my deputy?"

"Yes, sir, a deputy in disguise when she wears her Princess Tanacoa costume, just like you are when you're dressed up as Brother Law. She is a deputy, ain't she?"

"Hell, no! What does Tubbs plan to do with her? Use her to get to me?"

His relief vanished, and Artemis began to cry again. "Maybe, but mostly, I—I think, oh, God in heaven! I think Tubbs means to take her out, same as you."

"Take her out?" Morgan grabbed Artemis's collar with both hands, yanking him up tight till they were nose-to-nose. "You mean to tell me he's planning to kill her?"

His eyes crossed, and his teeth chattered like never before, but Artemis managed to say, "Y-yes, sir. That's exactly what I mean."

Inside his room at Ma Cherry's Hotel, Tubbs argued with Cletus. "It don't make a damn bit of sense to go wringing her neck already."

Cletus turned a startling blue eye on their captive, and winked at her. "I didn't mean right this minute. I thought we could have a little fun with her first." He blew Mariah a kiss, and then turned back to the piece of mirror he'd propped up on the dresser.

With a heavy sigh, Tubbs went over to where his partner stood preening. "If you could get your mind off your dick for a minute, you'd realize the girl's worth more to us alive than dead for the time being. Hell, that marshal is slippery. We might have to use her as a little 'persuader.'"

Cletus's gaze was intense, electric, as he forced himself to look away from his reflection long enough to study the woman. She was sitting on a wooden chair in a corner of the room, her hands and feet bound with twine, her lovely mouth silenced with wads of his very own blue cotton handkerchief. "You might have a point, Tubbs. So we keep her alive, but I still don't see why we can't have a little fun with her until it's time to board the train."

Tubbs turned a cold gray eye on Mariah, and slowly broke into a wide grin. "Neither do I." Then he reached for his belt buckle.

As Morgan and Artemis crept down the narrow, murky hallway at Ma Cherry's Hotel, Morgan pulled the young man to a halt. His voice barely more than a whisper, he said, "Let's make sure you have it straight before we go knocking on that door, son." Artemis nodded. "Just in case Mariah is not in that room, or if something else goes wrong, you're to pretend that

I've captured you and forced you to take me here, right?"

"That's right," he said, remembering to speak so only the marshal could hear. "Tubbs is supposed to think I'm still a member of the gang until you tell me I can show him different."

"That's right, son." And just to make sure that nothing had changed there, he said, "Things are different with you now, aren't they? You've sworn an oath to uphold the law."

And didn't Artemis know it! As of ten minutes ago, he was a sworn-in deputy on Marshal Slater's special posse. Artemis Doolittle, an honest-to-God deputy! Glory be! If that didn't beat all. Barely able to contain the squeal of delight which had built up inside him at the thought, he said, "Yes, sir!" And then saluted his hero.

"Let's go then, and remember—don't say a word about being my deputy unless I say you can. Make sure you speak to Tubbs the way you always do." Then he poked him in the back, encouraging him to go ahead.

When Artemis found the correct room, he beat on the door at one of the few spots where the paint hadn't peeled off. "Open up, Tubbs! It's me, Artemis."

A few moments later, a sliver of light appeared, and then the door swung wide open. Tubbs backed into the room, clearing a path for Artemis to enter. "What in hell are you doing here, kid? Ain't you supposed to be keeping an eye on the marshal over at the hotel?"

As the young man moved forward, Morgan

stepped out from the shadows, laid the barrel of his gun across Artemis's shoulder, and trained the sights on Tubbs. Pushing his "shield" through the open doorway, he glanced toward the far corner, confirming that Mariah was indeed in the room, and then said, "Evening, Mr. Tubbs. I decided to keep an eye on *him* instead. Now put your hands up slow and easy, because just like your little friend Artemis, you're under arrest."

Tubbs did as he was told, but something wasn't right. Morgan could see it in his eyes, and in the slight grin at the corner of his mouth. He didn't seem the least bit concerned over his arrest. It was almost as if— Something cold and hard slammed against the back of Morgan's head then, dousing all the light. He fell to the floor with a terrible thud.

"Get over here, kid," Tubbs said. "Help me drag him past the door."

Cletus stepped out from his hiding spot behind the door, brandishing the pistol he'd used to waylay the marshal. "You heard him, dummy—get moving."

Artemis, who wasn't quite sure what happened, or why the marshal had fallen, nearly jumped out of his skin as the other gang member came into view. God in heaven, how could he have forgotten about Cletus? His job was to warn the marshal about anything and everything! How could he have been so stupid as to forget an outlaw as mean as this? Would there ever be an end to his messing up?

Tubbs, who'd managed to drag the lawman inside the room by himself, said, "Jesus, kid! Get your ass moving! At least close the damn door."

Cletus brushed past Artemis and went to stand
over the marshal's prone body. After the kid had
secured the room, Cletus pointed his gun at
Slater's head, and said to Tubbs, "Say a few words
over the 'preacher man.' He's about to meet his
maker."

Behind him, the chair rattled in the corner, followed by a muffled scream. Cletus grinned at Mariah.
"I almost forgot that you and the fine marshal had a
little something going. Don't worry, honey pie—you
won't miss him a'tall once I get my hands on you."

Artemis, who was struggling against his terror and
trying desperately to think things through before acting, went over the marshal's warning—"Don't tell
them you're a deputy unless I say so." He repeated it
several times over in his head just to make sure he
wouldn't mess up again, and then rushed up beside
Cletus. "Please don't shoot him. I—I'm afraid."

"Oh, hell, Artie boy. You're afraid of your own
socks." He cocked the hammer.

Tubbs reached over and lifted the barrel of the gun
with his index finger, pointing it toward the ceiling.
"Hang on a minute. For once the kid might be right."

"Come on, Tubbs. Dead's how we want him. I'd
just love to do the honors."

"He's mine when the time comes, and the time
ain't here yet. We've made enough mistakes on this
job as it is. I'm not going to stand here and let you
shoot off that gun!" Tubbs paused, calming himself
before he went on. "Don't you think maybe Slater
checked in with Silverton's sheriff? We can't take the
chance of killing him or the girl here. Hell, even if we

broke their necks, their bodies could be found before we even get out of town."

Cletus slammed his gun into the holster. "Then what the hell are we going to do with them?"

Tubbs thought on that a moment as he squatted down next to the marshal's body. Chuckling over his own ingenuity, he rolled the lawman over onto his back. "We'll drag them along with us to the train in the morning, and do what I planned on doing in the first place—toss them over the side just past Elk Park."

Artemis didn't know what he should do next, but he did know that Tubbs's plan bought the marshal and Mariah a little more time. He grinned. "That sounds like a right fine idea to me."

"You see there?" Cletus pointed at the kid. "That's how brilliant your plan is—the dummy likes it! Hell—we won't get two blocks down the street with these two, much less smuggle them aboard the train! What in hell's the matter with you?"

"Oh, I think they'll come along nicely, Cletus, and we won't have to be doing any 'smuggling.'" Tubbs lifted the gold star off the frock coat, and then pinned it to his new sheepskin coat. "Especially since I'm a United States marshal, and they're a pair of murdering bank robbers I'm taking down to Durango to stand trial."

Cletus whistled his appreciation. "Hell, it might just work at that."

"Oh, it'll work." He flopped Morgan onto his belly and took the leftover twine to bind his wrists at the small of his back. "Or my name ain't Morgan Slater."

The pair shared a laugh as Tubbs bound the marshal's ankles. As he finished, his captive began to stir. Tubbs quickly got to his feet and stood back, ready for anything from the clever lawman.

Morgan shook his head, raised his chin as high as he could, and then glanced around the room. His gaze briefly skimmed across Mariah, touched on Artemis and Cletus, and finally landed on Tubbs.

With another shake of his head, he blinked and said, "What's happened to me? Who are all you people?"

19

The outlaws and their captives stayed in Tubbs's room until just after dawn, leaving Mariah to feel as if she'd been strapped to the wooden chair for five days, not five hours. Each step during the short, frigid walk from Blair Street to the train depot brought protest from her stiff, sore muscles. And as far as she could tell, Cain wasn't faring any better. He'd been forced to spend those hours on the floor trussed up like a pig at a barbecue.

Cain, that is, or whoever he thought he was now. Tubbs, who'd barely been able to keep from laughing at the time over the marshal's amnesia, informed him that he was Billy Doolittle, wanted for train robbery and murder. With three pistols trained on her, Mariah had been in no position to argue the point.

Now, as she stood near the entrance of the Silverton depot, she knew her position was even graver.

Obviously, killing those who might bear witness against them would be in the gang's best interests.

If only she could find some flicker of recognition from Cain, anything to let her know that yes, he knew exactly who he was, and that even now he was working on a way for them to escape. Mariah glanced up at him, hoping for just a tiny sign, but Cain stared straight ahead at the snow-dusted mountains, his profile rigid and unblinking.

It was hopeless. As long as he wore that same lost, cloudy expression he'd had the first time he'd been hit in the head—looking like neither Morgan Slater nor Cain Law, and not at all like the man who'd once said he loved her—Mariah knew escape was all but impossible.

Tubbs had bound Cain's hands behind his back, hers at the waist, and then added a length of rope around each of their middles, linking them together to keep better control of them. For that much, a shivering Mariah was grateful. Her thin wool dress no match for the frosty mountain air, she inched closer to Cain, seeking his warmth, and again, just a flicker of recognition. He glanced down at her as she snuggled against him, but as before, his features remained impassive.

Back in Bucksnort this reaction wouldn't have bothered her, but now, it nearly tore her apart. Mariah wanted him to remember, even as Morgan Slater, wanted him to recall the afternoon on the train when he'd crushed her against the window and told her he loved her, and that he'd love her forever. If he never remembered another thing as long as he lived, she wanted him to remember that much. Another shiver racked her body, but this time, it had nothing to do with the temperature.

"Cold, sugar?" asked Cletus, their lone guard. "I guess I never did get a chance to warm you up proper back at the hotel." He winked, and for a moment, Mariah thought he might actually desert his post to come dally with her, but the huge cross-beamed door of the depot opened then, and Artemis and Tubbs, who'd been speaking with the stationmaster, stepped outside.

His breath blowing white, dragonlike plumes, Tubbs laughed and caressed the shiny gold badge pinned to his sheepskin jacket as he approached his shivering captives. "Well, well, well, folks. It looks like you're in luck. It seems the officials from the Denver and Rio Grande are in no hurry to expose their passengers to a pair of desperadoes like you two. They not only think it's a fine idea, but very thoughtful of us, to board now before the decent folk show up, so none of them will be offended by the sight of you." Still laughing, he strutted up beside Mariah and pinched her cheek. "Shall we?"

Behind the trio, Cletus jabbed the barrel of his gun against Morgan's spine. "You heard him. Get moving."

And Artemis, still chanting "Don't tell them a thing unless I say so" in his mind, brought up the rear.

The prisoners were settled into a private compartment, with Cletus again as the lone guard, but when the train began to fill with travelers some two hours later, he and Tubbs took turns as the sentry in the cramped room. Artemis was shown to a seat in the adjoining parlor car, and told to stay put until further notice.

Mariah supposed she ought to be grateful that the outlaws were so preoccupied with the robbery and their clean getaway from Silverton. In all the confusion, they'd forgotten about their lewd plans for her.

In fact, no one seemed to notice that she was on the train—not even the man she loved. She sighed and turned toward the window, the long sugar-scoop brim of her bonnet bumping against the glass as the locomotive finally chugged to life. The private car lurched forward several times, and then caught, smoothing its path on the rails. It was then that a slight movement at the corner of the window caught Mariah's attention.

She glanced upward, noticing that the curtain had been torn from its moorings. All that remained were a few shreds of burgundy velvet, a pair of gold satin pulls and tassels, which bounced with the rhythm of the rails. Suddenly, hit full force with the intimate memory of exactly why the window dressing was in such a state of disrepair, Mariah gasped. She could almost hear the ripping of fabric, mingled with her own cries of ecstasy and, above them all, Cain's urgent words of love.

Her gaze darted across the aisle to where he sat. Their eyes met and held for a brief moment. Then he restlessly shifted his hips and quickly looked away, and in that moment, Mariah knew: The man across from her did indeed remember exactly who he was, and how close he'd once been to her.

Her response to it all—the memories, the knowledge that Cain was not only in his right mind, but thinking back to their wild, impassioned encounter right here in this room—was involuntary, instinctive, and impossible to harness. She turned bright red to her roots, and her gaze fell to the floor.

Tubbs, who'd noticed part of the exchange, and all of Mariah's reactions, said, "What's all this, sugar pie? Flirting with your old sweetheart, and blushing, too? You trying to make me jealous?"

"I doubt the lady had any such thoughts about me, Marshal Slater," said Morgan. "In fact, I can't believe I'm a bank robber or that this charming young woman is my partner. Are you absolutely certain you've detained the correct individuals?"

Tubbs let out a boisterous laugh. "Oh, I have the 'correct individuals' all right, Billy boy. As for the 'charming young woman,' she *was* your little bed-warmer. Now she's mine."

"I find it difficult to believe that I could forget a woman as beautiful as Mariah."

Tubbs laughed harder. "Now that's a crying shame. Why, to think that you had all that fine woman-flesh to yourself at one time, and now you can't even remember a minute of it. Amnesia. What a hoot."

Still laughing, Tubbs made sure his captives' bindings were still in place. In addition to the bonds at their wrists and ankles, Mariah and Morgan were strapped to their individual seats by a length of hemp.

When he was satisfied that they could not aid one another in escaping, he said, "You will excuse me a minute, won't you? I need to stretch my legs. You two be sure to stay put until my replacement gets here."

The minute the door closed behind the outlaw, Morgan whispered across the aisle. "Are you all right?"

"Cain—I mean, Morgan—is it really you?"

"It's me. I never had amnesia—just a hell of a knot on my head."

"But you were so convincing, I thought for sure that—"

"I've had recent experience with amnesia." His expression was grim. "I have firsthand knowledge of exactly what it feels like to be lost inside yourself. I also know how easily others can manipulate you into thinking you're someone else."

Any hopes she might have entertained that Cain would be the man to emerge after the blow to his head were dashed as Mariah recognized Morgan Slater's authoritative, accusing tone. She stiffened, but said nothing.

"You didn't answer me," he said, still demanding, not asking. "Did they touch you, any of them?"

"I don't see what concern it is of yours if they did."

"I'm the law, remember? It's my business to ask these questions." He paused to soften his tone. "I saw your room, your nightclothes thrown all over. It looked like . . . Jesus, Mariah! These men are animals. I have a right to know what they've done to you."

"You have absolutely no rights where I'm concerned." Mariah finally met his gaze, and finding at least a hint of concern in it, told him what happened. "Being dragged forcibly from my room at midnight wasn't, in any way, pleasant. Tubbs made me get dressed in front of him, and he did think about . . . about getting to know me a little better, but he was too afraid to do anything about it in case you came by to visit me. I guess he didn't want to take the chance of being caught in the act."

Morgan ground his teeth. "And when he took you to the hotel with his friend Cletus?"

She shrugged, far more concerned about her current plight. "I'm just glad you and Artemis came by when you did. They were talking about killing us! Why?"

"Because I'm a United States marshal, and those men are part of the Doolittle Gang. You, I'm afraid, had the misfortune of getting caught in the middle."

"The Doolittle Gang! But what about Artemis? Why is he with them, and why did you arrest him?"

"Artemis"—Morgan leaned as far forward in the seat as the rope would allow—"*is* . . . a Doolittle."

She gasped. "B-but, but how is that possible? He's such a nice young man, and so, I don't know, polite!"

"Whatever else he may be, Artemis is also the fox you hired to guard the henhouse, if my splotchy memory serves me correctly. You did put him in charge of keeping me from being killed by the Doolittle Gang while I still thought my name was Cain Law, did you not?"

"Oh, my God." Mariah recalled the day in the

Durango sheriff's office, remembering particularly how nervous Artemis had been at the time, at how flustered he got when she mentioned the name Doolittle. The gang must have been tracking Cain's every move even then! "Oh, my God!"

"Shush." Morgan glanced toward the door. "Lucky for us, your instincts weren't entirely—"

The door to the compartment opened, and Morgan quickly sat back against the bench seat, motioning for Mariah to do the same.

"Y-you folks okay in here?" Artemis asked as he stuck his head inside the room. "I, ah, I'm supposed to stand right outside your door, and keep an eye on you for a spell."

Morgan canted his head, calling the fox into the henhouse as he whispered, "Are you alone?"

His eyes huge, Artemis checked both ends of the car. "Ah, yes, s-sir."

"Get in here, quick!"

Artemis slipped inside the room and closed the door. "Ah, is your, ah, esthesia all gone, sir?"

"I never had amnesia." He slid down the bench to make room for the young man, pressing Mariah's legs against the outside wall of the car in the process. "Sit down, son."

"Yes, sir."

As Artemis sank down beside him, Morgan explained. "I've been pretending that I couldn't remember anything so I can get the drop on them a little easier. Understand that you've got to keep this information to yourself. Remember your oath?"

"Right. My sworn oath as your number one deputy."

"That's right, and now we have work to do." Morgan offered his back to Artemis. "Untie me."

Mariah, her mouth agog, shot Cain a look suggesting he'd gone mad. "Didn't you just tell me that Artemis is, you know, one of the, ah . . ."

Morgan smiled. "I deputized Artemis before we came looking for you. He wants to see these cutthroats brought to justice as much as I do."

"That's right, Miss Mariah," said Artemis, untying Morgan's arms. "I'm an honest-to-God deputy for the United States Marshal's Office. Cain made me one last night."

Incredulous, Mariah rolled her eyes and sank back against the bench seat.

Morgan, his hands now freed by Artemis, didn't notice her reaction or correct the young man on the use of his bogus name. He quickly untied his feet, and then rewrapped them, making it look as if he were still bound.

Then he reached down and did the same for Mariah, continuing to explain as he worked. "The gang is planning to rob the train a few miles down the road. They intend to blow up the tracks near Needle Creek to stop the train, but before that, somewhere between there and Elk Park, they plan to throw you and me over the side."

Mariah shuddered as she recalled the jagged face of the mountainside, the sheer drop to the canyon so far below. She held out her wrists, and as Cain untied them, she said, "What are we going to do? It's not like we can run away or anything."

"I'm working on it."

Artemis, who'd gotten up on his own to go check the aisle again, ducked back inside the room. "It's still clear out there."

Finished with Mariah's bonds, Morgan sat back in his seat and tried to look as if he were still a helpless captive. Then he asked his deputy, "Is there any way you can talk Tubbs or Cletus out of a gun?"

So proud of himself he thought he might burst, the youngest Doolittle flipped open his coat to reveal Morgan's huge peacemaker buried in the waistband of his trousers. "I asked Tubbs to give it to me in case of an emergency, and he did!"

Chuckling softly, Morgan held out his hand. "I'd say we definitely have us an emergency of the highest order, Deputy."

After Artemis dropped the weapon onto his palm, Morgan checked the cylinder to make sure the Colt was still loaded. Then he slid the gun between his thigh and the wall of the train, and rewrapped his wrists. "Where's Cletus?"

"Last time I saw him, he was stretched out in the parlor car."

"And Tubbs?"

"He went up to check on the guards at the express car, where they got the gold."

"In that case, why don't we take care of Cletus first." Double-checking both himself and Mariah to make certain they looked as incapacitated as before, he nodded to Artemis. "We're ready. Go tell Cletus that Mariah's taken sick and you don't know what to do with her. Tell him to hurry."

"Yes, sir!" He saluted, then ran out the door.

Looking back at Mariah, Morgan said, "It's going to get dangerous and maybe even a little messy in here pretty quick. The second I go for my gun, you drop to the floor and cover your head. Understand?"

"But I want to help. I have to do something."

"Just do what I said—and Mariah . . ." He hesitated, not sure how to say what he was feeling, not even certain *what* he was feeling, only knowing that he couldn't let things end this way. "If something happens to me, if I should—"

"No, don't say it," she warned, a sudden image of his blond wife coming to her mind. "Don't tell me anything you wouldn't have if we weren't in this predicament."

But Morgan wouldn't be put off. He had something to say, and by God, he was going to say it. "I have to let you know that, well . . . I forgive you."

"You *forgive* me!" Mariah's temper flared, sending her fears for her safety up in smoke. "For what, you arrogant bastard? For showing you how to live like a real human being for a few weeks, for caring about you? We ought to charge you for the privilege of having—"

The doorknob turned, and Morgan cut her off. "Put your head between your knees, and keep your eye on my gun" was all he managed to whisper before Cletus walked into the room.

"We got trouble in here?" the outlaw said as he leaned over to take a look at Mariah.

"Like you wouldn't believe." Morgan swung the Colt up to fit the barrel against the man's temple. The gun's hammer clicked back one notch at a time as he softly said, "Now straighten up, real slow." Rising along with Cletus, whose intense blue eyes had paled with fear, Morgan relieved him of his pistol. Then he dropped the firearm to the floor beside Mariah, and surprised the outlaw with a vicious left uppercut.

Cletus staggered back to the door and stood there wavering for several long seconds, his legs unaware of the fact that he was unconscious. Then, finally, he slid to the floor.

Morgan quickly bound him with the ropes he'd removed from himself, then used Cletus's handkerchief to gag him before dragging him up to where Mariah had been sitting. After stretching him out on the bench, Morgan turned to find Mariah standing by the door. She was helping Artemis to keep a watch on the aisle, despite Morgan's instructions to stay on the floor.

"Next time I tell you to do something, you do it!" he said, his voice gruff.

"Or what?" The set of her chin and look in her eye held more challenge than question. "Maybe you'd like to knock me down and tie me up, too, is that it? Why don't you just shoot me and get it over with!"

Morgan took two short strides and caught her by the shoulders. "Damn you, Mariah. Now is not the time for this, understand?"

She shrugged out of his grip with a haughty toss of her head. "There will never be a time for this again, Marshal Slater. Either arrest me now, or leave me the hell alone!"

His green eyes glittered with rage and something

else—a heightened sense of awareness, of what he'd had and what he'd lost—but Morgan didn't have the time to sort through it or figure it out. Not now, with another outlaw loose on the train. He did the only thing that he could do: He lifted Mariah off of her feet, swung her around in a half-circle, and set her on the bench across from Cletus.

"You may consider yourself under arrest, Miss Penny. From here on out you are under my orders, and you will do as I say!"

Mariah was speechless. Never had either Cain or Morgan spoken to her in such a manner, and never had she experienced such a strange reaction to him, this feeling of being both threatened and cherished. As she stared up at him, her chin trembling, her gaze locked into his, the door to the compartment burst open and Artemis stuck his head inside.

"Marshal! It's Tubbs, and he's a-coming this way, fast!"

Morgan jerked Mariah off the seat and pushed her down to the floor. "Roll under the bench. And stay there!" Then he turned back to the door and leveled the peacemaker toward the opening, just as the outlaw stepped into the compartment.

Spotting the barrel of the Colt immediately, Tubbs went into a crouch.

"Don't try it!" Morgan warned as the man reached for his gun. "Put your hands on your head."

Tubbs froze, and then slowly raised his arms. Speaking to Artemis over his shoulder, he said, "Don't just stand there, kid. Shoot the son of a bitch."

Offering the young man the ultimate expression of trust, Morgan never even looked at Artemis. He simply smiled at Tubbs and said, "I wasn't aware you were acquainted with my deputy."

The outlaw's features tensed. "Your . . . *what*?"

"Meet Artemis Doolittle, special deputy for the United States Marshal's Office."

Artemis puffed up his chest, straining the seams of his shirt, and elbowed Tubbs in the back. "That'd be me. Now put your hands on your head like the marshal says."

His gaze darting to every corner of the compartment, Tubbs continued to raise his arms. As the train rounded a sharp bend, Cletus rolled off the seat and fell to the floor with a thud, his limp body trapping Mariah in the narrow little hiding space behind him. In her sudden terror, she screamed.

Taking advantage of the distraction, Tubbs went for his gun. He drew his pistol, but didn't quite find the time he needed to fire it. A bullet from Morgan's peacemaker slammed into his chest, driving him through the open door and flattening him against the wall across the aisle. He looked down at the crimson hole in his shirt as if to say, "Well, imagine that." Then he pitched forward, dead before he hit the floor at Deputy Doolittle's feet.

The death of gang member Tubbs didn't go unnoticed by the other passengers on the train. The female occupant of a nearby compartment opened her door, saw the dead man in the aisle, and screamed. The conductor was none too pleased about the goings-on either.

After several long, tense moments of testimony by Morgan, Artemis, and Mariah, the conductor finally accepted the fact that Morgan was indeed the real U.S. marshal, and that trouble lay just ahead on the tracks. He notified the brakeman to slow down, as the train was rapidly nearing the Needle Creek area, and then left the logistics of capturing the Doolittle Gang up to the marshal.

Tubbs was temporarily "interred" in an empty compartment, his shroud the sheepskin jacket Morgan no longer cared to own. Figuring it would be best for the time being to leave Cletus where he was, Morgan secured his bonds and then lashed him to the bench seat, wrapping the rope around him several times over like a spider rolling up a fly. When he was certain the outlaw would be incapable of causing any more trouble, he approached Artemis with an idea for bringing the rest of the gang in—alive, if possible.

Morgan leaned against the door, his gaze skimming Mariah's tense features before settling on Artemis. "We'll be at Needle Creek soon."

Artemis nodded. "Y-yes, sir."

"You've done a real fine job as my deputy so far. I want you to know that."

Artemis's troubled brown eyes lit up. "Thank you, sir."

"I also want you to know that if you decide to back out now, I'll understand. I can't expect you to take part in the capture of your own brother, especially since there's a good chance he could wind up like Tubbs."

Artemis cringed, and beside him, Mariah bristled. She said, "You sound as if you're going to ask him to do it anyway!"

Morgan could hardly argue the fact, since it looked as if using Artemis might be the only way to surprise the rest of the gang. "I am," he said, careful not to meet her gaze. "But he has every right to decline."

"I ain't about to quit being a deputy! No, sir!"

Seething inside, Mariah shot Cain a narrow gaze, but said nothing more.

A female's sense of fair play would not have counted as much as a bean in a bucket to Morgan just six months ago, but now he found he had to think over his plans for using Artemis a little better. Morgan sighed heavily, no longer certain he was worthy of the badge he'd taken back from Tubbs, and sweetened the deal.

"You can stay on as deputy as long as I'm marshal no matter what you decide to do, and that's a promise. Now here's what I'd like you to do. Once the train stops, the only way that gang will come in is if someone they trust signals them. If you don't do it, they'll smell trouble and take off."

Artemis shrugged. "Don't sound too hard. What am I supposed to do exactly?"

"Stand outside the train, I guess, or maybe up on the tender, high so they can't miss you, and wave the men in. Once you spot them coming, your job is over and you can disappear."

"Sounds okay to me, except for the one thing: If I

disappear after the fellahs start coming at the train, who's gonna be left to round 'em up besides you?"

Morgan chuckled. "Me and my other deputy, 'surprise,' ought to be able to handle them, son. Don't worry."

"But there's three of them! Billy, Tate, and Shorty, and every one of them is meaner than a sidewinder on a hot skillet."

Touched by Artemis's concern, Morgan wondered, and not for the first time of late, if maybe he wasn't going soft. "I've faced worse odds and won. You just disappear amongst the passengers, and try to calm them if you can. Tell them you're an official deputy and that everything's going to be all right."

Mariah's agitated voice cut into the lawmen's conversation. "What about me? Can't I help in some way?"

Morgan didn't even glance her way. "You sure as hell can. Just stay right where you are and keep an eye on your fellow prisoner."

The train's whistles blew three short blasts, and then another long one as the locomotives slowly screeched to a halt, drowning out any protests Mariah may have had.

Morgan double-checked the peacemaker, making sure it was fully loaded again, and then said, "Time to go, son."

"Yes, sir!" Artemis leapt to his feet.

"Wait a minute!" said Mariah. "You don't plan to just leave me here unarmed and defenseless in the same room as this . . . this miscreant, do you?"

A frown building between his eyes, Morgan pulled

Tubbs's pistol from the waistband of his jeans, glanced at her, and said, "I don't normally issue firearms to prisoners, and even if I did, you might be in more danger with this than without it. Are you sure you can handle a gun?"

Mariah glared at him. "What do you think?"

"My mistake, ma'am." Morgan touched the brim of his hat, with just a brief flicker of amusement shining in his dark green eyes, and handed her the gun. Then he and Artemis hurried out of the compartment.

Still seething, Mariah secured the door and then marched over to the window to let off a little steam. As she peered out, scanning the trees for signs of the other gang members, she muttered to herself, mimicking the marshal's voice. "Consider yourself arrested, Miss Penny." She brandished the weapon, threatening a thicket of aspens, their bright green leaves quivering in the breeze. "Such a know-it-all bastard, so arrogant, and . . . and . . ."

Mariah let the sentence die in her throat as she realized Cletus was not only conscious, but moving. And staring at her. She whirled on him, gun leveled at his head. He was twisting inside his bindings and shouting into the gag, and worst of all, he had those crazed blue eyes of his fixed on her, making her skin crawl.

"Shut up," she said, her voice sounding far more confident than she felt. "Shut up, close your eyes, and hold still right this minute, you hear me?"

Cletus quit struggling against his bindings, but he continued to talk into the gag, and even though she couldn't see his mouth, she knew by the way his expression rippled all the way up to his ears that he was grinning at her.

Her voice low and dangerous, almost a growl, she said, "Can't you see what a bad mood I'm in? Do you think I'd hesitate for one minute to shoot you, you miserable no-good bastard!"

Mariah thought back to some of the things Cletus had said in Tubbs's hotel room, to the lewd comments and promises he'd made, and found the extra strength she needed to overcome the last of her qualms. In one swift movement, she slammed the grip of the pistol between both hands and swung the weapon in an arc until the barrel pointed directly at the outlaw's groin.

"Don't make me tell you again, you big sack of buffalo flop. It won't take much for me to make sure you never pester another woman for as long as you live." Her thumbs found the hammer of the gun. "So for the last time, shut your eyes and your mouth, and hold real still, or I swear—"

She cut the sentence off there, as further words were unnecessary. His body as rigid as the bench beneath him, Cletus grew silent. Then he squeezed his eyelids so tightly, his bushy brows practically kissed his cheekbones.

The gunfight itself, if it could even be called that, lasted for only ten minutes and featured just two casualties: Artemis, who did not take the easy way out by calming the other passengers, choosing instead to confront his brother; and the brother in question,

Billy Doolittle, who left Morgan no choice but to let the peacemaker intercede on his deputy's behalf.

The wound Artemis suffered was superficial, little more than a bloody but insignificant crease in his upper arm. Billy, on the other hand, while in no immediate danger of passing from this world, would have difficulty walking in it for the rest of his life. When the elder Doolittle had taken aim and fired at Artemis, Morgan's peacemaker had responded in an instant, shattering the outlaw's right kneecap beyond repair.

That had made it Billy's lucky day, as far as Morgan was concerned. Six months ago, he would have aimed for his heart.

Once the gang was subdued, they were all incarcerated in the parlor car, away from the other passengers, where they could be openly observed by Morgan, his deputy, and Mariah. Tate, Cletus, and Shorty were tied leg, belly, and chest to individual chairs situated in a semicircle, looking as if they were seated at an invisible poker table. Billy, in such agony that he could hardly lie still, was stretched out on a plush couch of mauve velvet, his arms strapped to his chest even though his injury made escape almost impossible.

At Artemis's request, all four outlaws were gagged as well. Billy Doolittle's cruel and cutting remarks had cost Artemis more than one moment's pleasure, and he wasn't about to let him ruin his debut as a deputy.

At a table situated directly in front of the gang, sat the trio of guards. With Mariah at his left and his new deputy at his right, Morgan oversaw his prisoners from the center spot, the freshly loaded peacemaker laying directly in front of him on the table, should one of the gang members be fool enough—or get free enough—to test him.

Artemis, who was so excited he could barely stay in his chair, leaned in close to the lawman and asked, "Just how long is my sworn oath good for, sir? I mean, can I still be a deputy a little longer, or is it over already?"

Morgan considered the kind of life the young man had led up to this point even more heavily than he did the question, and after weighing the benefits against the obvious drawbacks, he said, "I'm not sure how much longer I plan to stay on as a marshal, son, so it's likely I won't be needing a deputy again."

Artemis's bright expression faded.

"But I tell you what," Morgan went on, recalling his promise. "How would you like it if I were to make you an honorary deputy?"

"'Honorary'? What does that mean?"

"It means you'll be a deputy for the rest of your life, but that you can't go around shooting or arresting people. I'll even make sure you get a special badge."

"Wow!" Artemis scratched his head in the area of the cowlick, then seemed to suddenly remember something. "I'd be right pleased to be one of them honored deputies, Marshal! What about my job with the medicine show? Miss Mariah's daddy said he wanted me to stay on with them when the show packs up and heads to Denver, and well, I really like playing the banjo and all. Can I be a deputy and play music?"

"I don't see why not," said Mariah. "Zack could bill you as our 'lyrical lawman,' or something like that."

His eyes luminous, Artemis looked to Slater. "Is that okay? Can deputies be lyrical fellahs too?"

"Of course, son. The honorary title simply means that you're a hero."

"*Me?*" Artemis gulped. "People will think that I'm some kind of a, a . . . *hero*?"

"Yes, and I'll make damn sure that everyone knows what a hero you were here today. I couldn't have brought in this gang without your help." He offered his hand. "Thanks again, Deputy."

His chin quivering, and tears rearing to burst through his eyelids, Artemis quickly shook the marshal's hand, jumped out of his chair, and said, "I—I got to go, ah, outside a spell."

"I can take it from here. Go ahead, son."

As Artemis made his way toward the caboose, Morgan turned to Mariah. She immediately averted her gaze, but he caught the sparkle of tears, and knew that she'd been deeply touched by the young man's overwhelming joy. Until that moment, she'd been silent and withdrawn, completely uncommunicative.

In a way, he supposed he couldn't blame her. Not only had he arrested her, even if it was for her own good, but she probably hadn't forgotten all the hateful things he'd said to her yesterday—cruel, thoughtless remarks not only about her, but about her family and their way of life. He'd done everything but call her mother a madam, her father a pimp, and Mariah a whore. Morgan decided he was fortunate that she hadn't turned Cletus's gun on him and blown a hole through him when she had the chance.

He thought back to the things Artemis had said, particularly the part about the medicine show moving on to Denver, and sighed heavily. He wasn't ready for Mariah to go, nor was he prepared to ask her to stay, but the silent war between them had Morgan on the verge of surrender. He caught her in his gaze and said, "Haven't you wondered why I came looking for you in your room last night?"

Mariah shrugged. "I assumed it had something to do with Artemis."

"It didn't. Daisy came and got me."

Guilt-stricken, Mariah said, "My God! I forgot all about her! She ran off when Tubbs took me from my room. Is she all right?"

"She might have a sore throat, but other than that, she's fine." He went on to explain. "I heard her howling for a pretty long time last night before I realized it was her and that she was looking for me. I think she woke up the whole town."

"Umm, she probably did." Bone-weary and too exhausted to think, much less keep up this strained conversation, Mariah quietly asked, "What did you do with her?"

"I put her in your room."

"Thanks. I suppose I ought to be grateful you didn't take her over to the jail. Is that where you're taking me when we get back to Silverton?"

"Hell, no." His tone was sour, irritated. "I only

arrested you to keep you out of danger. I thought you'd have figured that out by yourself."

As Mariah opened her mouth to defend herself, the train's whistle blew three times, alerting passengers to the fact that they were pulling into Silverton. Above the screech of brakes, Mariah asked, "What about my family and the medicine show? Do you still plan to prosecute us?"

At that moment, Morgan honestly didn't know what he planned to do with Mariah, or her family. He, too, was exhausted, and clearly in no condition to be making decisions of any kind. Before Morgan could even form a reasonable answer, Artemis dashed back into the parlor car, out of breath.

"They's a big crowd up ahead, Marshal! Look out the windows! They's lined up for blocks just to see us come in! When you wired ahead, did you tell them about me being a hero and all?"

"I'm afraid I didn't, son, but they'll find out soon enough." There was no point, Morgan thought bitterly, in telling him the crowd had gathered to watch the humiliation of the Doolittle Gang, not to pay homage to the men who brought them in. "But your work isn't over yet. You have another job to do, Deputy."

"I'm ready!"

"The minute this train stops, you run get the sheriff. He's probably out with the crowd, but just in case he isn't, make sure he gets up here in a hurry, with every available deputy he can find. I'm asleep on my feet."

"Yes, sir!" Artemis saluted, and then bolted from the car.

Mariah, who'd been looking out the window as the train rolled to a stop, leapt up from her chair. "My God! My mother and father are out there! They must be worried half out of their minds." With that, she ran out the door behind Artemis.

Keeping one eye on the outlaws, Morgan slowly rose and strolled over to the window. When he finally spotted the Penny family, the three of them were huddled together, hugging one another as if they would never let go. Arms still linked, they began to walk up the street toward the hotel.

Just before they disappeared from view, Mariah pulled away from her parents and paused to look back at the parlor car. She met Morgan's gaze for a brief, intense moment. Then she rejoined Zack and Oda and continued on her way.

Feeling as if he'd just been crushed beneath an icy mountain avalanche, Morgan turned away from the window. He hadn't spotted any of the things he'd hoped to find in Mariah's beautiful violet eyes; no regret, longing, or even a little dash of love.

He just saw good-bye.

20

An hour later when Morgan walked into the tidy little white house at the end of Thirteenth Street, sleep was the farthest thing from his mind. Putting his life in order had suddenly become paramount to him.

To that end, he'd begun the process in Sheriff Teal's office after the Doolittle Gang had been secured behind bars. Morgan had laid his United States marshal's badge on the desk, and informed the sheriff that he was taking a long vacation—maybe a permanent one.

Now he passed through the parlor of the home on his way into the kitchen, and headed right for the stove. He lifted the coffeepot off of the burner and shook it. There was at least a cup left inside, and judging from the heat radiating up through the handle, it was still warm. He poured the remaining liquid, grounds and all, into a mug and then fell heavily into a chair at the kitchen table.

The little dining alcove sported a wide window which looked out on the backyard of the small home. As Morgan gazed through the peach organdy curtains, he spotted Amelia.

She was wearing a plain dress of heavy blue wool, her tiny legs wrapped in bloodred stockings, and her delicate little features were screwed into a frown, so intent was she on her assigned "busy work" for the morning. Brandishing her child-sized hoe, she flung aside load after load of damp earth, along with the few weeds that had dared to trespass in the rhubarb patch.

Morgan chuckled softly. Amelia had grown since he'd last been to Silverton, become longer and more slender of limb, and even more startling, appeared to bear a strong resemblance to him. He'd always thought of Amelia as a red-haired version of his wife. When had her features begun to change so?

As he observed his daughter, Morgan heard dainty footsteps and then felt a light tap on his shoulder. He turned to see Virginia's dove-gray eyes and pale blond hair—or a close match to them, anyway.

Prudence, the sister of his dead wife, gently said, "Amelia has really missed you, Morgan. She asks about you almost every day."

He felt a stab of guilt. "I guess it has been something like four or five months since I got this far north."

"It'll be nine months next week, Morgan. You missed her birthday—again."

Nine months? How was it possible? As he thought back over that period of time, the parts he remembered as Morgan Slater anyway, a great sadness washed over him. It wasn't that he didn't love his daughter—he'd loved her enough to make sure she had a good home after her mother died, hadn't he? He was, in his estimation, the best father he could be, given the circumstances.

But then he remembered Mariah's words the night she discovered Zachariah Penny was not her natural father, and the strength, love, and pride in her voice as she'd said, "A 'real' father need only meet two requirements as far as I'm concerned. He must love me, and protect me. Zack has never failed me in either way."

He'd done neither for Amelia, Morgan realized with a start. Oh, he loved her all right, but he had an idea she didn't know how much. How could she when he was never there?

Morgan gazed out the window, again making note of how much she had grown. Amelia was not a baby, but a little girl—a very needy little girl, he had to admit as he remembered the look in her eyes when she first saw him in the alley. What kind of young woman would she grow into if he continued to neglect her this way? The kind who looked for a father's love in every man she met, always seeking, but never finding?

Prudence, who had drawn back the pantry curtain and disappeared inside the closet-sized room, called to him from over her shoulder. "I have a little surprise for you." She lifted the item she'd been looking for off of the shelf, and then came back over to the table to drop it in front of her brother-in-law. "Amelia's friend Eloise brought this bonnet by earlier. She said the lady who was with you yesterday lost the hat in the street. It was pretty muddy, but I cleaned it up the best I could."

"Thanks, Prudy." One of the plumes was crooked and the supporting quill was badly damaged, although not quite broken. It reminded Morgan of Mariah, and of his fragile relationship with his daughter. "This Eloise—she said that Amelia calls every man she sees 'Daddy.' Is it true?"

"Oh, I wouldn't worry about it too much. She'll stop doing that once you're able to see her a little more often."

Morgan fingered the lemon-colored plumes, remembering how well Mariah's lush ebony hair had set them off. "Be sure to thank Eloise for me."

"Of course." There was hesitation in her voice, a catch as she went on. "This, ah, lady—is she someone special, Morgan?"

How was he to answer a question like that, and to his wife's sister? He'd never really had anyone special in his life before Mariah, not even lovely, gentle Virginia. She'd been his wife because they had agreed to the match as her father, Marshal George Singer, had lain dying. It wasn't that Virginia couldn't have had her pick of men—she was handsome enough, if painfully shy—but George had been so afraid she'd end up like her runaway sister, Prudence, that he'd begged her to marry his then deputy, Morgan Slater. And Morgan, feeling a bond with the old man he'd never had with his own father, had given his promise.

It had been the wrong choice for both himself and Virginia, but the union had produced Amelia—and from where Morgan sat, there wasn't a thing in the world wrong with that.

He had to smile as he glanced up at Prudence, the errant daughter who'd run off with Jack the dreamer, a man who'd dragged her all over the West, chasing one pot of gold after another before he'd finally settled down. He wondered what George would think of this foolish daughter if he could see her now: happy, content, a beloved wife, and the mother of three strapping sons. She was a far happier woman than Virginia had ever been, and much more fulfilled.

Morgan's curious expression and prolonged silence prompted Prudence's cheeks to go pink. "There I go again, poking my nose into places it doesn't belong. I had no right to ask such a personal question."

"That's all right, Prudy." Morgan reached for her hand and squeezed it. "I wasn't trying to ignore you or the question; it's just that I haven't slept for a couple of days, and it's taking me longer to think than usual. The lady—her name is Mariah—is a very special woman. One, I might add, who isn't too happy with me right now."

Her eyes lit up. "Maybe I can be of some help."

He laughed. "I don't think the entire Kickapoo Nation could help, but thanks for the offer."

"Kickapoo . . . ?" She started to inquire further, but then thought better of it. "You're exhausted. Why don't you go into Jack's and my room and get some rest. I'll keep Amelia out of the house for a few hours."

"Thanks, but no." Morgan pushed out of his chair. "She's another little lady who deserves some fence-mending from me. I'm going outside to have a talk with her." As he started for the door, Morgan paused to add, "I want you to know how much I appreciate all you've done for Amelia. It's meant a lot to me, knowing that I didn't have to worry about her well-being. Virginia would have been damn pleased with the way you've raised her girl."

Again, Prudence blushed. "No thanks are necessary. I love her as if she were my own, and you know it."

With a brief nod, he turned and walked out the door. Morgan stood on the porch for a moment, then sank down to the top step, content for the time being just to watch Amelia tend the plants. The sun was out, melting the icy puddles into small lakes of mud, and a gentle breeze carried Amelia's small voice to his ears as she sang a gibberish-filled song to herself.

Suddenly, she looked up, her curly little carrot-top bouncing. "Daddy!" she cried, flinging her hoe aside as she ran toward him. "Hi, Daddy. Are you leaving again?"

Morgan winced. She'd almost made it sound like leaving was his job. "Not for a while, Pumpkin."

Amelia whooped and clapped her hands. "Can I go on the train with you this time? I never get to go on the train."

"We'll have to wait and see about that, Pumpkin."

"Why do you call me *punkin*?" She frowned,

bunching her freckles at the bridge of her nose. "I don't want to be a pie!"

Chuckling, Morgan pulled her onto his lap and ruffled her already mussed curls. "I call you that because your hair is so red. I'm afraid if I ever lost you in a patch of overripe pumpkins, I'd never find you again."

She giggled, but then abruptly grew somber. "Would you miss me if I got lost in a punkin patch?"

"Oh, yes, sweetheart. I'd miss you so much I couldn't stand it." Morgan hugged her close. "I don't ever want to lose you again, Amelia, not even for one minute. In fact, I'm working on a way to keep us together from now on. Would you like that?"

"Really, Daddy? You mean live together?"

"Yes, Pumpkin."

"And you promise you won't go away again?"

Morgan weighed his next words carefully, bound and determined to do right by her. "Not if I can possibly help it."

Amelia sniffled, then wiped her nose, but big fat tears rolled down her freckled cheeks anyway. She buried her face against her father's neck. "Yes, Daddy. I want you to stay."

Morgan held her for a long time, hugging her, soothing her, knowing all the while that he had Mariah to thank for at least a part of his decision. Maybe she hadn't reshaped his soul during his bout with amnesia as much as rearranged it. She'd certainly done one of the two, perhaps even both. Mariah had turned him from a man who hated dogs to one who more than simply tolerated Daisy; from a man who loathed hucksters to one who'd come to understand the value of Doc Zachariah's Kickapoo Medicine Show—so much so, in fact, that he'd actually helped in the preparation of their tonics and herbs!

The ultimate alteration, the one about which he was most frustrated as well as most grateful, was the way she'd manipulated his heart. She had helped him evolve from a man who'd been taught at a very young age not to care too much about anyone or anything, to one who dared to test his emotions. The old Morgan Slater would never have let his guard down long enough to notice how badly his daughter needed and loved him, and he sure as hell wouldn't have seen past the Princess Tanacoa costume to the woman beneath it—to the woman he loved.

Amelia squirmed out of her father's arms, too excited by the idea of their new life together to hold still any longer, and began to shower him with little kisses. She stopped when something wet met her lips, and poked her chubby finger against his cheek. "Are you crying, Daddy?"

Morgan knuckled the moisture away. "Of course not, Pumpkin. My eyes just aren't used to this dusty little town."

Amelia glanced around at the mud puddles still lingering from the recent showers, and shrugged. Seeing the confusion in her eyes, Morgan climbed to his feet and lifted her into his arms. And then it came to him: a plan. A little bit of strategy that not even the most wounded of hearts could turn away. One that would most surely get his foot into Mariah's door. And maybe even back into her life.

Swinging his daughter up high on his shoulders, Morgan said, "I have a really special job to do, Pumpkin. How would you like to be my new deputy and go with me?"

Mariah hadn't fared any better than Morgan in the rest department. After she'd assured Zack and Oda that the only harm she'd suffered was sleep deprivation, they'd filled her with a warm, nourishing breakfast, then hurried her off to her room, where they instructed her to sleep for as long as she liked, around the clock if necessary. The medicine show would be canceled, they told her, until further notice.

She'd been grateful at first, her body weary and aching as she slid between the sheets. But sleep hadn't come. She closed her eyes and saw Cain. She clamped her pillow over her ears, but continued to hear those wonderful, painful words of love he'd uttered not three days ago. How long did it take to recover from a broken heart? she wondered. Or was recovery even possible?

She thought back to the look in Oda's eyes as she'd spoken of her time with Patrick O'Conner, and a kind of hopeless despair swamped her. Her mother had never forgotten the first man she loved, and neither would Mariah. The tears began to fall, when a knock sounded at her door.

Slipping into her robe as she crossed the room, Mariah called out, "Who is it?"

"It's me, Amelia!"

The little girl's voice startled her, but Mariah recognized her name in an instant. She quickly wiped her eyes, then turned the key in the lock and opened the door. Outfitted in his Brother Law apparel, Cain held his young daughter in his arms. She was wearing the lovely leghorn shade bonnet he'd purchased in Durango—or more correctly, it was wearing her.

Morgan touched the brim of his own hat with his free hand. "Afternoon. I'd like you to meet my daughter, Amelia. May we come in for a moment?"

"Oh, ah, sure." Mariah backed into the room, fumbling with the buttons at the throat of her best white robe.

"Amelia, this is Miss Penny. The lady who owns the hat."

The girl lifted the bonnet off of her head with a little help from her father, and handed it to Mariah. Flashing a broad grin, one which clearly revealed the space her front teeth had once inhabited, she said, "You're pretty!"

"Thank you, Amelia. So are you." Her mind afire with questions, Mariah took the hat to her dresser and laid it down. Daisy, who'd bounced down off the bed the moment she heard Morgan's voice, was dancing around his legs, begging him for just a scrap of attention.

"Daddy, look!" cried Amelia. "She gots a puppy!"

"She sure does, Pumpkin." Morgan leaned over as if to set the child down, but paused to ask Mariah, "How does Daisy feel about youngsters?"

"She doesn't bite them, if that's what you're asking, but I have to be honest: Daisy doesn't, as a rule, like children. She'll probably run away and hide under the bed." As Morgan set Amelia on her feet, Mariah cautioned the girl. "Be real quiet around Daisy at first, let her sniff your hand so she will understand that you don't want to hurt her, and she might play with you."

Giggling as the dog's cold, damp nose touched her fingers, Amelia sank cross-legged onto the floor and let Daisy make her acquaintance.

Assured that his daughter would be preoccupied as well as safe, Morgan took Mariah by the elbow and steered her over to the window. Before saying a word, he tied one of the heavy velvet drapes back out of the way. Sunshine spilled into the room, lighting Mariah's dark hair with a fiery glow.

"I want another chance," he said simply.

"'Chance'?" He couldn't be talking about her, not with his daughter in the room. Mariah held her heart at bay. "What kind of chance?"

"To apologize first. The things I said to you yesterday, the awful accusations, especially the way I tried to blame you for my neglect of Amelia. I was angry, and—"

"You had every right to be angry," Mariah said, cutting off his apology, her heart all too eager to welcome him back, to love him again, if even for just this moment. "If anyone needs to say I'm sorry, it's me. And I am."

"For what?" He grinned, his green eyes twinkling. "Taking my blank mind and transforming me into Cain Law? I thank you for that rebirth, princess. Say you forgive me. Say that you . . . love me, if only just a little."

Mariah's treacherous heart pounded in her breast. God forgive her for the wicked, wanton woman that she'd become, but all she really cared about was this last moment with Cain, and all she wanted to do was throw herself into his arms and bury herself there forever. Strangling on the words she knew she had to say, Mariah managed them somehow. *"Love you?* B-but what about Amelia's mother? Surely you can't just—"

"Christ in a whiskey barrel! Between the Doolittle Gang and all that's happened, I guess I never did get around to telling you about her, did I?"

"No." She swallowed hard. "You never even mentioned her name."

Morgan glanced at Amelia out of the corner of his eye, and then quietly said, "Her name was Virginia. She got caught in the cross fire during a holdup almost three years ago."

With a soft gasp, Mariah said, "Oh, Cain. How horrible."

He nodded. "It was all of that and more for Amelia at her tender years. I knew I couldn't raise her alone, so when Virginia's sister Prudence offered to take her in, I let her. I see her as often as I can, but . . ." Again he glanced at Amelia, who had already managed to make herself a mighty good friend of Daisy's. "We haven't been together nearly enough."

Because she didn't know what else to say, Mariah whispered, "I'm so sorry. For you both.".

"Don't be. Virginia's death isn't something I dwell on anymore. We were, in many ways, polite strangers." Suddenly, Morgan could no longer bear not touching

Mariah. He reached over and brushed his fingertips across her long, loose hair, and then let them fall to her throat, caressing the delicate skin there as he said, "I'd rather talk about us. I love you, Mariah Penny. Did you hear me? I love you. That's something I never could say to Virginia, or anyone else for that matter. I take it as a real sign that we belong together."

His touch, as always, was magical; her body, as ever, eager to believe his every word. But something disturbed her, a concern that would not be denied. "Cain Law once told me that he loved me. I loved him back with all my heart." He looked as if he was about to take her into his arms, so Mariah stepped out of his reach, evading him while she still had the strength. "I never thought I'd hear those words from a man like Morgan Slater, and frankly, I'm not sure what I think about hearing them now. I don't even know what I think of the man."

Morgan had halfway expected this kind of reaction to his declarations, so he'd come prepared. "I didn't want to have to get tough with you, Mariah, but I should warn you that Amelia and I decided to make a little stop on the way over here in case we needed some more ammunition." He reached into his jacket pocket and pulled out a bottle of #20 love potion. "I don't want to have to use this on you, princess—it tastes like old socks—but I'll force it down your throat if I have to."

Her heart lurched, and she began to laugh. In spite of all her doubts and fears, Mariah laughed, and laughed, until she discovered that she was crying as well.

Morgan pulled her into his arms, thumbing a tear

off the corner of her mouth. "If you still have doubts about this Morgan Slater fellow, we'll just get rid of him again. I'll be anyone you want me to be—anyone at all—just as long as you tell this man standing before you that you love him. And that you'll marry him."

"Oh . . . oh, my God." Mariah fell into his embrace, her tears soaking his frock coat, and through a sob of sheer joy, she finally said, "If I say yes, you won't mind if I call you Cain, even though the name belonged to my dog?"

"I don't mind, if you don't mind being called . . . Mommy." He took her face between his hands, staring hard into her moist eyes. "I'm serious about that part, princess. I do understand if you have some doubts about Amelia, but I can't neglect her any longer. I intend to keep her with me—with us—even though I don't know what to expect, since I haven't been around much the past few years. I don't know if she's willful or obedient, spoiled or charitable, incorrigible, or even—"

"Shush." Mariah briefly pressed her lips against his, making sure they would stay sealed, and then glanced over to where Amelia and Daisy were playing on the floor. "That's all I need to know about your daughter, Cain. I trust Daisy's judgment completely. She only cottons to very special people, remember?"

Remembering that he, as Cain Law, had been special enough for Daisy to "cotton" to, again he drew Mariah into his embrace. As her body molded against his, surrounding him with her intoxicating scent, for a moment he thought he might happily drown in that sea of cinnamon, rosebuds, and silken skin. Gathering himself, he whispered against her hair, "Is that a 'Yes, I'll marry you,' princess?"

Mariah's emotions exploded inside of her, as wondrous a feeling as the dawning of a new day. "Yes, darling. I'll marry you. Oh, yes." Their lips met again, their hearts beating as one, and the world seemed to spin beneath her feet.

From across the room, Amelia glanced at the couple and screwed her pert little mouth into a frown. "They're kissing, Daisy. Just like Aunt Prudence and Uncle Jack." She called to her father. "Is there going to be a lot of that kissing, Daddy?"

Cain broke away from Mariah's mouth long enough to say, "As much as possible, Pumpkin." Then he returned to the decidedly pleasurable task at hand.

Amelia let out a noisy sigh, and muttered to the little dog. "Kissing. I don't think I like all that kissing!"

Daisy hopped into Amelia's lap, her pink tongue laving the girl's cheeks, and confirmed in her own way that, like it or not, there would be a lot of kissing going on in the Slater household from now on.

COMING NEXT MONTH

FLAME LILY by Candace Camp
Continuing the saga of the Tyrells begun in *Rain Lily,* another heart-tugging, passionate tale of love from bestselling author Candace Camp. Returning home after years at war, Confederate officer Hunter Tyrell only dreamed of marrying his sweetheart, Linette Sanders, and settling down. But when he discovered that Linette had wed another, he vowed to never love again until—he found out her heartbreaking secret.

ALL THAT GLITTERS by Ruth Ryan Langan
From a humble singing job in a Los Angeles bar, Alexandra Corday is discovered and propelled into stardom. Along the way her path crosses with that of rising young photographer Adam Montrose. When it seems that Alex will finally have it all—a man she loves, a home for herself and her brother, and the family she has always yearned for—buried secrets threaten to destroy her.

THE WIND CASTS NO SHADOW by Roslynn Griffith
With an incredibly deft had, Roslynn Griffith has combined Indian mythology and historical flavor in this compelling tale of love, betrayal, and murder deep in the heart of New Mexico territory.

UNQUIET HEARTS by Kathy Lynn Emerson
Tudor England comes back to life in this richly detailed historical romance. With the death of her mother, Thomasine Strangeways had no choice but to return to Catsholme Manor, her childhood home where her mother was once employed as governess. There she was reunited with Nick Carrier, her childhood hero who had become the manor's steward. Meeting now as adults, they found the attraction between them instant and undeniable, but they were both guarding dangerous secrets.

STOLEN TREASURE by Catriona Flynt
A madcap romantic adventure set in 19th-century Arizona gold country. Neel Blade was rich, handsome, lucky, and thoroughly bored, until he met Cate Stewart, a feisty chemist who was trying to hold her world together while her father was in prison. He instantly fell in love with her. But if only he could remember who he was . . .

WILD CARD by Nancy Hutchinson
It is a dream come true for writer Sarah MacDonald when movie idol Ian Wild miraculously appears on her doorstep. This just doesn't happen to a typical widow who lives a quiet, unexciting life in a small college town. But when Ian convinces Sarah to go with him to his remote Montana ranch, she comes face to face with not only a life and a love more exciting than anything in the pages of her novels, but a shocking murder.

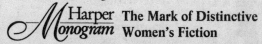 **Harper Monogram** The Mark of Distinctive Women's Fiction

Harper Monogram *By Mail*

Looking For Love?
Try HarperMonogram's Bestselling Romances

TAPESTRY
by Maura Seger
An aristocratic Saxon woman loses her heart to
the Norman man who rules her conquered people.

DREAM TIME

by Parris Afton Bonds
In the distant outback of Australia, a mother
and daughter are ready to sacrifice everything
for their dreams of love.

RAIN LILY
by Candace Camp
In the aftermath of the Civil War in Arkansas, a
farmer's wife struggles between duty and passion.

COMING UP ROSES

by Catherine Anderson
Only buried secrets could stop the love
of a young widow and her new beau
from bloomimg.

ONE GOOD MAN
by Terri Herrington
When faced with a lucrative offer to seduce
a billionaire industrialist, a young woman
discovers her true desires.